BLOOD ON THE SADDLE

BLOOD ON THE SADDLE

Dan Cushman

GUNSMOKE

This hardback edition 2011
by AudioGO Ltd
by arrangement with
Golden West Literary Agency

ISBN 978 1 445 85658 2

British Library Cataloguing in Publication Data available.

Printed and bound in Great Britain by the MPG Books Group

"Blood on the Saddle"

A Cowboy Ballad

— Anonymous

There was blood on the saddle and blood on the ground,
And a great big puddle of blood all around
Oh, the cowboy lay in it, all covered with gore,
And he won't go a-riding his broncho no more.
Oh, pity the cowboy, all bloody and red,
His broncho fell on him and mashed his head.

[To be sung stoically but not to be taken seriously.]

CHAPTER ONE

Clyde rode, taking his time. The June sun was very hot. A slight smell of skunk hung in the air. Hens poked around in the litter of old wagons, machinery, and of steam parts from a wreck on the Missouri River that Billy had hauled up, intending to fit them together and make a power sawmill and never had. The litter ended when he neared the house. Everything was clean and raked where Ma took care of things. A rose bush was in bloom. New, yellow-green, wild cucumber vines grew over the porch. There was a bench, pail and dipper, and a wash dish. The kitchen door was propped open. Ma always propped the screen open so the flies could leave, and closed it again when she started supper. There was a strange horse tied up to the post. It was a rangy gelding with a Flying A, and also a newer brand, a half Circle H for Hancock County. He figured it was the sheriff, Earl Hankey.

They were old friends, Ma and Earl Hankey. They had been friends in the Beaverhead, and Idaho, and even Colorado as far back as 1859. Earl had followed Pa into the Musselshell country east of the Judiths in the year of 1871, the year before Clyde was born, and had worked for him as driver and general traveling boss when he had the freight company and the U. S. Army contract. It used to be they could look for Earl to visit at least twice a year and spend a week, one when the spring work was over, and always one at Christmas. He and Pa would talk old times, and Clyde would listen. But Earl wouldn't be talking old times with Pa *this* afternoon. Pa wasn't here. He was six feet under the sod.

They were sitting inside, and Clyde, entering by the back door into the kitchen, heard the sheriff say: "Where's that tan sheep dog you had? Toby? He used to bark at me every time when I came up that pitch from the creek."

"Somebody shot him," said Ma. "Clyde found him dead last week

7

about a mile down the road."

"Why, who'd do a thing like that?"

"I don't know. I thought maybe you could tell me."

"Me?"

"There's been people hanging around here lately, keeping watch of this ranch."

"Oh?"

"And the reason that poor, old dog got shot was that *somebody* didn't want him barking and giving them away."

"Nobody in my office has been hanging around here or shooting dogs, that I guarantee."

"You asked me who'd do a thing like that? I'll tell you who'd do it . . . that evil, whiskey-rotten undersheriff of yours is who'd do it."

"Well, Ted Danner may have his faults, but he's not going around shooting dogs. Not by stealth. He's meaner than that. Danner would ride right up here and shoot that dog in your front yard."

It became quiet. Clyde, standing there in the kitchen, couldn't understand what was going on, then he heard the front door close and realized Ma had been outside, looking around. If she had seen him ride up and past the front, she hadn't let on.

"I'm alone," assured the sheriff.

"Maybe you are, but this place is being *watched.* They been skulking from on top of that ridge. I knew it when I saw the eagles veering around. I haven't lived in this god-forsaken place sixteen years for nothing, and there's always a *sign* when somebody comes poking around."

"Sixteen years," Earl said, wanting to get off the subject, "can it be possible?"

"Seventeen this autumn. I stayed away until Pa finished the cabin. We moved in about two weeks before the big blizzard. We didn't even have a door. Just a buffalo hide he'd bought off a dirty, old Indian, and it got so stiff from cold it was like a board. The cabin was ten by fourteen, and we denned up like wolves. I don't know how cold it got. We didn't have a thermometer. I heard it got down to fifty-six below at the fort. That's what the Buttons went through, bringing in the first beef so those Englishmen . . . Major Morrison and the rest . . . could come in here with backing to hog it all."

8

"I know, I know." He'd heard it all before.

"And now it's come down to where they shoot poor old Toby and sneak around with spy glasses. I suppose they want to know how long we're going to hang on. One little corner of the country they don't own. That they don't *control,* I should say, because they don't *own* much of anything." She added with vehemence: "Why do they control this entire territory?"

"No, they do not. There's more brands registered now. . . ."

"Well, I say they do!"

Earl decided not to argue. He took a big, deep breath as Ma waited.

"Is Billy around?"

"I haven't seen Billy in weeks. He stays here a day or two and gets so impatient. . . ."

"He's got to come in, Kate."

"Why?"

"You must know why! Everybody in the country knows."

"Well, *I* don't know. Stuck way out here. . . ."

"Kate, this is serious. This has nothing to do with title to a few cattle, anything like that. This is . . . homicide. And no crazy, drunken shoot-out. He's in trouble as bad as anybody can be."

Forcing strength into her voice, she stated: "I don't know what you're talking about."

"Well, Gannaway's been shot. *He killed John Gannaway!*"

If he'd said Billy killed the governor, it couldn't have been more stunning, because Gannaway was head of the Omaha & Montana Cattle Company. If you'd been asked to pick the most important man in all the broad ranching country between the Yellowstone and Missouri Rivers, it could likely be John Gannaway. He had run the Big G Freight Co., was a director of banks, on the board of S. C. & P. and the Dakota Southern Railroads.

"*You* say my boy did it?"

"No, *I'm* not saying it. That's not my task. Three witnesses say it. They say Billy met John Gannaway at the Willow Creek crossing where that road runs from the old Northwestern home ranch to Camp Griffin and shot him. It was no gunfight or anything of the kind. Gannaway was unarmed. They were in plain sight, and Billy shot him. He shot him while his arm was raised for mercy. It was a fearful

9

deed, Kate. This country is all wrought up."

Clyde's heart was beating so fast, and he was so dizzy and buzz-eared that he didn't hear what Ma said, or what Earl answered, but then he heard her say: *"That's one side of it, and one side only!"*

"Sworn testimony at the inquest and the grand jury."

Grand jury made it seem that Billy was convicted already; grand jury sounded bigger and more final than any court, such as the second district court in Fort Benton.

"Sworn testimony? Whose sworn testimony? Were they Omaha men?"

"Yes, there were three Omaha men, but one was Avery Carns. He's a hard man, but not a liar. The two others were cowboys. Witnesses with nothing to gain."

Ma said bitterly: "I know all about *witnesses*. Us Buttons have had sad experience with witnesses. I have a long memory. I recollect how they got the witnesses out of the country, the time they shot down Walter, Junior. I didn't hear them talking about cold blood then."

"Well, you did me. If I'd been sheriff then, I'd have gone to the ends of the earth to get those witnesses, only it would have done no good. All they could have proved was that it was Bob Shields, and he was authorized by a federal judge. He was wearing the star of a deputy United States marshal. Anyhow, it's too late now. Both're dead and gone."

They were talking about Clyde's brother, Walt, next oldest of the boys, who had organized the so-called Badlanders' roundup. There was a big outcry, but nothing could be done. Shields had a warrant of some sort. Then the bad winter came. Most of the big outfits went under or took a terrible loss in the hard winter. Now people wanted to forget the past. Marshal Shields was dead. It was all water over the dam.

Ma said: "Oh, it's easy for you to talk."

Earl answered back: "No! It's *not* easy for me. I carried your boys around on my back when they were babies. I taught Walt to drive a team. It ain't easy for me. But we can't start in with that Bobtail Coulée business all over again. As sheriff, I'm going to do all in my power to stop it."

"What happens if Billy does come in and gives himself up?"

10

"He'll be charged and put in jail. There won't be any bail. There can't be, because it's a capital case. However, his willingness to face charges will be in his favor. One lucky thing, it won't be a long wait for court. There's a big docket of civil cases, and they promised a judge will come in six weeks or two months. It will either be Judge Minough or Judge Newby. Both are absolutely fair. If the decision goes against him, there'll be automatic appeal to the other judges sitting as supreme court in January. If Minough sits, then McCabe and Newby will sit in appeal, and if Newby, then Minough and McCabe. It's a far cry from the kind of short-rope justice we had in the old days, Kate. I'm not here asking Billy to surrender to any vigilante court."

When she didn't say anything, he went on: "What happens otherwise? He'll be a fugitive. An outlaw. How long do outlaws last? A year, maybe? Two years? It used to be they could head to the frontier. Over the border, they used to call it. That time is past. There's no border left. They're opening the Blackfoot lands all the way to Canada. We're about to become a state. They're building another transcontinental railroad. Arlington will be on the new line, linking it to the N. P. Billy would have to go to Alaska or the Argentine. But he won't. You know he won't. He'll shack up in the badlands and then try sneaking back for a night in town. They'll put up a reward, it'll be a big one, and it'll be only a question of time before one of his good friends decides to collect it. His only chance is to face up."

She started moaning and sobbing, telling how she'd lost her children one after another, that the trail from Vandalia, Indiana, to Kansas and Colorado and Idaho and Montana was marked by the graves of her children, and she enumerated them — Prescott, Orville, Carlot, the twins, Hope, Willard, Jenny, Walter, Jr., and Billy. Clyde was the only one she had left, except for Irma who had her own family. And Pa was gone, too.

"You have some wonderful grandchildren."

"Yes," said Ma, "but it's not the same. Clyde's the only one left, but I'm not going to stand by and let this country ruin him like it has Billy, or see him shot down in cold blood like Walter. No, I'm going to get him out and away from here. I'm going to realize what I can from this ranch and take him back East to school. That boy is

11

going to amount to something. That boy is going to be a *doctor!*"

After a long quiet, Earl cleared his throat and said: "Well, Kate, you get word to Billy, will you? You tell him to turn himself in, otherwise I can't guarantee. I have forces to contend with."

What he meant was he didn't have the complete power of office. He was only half a sheriff actually. It had come about when they had tried to form a new county with Arlington as the county seat, but Fort Benton had bucked it. They wanted to keep it all part of Chouteau County, and not promote any rival steamboat ports on the Missouri River. So they had got busy over at the territorial legislature and had the ordinance act pigeonholed. What happened was that a version of the act had got signed by the governor, but there had been an amended resolution, a grand mix-up. People in Arlington claimed there was a new county, Ricketts County, and Fort Benton claimed there wasn't. But Arlington had gone ahead and elected county commissioners. The commissioners had filled other offices by appointment temporarily — sheriff, county attorney, assessor, treasurer-recorder — and set up offices, tax rolls, and archives. Land had been set aside for a courthouse. All this was during the good times. After the dreadful winter of 1886 had all but wiped out the cattle business, ranchers who paid most of the taxes had had second thoughts. But the people in power at Arlington went ahead with an election. There had been a big contest for sheriff. Quite a number of candidates had jumped in, most on the Democratic ticket. The voters, all men, of course, had seemed to come from Missouri or New Mexico — Earl Hankey had been "The Peoples' Candidate" and Ted Danner, range detective for the old Anglo-American Company (in receivership), had campaigned as "Fair, Fearless, Experienced." The big outfits had all been for Ted Danner, but Earl Hankey had won easily, getting more votes than all the other candidates combined, with Danner coming in a poor second. The big outfits had been finished, however. They had threatened to pay their taxes to Fort Benton, which would have put Ricketts County out of business, unless they got their man in the sheriff's office, so Earl Hankey had made a deal. He had offered to take Ted Danner on as undersheriff. Earl had got the title and the wages, also the sheriff's usual share of the fees (which were said to run as high as five hundred dollars a month!), but Danner was to have a free hand, disputes between them

12

to be submitted to the county attorney. As Billy had put it: "Uncle Earl couldn't wipe his ass without asking Ted Danner for the paper."

Ma was saying: "Oh yes, you *promise* Billy'll get a fair trial, but can you keep your promise?"

"What do you mean?" Earl asked sharply.

"I mean, you have that evil Ted Danner to contend with."

"Danner wasn't my choice. He was rammed down my throat. But what would you have had otherwise? A Fort Benton sheriff, and Danner here as deputy-in-charge? The handwriting was on the wall. But I'm still sheriff. And whenever I don't exercise the power of that office, I'll resign." He let that sink in. "Right after the inquest they were ready to put a posse together and come out here, and I don't know what action they'd have taken. They'd have hung Billy, if they'd caught him, that I know. I stood up to them, Kate. I threatened to resign. I put it up to those Arlington merchants that it would be bad for the county if there was vigilante action. News stories in the Eastern papers. I told them they could just bid good bye to attracting capital investment into a lawless country. So they said all right. I could have one week to see what I could do. If Billy comes in, and gives himself up, the leading men of this county absolutely guarantee he'll get a safe surrender and a fair trial. But after one week I give my approval to a posse. I'll have to."

Ma grumbled: "Anyhow, I haven't seen him."

"Send Clyde to find him."

"No, I'll not have Clyde getting mixed up in it!"

There followed a long quiet, and Clyde was just preparing to slip back out the back door when Ma came into the kitchen and saw him. She didn't say a word, but started to take off the stove lids to kindle a fire. She was a big woman, solid as a man, and there'd been a day when she could hoist like a man, but lately the smallest tasks seemed to tire her, and she stood for a time, resting from lifting the lids before putting bacon grease on the wood and striking a match.

The sheriff's voice came: "Don't go to any bother, Kate. Just a cup of tea. I don't like to ride on a full stomach."

"No. You'll come in here and set down."

She didn't even glance again Clyde's way, so he got the idea and did slip out the back door. He went down to the barn.

13

CHAPTER TWO

"Well, what does dear old Uncle Earl have to say?" asked Billy, lying at ease in the hay. "Did he enumerate my crimes and short-comings?" Clyde hesitated. "Go ahead. These are my friends."

He didn't want to talk in front of Ace Carter, whom he didn't completely trust, or Kid Nehf whom he didn't like.

"He says you shot John Gannaway," muttered Clyde.

"Uncle Earl say that? Do you hear that, fellows? They're trying to make out I shot Gannaway."

Carter let out a cry and pretended to fall prostrate at the news, but he was always showing off for Billy. Kid Nehf just looked narrow-eyed and chewed a piece of hay.

Billy asked how he was supposed to have shot him — in a fair fight? Clyde said no, unarmed, while his arm was raised for mercy, and Billy just lay and looked at him from under the brim of his hat. He was perfectly direct and serious. No more sarcasm about dear old Uncle Earl. Not in front of Ace Carter.

"Well, how about it, Clyde? Do you believe him?"

He had to look at Billy again, and then he said: "No. No, I don't believe 'em."

"Fine! You're what a brother ought to be. Of course, you wouldn't believe it. You're smart enough to see it makes no sense. A man that'd do that would be a dirty coward. Run for his life. Do I look like I'm running? I'm not running from Uncle Earl, or Danner, or any of those English sons-of-bitches at the Omaha."

Then, although the sheriff was right up at the house, and there were probably men with rifles watching from back on the rimrocks, ready for a signal to swoop, Billy got to telling about how the country used to be, full of deer and elk, and the badlands full of mountain sheep, and even the last of the buffalo, when he and Pa had first ridden into it. The grass was so high it polished the bottom of the wagon. It made that oak shine as if it was varnished. Oh, God, the grass! You could see the wind blow through it in waves. But that was before the Englishmen came in, and Major Morrison with his Eastern corporations, to harvest it all in the form of beef. You'd see an antelope, only you wouldn't see *him,* only his white tail, the grass was so deep. And you never saw anything like the mountain sheep any more, so tame you could kill them with a rock. The old-timers hadn't done it. They had just taken what was needed for food. But those English sons-of-bitches and the Eastern dudes slaughtered them. They shot them till their guns got hot in their hands. Deer, elk, sheep, antelope. They would come in after a week of hunting with wagonloads of carcasses and choose the best heads to be mounted by a taxidermist, but the meat all lay and rotted. The Indians came around and got the hides, not minding the smell.

Billy wasn't a damned bit sorry about the hard winter. The cattle had stacked up in the coulées, belly-deep in the snow, looking for protection from the storm, and Pa, who was also seeing his last winter, moaned disaster. Then Billy had come home. He'd been away off somewhere on one of his trips. He had got back along about Christmas, riding all the way from Billings in the awful cold. He had on hair chaps over blanket-lined pants, with gunnysacks full of hay hanging like *tapaderos* to put his feet in. He had started quite a row by saying he was willing for all the stock to die if it meant ruining the god-damned dude sons-of-bitches, freezing them out of the country. He had said that to Pa. In fact, Billy had said he hoped there'd be another winter just like it (though it was Pa's last.) That's the subject he was on now. It was his favorite. "I'd like to see it get a hundred below zero and bankrupt them all, their railroads included. I'd like to hear the wind howl through their rotten bones."

Despite the awful things he said, there was always something very attractive in the way Billy talked. He had a certain quality that made people take to him. Total strangers would know him for half an hour and like him the best of anybody they'd known all their lives! He wasn't handsome, not by a long shot — his face was too long and narrow, but he always smelled a certain way. He might not have had a swim for a month and have slept in his clothes, but he smelled of wind, as if he'd been rained on and had sat in the smoke of campfires, and had ridden wild horses, stagecoaches,

15

and trains. He smelled of far places.

After a while Billy got up and had a look at the house, and wondered out loud whether Earl knew he was here, and if, maybe, he had somebody posted in case he was flushed out the back way, down past the narrows of Arrow Creek? "You don't suppose he'd do that, Clyde? Dear old Uncle Earl?"

Clyde didn't really think he would — and said so.

"Just the same, here's what I want you to do. I want you to saddle up and drift up along the creek, as you naturally might do, this being our ranch. But when you get to the forks, head south and swing around east. Stay a good two or three hundred yards from Birdtail and those broken rocks, because that's where they might have set an ambush. They'd have set it for me, but they might take any Buttons that came handy. It wouldn't surprise me if they were the ones who hung that U. S. marshal. The one that shot Walt. Afraid of what he might give away some night when the dead got to calling on him. I want you to wait for twilight and see where our noble sheriff goes. You know, the old family friend? The one who did his best, almost, to get warrants charging Marshal Shields with shooting our brother Walter."

It was as if Billy had been listening to them talking, Ma and the sheriff, away off at the house.

Anyway, nothing needed to be done about the marshal — U. S. Deputy Marshal Bob Shields. He had died, and in a way not the last person in the land would have predicted. He had been headquartered at Miles, seeming the same as ever, full of steel and untouched by care, playing poker and having his evening toddy, sometimes a bit too much but never showing it. He stayed upstairs at the Drovers Hotel. Would go to bed as usual, about twelve or one, but uneasy lay the head. Slats Sweeney, the barber, told him about it. Clyde would get his hair cut, sitting upright in the chair where Sweeney could talk in his ear, as was his wont — keeping the customer interested with all the town news better than the paper, lots the editor didn't dare print, only making oblique references — and, while Clyde listened, would give him part of a shave, a dab of lather at his silky, young mustache, two whacks with the razor on each side, also side-burns, not charging a cent extra, and tell how Shields would get to talking in his sleep. Actually, it had been shouting out. Along around the gray of dawn, he'd get to screaming: *"Ya-ya-ya!"* and "Go away, go away!" He had named people you might never have heard of, the men he'd killed. People would refuse to stay in the next room, fearing he might get to shooting through the wall. It would freeze the blood in your veins, and finally Mrs. Eddington, the proprietress, would have to go up and hammer on the door to wake him. Well, he'd calm right down and say: "Oh, I must have been dreaming." Sweeney had said: "They never forget the glass in their eyes, meaning that stare, when a man dies. They look not at you, but at eternity, in that awful way."

Well, they didn't have to worry about Marshal Shields any more! It had been a relief to all when he was found hung. It had been by his own hand on a tree, away down by the Wyoming line. What he'd done was ride under a limb, sitting behind the saddle, tie a noose, and ride from it. The rope slid him off the horse's rump and did the job. At first they thought he had just been standing there. It was a big, old bullberry tree, and the limb had bent, from days in the fierce sun, until his feet were on the ground, his knees slack. The magpies had been having a regular convention. They had picked his eyes out so there were just holes, so he seemed from a distance to be staring. His whole head had been puffed and purple black, like a withered Hubbard squash. All in all, no pretty sight, to say the least.

A cowboy no older than Clyde had found the body. It had been down at the Chalk Buttes, near Wyoming and Dakota. He had been riding for the Canton outfit. This was a ranch with a name having nothing to do with the Chinese city, but with a cantonment, where the U. S. Army once had a summer camp to watch for the war-like Sioux so Custer would know where to find them, if needed.

Anyway, the young cowboy had wisely stayed clear and had ridden to the ranch for help, which meant witnesses and testimony. So quite a number were on hand to get a view and decide on burial at the spot. There later had been talk about digging him up and burying him with rites over at Belle Fourche, but it was not done. *Sic transit gloria.*

Billy was talking. "Clyde, why don't you ride up the coulée and find some place to keep watch? See where dear old Uncle Earl goes. See if he's meeting someone. The brave Undersheriff Danner, for instance. But stay clear of banks and draws. Danner would shoot you

17

like he did poor Toby. Find out if our noble sheriff is out here on his lonesome, like he says."

The bottoms of Arrow Creek lay half a mile wide between sand-rock rims. The warm stream was full of frogs and bloodsuckers, but no fish to speak of, although you could catch rainbow trout about eight miles up, toward the foothills. Cattle — chiefly cows and their spring calves — rested in the shade of box elder trees that formed scraggly groves. A few were longhorn half-bloods, but most of the cattle were the old-time Buttons stock, descendants of the Oregon Reds Pa had driven into the country in 1872.

Clyde wasn't too worried about being ambushed. If anybody was around, he'd know it by the cattle. You could always tell when anything had stirred them up. He rode and checked the brands by habit to see if any Omaha cattle had got that far down onto the Buttons range. You couldn't hold a range unless you occupied it, so Ma didn't dare sell so much as a hoof or a horn after the hard winter, or those Omaha cattle would move in and take it. It was all Public Domain — ninety percent of the entire country was U. S. government land — and there was no right except the right of possession. You had what you could hold, and that was that. Clyde spent half his time driving those Omaha cattle back over the Piney Ridge that since time immemorial had been the Buttons boundary. He would ride out and cache himself somewhere with his air rifle. It was a genuine French Baille rifle that Billy had won in Sioux City in a raffle. It was worth fourteen dollars, Billy said, and put together like a watch. You pumped it with a lever that folded out, one pump for target practice, but give it three and it would kill sage hens at fifty yards. It shot size F buckshot from a magazine of a hundred. What Clyde did was put a dab of salt-gritty bacon grease in the muzzle, then he'd give the gun three full pumps, take aim at an Omaha critter's rump, and *whfft!* God, how it'd go! He shot at longhorns or anything with an Omaha brand, but what he liked most was to get one of their new white-faced Herefords. Everyone hated them. People said there wouldn't be a longhorn left in the country in another five years. When Billy heard that, he said: "Shee-it!"

It had been over at Rimfire Butte last year. They were branding — Simon Arbogast, Gannaway, Ewell Ethrington, all the great and

18

powerful were there — and Billy said it right in their teeth. "Oh, shee-it," Billy said. "Wait till we get another howling winter and your Herefords will freeze like posts." They stood there and looked at him without saying a word. "How much you willing to pay for skinning crews? Me and my boys will do it on contract, but we'd like to start right after the thaw before the carcasses begin to stink." That's what Billy had told them.

Clyde saw nothing to shoot at. It was very hot during the drag end of the afternoon, dense and absolutely windless, with clouds of flies wherever the cows had been. He rode slowly, taking all the time in the world, never forgetting that somebody *might* be watching him. Finally the sun dropped away, and there was a towering sunset, with a dark thunderhead in the north. He could feel the electricity in his hair and in the way his shirt clung to him. Then, in thickening twilight, early because of the clouds that silhouetted far-off lightning, he left the creek and set off at a good clip, the way Billy had told him, and, sure enough, somebody was at the old stage station. He could see it away far off in the bottoms of Salty Creek and a point of candle light.

He kept riding, and the candle went off and came on again, off again, on again. It was very peculiar until he realized somebody was walking back and forth in front of it. He stopped in a clump of chokecherry bushes dense in a little draw, tied his horse, his favorite gun-powder roan broncho, and decided to proceed on foot. It was growing lighter with the clouds swinging around over the Judiths. A few stars were out and a glow of sunset. There was a smell of rain, wet dust where it had come down somewhere in a torrent, and fresh manure. He took his time. He certainly didn't want to walk in on Danner, but he had to get close to see if the sheriff was there. He reached the brush. He could hear water running. Mosquitoes swarmed up. He waited and listened, and the moon climbed over the hills, big as a dish pan. He could no longer see the stage cabin. He had just started to cross through the mud, the cool water telling him where the holes in his boots were, when a man spoke. The voice seemed right beside him. Perhaps it was some fellow, camping for the night.

Then Earl's voice: "Yes, times are kind of hard all over."

"I figured once they opened all those Blackfoot lands. . . ."

19

"They're still branding north of the river," Earl said.

"Who's the fellow down by the corral? Friend of yours?"

"Yes."

Clyde wondered if they meant him — but they couldn't possibly.

"Is he coming up here? He better hurry, if he wants to use this fire."

"Let him go." Earl's voice became hard with command. "You stay here, understand? This doesn't concern you."

"All right. I ain't butting into your private business."

Clyde was right out in the open, on the creek, and he had to get under cover. He went forward, very quiet in the dark, careful that his boots didn't suck mud, and came up against a bank. The bank was straight up and down, slightly higher than his head. It was more than straight up and down, it hung over some, so it gave good cover. He'd have been safe there in broad daylight. It was just as well, because he realized they were right above him, between the bank and some corrals.

"You better come along and have a bite," Earl said.

"Not hungry."

Clyde recognized the voice now. It belonged to Ted Danner.

Earl said: "You're here, now. You might as well come in."

"I said I wasn't hungry."

They weren't getting on, and the next was shocking, because Earl said: "I'm still sheriff, here, you son-of-a-bitch."

Danner, for all his reputation, made no response at all. It didn't bother him a bit to be called a son-of-a-bitch. He was strictly cold meat, as Billy said. He didn't have the feelings of a normal man.

"God damn you," Earl said. "I told you to keep out of this."

"How about a shot?" said Danner.

Clyde didn't understand what he meant until he heard a cork squeak and caught the smell of whiskey.

"It'd make you feel better," said Danner.

The sheriff didn't drink. He'd have had all liquor outlawed for white men as well as Indians if he'd had his way.

"Don't you ever touch the stuff?" asked Danner.

"I've touched it."

"That may be the trouble with you, Earl. What you may need from time to time is a good shot of whiskey."

"Who you got with you?"

"If you look all around, you'll see nobody's with me."

"Answer my question!"

But Danner didn't.

"Who have you got watching the ranch?"

"That sounds like an accusation. If you'd count noses in town, you'd see nobody could be watching the ranch, and I haven't hired anybody out of my own pocket. That's the trouble with this goddamn' sheriff's office, it has no income. Deputies at twenty-five dollars a month. Nobody will stir a foot unless there's a fee to be had. We ought to have a special mill levy earmarked for criminal enforcement. If we could pay a three-dollar *per diem,* we could afford to have men watching the ranch."

"That woman's no fool." Earl said, then, giving it to him hard. "Who shot her dog?"

Danner took his time before he said: "If I shoot anything out there, it won't be a damned dog."

"Somebody shot her old sheep dog, and it was done for one reason only, because someone didn't want to be found out snooping around the ranch."

Danner seemed to be having another drink.

"And I know where the *per diem* comes from," said Earl. "I took you on as undersheriff with the strict acknowledgment that I was to run the office."

"You're running it. And you can keep right on running it. But I'm going to tell you this . . . if Buttons isn't brought in by the end of this week, I'm going to head an independent posse, backed not by this county, but by the stockmen, and we're going for him."

"Are you resigning?"

"I'll let you fire me, Earl. I'll let you give me my ticket. Write it out and see who fares best. The taxpayers aren't going to put up with your pussyfooting."

That was the end of it. Earl walked toward the cabin, mounted, and rode off. Clyde was left with Danner not twenty feet away.

"Ach-pah!" went Danner, clearing his throat and spitting. Then he walked some distance and a tiny jingle of bridle links told Clyde he was fussing with something around his horse. After a while, Clyde stole across the stream, and, as soon as he dared, he lit out on the

21

rim, badger holes and snakes no matter, running the fear out, ready to fall down from effort and relief when he found his broncho, Gun Powder, waiting in the chokecherry brush. He set out for the ranch to tell Billy what he'd heard.

CHAPTER THREE

It was very late. A light burned in the house. Ma was waiting up for him. He rode around by way of the creek, through the corrals where the gate bars were down. Everything was perfectly quiet.

"Billy!" Clyde called into the barn, as he led his horse through the door.

The barn had an empty sound, no smell of confined horses. Clyde heard someone and spun around. A man had come up behind him. It was only old Tom Shipley. He had his six shooter strapped on.

"They couldn't wait no longer. They pulled stakes about an hour ago."

"Are they coming back?"

"I don't know, but, judging by what he took, I wouldn't make case on it. He took his rifle, and also the carbine, and his pistol. Oh, he was armed to the teeth. They all was. I'd hate to be the sheriff try to take them."

"He leave any word for me?"

"Just if you missed that old Nero horse, or Fiddles, that bay gelding with the shoulder scar, well, don't go looking."

Clyde pulled off the saddle and bridle, just letting them drop, he was so tired, and went over to wash up in the creek where it flowed into the corrals. Old Tom followed him, talking gunfight, about all the wild bunch he'd known in the old days, and had rode with, implying there was plenty that even to this very day he couldn't talk about.

"Take my gear in, will you?" asked Clyde.

"That's not my job!" old Tom said querulously, cut off in the middle of his story.

"Well, get it anyhow." Clyde was suddenly so sick of him, his gun, his lies and bragging, and he knew very well he'd buckle at the first showdown and tell everything he knew about Billy. "And take off that old pistol. You know Ma won't stand for it."

"Well, all right, I'll pick up your gear, but I'm not taking off this pistol. By God, I'm goin' heeled. And I'm not taking orders from you, young fellow."

"That old gun! I'd as soon stand in front of it as behind it."

"It shoots where I point it."

It was so worn the click wouldn't engage, so you had to line up the cartridge chamber with the barrel or risk getting a sliver of lead from the side. Clyde walked to the house. Ma was sitting, asleep, with the lamp lit. The chimney was all brown. She roused up when Clyde came in and laid aside a copy of ROB ROY. She'd been reading her complete Sir Walter Scott all the way through again.

"Oh, there you are. I been worried sick. Where have you been? Did you ride off with Billy and those fellows? What did he decide? Did he decide to give himself up?"

"I don't know where they went. I rode over to see what the sheriff was up to."

"What do you mean . . . up to?"

"You know who he met over at the stage station?"

She was waiting.

"Danner, that's who."

"Well, what if he did? It's no business of yours. Billy got himself into this awful trouble, and I'll not have him dragging you into it."

She went on, telling how no-good Billy was, going into a lot of ancient history, how even when he was sixteen or seventeen years old he'd go out and run with cheap, flashy no-goods, the very riffraff of the country. And how Pa had encouraged him. "Let him grow up," Pa had said. "He'll get it out of his system when it's time to assume a man's estate." Well, he grew up, and here he was going on twenty-eight years old, and he still thought the greatest thing in the world was having people laugh at his jokes and admire him and making big wads of money by outfoxing the other fellow without work.

Clyde said: "He never shot Gannaway in the back."

Ma didn't argue. She heaved a sigh and said: "Well, let's see if we can get some sleep. Oh God, when is this tribulation ever going to end?"

Thursday was mail day, and Clyde rode over to Hayden's post

office. There was always a thick bundle because of the magazines and newspapers Ma subscribed to, and the advertising letters from cattle and horse breeders still addressed to W. B. Buttons, Esq. He got it all together and tied a saddle string around it while some fellows stood and watched. Slim Weekins was there, and Ev Bartley, a fellow they called Slick Ear, and Big Mace Kuykendall. He knew they were waiting for him to read the newspapers, but Clyde wouldn't give them the satisfaction.

Finally Kuykendall said: "Hey, ain't you going to read what's in the paper?"

"I don't care what's in the paper."

Kuykendall used to be chief engineman on a river boat and was accustomed to being obeyed by a very rough lot now that he'd turned rancher. He ran only about four hundred head of stock, but he fancied himself right up there with the high and mighty, with Major Morrison, the Ethringtons, and Arbogast.

"What do you mean, you don't care? Ain't you interested in the big news of the day?"

Kuykendall pretended he was being funny, but he grabbed Clyde's bridle from in front, mean about it, showing off his strength, his mastery.

"Leave off that bridle," said Clyde.

"Why, you folks is getting famous. Don't you want to read about that cold badman, Billy Buttons?"

Clyde was tempted to sing out with his quirt, he really was. He kept trying to get the reins away while Kuykendall showed off his power and laughed at him.

"If you'd like, I'll hold your horse while you read the paper."

The others were laughing, but not too hard because they didn't care for Kuykendall, either. Rose Hayden came from the long, low, filthy log house where she lived with her husband and six or seven kids. She was a lean, rough woman who rolled cigarettes and smoked them like a man and could match a man for invective. "Lay off him, you son-of-a-bitch," she yelled. "Let him go. Who do you think you are, one of the Ethringtons?"

People joked about how Kuykendall courted the Ethringtons, but not to his face.

"What have they got to do with it?"

25

"You kiss their British asses every chance you get is what they got to do with it! All they need do is pucker up their assholes, and there you are on one knee with your hat off. Who in the bald-headed Jesus do you take yourself for? Who are *you,* siding against the Buttons? One of these days you'll get in those dudes' way, and they'll kick you right in the butt out of here."

Kuykendall laughed and let Clyde loose. "You lining up with the Badlanders, Rose?"

Paying him no more attention, Rose Hayden handed Clyde some baked stuff in a flour sack. "Here, take this home to your ma. Don't eat it all up on the way. And I expect to get the sack back."

Clyde didn't stop until he got to Blackfoot Springs where the old Army redoubt had been. He rode down among the cottonwoods to make sure nobody could possibly see him, but he didn't look at the papers right away. The area smelled vaguely of rattlesnake. He dismounted near the muddy bank where the spring came out. He scooped a basin and let it clear, and lay flat and drank the cold water, coming up with his nose and chin dripping. He let the water run down inside his shirt, cold and refreshing. Then he still didn't rush to read the papers. He made a test of character and decided first to eat one of the fresh rolls. There was a note in the sack, printed and drawn, all capitals:

UND. SHERRF CAMPT LAST
NIGHT AT OLD FORT 18 STRONG
HEADED FOR BROWNS LANDING

He held the note and felt empty from helplessness. There was not a thing to be done. If Billy was at Brown's, there was no warning him. And well he might be. It was one of his favorite hangouts, a wood yard and trading post where boats seldom stopped except on flag. There were always a number of loafers at Brown's — trappers, wood hawks, cowboys out of work, and men on the lope from the law. About once every year there would be a big, drunken ruckus, and somebody would get killed. Then the sheriff, who in former days had been the resident deputy, would say: "No, I'm not going to investigate. They know what it's like when they go down there." Pat Brown owned the store, wood yard, saloon, everything, and ran a

26

herd of cattle. The cattle were branded P Lazy B for his initials, but everybody called his ranch the 2 Lazy 2 P. He was a real old-timer, a squawman with half-breed kids from age forty down by at least three Indian wives, two of whom he'd had at the same time, or so they said. He had a real pretty daughter named Lola who the fellows joshed Billy about, calling her his dusky maiden.

Well, thought Clyde, *Brown's is the last place they'll catch Billy napping*. No matter how empty the badlands seemed, you could never ride through without people seeing you, and, if it was a posse, it would be known a long way ahead. That was Bill's country; it was his native land. By now he'd be over the hills and far away.

Clyde's appetite came back. He started wolfing the fresh rolls, one after another. Then he opened the newspapers to see what they said about Billy.

The weekly *State Post* from Helena had a big headline about **TERRITORIAL FAIR OPENS**, and another, **STATEHOOD ASSURED, ALDRICH TELLS CHAMBER**. But in smaller type toward the bottom:

PROMINENT CATTLEMAN SHOT DOWN
John J. Gannaway, Prominent Rancher of Musselshell
Country, Former Kansas Legislator, Freight Operator
Killed by Man Going by Name of Billy Buttons

The editor must never have heard of the Buttons family, even though Pa had served a term for eastern Chouteau County as representative in the legislature. Clyde read the article. It was long and had hardly one sentence of truth in it. It said that "a man, bearing the sobriquet of Billy Buttons, reputedly leader of a gang of rustlers and outlaws known as The Badlanders, or The Hole-in-the-Wall gang," had lain in wait for John Gannaway, "the prominent and well known rancher-capitalist," and shot him down without warning. But in another place it said Billy Buttons was "captain of the Little Snowy Roundup Association, rival of the Big Draw and Judith Roundup Associations, which has drawn into its membership many small owners. A chaotic condition exists in the cattle ranges after the disastrous winter of 1886–87" — which didn't square with all that about rustlers, outlaws, and the Hole-in-the-Wall gang. The Hole-in-the-Wall gang was away down in Wyoming, showing how little the editor knew. "A wide search is being conducted by Undersheriff T. S. Danner of Chouteau County." Danner had nothing to do with Chouteau County. He was Undersheriff of Ricketts County. "Danner is known here to many, having served some months as a policeman at Park City. Until his appointment as Undersheriff he was Chief Range Detective for the Anglo-American Land & Cattle Co., recently gone into receivership." And that was about the only accurate thing in the entire story.

The other paper came from Miles City, and they had it on the back page, which was the main Montana news page.

J. J. GANNAWAY DIES

Then it had a lot about where he was born, and how he'd been prominent as a freight operator, one of the founders of the Council Bluffs Beef Packing Company, Sioux City Yards Company, and the guiding genius in reorganizing the Anglo-American, the Northwestern, and several other companies into a new combine: the Omaha and Montana Cattle Company, of which he was president at the time of his death. It told about his family, two sons and a daughter, and a wife living in Council Bluffs, and that she was ill. (She had actually been in an asylum for years, and John, Jr., had told Billy once that he held his father responsible, that his cruelty had sent her there. Yet the article referred to him as a "devoted husband.") The body had been taken to Billings and shipped east for burial. Then in an item that seemed to have been added at the last minute, it said there were "conflicting reports" of Gannaway's passing, but that a search was going forward for "Wm. T. Buttons, a former business associate," it being reported that the shooting was "culmination of a dispute over co-ownership of cattle."

The "dispute over co-ownership" dated to three years back when Gannaway wanted to have a herd of blooded shorthorn cattle driven up from Wyoming. The range was bad, and the weather hot, so he conceived the idea of driving west around the Big Horn Mountains, instead of the regular trail via Tongue River. His problem was crossing the Crow Indian treaty lands, from the Wyoming line all the way to the Yellowstone River, and then the Bull Mountains, an area of

28

wooded hills full of rustlers. Naturally Billy came to mind. He knew everybody and was trusted. Especially, he knew the Indians. He would be away from home two or three months at a time, and, when he did come in the house, it would smell just as if you'd opened a box of smoked herring, and Ma would say: "Oh God, he's been lying around the Injun camps again!" And she'd say: "The least you could do is bathe the teepee smoke off in soap and water." But Billy had bathed. It wasn't teepee smoke you smelled, but leather stuff squaws had made for him — gloves, moccasins, beaded wallets. The squaws tanned their buckskin by scraping and pounding and then squatting down and taking a pee on it, Billy said. He'd seen them do it a hundred times, and that's how you picked out the squaw you wanted. He swore it was the truth. Then they dried it in the sun, and chewed it soft, and finally they hung it in a willow smudge; they smoked it for days until it got full of a certain oily tar, and it never stopped smelling. You might have a beaded buckskin shirt you liked, so you'd let it hang outside for a year or two until you couldn't smell a thing, but, when you put it on and it got warm from the heat of your body, that smoky smell would come pouring out again. Billy was great friends with Elk Calf Man, chief of the River Crows, and claimed to have been offered his daughter in marriage. Whether that was true or not, he was just the one to deal with them. He could save Gannaway's having to go around the Bulls, too, because he had no trouble there at all. He rode everywhere he wanted, and the doors were always open. In fact, they weren't rustlers, he said, but small ranchers, trying to get along.

So they made an agreement. Billy was to serve as guide and furnish half a dozen riders — Ace Carter, Long Tom Cooper, and some other trusted men — and receive five hundred dollars plus a certain percentage of the cattle saved. That is, on drives during poor condition a ten percent loss might be expected. If there were fifteen hundred head total, it would be one hundred and fifty. So, if they delivered one thousand four hundred and twenty-five, or a five percent loss, Billy was to get half of the difference, or thirty-seven and a half cattle. That's how Billy always told it. People liked to hear Billy retell things because it got funnier and funnier.

It hadn't worked out. They had got the cattle as far as the Yellowstone, and there had been a "misunderstanding." According to

29

Gannaway they had been waiting to cross the river, and Billy and his riders had gone into Billings on a big toot. Gannaway said Billy had got into a poker game, and they couldn't get him to leave. Finally, Gannaway said, he couldn't wait any longer, so he took the cattle up through the Bulls himself, danger notwithstanding. Billy said it was a lie. They'd agreed to spend six, seven days on some good pasture before crossing the river, and Gannaway had said: "Go on into town, take your boys, my riders will tend to things, then it'll be our turn." That would have been three days apiece, but as soon as Billy was out of the way, John Gannaway had larruped the whole herd north, Billy having made the mistake of already fixing up a safe passage with his friends in the Bull Mountains. Later, Gannaway wanted to settle with Billy for a cash amount, but Billy claimed he was owed fifty of those fine shorthorn cattle. He didn't get them. The hard winter followed the dry summer, no more than half the herd saw it through, and Gannaway sold them off to an outfit on Smith River, having decided that Herefords would be better in that climate than shorthorns.

Billy kept after him, saying that was all right, he'd take white faces instead, *plus* the increase. You never knew whether Billy was joking or not, but it turned out he wasn't, because last fall he had tied into Gannaway at the River House Bar in Arlington. Gannaway was supposed to have said: "Take off your pistol and I'll fight you hand to hand." That was one story. Another was that Billy had called him every name he could lay his tongue to, and Gannaway had just taken it, and later he'd walked out to find Ike Thrift, or one of his other Wyoming gunfighters, and, as Billy had his backing, it looked like trouble. But Earl Hankey had come around and ordered them to shake hands. Neither version could have been true, because somewhere along the line Billy and Gannaway had been Indian wrestling with their elbows on the bar, and Gannaway had won, and then Billy offered to throw him by another method, and they both ended up with their shirts torn off, and that was when the sheriff had come around.

Clyde sat under the cottonwoods and thought about all the ways Gannaway had tried to get the ahead of Billy, and how Billy had been too smart for him. For example, there had been Billy's estray business. Ma wouldn't let him have much say about the home ranch, so he'd gone into a partnership with Art Rooney on the O X, also known as the Spider Brand, out by Crazy Buttes. Fellows would work the badlands of the river for strays, and Billy would buy them. He'd buy their rights in them. It was all perfectly honest and above-board. So many outfits had gone broke, their brands vacated, or cattle had wandered so far in the great blizzard, that it was generally impossible to locate an owner. Billy would impound the stock before signed witnesses and advertise for claimants. If there happened to be a claim, he would charge for the ad plus expenses, which was his legal right under the estray law. When Arlington still had a weekly paper, hardly an issue came out, but there would be six or eight head of stock advertised, each with its brand inscribed on a blank of type. People used to say Billy would have several with the same brand, but he'd only advertise one. Also that cowboys with nothing else to do would drive cattle from away off somewhere, and make them estray. One time the Mill Iron Company from halfway to Dakota threatened to sue, and Billy showed up in Arlington with a lawyer from Kansas City who examined all the records. He said he and his client were ready to meet all legal action with appropriate counter action. The Mill Iron didn't carry it further, but what a howl had gone up from the newly organized Omaha Company when they found out Billy was claiming some calves with white faces. The association had a meeting, and Avery Carns, the Omaha boss, stormed around that any white face was theirs, *prima facie,* because they were the only ones who had ever brought them into the country, but Billy had backing, too, because Omaha had brought in bulls, and a great many more bulls than they needed. In fact, their white-face bulls were ranging very freely, and, if the issue had white markings like their sires, then it was only a matter of time before a claim could be made on every calf in the country.

"You keep your runty-legged Eastern bulls away from my long-horn cows," Billy had been quoted as telling Gannaway during their row at the Mountdouglas House, "or I'll sue you for mongreling the breed."

However, Billy, or rather the Buttons, had something that concerned the Omaha much more than its claim against a few white-faced cattle. Before railroads came, the cheapest way to get freight into Montana Territory had been by steamboat from St. Louis, Sioux

31

City, or Bismarck, whichever was head of rail transportation at the time. When the water was high, boats went all the way to Fort Benton, but many seasons they could get no farther than the mouth of the Musselshell, so a road was laid out, slightly south of west, to Helena. The distance was two hundred miles by the map, closer to three hundred because of the mountain ranges in the way, and still the domain of wild Indians, but Helena needed the river traffic, otherwise the origin of most traffic would be Corinne, Utah, on the Union Pacific, and the natural commercial center would be some town farther south. A great deal had been at stake. Helena was also battling Virginia City for the capital, and so the road had been finished, and pressure had been brought on the federal government in Washington to protect it, with the result that the Army had set up a permanent post called Fort Howe at the foot of the Castle Mountains, and semi-permanent summer posts called Fort Hardee and Fort Griffin. As several hundred Army mules and horses had to be fed, plots were set aside for hay reserves. The plot near Fort Griffin had been the only one used. The other, known as the Buttons Reserve, had been given away for use by various freighting outfits having Army contracts. Chief among those, and the only one to remain after the railroads had come and traffic on the Helena road had ended, was Pa who had operated the W. B. Buttons Freight Company.

Now, here was a very amusing thing: everybody thought it was called Buttons Reserve because of Pa. This was not the case. It was named for the Buttons Buttes, two flat, circular outliers of sand rock that looked like buttons on a coat, and had been so named by trappers when Pa was still a kid back in Kentucky. But now there wasn't a soul outside the family who doubted they were named for the Buttons. It gave them a good claim on that part of the range. The same held for the Buttons Rreserve, and, when the Army had moved away, Pa had treated it like personally owned land, except that he never paid taxes on it. That's how it had been for better than twelve years, but when the Omaha was organized, its lawyers searched title of all lands in the area, and went to Washington and leased all the Army reserves, including the Buttons Reserve — the Buttons Reserve most of all, because even in poor years it grew grass to your knee, and in good years Clyde had seen it in grass to his armpits.

Billy was gone, as usual, when Ma had heard about Omaha's

trying to claim what had always been part of the ranch, so she got dressed up, and Clyde drove her to town to see Paul V. Stewart, the county attorney. Stewart said he'd look into it, but there wasn't much could be done. He asked to see her tax receipts, and, of course, there weren't any, and he said that was unfortunate, that evidently the late Mr. Buttons did not believe he owned the land, or else he'd have paid. Ma was just sick about it, but there didn't seem much she could do. However, when Billy came home, he said, by God, they did have a right, a right that was acknowledged by custom, a common law right, to wit, the right of occupation, use, and possession.

The Reserve had never been fenced, but Pa had a shack on it, down near the sloughs of Hay Creek, where he would go to hunt ducks, or just to sit around for a few days when he wanted to be alone. Billy got to calling it "the farmstead," and he brought in some rolls of barbed wire and had a mile of fence put up — just a straight line, it didn't enclose anything — and next he rented the place to a family by the name of Harbison, on credit, provided they'd plow a few acres and keep some clothes on the line. There was nothing like clothes on a clothesline, Billy said, to make a place look occupied.

Lyle Weaver, U. S. commissioner, drove out and tacked a notice on the house, ordering all trespassers off, under penalty of federal statute, so Harbison rode over to Ma's as hard as he could cut, bareback on an old, gray, plow horse. Clyde wasn't home at the time, but Ma had Jim Walsh working for her, and he hitched up and drove her over to see what was what. Weaver must have figured she'd respond, and he could serve a paper on her. At least he had one in his possession, and he was waiting. He handed her the paper, and Ma tore it up. She ripped down the one he'd posted and tore it up, too. Nobody had ever seen her so mad. Weaver said, all right, he was only acting as an officer of the federal court, that the next visit would be by the United States marshal. This scared Harbison who was ready to pack what he had and move off, but his wife wasn't. They had about seven kids, and she didn't seem to think the government would put them in jail. When Ma asked him what kind of a man was he, and didn't he realize that a man's home was his castle?...Harbison decided to stay. Besides, he had no other place to go. If he'd left, he'd probably have had to go to work. As it was, Billy kept hauling grub to them. So the farther off Weaver got, driving back to town to tell the powers-that-be what·had happened, the more Harbison got outraged, and said, yes, by God, all the sheriffs and marshals in the land weren't going to put him out of his home, which he had rented and built up with the sweat of his brow.

Nobody bothered Harbison again, but a few days later Gannaway drove out to see Ma, telling her he was sorry that Weaver had made a fool of himself with all his threats, but nevertheless Omaha did have the land leased and had paid money over and would be perfectly within its rights to bring in the U. S. marshal to effect an eviction. However, they realized the Buttons had always used the land, and, while they had no legal claim, there was sort of a moral claim grown up through habit and custom. Hence it had been decided to offer her the sum of five cents per acre, or four hundred and seventy-five dollars, and another two hundred in consideration for the improvements.

"No," said Ma, "it's always been Buttons land. Why, it's marked right on the map as Buttons land."

Gannaway said, well, that might be, although he hadn't seen any such map. Ma said it was marked Buttons Reserve on the books in the Fort Benton land office. And what was more, it was flanked on the east by Buttons Buttes. Then she reeled off all about possession, common law title, and "moot acknowledgment of the community," all the things that Billy had said and she'd scoffed at when he'd said them.

Gannaway, who despite his beaming Irish manner had a short fuse when crossed, sat right there in the parlor and heard her out, redder-faced by the minute, and said: "Missus Buttons, you must know deep in your heart you can't take over the Army lands in this manner."

"You mean you'll bring the Army in?"

He laughed and said: "No, of course not. The Army has made over the administration of the lands to us on leave. But they still have ownership."

"That remains to be seen. It's my understanding they merely usurped those lands from the Department of the Interior, and their claim, whatever it was, vanished with the abandonment, so, if all you have is an Army lease, then you have nothing at all."

This was a new one on Clyde who was listening from the kitchen, but from the peek he got at Gannaway, it really struck home. Gannaway acted for a second as if he were going to rise up and let Ma have one right in the chops. His neck turned as red as beefsteak, while his face was white.

"You've been traveling around, talking to cheap lawyers," he said when he was able to speak. "Well, let me tell you, nobody gains when they get involved with lawyers. There'll be nothing left for you when *they* get through."

Ma remained perfectly cool. "Mister Gannaway, the title of those lands is not up to you, or the Army, or the marshals. We are in possession, and our possession dates a long way back and has never been challenged. I'll tell you this! There has been ample precedent for so-called squatter sovereignty. The courts time after time have held for those in actual possession, tilling the soil. You Easterners and Englishmen may be able to come out here and run us old-time settlers out of our homes, I don't know, but this I guarantee . . . if you run the Buttons off, you'll do it in the full light of public knowledge. Because we're standing fast."

Ma didn't really mean it, though. She was just sick when Gannaway went.

"Oh, they'll find a way," she said bitterly. "They always find a way. Oh, God, I wish we were gone from here. I wish we were gone to where we could live in peace and decency."

She was building herself up to take the offer. Billy said all right, if Ma played her cards right, she could get as much as twenty-five hundred for the Reserve, plus another twenty-five hundred for the Buttons home ranch. It would be worth five thousand dollars to the Omaha just to get the Buttons out of the country.

"That's pretty good," he said. "They ought to call us the Skunk family. It's not every family has a five-thousand-dollar pest value." Then he slapped Clyde on the shoulder and said: "We'll get that money and send you to college. You'll be a credit to all of us. That's what Ma wants, and that's what I want. And, by God, we'll make those Omaha sons-of-bitches pay for it!"

For years Ma had been talking about going back East to visit her relatives. With five thousand dollars, they could do it in style. Even the interest off five thousand dollars amounted to considerable. Clyde would get to ride on the train, which he'd never done, and attend some of the big Eastern state fairs. Then he'd go to medical college and become a doctor. First he might have to go to Latin school for a while, but inside a year he could enroll, and by the time he was twenty-one, if he worked hard, he'd be graduated, full fledged. He could practice in some city, maybe in a hospital, doing whatever came his way for a small fee, but in a year, or at most two, he'd be all practiced up, and then he could go where he liked, and be on his own. He could go all over the world, free, on steamships, just for his services. He could get jobs with big companies like Heccla, or Standard Oil, and they'd send him to foreign lands. He could go to Mexico, or Alaska, or go into the Army and be an officer right away. There was absolutely nothing that would let a fellow go where he pleased like being a doctor. "You can just hang up your shingle and wait for the wounded," is what Billy said. Chiefly, though, Clyde wanted to be a doctor because he'd be *somebody*. "There goes Doctor Buttons," people would say. "Hey, Doc, don't forget to *button* him up when you're through operating." That would be a joke he'd have to get used to. He could imagine himself smiling when they said it, just smiling, friendly but keeping his distance, demanding respect.

So much for that. Clyde got back on his horse and rode home. He gave the newspapers to Ma, and the note, which she burned.

"Rose Hayden could get in trouble doing this," said Ma. She went about her work and got supper, and never mentioned Billy, or what it said in the papers, or anything.

CHAPTER FOUR

"Clyde!"

"Yeah?" He was scared by Ma's tone.

"Get up quick!"

Riders were fanned out in a sweep from one side of the bottoms to the other. He looked toward the ridge and saw riders coming from there, too. By the time he was dressed and outside with Ma, the first of them had spurred to reach the corrals. They went through the barn on foot, and through the sheds. There seemed to be men everywhere. Then two of them came out with old Tom. He was arguing and fighting back and getting shoved and knocked around for his trouble.

"Mister Kilpatrick!" Ma cried out. "Mister Kilpatrick, you leave that man alone!"

It was Luke Kilpatrick who'd been fired as warehouseman by the Baker Steamboat Line. He had the biggest mustache in the county, and he always looked as if his pants were falling off. Hearing himself named, he stopped roughing up old Tom and looked toward the house. He didn't answer. Ted Danner saw Ma and walked toward her.

"Missus Buttons? I'm T. S. Danner, the undersheriff."

"I know who you are. Where's the sheriff . . . the man duly elected and constituted to enforce the laws of this county?"

"Sheriff Hankey went to town. I'm in charge. We're looking for your son. We have a warrant. If he's in the house, or anywhere else around, it would save a lot of trouble if he gave himself up."

"Well, he's not here. I haven't seen or talked to him in weeks."

That was true, she hadn't *seen* him, and she hadn't talked to him.

"We're going to have a look in the house."

"Well, look!"

Danner waited for help. He had his pistol in his belt, and he didn't put a hand on it. He was too proud and evil-arrogant, but just the same he didn't walk in alone. He looked at Clyde.

"That's my youngest son," Ma said. "You leave him be."

Danner laughed, and they went in, three of them by the back door and then two more in front. They went through the house, looking under things, and down the cellar by the trapdoor, and in about three minutes came out again, obviously no longer expecting to find him.

Danner sized Clyde, up and down, perhaps considering a bit of arm twisting to see if he would tell where Billy was, but he didn't do it. He looked sour, bilious, and tired. He probably wanted to get back to town where the liquor was. The horses bore signs of having traveled many a mile. There was even a small remuda of about seven head being driven by a wrangler who had had no part in the search. It must have been quite an expedition, and now it was going back empty handed.

"Missus Buttons, if Billy gets in touch with you, tell him to come in," Danner said. "Tell him to send word ahead and not one move will be made prior to his surrender. Fairer than that, nobody can be."

"He never gets in touch with me. You're wasting your time talking to me."

"All right, come on. Let's get out of here."

They rode off. The dust settled. Later in the day it rained, washing their tracks away. There were cloudbursts in the mountains, sending torrents down the creeks, filling the potholes, giving Clyde an easier time patrolling between Arrow Creek and the Big Piney.

For weeks there was no sign of anyone watching from the ridge. It was very hot all through July, but a succession of sudden rains kept the range green. They were having a good year; the country was coming back. August came on, hot as usual, but as soon as the sun went down, you could feel a cold current reminding you that autumn was not far away. Travel along the roads picked up with the approach of roundup time when the worst loafers in the land worked for at least a month or two, trying to earn a winter's grubstake.

Harry Doty and Hank Reynolds came around to talk to Ma about the roundup. How many riders was she willing to furnish and who would her reps be? Some of the beef was going south to the Northern Pacific, but the Association and some non-members from across the river had contracted with one of the Dakota packet companies to ship by flatboat to the Sioux City yards at a guaranteed saving of one third. Ma as a member of the Association was, of course, welcome to participate, but arrangements had to be made.

In other years Billy was on hand, and he could always find some of his friends to ride in the Buttons' behalf, but Billy was gone now, and Ma didn't know what to do. She was in no position to hire anybody, so she asked for a few days and had Clyde drive her to Dave Young's Square 6 ranch in the buggy. Pa had helped set him up in the cattle business back in the spring of 1879 and had lent him money, and, when he had died, Dave said if there was anything, ever, he could do for Ma, she should just ask. So now she asked him to furnish riders for her share in the roundup, and she'd pay him after the beef sale.

She and Clyde didn't get what would be called a cordial welcome. He listened leather-faced and said: "No, I can't be put in that position."

"In what position?"

"You know what position."

Ma kept a tight grip on her voice. "I want to hear you say it."

"Well, if it was last year, I'd have said, yes, but I can't partner with you after what happened to John Gannaway. I can't have them say I'm lining up with the Buttons."

Ma still held her temper, but Clyde was so damned angry he just let go. "You liked the Buttons pretty well when you needed money and the bank wouldn't lend you a cent!" But Ma gave him such a ram with her elbow it almost knocked him off the seat, so he didn't get any more out.

"Yes, I know," admitted Young. "I came to W. B. when I needed five hundred dollars that time, and he let me have it. And I paid it back. I gave him interest . . . not that he asked for it. Still, we've been friends a long time, and I owe a debt of gratitude, but things are to the point now where I can't be seen lining up with you. Even if Billy hadn't had that trouble. . . ."

"I don't think there's been any proof yet my son is guilty."

"Then let him come in and clear things up. But even so, there's that matter of the herd he's running with Art Rooney over on the Spider."

"That's his business, not mine."

"At any rate, I can't do it."

39

"You're knuckling under!" interjected Clyde. This time he was going to have his say. "You're scared of the Omaha."

"I'm staying in business through a hard situation. Wait till you get a few years on you, kid, and you'll see things aren't ever so simple."

"Clyde, stop it!" Ma said.

They must have been causing more commotion than Clyde thought because several fellows came up on the corral rails for a look, and Con Sharpless, the cook, looked out from the kitchen.

Clyde continued: "Pa set you up with your first cattle and then stood against the English outfits from Wyoming when they'd have run you off the range."

"You whelp. You god-damn pup." Young started toward him.

"What kind of a man are you?" asked Ma. "He's only a boy."

"Get him off my ranch."

"We'll get off."

"I'll tell you what kind of a man I am!" Young went on. "I'm a man that spent his whole life working night and day, winter and summer, never had a family or anything, no comfort, nothing, living worse than a coyote in the coulée, and finally, by God, when I get a little bit ahead of the game, I'm not going to toss it all away."

But his voice was lost, mixed with the rattle of the buggy, as Ma whipped the horses herself, and Clyde managed them.

"I shouldn't have gone over there," Ma said, "and *you* should have kept your mouth shut."

Clyde was sick about it, feeling he'd done the wrong thing.

"I'll go on the roundup, Ma. I'll rep for us."

"No, you won't. You'd just get in trouble."

Every day or two somebody dropped in at the ranch. Art Rooney came and asked Ma if she wanted to join the Central Roundup Company. Again there'd been talk about a roundup made by the small outfits, but nothing would come of it.

Then one evening, at just about sundown, the kitchen door opened and in walked Billy.

"Is supper ready?"

He acted as if he didn't have a care in the world. He had a gun, but it was off, rolled up in a belt and holster because Ma would allow nobody to come in armed. He laid it on a shelf. He had on a new outfit, not brand new, but nothing Clyde had seen before — a floppy Panama hat, gray-white shirt, jersey pants, and chocolate-brown, knee-high, riding boots. He certainly didn't look as if he'd been sleeping in any wolf holes.

"You shouldn't walk in here in broad daylight," Ma told him. "They've been combing the country for you."

"I know."

"Are you alone?"

He didn't say. He laughed and winked at Clyde. "Don't see anybody, do you?"

"Do you have a gang down in the barn?" Ma asked.

"No." (But he had somebody watching from the hills, you could bet on that.) "I came back here to see what the rumpus was about. You didn't think I'd let 'em run me out of the country, did you? No, sir. This is my home. I lived here longer than any of 'em. I lived here longer than you, Ma. I rode in here with Pa when you was still back on Smith River. Why, I helped chase off the buffalo."

"I'm telling you this won't blow over, Billy. This isn't any ordinary thing."

"You're right."

"Don't think you can ride in and just explain things."

"Not even if I'm innocent and can show it?"

"If that Danner gets hold of you, there'll be no chance to show anything."

"That's not going to happen. I'm going to put my trust in Uncle Earl to see I get a fair and proper trial."

"You'll show up with witnesses, I suppose. You'll prove an alibi, or you'll try to prove self-defense."

"No, I'll just present the truth, Ma."

He wanted to let it drop, but Ma stayed after him. "Who'll your witnesses be? Ace Carter and that no-good Grover Nelson? Art Rooney? That bunch of Badlanders? Who would believe them?"

"Well, who'd believe the Omaha? At least, my witnesses would come in free and unpaid, they wouldn't be hirelings of the English and the Easterners."

"Oh, go away. Get your horses and ride. Just ride. Go to Canada or Alaska."

"Now, Ma! I'm here to clear my name. I'm doing it for me and all the Buttons."

"You think there's nothing you can't do and get away with? Well, this time it won't work. So, go! Go!"

"No, Ma. I've talked it all over with a lawyer. I've laid the cards right on the table. I went there with my mind made up to take his advice. His advice was to surrender, but to do it in such a way that nobody could possibly doubt that it was my own free will and volition. I'm taking that advice. I'm going to ride right down the main street and up to that jail. I'm doing it the very best time I can find, on Saturday morning, just after sunup. I'm going to ask Clyde to come with me. There we'll be, the last of the Buttons."

"Well, Clyde's not going!"

Billy looked at Clyde. He was scared, but he was proud. He wasn't scared of riding with Billy, he wasn't scared of anything if Billy was along, but he was scared that it would go all wrong, that it would be suicide for Billy to stand trial.

"How about it, Clyde? Are you riding in there with me?"

"He's not!"

"Yes! I am."

"Shoulder to shoulder. Stirrup to stirrup. The last of the Buttons! We'll show 'em, kid. We'll show 'em or go out in a blaze of glory, I'll promise you that. We'll teach those dude sons-of-bitches a lesson they'll never forget, that's my promise to you."

"What time is it?" asked Clyde, his ears still buzzing from sleep.

Billy's voice came from close in the dark: "Just grab your things. Put 'em on outside."

He did. It was so night-cold Clyde's teeth chattered. He was shivering all over, uncontrollably. He tried and tried to get his legs in his pants.

"Take your time. I didn't want another go-'round with Ma. I don't think a man should have to argue with women."

"I don't pay her too much heed," said Clyde.

"I know it's been pretty rough on you here . . . Ma running things. She's getting along in years, Clyde. Ma's a fine woman. I think the world of her. But even when Pa was alive, he could stand it just so long. He had to hide out on Hay Creek about one week in four."

"I don't mind. It goes in one ear and out the other."

In the corral the horses were dark shapes, aware of them. The moon shone on slicks of mud and water, hoof-track mirrors. It was so quiet you could hear the creek running.

"This is a good time of night," said Billy. "I like it this time of night." He talked as they saddled, and let the corral bars down, and rode. "A man will be sleeping and wake up at this time of night, and look, and wonder what the end is and how anything happens to be." It wasn't everybody Billy would talk to that way, and it warmed Clyde, knowing how close they were as brothers. "There's a certain time away deep in the night when there isn't a sound or a movement anywhere. It will be just absolutely empty and then you'll be lying there, the only living thing left in the world. And then there'll be some little thing. It may be no more than a blade of grass, but it will be a sign that things are starting to wake up. Then, one by one, everything will start to stir. You can't imagine how many things there are unless you lie through the blank time of night. Did you know you could even hear the gophers under the ground? I don't mean putting your ear down to their holes, but right through the ground under you, if you lie quiet enough. Stirring about, scraping the dirt, gnawing. Those gophers away down there in the dark. It gives you a strange feeling to know that they have their lives and worries just like we do. That's what I like to do, Clyde . . . lie out there in the long lonesome . . . or just ride and ride with the wind blowing. I don't know how I'm going to make it in jail. But you know what Ma says . . . 'Stone walls do not a prison make, nor iron bars a cage.' "

"Yeah, that's right," said Clyde, trying to sound off-hand. "Think you'll be safe, going in there?"

"Why, no. There's nothing safe in this world. Not if you face it, and not if you turn your back on it. But there's certain things a man has to do."

They rode and rode with the night getting on, following no road or trail. Just the prairie, the heights and bulges of the prairie. They rode where they could see. In some respects they could see better than by daylight. The river and all the coulées were planted in purple. Crazy Buttes, away off above Brown's Landing, were sharp in every convolution. Then, swinging your eyes about forty degrees east, making a distance of about twenty miles along the river, you could make out a faint glow, a shine as if from a fire in the valley. That was Arlington with its new, steam-powered, electric generator, running all night long to keep the street and dock lights burning. It gave Clyde an eerie feeling, as if it was a fire burst out of the earth.

They rode and rode, and slowly the details faded, a thick darkness settled over the land. It was the darkness before dawn. Then dawn came, and the sun. When the sun got hot, they rested. Clyde could spit dough balls from thirst. A white puff of dust appeared far down the road and hung, apparently unmoving, for a quarter hour, then an object took shape — the Billings stage.

"They're using the omnibus," said Billy. "That's the same omnibus they had between Helena and Butte before the railroad was finished. It has genuine coiled springs. It rides like a railroad coach. Holds twenty-four passengers. Things really must be booming. Well, that's what I wanted, everybody on hand, and we'll ride right down that street. I want the whole country to know that I came in completely of my own free choice.

"You worried about it? You think maybe they'll shoot me on sight? They wouldn't do that. It would look bad for the town. They'd look Wild West, and nobody would want to invest money. Besides, Clyde" — and he winked — "the man who raised a gun against me would never live to tell the tale."

That was what worried Clyde, the friends Billy may have sent ahead to give him backing, just in case. They would get to drinking and shooting their mouths off, bragging, and let the cat out of the bag. You could trust Long Tom Cooper, but Grover Nelson would tell everything he knew, and Kid Nehf was a sneak. Clyde didn't say so, however, because Billy would get his back up whenever you said the least word against a friend. The more no-account that friend was, the surer Billy would be to resent it. He wouldn't say anything right at the moment — in fact, he'd be as nice as pie — and then he'd say something that was really cutting.

"He's got the same mean streak as Uncle Josh," Ma would say. Billy would do something Ma didn't like, and she'd say: "He's Josh, all over again." Josh was Pa's older brother who had been town marshal of Atchison, Kansas, after it was taken over by anti-slavery forces before the war, but he was voted out of office and later became a captain with Berge's Sharpshooters — the Fourteenth Missouri —

44

and was killed at Shiloh. "You could always tell when Josh was holding a grudge by how polite he was," Ma would say. "Oh, it would be Mister This and Mister That, but when it came handy, Josh'd do some utterly vicious and vindictive thing." And that's what Billy was like. But, by God, he was loyal! Nobody could say he didn't stick by his friends!

They couldn't have timed it better. A glint of sunlight still hung along the sandrock cliffs a mile beyond town. Everybody seemed to be out, along the sidewalks. They seemed to be waiting for Billy.

"Back straight, eyes ahead," Billy said. "Little jog, tight rein. Just enough to make your spurs jingle. Make it a sight they'll never forget. The Buttons boys, riding into Arlington."

God! He was cool about it, and Clyde could hear them — "Hey, it's Billy Buttons!"— racing down the street.

He could hear the boots and the doors, as men hurried to see. Billy was enjoying it, but Clyde was scared. He was so scared he felt as if he might fall off his horse.

It wasn't a long street, built mainly on one side with a view of the river, and they didn't have to cover more than half of it before reaching the jail and county offices. Earl Hankey had got the news and was outside to see.

"Hello, sheriff," said Billy. "They say you been looking for me."

CHAPTER FIVE

"That's fifteen two, fifteen four, and a pair makes six, and one for his Nobs, and there's the crib. I'm going to peg out on you."

"I never saw such luck. A dollar eight already, and two I owe you from yesterday."

"Your luck's about to change," said Billy.

"Just so *your* luck doesn't change . . . and at the wrong time, hey, Billy?" said Luke Kilpatrick, part-time deputy, part-time town marshal, looking through the cell door.

"Why, Luke, if you're referring to the trial, there's to be no luck about that, one way or the other. The trial will go strictly on the facts in evidence. Now, I know what the facts are. And I pretty much know they're going to be put in evidence. Otherwise, I wouldn't have ridden in here of my own free will and choice. No, I'm not playing cards with my life and liberty. I'm not that kind of fellow at all."

Billy sat cross-legged on his iron cot with his boots off, playing cards with Oscar Friedahl, a very tall, red-faced Swede who had the cell's only chair. There was a box for cards and cribbage board between them. Billy's hair was slicked, and he smelled of hair tonic. He had just been barbered, and the barber had tarried to watch the game. There were two others in the small, log-sided room that looked more like a cabin than a jail cell — Jack Wallin and Grover Nelson. There wasn't room for more. The air was thick-layered with tobacco smoke, but others were sitting around the main office — Ace Carter, Long Tom Cooper, Dirty Jake Skinner from the coal mine, old Andy Weaver with his walrus mustache, a pensioned soldier named McGrath, and Kilpatrick. Kilpatrick made sure everyone left his weapons at the counter, but he didn't keep the cell locked. It was locked only at night.

"What I ought to do," said Billy, "is get 'way deep in debt to you fellows in hopes you get on the jury."

Oscar said: "I can't serve on no jury." He pronounced it *yoo-ry*. "I'm not on voting rolls. I'm not American citizen."

The fellows got to arguing about whether you had to be a Montana resident, seeing it was a territorial, and hence federal, court.

"I don't know," said Billy, starting to play solitaire. "Ask the sheriff."

Sheriff Hankey had come into the outer office where, though speaking civilly enough, showed by his manner that he wanted the crowd to leave. "Anything I can bring you?" he asked Billy.

"Yes, if you get any catfish on your set line, have the Chinaman fry some for me."

"You want it tonight?"

"No, I have T-bone ordered for tonight. I'd like it tomorrow morning. I love fish and cornbread for breakfast."

"You sure eat good," said Grover Nelson. "I wish I was in jail so I could eat so good."

"I have to pay for it myself," Billy said. "What's on the menu for tonight, Sheriff? The free menu?"

"I don't know."

"Salt pork and biscuits?"

"There's worse," replied the sheriff. "I've fed on a lot worse."

"You didn't come here to talk about grub. Something's troubling you."

The sheriff took a paper from his pants pocket and handed it to Billy. It was a telegram written out in pencil on blue paper, a notification to Sheriff Hankey and County Recorder Pennecard that the Honorable Curtis Minough, judge for the third Montana judicial district, would arrive on the twelfth, which was the next day.

"It's pretty sudden," said Hankey. "I want you to know it's a surprise to me, too. I wasn't holding out from you."

A shadow hung on Billy's face, but he handed the paper back, and then he was the same as before.

"How about that lawyer of yours?" asked Hankey. "I don't know what arrangements you made."

"He'll keep up with things."

"No word from him?"

"No."

"What if he doesn't show up? You'll have to think about it. If he

47

doesn't come, you'll have to get a court appointee."

"Paul Stewart? He's tied up with the companies."

"I wasn't thinking of Paul."

"The only other one is old Jerry Scruggs. He's not a trial lawyer. He just draws up papers."

"No, but you could get a lawyer from Billings. They have three lawyers down there. A young fellow named Cartwright is supposed to be good."

Billy was non-committal.

"I just wanted to lay it out. I thought you might want to telegraph. If they refused, or didn't answer, you might have a good cause to ask that the trial be put over."

"You must like my company. We won't have another term of court here till next summer."

"You could ask to have it moved. They hold court in Fort Benton every three months, regular as clockwork."

"Afraid you'll have the job of hanging me, Uncle Earl?"

"I wouldn't fancy it. But I'd do it. I ran for the office."

"You could give the job to Danner. He'd fancy it."

"The judge will have a civil docket long as his arm. If you could prove you'd hired a lawyer and he didn't come, Minough might move it. That way they'd draw a Benton venire. You'd stand a better chance."

"I don't believe that. I think secretly three-quarters of the people in this town are on my side."

"No, they're not. These fellows that hang around here are on your side, but they're not going to be on the jury."

"You mean it's not going to be an impartial drawing?"

"It'll be impartial. But they'll be property owners mainly, because they're the ones on the books. I could turn the list over to you, and you'd have a hard time picking a jury that'd turn you loose."

"How do you know that, Uncle Earl, without hearing the evidence?"

"I've heard the evidence."

"You've heard *their* evidence, but not mine."

"I know what testimony they have, and it'll nail you down absolutely. As for your testimony . . . nobody's going to believe Ace Carter, or any of this bunch here. Maybe you'll bring in a surprise witness. Even so, they won't believe him. You don't know how solid this country is against you. A lot of them didn't like Gannaway. He was stubborn, and he made enemies. But just the same they're not going to stand by and let that kind of citizen get shot down. If you go to trial here . . . and I don't care whether your lawyer comes or not, or how good a speech he makes . . . you haven't got a chance. I'm telling you this because I feel responsible. I rode out to the ranch and asked Kate if you'd surrender. I feel morally bound to tell you your only chance is in Benton, and maybe, if you delayed six months, they'd let you plead guilty to second degree."

"Uncle Earl, I got more faith in people than you have. And I'm going to walk out a free man. I know it, because I got right on my side, and a man with right on his side is protected as by a host of angels." And half smiling, with his Panama hat on the back of his head, he sat looking at Hankey with his wonderful eyes.

"It's no joking matter. And you'll find that out, Billy."

Judge Curtis Minough, his clerk and nephew, Alfred Bunting, and Roman Wardrope, assistant United States attorney, arrived in Arlington on the omnibus stage late next evening and were installed in specially opened and renovated quarters at the Mountdouglas House. It had been a very long and dusty journey, covering almost the whole of two days, and Minough could be seen to reel from weariness, or from land legs after the interminable jouncing of the coach, but he retired to the privacy of a hot toddy and hot bath and emerged in very good fettle.

It was very important to the judge's plans that he appear so because, although nearing seventy, an age when other judges might look toward retirement, events had suddenly presented the opportunity to sit in the Congress of the United States. Twice he had discreetly sought nomination by the Democratic territorial convention for Congressional delegate, losing both times. Now that Montana was about to become the thirty-ninth state in the Union — there was not a doubt in the world that Congress would pass the statehood bill at its next session — it would send two senators to Washington, and Judge Minough intended to be one of them. It was to this end that he had decided to hold terms of court at various remote places in the eastern part of Montana Territory. He wished to be known to as many as possible of those who would attend the first state legislature. It was this legislature that would elect the senators.

"Hello, Mister Mayor!" cried Judge Minough, striding to shake warmly the hand of John T. Wright, Arlington's mayor, and then in correct protocol Ewell Ethrington, R. E. Pennecard, and others who formed a welcoming committee in the lobby. He called each by his correct name, a thing that surprised and pleased those who had not met him before, unsuspecting he had been briefed from the vantage of a heavily balustraded mezzanine before descending.

The judge had shaved, his face was still pale, his snow white hair was swept back of his ears and down his collar in just the correct absence of care. He was an upright, but not a starched and severe, man, and the chief thing one noticed about him was his buoyant good health. Had it not been for his white hair, and for the turkey-gobbler's droop of skin that jiggled between the wings of his low, turn-point collar, one would certainly have underguessed his age. In fact, when dressed in sportsman's garb — he was an avid hunter and had brought along his three-hundred-and-fifty dollar Greener shotgun in a leather case — he looked a young sixty.

Judge Minough brushed off any solicitude concerning the difficulty of his journey. It was a rare privilege to see "your wide vistas" at first hand. "This great, broad-chested country, of red beef and golden grain." He knew that as a potential senator a certain grandiloquence was expected. He led the way outside, easily taking charge from the mayor, and on the high front porch stopped for a deep breath of the evening air. It smelled softly of the river, of fishy shallows, and of cattle, for herds had been coming in steadily to graze on the public meadows while waiting for the flatboats that would transport them downstream.

"Gentlemen, it is no longer a question of whether this town will prosper as a shipper of beef. That is a foregone conclusion. The question is, which will win as they vie for its favor . . . the steamboats of the river or the iron horse on its webs of steel? Because there *will* be a railroad. Yes, the line connecting the Northern Pacific with the Saint Paul, Minneapolis, and Manitoba will most assuredly pass through here. I wonder if you realize what this boon will mean to the town, to the entire area? This choice of water and railroad, northern route or south? However, let me caution you not to sit by passively and wait. Yours is the ideal situation, but I urge you to demand it be recognized. Let me ask *why* has the survey not been carried through? Why has approach land not been set aside for the bridge? What do we hear from our elected officials on this score? I have nothing against our delegate in Congress. After all, he has no vote. He has no power except that of persuasion. Thank God this will change when we are represented in the Senate with the same potential power as New York, Ohio, or Pennsylvania . . . as, indeed, we deserve, standing as we do third only to Texas and California as the largest state in the Union, but if you are to be heard, if this area right here, as distinct from the state of Montana, is to be heard, then I tell you that your county representatives must be heard when the legislature meets in Helena, and when those two senators are chosen. Also, you must see to it that those senators make the proper commitment. Ah! I wonder if you truly realize the richness, the potential of this land? Yours could be the breadbasket of the West, with corn and feed to double your beef production, allowing you to ship fat cattle ready for slaughter to double your income. The railroad! Aye, the government could well subsidize a railroad because it would be paid for many times over through increased property values and resultant taxes. I assure you I call for no new land grants carved from the Public Domain. Your senators will have to guard against that. But there are other ways, strong fiscal inducements, and, by gad, sirs, they will have to be explored. Ah, it boggles the mind. Do you realize that this undeveloped area of yours is as large as New Hampshire? With a railroad, and with the river development due to come, this town will become a city of five thousand souls practically overnight, and potentially twenty thousand. Ah, gentlemen. You smile. But remember who said it. Remember five years from now, and see who smiles then!"

They all looked serious, and looked at the naked river bluffs as if for the first time. Judge Minough then confessed some regret that the frontier would have to go. He had loved it when it was wild, the land of the Indian, the wandering prospector, and the buffalo. He had seen it all happen, from wilderness to tomorrow's statehood, having been the second federal judge appointed to Montana, and had made the long journey up from California by stagecoach when Virginia City was still capital of the territory. He was the only judge to have set in all three of the judicial districts. From the prairies to the mountains he was proud to have familiarized himself with the problems of the whole territory. And if those others, estimable gentlemen all, who aspired to high office, who esteemed themselves tomorrow's leaders, would bestir themselves and forego for a time the cloying luxury of Helena and Butte and get out and see what lay beyond the veil of the smelter smoke, to forget for a while queen silver, king copper, and royal gold and see the vast herds, roaming the prairies, already outnumbering the buffalo of old. But he did not censure. They had their orders of preëminence, and he had his. Tomorrow would be another day. The oversight would, he knew, be brought home to them in sorrow. For himself he deemed it a privilege. Then he laughed and said: "No, no, in answer to your questions, I am not wearied by my voyage over this prairie sea, this ocean of grass, rather do I feel as a galvanic charge my traverse of this land. Its breadth does not fill me with ennui, but with wonder. And you men who have crossed its trackless reaches and are causing it, in the teeth of old disappointments, to blossom as the rose, my hat is off to you. It fills me with pride that I have been ordained to serve, and I shall continue to serve in any way I am called."

William Westmore, printer, who had just taken over the Arlington *Herald*, interrupted rather rudely: "Judge Minough, is it true your hat is in the ring for senator?"

Minough did not care for the form of the question. "No, my hat is not in the ring. I am judge of the federal court. There are several avowed candidates . . . from the mining districts. It is my opinion that the office should seek the man. All I wish to point out is this . . . at least one of the two senators chosen should have a first-hand knowledge of the ranching half of the state."

He turned away, but the printer, scribbling, was not to be set off so easily. "How about the murder trial?"

"Indeed?"

"The Billy Buttons trial. Is it to be moved over?"

"I can't discuss such matters. I can tell you that no continuance has been asked, but if one is, it will be considered and ruled on in that manner which best serves the needs of justice and the whole community."

"You feel you have jurisdiction?"

"This is a territory of the United States, and I am federal judge of this judicial district. I anticipate no *quo warranto* proceedings. . . ."

"I mean that the state courts will supersede in criminal matters?"

"We're not a state yet. The enabling is held in abeyance. There is some gray area. It is true that some county judges have been elected, and some have taken over criminal procedures. Nothing of that here. We can't anticipate."

"Half the people in this town are sticking around for the trial. I'd hate to go to press telling 'em there'd be a trial and then have it set over or moved to Fort Benton."

Most of the fellows wanted to elbow him away, shut him up, but Judge Minough signaled, no. "Wait, now. The public should be considered. Every court is a compact between the judge and the community. We have with us Mister Roman Wardrope, the deputy United States attorney. This gentleman is, of course, Alfred Bunting, my clerk. And we have made arrangements for the good offices of your own Mister Paul Stewart. We intend to make the fur fly, as the saying goes, in regards to a very long docket . . . civil and criminal. Yes, I think you can print that your Mister Buttons will be tried . . . fairly, impartially, and with an absolute economy of time."

"By God, he'll be fair," one of the fellows said.

"Billy will get a fair trial," the judge affirmed, "but no nonsense."

At nine the next morning Judge Minough climbed the stairs to Spokane Hall, over Schine's Hardware, where court was to be held against a background of dusty theatrical scenery. He'd had a hike along the river. Now he took his seat and had a breakfast of coffee and rolls served to him at the bench. His nephew and the two lawyers had already been at work for several hours. They had gone through the docket with the idea of getting as much disposed of as possible, and within a quarter hour of Minough's appearance, breakfast still at hand, the smell of coffee filling the room, the first case was called — Bob White Cattle Company versus Theodore Hallack in the matter of water rights on Otter Creek. Judge Minough rapidly appraised the situation. He asked a number of questions, then issued an order that Hallack desist from impeding the free flow of the waters of Otter Creek, if at the same time any appreciable amount of the waters were also not *consumed* (a wording that would not alarm the placer mining interests whose activities impeded and diverted but did not *consume*), and called the next case. No response. Nor was there for the next. And with the help of Paul Stewart, county attorney, who had information at his fingertips, the judge was able to get what had seemed a hopeless docket down to manageable proportions by night.

There remained mainly a land case of Mrs. Mary Lively, Harry Wilson, *et al.,* versus Judith Cattle Company, Inc., for fifty thousand dollars in damages (the largest claim ever brought in the region), but the judge had a telegraph in hand from Major Morrison of the latter concern advising of his imminent arrival, the Gravely Bar Association against the Dakota-Far West, a steamboat company, and, of course, the criminal cases.

"We will recess, then, until ten tomorrow. I believe Major Morrison is also to arrive tomorrow?" The judge looked at Stewart. "We will hear then, either the case of Gravely Bar versus Dakota, or Lively, Wilson versus Judith, whichever first stands before us in full array. This has been a productive day."

Clyde and Ma were all day getting to town in the buggy. Clyde drove the team, and Ma sat beside him in her black, silk dress with a cheesecloth over it. It was lifelessly hot, not a breath stirring, but Ma never complained. When they dropped down the bluffs and the draught of the river valley hit them, suddenly so cold, Clyde had to stiffen up to keep from shivering, but Ma didn't react to that, either. She had steeled herself for the worst; she was ready to endure anything. Clyde drove past camp wagons and shacks, tents, the rail fence along Ollie Haynes's crabapple orchard, and around the huge, unpainted hulk of Boland's Livery Barn into the main street — River Street, although nobody ever called it that — and people were everywhere. Men sat on every available bench and along the platforms, or they were walking and standing, kids were running and yelling, dogs barking.

Ma said: "Just drive right on. Make 'em get out of your way. We got nothing to apologize for. We got as much right here as anybody."

Actually they didn't cause too much excitement, nothing like when Clyde had ridden in with Billy. Once a man came out into the street with his hand raised and Ma said to stop.

"Hello, Mister Shockley," Ma said.

Grant Shockley was so dressed up in a stiff hat and long coat that Clyde almost didn't recognize him.

"Hello, Missus Buttons." Shockley walked around to her side with the hat doffed. "We're glad you got in. We was just wondering whether we had ought send a rig after you."

"Thank you kindly."

"Do you have a place to stay?"

"I'm going out to Maud Hemphill's."

"If she can't put you up, then let us know, will you?" Shockley was apparently on some sort of a committee. He was known as the foulest-tongued man in the country, but tonight butter wouldn't melt in his mouth, bowing and choosing every word.

"Mister Shockley, has my son got a lawyer?"

"Yes, he has. And a good lawyer, from what we hear. Thomas F. Boe from over at the capital. We're expecting him on the stage, which is a trifle late, but a telegram so advised. Your son will be in the very best of hands."

"Is the sheriff around?"

"He's right now taking care of matters at the court. The court is in session, trying Gravely Bar versus Dakota-Far West for damages claimed at fifty thousand dollars."

"Tell Sheriff Hankey I'm in town, will you?"

"Yes, ma'am. I most assuredly will."

Clyde drove on through town to Maud Hemphill's peaked two-story house. Maud was an elderly widow who took roomers. She had no room to let, but she said Ma could sleep on a couch in the tiny parlor, and, if the couch was too short for Ma's legs, she could put a footstool out. "But I don't know what I'll do with you, young man."

"I'll put up at the yards."

"No, you're not sleeping at the Square Deal," said Ma. It was a feed yard run by S. D. "Square-Deal" Hackersmith who had poker and put-'n'-take games in the bunkhouse office and who sold booze, but worse to Ma's thinking he catered to the Badlanders, the so-called rustlers. Whenever Clyde had come to town with Billy, they had stayed there as a matter of course. "That evil gambler's den!" Ma said. "I won't have you there."

Clyde didn't argue, but he still ended up at the Square Deal.

"All right, Buttons," said S. D. Hackersmith, "I'll find space for you but no gun play."

It was just a joke, but it made Clyde feel good. He put up the horses and drifted around town. Nobody paid any attention to him. He stopped in front of the jail. The office was full of men. He couldn't see through to the cell where Billy was. Ted Danner walked up, a cold cigar in his mouth, mustache drooping around it. Nobody spoke to him, just made way. Pete Wall came out, badge on his vest, gun at his hip. The gun was unusual. He liked to go unarmed and avoid trouble. Danner carried one gun at his waist and another in an armpit holster, but he was wearing a coat, and you couldn't see either of them. It didn't look like a very handy arrangement. All his life Clyde had heard talk about the fast draw. Old Tom was always talking about gunfighters who had been fast on the draw, but Billy said it was all dime-novel foolery. About the time you built yourself a rep for a fast draw, somebody would decide to equal it with a squaw gun and buckshot. "Forget about the fast draw and just hit your mark. Point your gun and wait just a fraction of time before you shoot. Always look right at what you're shooting at." That's what Billy said.

Everybody started to clear out as soon as Danner went inside the jail. It was as if they didn't like the smell of death on him. Clyde would have gone inside, but he didn't want to get close to Danner. He wasn't afraid of him. It was just something he didn't want to do.

Anyhow, somebody yelled: "Here it comes!" God, how the dogs were barking! It sounded as if all the dogs in the country had cut loose in concert. Then the stagecoach rolled in, around the livery barn corner. It was the omnibus with three teams. Polly Levinger was driving. He was swinging his long whip, giving a show, and, when he was about even with Clyde and fifty yards shy of the express station, he turned and curled that whip out, wrapped it right around a dog, and sent him rolling. How everybody yelled and carried on, because it was a sight to behold, and the older men said it was like the old days, and they could remember when Holladay's Overland Mail had fought it out with A. J. Oliver & Company, setting a record of nineteen hours from Three Forks to Fort Benton — which figured out at ten and a half miles per hour.

Polly got on the hand brake, which was as tall as he was, with enough leverage to put the wheels skidding. He simply manhandled that big omnibus in against the high platform of the express station. There were at least fifteen passengers. It was hard to tell exactly because some got off through the back. The omnibus had no doors and roof like a regular stage, just the high seats, higher than the driver, even, who had a perch out in front where he could look right down on the rumps of the wheelers, and a canvas canopy with side curtains. A crowd quickly gathered, so a second vehicle, of the mudwagon type, loaded with express, had to stop a good distance away. Dogs kept barking and barking. Men tried to beat them away, and a couple were sent howling, but the racket continued, and Clyde, when he came up, saw the reason — there was a dog in a crate in one of the side baggage compartments, a curly retriever.

"Ain't we got enough dogs without you bringing more?" a bystander asked Polly.

"He's a paying passenger. This is Major Morrison's pure-bred retriever. They'll go right off a block of ice to fetch a duck. They're from the north of Ireland and are the toughest dogs alive. This one's worth forty dollars in Chicago. We had a telegram to get him off the express in Billings, and I near had to blow up the train to get him. He was billed through to Helena, but the major wanted him to go shooting with Judge Minough."

Major Morrison was not on the coach, but his wife and two stepdaughters were. Mrs. Morrison wore a veil that hid her face. One of the daughters was about nine years old; the other was twelve or thirteen. There were other women on the coach, some heavily veiled, like Mrs. Morrison, and some who weren't. They mostly alighted the best way they could, holding up their skirts to keep from getting tangled in the step, but Mrs. Morrison and her daughters got more attention.

The elder daughter was so beautiful she took Clyde's breath away. Actually he felt as if he couldn't breathe as he waited right where he knew she would pass close by. He could have reached out and touched her, but wouldn't have dreamed of doing it. She seemed like a holy object, from another world, while he was an ox, crude, cloven, and dirty with a touch that would defile her. She stopped right there and turned and addressed her mother about her chantilly puff, whatever that was. The smell of her came to Clyde, scented soap and tender skin. Oh, God, it made him feel like slumping into the ground like a warm candle. Then she turned and her eyes swept right over him, as if he wasn't there, and, when she walked past, he could see where she'd been sitting on her voile dress because the imprint of her hind end could still be made out, wrinkled and sweat-pressed into the cloth. The cloth was a very light, starchy material that Ma called percale, or French lawn, or something. The girl stopped and twisted from side to side, scrunching deep down at her clothes, and then she seemed to be looking right at him. An instant later he realized she was looking out past him, because she cried: "Oh! Here comes Father!"

It was Major Morrison in his carriage. He was riding in the back, and his mulatto man was driving. Clyde had never seen a carriage like that in Arlington, so the major must have been driven all the way from his ranch at the mouth of the Judith, either that or had it shipped, matched team and all, on one of the downriver steamboats.

Morrison, a short, thin, very erect, and gingery man, got down from the carriage, tossing aside his cigar although it was no more than one-fifth smoked. He walked to his wife, while people made plenty of room, and she lifted her veil to kiss him. He was in his middle fifties, a long-time widower recently remarried, his wife much younger, little more than thirty. Both the girls, his stepdaughters, called him "Father" — (pronouncing it Faw-tha) — and also kissed him. He seemed much pleased.

"How was the trip, Clara?" Clyde heard the major ask his wife.

"Dreadful. I'm just filthy."

"You are now a pioneer woman."

"Can't we bring poor Nero?" asked the younger daughter. Nero was also the name of one of Billy's favorite horses, but she was talking about the crated dog who whined piteously.

"No, we can't have him in the carriage," said her mother. "Can't you see there isn't room?"

"I feel sorry for him. Poor Nero. Poor, poor Nero."

The dog was now howling.

"Don't get too close to him," said Mrs. Morrison. "He smells to high heaven."

"Mother doesn't like dogs," said the major, "but we like dogs, don't we, little Chin-Chin?" This was evidently his term of endearment for the younger stepdaughter. "We'll have him brought, and then there'll still be some time to exercise him in the river. What he wants . . . and needs . . . is a good swim. We'll have to see he has the proper edge for hunting."

"Are you and Judge Minough really going out to hunt ducks tomorrow?" asked Mrs. Morrison.

"Not tomorrow, I'm afraid. He has a case to try."

"Is it the one where they're going to hang the man?" asked Chin-Chin.

"Stop it!" said her mother. "It's too degrading to think about."

The elder daughter didn't say a word. She was perfectly serene and beautiful. She seemed to float on the air. They all got in the carriage, four of them in the back. Chin-Chin on the major's knees, the Negro driver in a seat alone, and they rode off.

"Ow-ooo!" Nero howled after them.

One passenger was still aboard the omnibus. He was a gangling, ill-proportioned man, clean-shaven, with big bones in the cheek and jaw, with a heavy shock of hair pulled all to the back and held there, over his collar, by a sort of campaign hat, only floppier.

"Help Mister Boe to get down, what the hell's the matter with you?" the driver asked at large, reappearing after his first drink.

It was T. F. Boe, Billy's lawyer. The trouble seemed to lie in his right leg which wanted to bend inward at the knee. "Mister Levinger?" he said, still not attempting the descent.

"Yes, sir."

It was really something when Polly Levinger called anybody sir. One of the most famous drivers in the entire West, he wouldn't have said "Yes, sir" to the major.

"Will you have them bring that portmanteau and put it by the satchel? I want to keep all that stuff together."

"Jesus! What you got in here? Gold bricks?"

"Just some law books."

"You may need 'em!" some smart-aleck called.

Ignoring him, Boe said: "Now, if someone will just take hold of my leg. Guide it down. There, once I get on the ground, I'm all right. Hand me my cane. Thank you."

"Are you going to plead him guilty?" a man yelled.

"Somebody carry his bags!" said Levinger, looking around in a way that said: "and keep your damned mouths shut!"

Delbert Sperry from the livery barn volunteered.

"There goes the best god-damn' criminal lawyer in the territory, or any territory," Polly Levinger said to town marshal, Tip Power, when Boe was out of hearing, headed for the steps of the Mountdouglas House. He was talking to Power, but others came around to listen, and he let them in on it. "I heard him plead the Mixler shotgun murder case in Butte two years ago, where that woman shot her husband and brother-in-law. He had grown men crying like babies. You never can tell what he might do. He always hits 'em with the unexpected. Take that rape case down in Wyoming when he defended C. W. Shurkley's son. He was accused of raping that girl in a sleeping coach. They had him dead to rights, and the whole country was down on that kid, and I'll be damned but Boe got him off! I hear it cost old Shurkley three thousand dollars, fees and everything else."

Things quieted down. The vehicles remained, but everyone started drifting away. Levinger, with men following and Power at his side, went over to the Mountdouglas' bar entrance. Clyde thought about going over to the jail, Danner or no Danner, when Earl Hankey drove Ma past in a buggy. They didn't notice him. It was growing twilight, and he remained back against the recessed front of the Madrid Harness Store and watched them go over to the jail, and inside. After a decent time, so it would look like he wasn't tagging along, he followed. Billy and Ma were having an argument.

"Oh, you shut up!" Ma said. "You listen to me . . . !"

"Damn it all . . . !"

"Swear, go ahead! Curses don't hurt me. The pain I have goes a *lot* deeper!"

"Ma, just go home. Get in the buggy and. . . ."

"Now, you listen to me!" That was Earl Hankey getting in on it. "This is your mother! . . . and she's had more than her share of suffering in this world."

"Good God, I'm trying to save her from more suffering, can't you see that?"

"You should understand what you mean to her, in spite of everything. She's here for your own good."

"I don't want her here. She looks like she was in mourning. All you need, Ma, is a crêpe veil . . . !"

"You know very well this is the only decent dress I got. What would you expect me to wear?"

"Go buy yourself one. I'll give you the money."

"Where did you get the money, that's what I'd want to know? I don't want any of your ill-got money."

"Do you think I robbed a bank?"

"No, but it would be gambling money. You can rest assured, if you have money, it don't represent. . . ."

"Ma, cut it out."

"*I'm* not the one that had no appreciation and started finding fault! Oh, dear, why can't we be like other families? Why do we always have fault and quarrel?"

Finally they proceeded with a decent enough mother-and-son talk, until Uncle Earl told Billy his lawyer was coming.

Boe entered, smelling of whiskey. The sheriff introduced him.

"Missus Buttons!" he cried, scarcely paying any attention to Billy, or even to Clyde. "I am *very* pleased to meet you."

"Well! You seem to be the only one. My son just the same as told me he didn't want me to come around. He wants me to go home."

"We most certainly do *not* want you home! We need you here. Whether your son knows it or not, he needs you as never before."

Ma was all prepared to dislike Boe. She strongly disapproved of him, referring to him once during the journey as "the devil's spokesman for men of evil," who got the guilty set free "by ruse or stratagem." Being a reader, Ma said it that way instead of "by hook or crook" as most people would.

Boe said: "We call upon you for a mother's trust when all other trusts fail."

Mollified in spite of herself, Ma said: "That's about all a mother dare ask . . . to answer her call, when needed."

"Why, your leaving would have the most dreadful of implications. It would be abandonment of your son in his hour of sorest trial. There is nothing, nothing in all the world, as ennobling as a mother's love. It does not ask to be requited. It asks no reward, or even gratitude. It is most holy and god-like. And so, when all else abandons your son, I want them to see that you stand by him."

After a while they all withdrew — Clyde and Ma and Sheriff

Hankey — leaving Billy alone with his lawyer.

"That man's been drinking," Ma observed.

"He may have had one, Kate," the sheriff mollified. "It was a long, hard trip. He suffers a lot from his legs and back."

"He's a heavy drinker. I could tell it."

"He may be a heavy drinker, but nobody ever said he wasn't a good lawyer," the sheriff insisted.

"He don't look like anything. Why didn't Billy at least get a lawyer we could be proud of?"

"Kate," the sheriff assured her, "tomorrow when you see him all pressed up, in a clean shirt and rested, you won't even realize he's the same man."

CHAPTER SIX

"All rise!" cried Alfred Bunting.

It took some time in the packed room. The benches had all been filled as early as seven o'clock, additional chairs carried upstairs from time to time so elderly men could sit, and a chair for Ma which was placed at the very front, at the foot of the one-step stage. Late comers jammed the back of the room. They crushed tight, back-to-chest and shoulders rubbing in the tiny entrance hall, and made dangerous the outside stairs where they could neither see nor hear, but could ask questions and have information relayed. A hand-lettered **NO SMOKING** sign had been raised, but men held unlighted cigars, or they kept cuds of tobacco and found places to spit without hitting anyone's boots. None of the windows would open. They were plain windows, not the lifting kind. Already, although cool outside, the place was stifling.

After what seemed a considerable time Judge Minough entered by way of the narrow rear stairs. His hair was brushed flat and shining, and he wore a black robe, his first appearance so garbed.

"No wig?" whispered attorney Paul Stewart to U. S. Attorney Roman Wardrope at the prosecution table, and Wardrope substituted a pensive look for a smile.

"Be seated," said the judge.

Everyone started to sit, but they got up again when Judge Minough remained on his feet. He was waiting for Ma who was the only woman in the room.

Clyde whispered — "Ma, you're supposed to set." — and she sat down.

Minough then followed and said: "We welcome you all here to observe your federal territorial court, probably your final opportunity to do so before a commonwealth jurisdiction obtains and this chair is occupied by a county or district judge of your choosing. Because there has been some question voiced . . . and justifiably so . . . as to the nature of this jurisdiction, I will say I am Curtis Minough, judge of the first Montana judicial district, that the statutes administered are those of Montana Territory, based on the codes of California, chiefly as codified in 1872 by Attorney Longworth, the late T. E. Boles, and . . . myself." He bowed with a slight inclination of the head. "However, much as one may love the old days and ways, one cannot contravene progress, and it is now Montana's turn to join the Union of States as a full, acting member.

"Now, I am a plain, frontier judge, and I run a plain, old-fashioned, no-nonsense court. I know that many of you have come long distances at some hardship to attend. I do not intend to waste your time or let others waste it. If we apply ourselves diligently to the matter at hand, and only to the matter at hand, it is my belief that this case can be disposed of without harm to justice in a single day. No willful delays will be tolerated, and none is expected. May I introduce our clerk, Alfred Bunting, who is also an attorney-at-law, distinguished in having qualified to plead before the Supreme Court of the United States. We are honored to have for the prosecution Assistant U. S. Attorney Roman Wardrope. The distinguished attorney for the defense is Thomas F. Boe, bachelor of law, University of Michigan. The jury venire, selected from the voting rolls, are known to all. I would be surprised if any was to be excused for cause, but allowances have been made, and we have two extra veniremen. In addition, each side will be allowed to excuse any three of the venire they so wish. This is a firm limitation, but in my judgment not a severe one due to the esteemed quality of the men called on to serve. We cannot indulge here in the time-squandering luxury of legal thrust and parry, of riposte. We will cut through some of the niceties, but in a straight and forward frontier manner which has yielded a high degree of fairness in our past."

The judge leafed through a sheaf of papers, reading here and there. He said to Boe: "You have a copy of these charges, the complaint, coroner's jury findings, coroner's jury serving as a grand jury, indictment, *et cetera?*"

"I do," said Boe, standing and turning with his cane as a pivot so everyone could satisfy their curiosity as to what he looked like.

"May we dispense with the reading? It seems to be very long. To read it all would be in effect an opening statement for the prosecution."

Paul Stewart also stood: "Your Honor, this was read, in essence, to the defendant at his arraignment."

Boe said without looking up: "There seem to be *two* attorneys for the prosecution."

"Oh, excuse me. In my introduction I overlooked Mister Paul Stewart, county attorney. He will be associated with the deputy United States attorney. I hope you have no objection to being outnumbered numerically on the scale of two to one?"

"The defense is flattered."

"The county attorney will advise chiefly in matters of background, terrain, regional relationships, *et cetera,* is that correct, Mister Stewart? As you know, it is difficult for the United States attorney, traveling his first time by stagecoach across this broad land, to become familiar on short notice with each situation as he might in a more settled service of the law."

Boe said: "I do not ask that those charges, *et cetera,* be read in their entirety. I would like some of it straightened out, however. What of this so-called grand jury? Am I to assume this is a coroner's jury that later changed its name? Also in this matter of the indictment. I find no signature or paraph of the prosecutor here. Did Mister Stewart present a bill of indictment to this coroner's grand jury? If not, why is it labeled an indictment rather than presentment?"

"Your Honor, I think I should clear something up," Stewart responded. "I was never formally elected as county attorney, only retained by the board of county commissioners. I have never been designated county attorney or county prosecutor. Now, as to the coroner and subsequent inquest and constitution of a grand jury . . . Doctor Adams was gone, hence Mister Wright assumed as coroner. We had no magistrate, Judge Wall of the justice court also being absent. For that reason the citizens in public meeting caused the coroner's jury to serve a dual rôle and bring in, if warranted, a true bill. I believe the old-time miners' meetings served much the same function, Your Honor."

"They served more *function* than that," Minough said dryly, "and often far too much for the cause of justice. Why is this called an indictment rather than a presentment?"

"I wasn't present, Your Honor. I was out of town."

"It seems that an awful lot of folks were out of town!" interjected Boe.

Stewart went on, ignoring Boe, but raising his voice: "It is, nevertheless, a true bill of indictment. The grand jury acted on a complaint delivered orally by private citizens. Now, although this was signed as a true bill by Mister Wright, foreman, my subsequent procedure was to formulate an information, now in your hand."

"Well, this seems to go over the ground at least once. If we are to accept the indictment, the information is redundant."

"I wished to be sure of the exact points of time, place, offense, *et cetera*."

Boe interjected: "It does seem a piling of Ossa on Pelion, this indictment on complaint, and information on both. May I ask the county attorney if it is common to this jurisdiction to accept an information in charges of capital offense?"

Angry, with his voice shaking, Stewart replied: "The citizens of this town are much to be commended for their decision to form a grand jury and act in their emergency . . . albeit they may have neglected some of the niceties Mister Boe may have grown accustomed to over in the capital."

"Are you, or aren't you, the county attorney?" Boe pursued. "There seems to be some qualification in that matter."

"I merely stated that there was not a formal election, but the commissioners. . . ."

"Are you, or aren't you, yes, or no? You either *are* or you *aren't?*"

"I am. In fact, I merely wished to. . . ."

"Isn't it true that you are also the local attorney for Omaha Land and Cattle, Incorporated? And isn't that why you were loath to come here, wearing two coats?"

"I have served as its attorney, yes. I am the only attorney now in practice in Ricketts County."

"And isn't it true that the Omaha Land and Cattle Company is your chief client?" Boe pressed.

"This oversteps the bounds!" cried Stewart. "This reflection on my ethics is entirely uncalled for. It is a clear attempt to impugn and discredit the motives of the charge."

"Oh?" said Judge Minough. "Before whom?"

"Why, before this court."

"Well, now, if your concern is for me," responded the judge, "you can *dis*concern yourself, because this cynical old court will not be influenced by any such stratagems. This old court has seen them all."

"Discredited before the jury," Stewart amended.

Boe asked: "Is the prosecution suggesting that the jury has already been selected? If so, he suggests an impropriety of the very worst sort."

The jury venire was in a back room used for storage, but the door was open slightly for ventilation and heads could be seen.

"How about that, Mister Stewart?" asked Judge Minough.

"Of course, I make no suggestion of impropriety! But these statements are made in the hearing of the venire. . . ."

"The statements were made in the hearing of the community, as have many statements in regard to this matter, a situation which always obtains, and is one of the penalties we pay in following the common law dictum that crimes be tried in the locality of their occurrence."

Stewart sat back down, breathing heavily, and wiped perspiration from his brow. He was the only one who seemed perturbed. The judge kept looking at the papers, and Boe, still standing, took ample time to let the audience view him from his most advantageous profile.

"Your Honor. A final word before the venire is called. I do wish to deplore . . . and in the strongest terms . . . what appears to be the influence of those great Eastern and foreign corporations, the huge cattle companies, which is implicit in preparing this charge. Specifically I call attention to the absence anywhere of the prosecutor's identity. To read these charges one would never know there was a prosecutor in this county. Was this a deliberate act? If so, why? Did Mister Stewart feel that as the cattle company attorney, his double rôle would discredit the action? He would make it seem that the so-called grand jury spoke out spontaneously, the voice of the people. Ah, yes! . . . the voice may be the voice of Jacob, but the hands are the hands of Esau."

Judge Minough knew the crowd had come partly to hear a celebrated criminal lawyer in action, so he allowed Thomas F. Boe his say before calling out. "William T. Buttons! William T. Buttons, are you present?"

Billy stood, and everybody could see him. He was dressed in a black suit, white shirt, stiff collar, and a black bow tie, but he stood as easy and comfortable as if it were his everyday garb.

"William T. Buttons, you are here charged with homicide by firearms, specifically by a pistol held in hand, willfully, deliberately and through premeditation, with malice, a felony, against the person of John J. Gannaway, at or about the time of midday on the eleventh day of June, this year, same taking place at Willow Creek Crossing on old Gravely Landing Road, township eighteen north, range twenty-four east, Ricketts County, Montana Territory. You appear here represented by attorney of your choice and stand aware of these charges, copy thereof in your hand. How plead you, William T. Buttons?"

It was very impressive, the way Judge Minough did it, and Billy Buttons sensed the breathless instant as he stood there.

"I am not guilty," he said.

("And do you know," one of the spectators said afterward, with a laugh, "you almost had to *believe* him?")

"The venire has been sworn?" Judge Minough said to the clerk. "Very well, we will then proceed with the *voir dire* examination, the venire chosen by lot from the voter registration rolls, am I right?"

Sheriff Earl Hankey at the door nodded.

"Speak up, sir!"

Hankey said: "They were chosen by lot, but we had to pass over all those not in town or nearby."

"Time and distance precluded the issuance and serving of summons? Call the first venireman."

"The court calls Milford Spear," said the clerk.

Everyone looked blank. Nobody had ever heard of a Milford Spear — they did not realize who it was for a moment until Rusty Spear came, tall, shambling, into the room. There he stood, blinking and passing his fingers through his straw thatch of hair, not knowing what he was to do. "Milford!" some seemed to say in unison, and there was a release of pent-up laughter.

Minough gaveled them down in an instant. Spear sat in the witness chair and was told he was already under oath.

"Do you know the defendant?" asked U. S. Attorney Wardrope, whose voice was being heard for the first time.

After a moment's hesitation, deciding what defendant meant, he said: "Yes."

"Friend of yours?"

"Well . . . yes."

"Good friend?"

"Well, I've known him off and on."

"Not a bosom companion?"

"No, I wouldn't say. . . ."

"Ride with him?"

"Well, I rode on the roundup with him."

"Worked for the Buttons, didn't you?"

"No, sir!"

"Weren't you hired and paid by the Buttons for your riding two years ago?"

"Oh, that. Well, I rode on the roundup, you see, Ma Buttons" — he nodded toward where she was sitting — "had to pay for three riders, and I was one of 'em."

"Ever been a guest at the Buttons' house?"

"Well, I stayed overnight at the bunkhouse. Everybody in the country has done that. When you head over toward the Judith and want to put up, it's about your last chance unless you want to stop at the Omaha, and not many fellows do that. Those bosses there don't give you a very warm. . . ."

"We ask this man be excused," said Wardrope, cutting him off.

Judge Minough was about to excuse the juror, but Boe stood, doing his usual leaning balance with the cane, and the judge looked toward him.

"May I question this venireman?"

"There is no point in questioning him," said Wardrope. "He is excused."

"Excused, Mister Spear," said Judge Minough, leaving Boe standing there.

"Patrick McGraw!" called the clerk.

McGraw was a former pugilist, gone to fat but still powerful, a bartender at the River House. He, too, was excused by the prosecution, using two of the three challenges. Wardrope was unperturbed.

It was obvious to everyone that Stewart had had time to study the list and check off those most likely to favor Billy.

The third venireman was Lloyd Wagner, owner of a coal mine, who had no known bias one way or the other and was quickly passed by the prosecution.

"Mister Boe, will you question?" inquired the judge.

"Mister Wagner, if you sit on this jury, do you promise to decide the guilt or innocence of William Buttons on the basis of the evidence presented in the court, and only on that evidence?"

Wagner glanced at the judge who said: "Yes, that is what you must do."

"Do I have your word for it?" asked Boe.

"Yes."

"I accept your word. We accept Lloyd Wagner for the jury."

Boe did very much the same thing with each of the jurors. "There was just something about him," George Carew said afterward. "He didn't look like much, wobble-kneed on that walking stick, coming up there, but all of a sudden you saw those eyes of his, and it was like being hit by lightning. You realized what an awful responsibility you'd taken on! You just all of a sudden resolved to do your god damnedest!" Carew, who was semi-retired after a very bad bout with the black pneumonia, called frozen lungs, was the fourth juror accepted. Before him came Ed Schuman, hardware owner, and Ralph Richardson, a small stockman from the Little Teton. The prosecution then used its third, and last, challenge rejecting Walter Cole — rancher and one-time partner of Billy's in the horse-ranching business.

"They must be pretty sure of themselves . . . who's left in there?" asked someone back of Clyde.

"Doc Coglister, Stefling, Bob Martin . . . oh, Jesus, look who's sitting in there!"

"Who?"

"Major Morrison."

"No!"

"Yes, he stood up to light a cigar and sat down again."

"Well, there's one challenge for the defense."

"You can be sure of that!"

"Doctor Coglister?" called the clerk.

"As a dentist, under the common law, you don't have to serve," said Judge Minough.

"I'm willing to serve."

Coglister was accepted by the prosecution, but Boe said: "I ask that Doctor Coglister be excused for cause."

"The bench sees no reason for that."

"Were you present at the inquest?" asked Boe.

"Yes," said Coglister.

"Isn't it true you sat on the jury?"

"No, it is not. I advised the jury on certain matters."

"What matters?"

"Medical matters."

"Isn't it true you sat with the jury during its deliberations?"

"No. I was in the room, but I certainly did not sit with the jury."

Boe questioned the doctor for some time, but Judge Minough refused to recognize his part in the inquest and subsequent findings as cause, so Boe had to use the first of his challenges.

Claude Stefling, an old Texas cowboy, and Monte Howell, harness maker, were seated without trouble. Tom McAdams, rancher, was questioned sharply by the prosecution — he was the father of Buzz McAdams, one of Billy's pals — with the hope the court would excuse him for cause, but Judge Minough, it was apparent, had already satisfied himself about all the venire, and that none was to be excused for cause. Jurors number seven, eight, and nine — Eaney Leavitt, Anton Bemer, and Cal Reims — were seated, also old "Soldier" Frederickson, an historic liar who claimed to have taken part in almost all the Indian campaigns of the West.

Then the clerk called: "Tyler F. Morrison."

And Major Morrison came out. He had one of his favorite, thin, Havana panatela cigars in his hand. He laid it on the edge of a table before sitting down. Although only about five feet six, and preferring soft, gaiter-type shoes in a high-heeled, booted, and spurred country, there was something of the cavalry in his bearing. Actually he had served in the artillery. He had attained the rank of major and had been breveted out a colonel, but he preferred to be called major, the grade which he had earned. There was a story common that he had come to the country a major in the standing Army and had made his fortune in the remount service, collecting under-the-table commissions, but it was categorically false. He came West as traveling manager of Diamond D Steam Transportation, and later founded Judith Cattle.

Wardrope indicated he would ask no questions, that Morrison was impeccably acceptable to the prosecution, and the judge started casting glances about, apparently wondering where he could seat him as a spectator.

"Mister Boe?"

Boe repeated the business of getting to his feet and walking to face the juror. He looked straight into Morrison's eyes and asked his question about promising to decide the guilt or innocence of William Buttons strictly on evidence presented to the court, which seemed pointless, seeing he was going to reject him.

"Yes," said Morrison, rather surprised, "yes, I would."

"Accepted."

The effect was startling. People couldn't believe it, and a buzz went up. "Yeah, he accepted him!" somebody said. The judge rapped for order. He looked at Boe. It occurred to him, apparently, that he did not realize who Major Morrison was, that if one searched the broad land over, he couldn't find a man with more reason to hate and fear a knight errant like Billy Buttons, and to make it worse he would be no ordinary juror, merely one in twelve, but a force that few would be willing to oppose when closeted for a verdict. He had been placed on the venire chiefly to off balance Walter Cole. Judge Minough had not been a party to this, but he had said nothing, seeing a chance to seat his friend as a favored spectator when challenged by the defense. Clearly unwilling to accept Boe's decision as final, Judge Minough indicated Morrison was to stay where he was. He cleared his throat, rubbed his chin, cleared his throat again, and looked at Boe, but Boe remained in profile. He even looked down at Billy as if to indicate a challenge by him would be entertained, but Billy gave no sign.

"I am not at all certain," said the judge, picking his words, "that jurors should be accepted with no questions whatsoever . . . if for no other reason than that they may wish, on second thought, to disqualify themselves."

Boe responded: "Your Honor, I would not presume to question

Major Morrison. Or challenge his qualifications to sit with fairness and impartiality on this jury. As Your Honor pointed out, this is a very well-chosen group, a fair cross-section of the country. All of these men have long had the opportunity of expressing any preconception which would rule out their ability to hear this case, not on the basis of wild reports and ugly rumor, but strictly on the testimony and the real evidence. We do not ask or suppose that a juror could come here without feelings in regard to a case such as this. We ask only each man's assurance that he will do his best to judge fairly within the rules. Major Morrison's very presence is implicit of that assurance, even had not a word been spoken. If we cannot put our trust in men such as Major Morrison, then, pray, whom can we? I gladly accept this juror."

Major Morrison heard him out unsmiling, watching him with a long, narrowed gaze, untouched by praise.

"Well, I guess you're on the jury, Ty," said Judge Minough. However, he stayed him for yet a moment. He still couldn't understand Boe's accepting him. Boe wasn't drunk, but he was making a very strange mistake in accepting Morrison. Sternly, to bring the defense attorney to his senses, the judge said: "Mister Boe! One more man and this jury will be complete. No juror will be excused for cause after this trial starts, and any hope of a mistrial will be very wishful thinking."

"That is my hope also. Neither I, nor my client, would care to go through the ordeal again."

Right up till that moment, Clyde, tense and barely breathing, had waited for Boe to spring some surprise whereby Morrison would be sent packing. Then the gavel fell, and Morrison quietly, in his precise movements, with death-like precision stood, retrieved his cigar, and took his seat beyond the two-by-four railing of the jury bench. Clyde wanted to shout out: "No, no!" He couldn't understand why Boe was doing it, or why Billy was letting him. It was too late. All he could do was sit, feeling as if his insides were going to drop out of him. Oh, God, he wished he could get out of there, but people jammed him on every side.

The last juror was Casey Sauer, woodcutter, prospector, trapper, about fifty years old. When he was seated, the judge recessed for five minutes, retiring down the back stairs obviously to go to the privy. Only briefly so. Skip Johnson, the barber, sitting in his shop all alone, stood with surprise when the judge walked in and sat in the chair. "A cold rub," he said. This consisted of several cold towels across his head and the back of his neck, a scalp massage, and a brisk combing. Then, after a few puffs on a cigar, Judge Curtis Minough returned for the long session facing him.

CHAPTER SEVEN

Roman Wardrope, thirty-five, six feet tall, with good depth of chest and shoulder, stood with his best view toward the jury, and particularly toward Major Morrison. He did not court political favor. He had secured an appointment as assistant U. S. attorney only as means to an end, to meet the leading men of the territory. He intended to set up private practice, and they would be the largest potential clients. Until only a few days ago he had thought of them strictly as mining men. However, his long and involved journey by train and coach had caused the scales to fall from his eyes. He had seen the plains and the distant mountains, country without end, the valleys bespeaking mighty rivers, the distant blue of timber, and the black lines around dull, gray hills that he had been assured came from the weathered carbon of deeper coal, all an estimable potential for the future, with the inevitable conflicts of right-of-way, trespass, bribery, preëmption, cross-filing, show cause, and replevin, the legal wilderness in which a good lawyer must show the way. He now held the floor with Major Morrison, probably the single most important man of Montana east of the Rockies, a prisoner to attention, and he recognized a heaven-sent opportunity when he saw one.

"Your Honor, it is with some hesitation that I address myself to these charges." He spoke quietly, testing his voice, a voice, he felt, that was more suited to great auditoriums and hardly at its best in this jam-packed heat and under this low ceiling. "Seldom in my experience has this office been presented with a more definitive, or, I should say, open-and-shut instance of capital crime, crime unmitigated by any conceivable excuse, any humanity, any passion, but a cold, planned, and with. . . ."

"The attorney should describe the other capital cases he's tried," interrupted Boe, "or otherwise we lack a basis for comparison."

"Your Honor . . . !"

"Let's not start *this,*" said Minough.

Boe clarified: "The attorney would leave the jury with the impression of heretofore numerous criminal prosecutions. In fact, the only criminal case the attorney has prosecuted in this territory was a fake mining stock case . . . which he lost."

Boe didn't stir, but no one doubted who was speaking. He had none of the full roll of the U. S. attorney — "the Roman tones of Roman Wardrope," as William Westmore put it later in the *Arlington Herald* — his voice was a mordant quack by comparison, a corrosive timbre, and seemed to stick to whatever it hit, cutting, derisive, and bringing postures down to size.

"Oh, Your Honor, I protest!"

"And I!" agreed Boe. "What say you to this traducement, this comparison with other capital cases? Does the assistant U. S. attorney intend to produce them here for a comparison of iniquities? If so, the transcripts should have been submitted. . . ."

Bang! — it was the judge's gavel.

"Mister Wardrope, I am sure, offered this only in the form of preoration . . . figure of speech or hyperbole. The preoration has now been taken care of. If you would proceed with your preliminary summation as succinctly as possible, please. Bear in mind that everyone here is perfectly familiar with the background."

Wardrope said: "I only hoped that in setting forth clearly the nature of this case, its hopelessness from the point of view of the defense" — he raised his voice to overwhelm Boe who was now, one limb at a time, getting to his feet — "that a plea of guilty might yet be. . . ." He had to shout: "I must admit my initial perplexity that so eminent an attorney as that for the defense . . . allow me to conclude, please . . . would not for the sake of the defendant, and to spare the relatives of the accused, who cannot but be pained, and unnecessarily pained, to have the shocking events laid forth. . . ."

"I *do* object to this!" said Boe.

"Yes, Mister Wardrope," asked the judge, "does the prosecution have a motion to put before the court?"

"No, Your Honor. I only hoped, even at this late moment, the defense would reconsider and enter a plea of guilty. If Mister Boe would care to discuss this, I would be more than glad, if Your Honor so decided, to retire in privacy. . . ."

"The state's attorney apparently wishes to secure a guilty plea on some lesser charge," said Boe.

"I suggest no such thing. . . ."

But Boe went straight on, voice in command. "I think you do, but the offer is refused. My client will not accept a sentence of ten or five years, or one year, or anything else just because the state's attorney may have, on closer scrutiny, discovered the glaring weaknesses in his case. No, we will not pull his chestnuts out of the fire. My client welcomes this charge, and this forum, to show his innocence before this jury, and the neighbors among whom he grew to manhood under these skies. So, be the sentence only one year, and that suspended, it would be too much, because I tell you that Billy Buttons will walk from this room a free man."

"Now everything is even," said Judge Minough. "Perhaps we can get on with the opening statements."

"Not exactly even," said Boe. "Your Honor, state's attorney has expressed surprise that I would take this case and wraps this dagger in flattery . . . that I have successfully defended many cases, but that this time I have gone too far, that I have 'come a cropper,' as they say in Eastern circles. Well, I say I have not 'come a cropper,' as the events will soon show. I have not seen here even a very serious problem, and I tell you I am going to win this case, but not because of any imagined forensic powers. No, I am going to win it because Billy Buttons is not guilty."

"Now you *have* had your way," said the judge. "Mister Boe, I am going to consider that to be your opening statement. I deem now the opening statements on both sides are complete. Will you call your first witness?"

Wardrope, angry, was on his feet with answers, but the judge left him with them.

"Call your first witness," the judge repeated.

"The people call Doctor Hingham."

The idea of Doc Hingham being called *Doctor* was greeted with laughter that Minough quieted. Hingham was a retired hospital steward from the Army with a regional reputation in the treatment of wounds and the setting of broken bones. Generally he loafed around town, living on his pension, but when Dr. Fairleigh Adams was absent, which was about one month in three, he was called by the sick, prescribing such medicines as quinine, calomel, laudanum, and Epsom salts. He also pulled teeth after freezing the gums with cocaine, and served as a veterinarian. "How much do I owe you, Doc?" a patient would ask after a bone was set, and Hingham would answer: "Well, now, that all depends on how much that arm is worth to you." Dr. Adams had been in far away Pennsylvania where he had attended graduation exercises at his old college on the evening they brought in Gannaway's body, stiff and jouncing in the bottom of a wagon, and hence it had been Doc Hingham who had examined it.

"Do you swear to tell the truth, the whole truth, and nothing but the truth, so help you, God?" said Bunting, getting in front of the witness with a Bible.

"I do . . . except I'm not really a doctor."

"What are you, Mister Hingham?" asked Judge Minough.

"I'm an Army hospital and ambulance steward, retired. I served as assistant Army surgeon, in fact, but I was never commissioned. Hereabouts I call on folks when I can help. I'm a doctor when the real doctor isn't here. When Doc Adams goes away, I call on his patients for him. I sew up a lot of people. They're glad to get me when. . . ."

Wardrope interjected: "Now, Doctor Hingham . . . I'm sure the defense does not object to the honorary term of doctor!"

"It does," said Boe. "Doc Hingham does not claim to be a doctor. He's just a mighty good man to have around when you're hurt, that's all. The term doctor would either imply something not a fact, or be . . . which seems worse . . . patronizing. Isn't that right, Doc?"

"Sure is," said Doc before Wardrope could object.

"Your Honor, I want to stop this right at the outset. The defense knows better than direct questions to the witness."

"Your turn will come, Mister Boe," reminded the judge.

It was apparent, however, that Doc Hingham, very on edge, was more comfortable with Boe than with Wardrope, whose witness he was.

"Mister Hingham" — the Mister was a sore handicap — "where were you on the twelfth of June, last?"

"Twelfth? Oh, that was the day they brought John Gannaway in. Well, I was right here in Arlington. Doctor Adams had gone East, and I was sticking around. They brought him in around seven in the evening. Tom Putley had come in and said there'd been a shooting. He'd rode in around noon. John had been shot the day before. It was about forty miles out there, you see. He'd been shot about one in the afternoon." He looked over to Billy as if for verification. "Well, I don't know *when* he was shot, not being there, but it all came out in the inquest."

Boe didn't object, so Wardrope said: "It will also come out in the eye-witness testimony, Mister Hingham. What we want from you is what your examination showed."

"Well, everybody in town saw him. Sheriff Hankey came around and asked me to serve as doctor. He'd been dead quite a while, but he was still dressed just like when he'd been when he was shot. That is, nobody had taken his clothes off. They hadn't disturbed anything. . . ."

"Now, how can you be sure of that?"

"Well, there was holes in his shirt and in a canvas-type vest he liked to wear. The holes in the cloth matched up with the holes in him." This caused some laughter that the judge stonily ignored. "You see, you could tell he hadn't been undressed because the wounds had glued themselves fast to the cloth. He'd sort of threshed around on the ground. You take a real fine clay dust and it will mix with blood and get hard as glue, only tougher than glue. You can soak it off, but it takes hours. What I wanted to do was transport the body to the river, but they wouldn't stand for it."

"Who wouldn't?"

"Chiefly the undersheriff, Ted Danner. He said to get busy and perform an autopsy. I told him I wasn't a doctor . . . I couldn't perform an autopsy. Then I asked if I was to be acting coroner? If so, it would make me kind of a judge. I'd have the same kind of power vested in me."

He glanced at the judge who dipped his head in agreement.

"He said, yes, but then the sheriff came along and said, no, it was to be John Wright. That was fine with me. I got his clothes off the best I could. I found the bullet holes in the cloth, but I had to do some cutting and tearing."

"How many bullet holes did you find?"

"Three or four."

Evidently this did not square with the coroner's report that

Wardrope had at hand. "Are you sure?"

"Positive, but that was in the cloth, not in him. The cloth had folded over."

"We introduce the clothing of the victim."

There it was — a shirt, vest, and pants. With a flourish, like Anthony showing the cloak of Cæsar, Wardrope shook out the shirt and vest and put his fingers here and there through ragged holes, blood-stiffened.

"Examine?" Wardrope asked.

He put them down in front of Billy, who gave them a distant regard. Boe, however, gave the clothes a good going over, nodding his head, yes, yes, as if all previous convictions were substantiated.

After Bunting had affixed his tag, Wardrope carried the clothing over and spread it out on a bench in front of the jurors so the bloody evidence would remain in mind. There was no objection.

Doc Hingham went ahead on his own. "Some of the cloth stuck to the wounds, and I suppose got cut off when he was embalmed. He wasn't embalmed here. He was embalmed. . . ."

"What was the state of the body?" Wardrope asked, not appreciating such gratuitous statements.

"Well, now, it was in about as good a shape as you could expect under the circumstances."

Even the judge smiled at that, but Wardrope was patient, and Billy, obviously schooled by Boe, sat perfectly poker-faced.

"You could see where that old Forty-Five slug had hit him under the arm, and that he had his arm tossed up. It wasn't in the armpit, but almost. Left arm. You can see the shirt and vest, both. It was like he saw Billy about to shoot and tossed his arm up."

When Boe merely sat and listened, Judge Minough turned and said: "Unless you personally saw who fired the shot, don't say it."

"Well, I'm just repeating . . . they all said it."

Wardrope interjected: "Tell us how, by your examination, you determined the posture of the victim to be?"

"The clothes had been pulled up. Like this. If I lift my arm, with the elbow bent, it pulls the shirt and the coat, each a different amount. The holes are staggered. It was like that. Then you could see how the bullet went through the skin and muscle. Muscle looks different

80

when you lift, or something. What I mean, if a man's running and gets hit in the leg, it looks different than if he was just sitting. The bullet wounds are more oval shaped in the former. And smaller. Limp muscle bruises more. But I'm not saying that's how these were. They were too ragged, and I didn't see them soon enough. They were soft and tender. Sort of rotten. The flesh pulled away. That Forty-Five wound was the size of your fist. Well, no, that's an exaggeration, they were big or bigger than a dollar. In fact, it was a while before I could decide whether the bullet had gone in there or come out."

"Will you describe the relative wounds as to size, and your conclusion as to the shot which caused them?"

"Objection."

"Mister Boe?" asked the judge.

"How does he know it was a bullet or bullets? Let's not prompt the witness. Let him volunteer as to the number of wounds."

"Withdraw that portion of the question," Wardrope conceded. "What was your conclusion as to causative agent or agents?"

"As I said, I decided he was shot from the left. It went in on the left and come out on the right."

"What evidence in your observation led to that conclusion?"

"The right side hole was bigger, and you could poke a finger in and feel the bones crunch around. Then, the right side wound was much lower down. You'd almost think he was sitting on the ground, and Billy had come up and shot him . . ." — there was no objection, but he hurried to correct himself — "that a party or parties unknown had ridden up and shot him. Only the bullet must have come in straight and veered down."

"In your experience is such a deflection unusual?"

"No, it's usual. You get so you expect the unusual. There really isn't any usual. I've seen everything happen to a bullet that could happen. I've seen bullets, brittle from too much impurity in the lead, and they just fly to pieces . . . high-velocity bullets especially. Bullets sometimes almost turn around. I saw a bullet one time hit a man in the chest and come out the top of his head. It lifted his skull off like a lid. That was in the Army."

"Now, let me review this. To the best of your judgment he was hit by a Forty-Five caliber bullet while the arm was tossed up, so?"

81

Wardrope gestured appropriately.

"Right."

"From what range?"

"I wouldn't say it was from too far. You wouldn't toss your arm up like that unless you saw somebody and was surprised. You wouldn't do it if somebody was across the street."

When again Boe didn't object, the judge said: "You may leave such applications of logic to others. You are to tell us about the wounds, and those correlations within the area of your expertise."

"Well, I was just . . . anyhow, a Forty-Five hasn't too much range. I'd say it was fired from thirty feet. Closer, the cloth would have been burned . . . especially when it was hot and dry. I've seen cotton cloth actually catch fire. I've seen the shirt burn right off a man's back from a pistol close on. If you were to ask me to say how it happened, well, I'd say a man rode up and drew a gun, and John tossed his arm up like this, you see how it would pull his shirt and vest, and then bang . . . or bang, bang . . . it could have gone twice right in the same hole, I suppose, and off he went, off his horse."

"How can you testify he went off his horse?" asked Wardrope. "You weren't there. You didn't see him."

"He'd been on a horse because you could see the burns where he'd held the reins. He'd clutched, and the horse had shied, or something, because the burns were very plain. Then, his whole right side was skinned up . . . shoulder and hip, where he'd hit the ground. He was a two-hundred-pound man and hit the ground pretty hard."

The witness was turned over to Boe to cross-examine.

"You say it was a Forty-Five caliber bullet?" he asked.

"That's what we figured."

"Based on experience?"

"Yes. It's the caliber 'most everybody carries."

"On the other hand, you never found a bullet."

"No. It must have gone through. Well, naturally. . . ."

"Or one bullet went through, and the other was still there? Bang, bang, remember?"

"Yes."

"You didn't probe?"

"Only with my finger. I could feel the broken ribs."

"Who took charge of the body after your examination?"

"The coroner, and then Harvey Ferris."

"Is he the undertaker?"

"Yes."

"What function did Mister Ferris perform? Did you observe?"

"No, he's just an undertaker. He lays out, but don't embalm. He sent the body off to Billings."

"You observed this?"

"Yes, I helped load it on the stage."

"On a stagecoach? How could that be managed?"

"Oh, they didn't set him up, or anything. It was the express wagon, really. He was rolled in a tarp, packed in ice."

"But Billings was not his final destination?"

"No, he was to be embalmed there and sent by express train to Omaha or Council Bluffs, which is across the river."

"That's where his wife is?"

"Huh?"

"That's the home of his wife, Missus Gannaway? Council Bluffs?"

Wardrope interjected: "If Mister Boe is interested in the victim's family affairs, I suggest this is not the right person to ask."

"Whom do you suggest I ask?" queried Boe.

"It's not my province to suggest anybody. I am objecting to this wandering line of questioning from a witness called to testify specifically on. . . ."

"If you were objecting, why did you say *suggest?*"

"It was only a figure of speech to. . . ."

"Then let us hear those definitive words . . . I object."

"I *do* object."

"Sustained. Mister Boe, you may inquire as to the disposition of the body only insofar as Mister Hingham, from this end of the line, is competent to answer from personal observation, inspection of manifests, *et cetera*."

Instead Boe said: "No bullets! Not even a sliver of lead?"

"Well, there was a lot of corruption, especially on the right where it came out . . . cloth, flesh, bone slivers. It was pretty bad, so we threw it away. When it gets down to a sliver of lead, there might have been one, but we didn't see it."

"So you couldn't weigh the bullet?"

"No."

"It could have been a Forty-Four, say?"

"Sure, there lots of Forty-Fours."

"The bullets weigh almost the same?"

Hingham liked this question because he was on familiar ground. "I think the average Forty-Four is two hundred grains, and the Forty-Five is two hundred and fifty. The Forty-Four shoots harder, though. That is, it won't knock you down better, but it has more powder to weight-of-ball." He had to be careful because this was a subject on which half the men in the room also considered themselves expert. "Lots of fellows use the Forty-Four because it's a bottleneck and has more steam."

"How about the Thirty-Eight?"

"Yes, there's Colt six-shooters made in Thirty-Eight caliber, but they're not too common. Actually the Forty-Five, Forty-Four, and Thirty-Eight are about the same as to power. Then there's the Forty-One caliber. Most of the Thirty-Eights and Forty-Ones are double-action . . . self-cockers. You see more Forty-Ones in town . . . detective specials, shoulder guns . . . I don't know why. They're quite a bit smaller."

"That Forty-Five or Forty-One refers to the diameter of the bullet, doesn't it?"

"Yes, hundredths of an inch. Forty-Five is just under half an inch."

"I have a ruler here. This is a surveyor's rule, marked in tenths of an inch. Show the jury how wide a Forty-Five is and how wide a Forty-One."

"Here. And about here."

"Almost the same. Difference about the width of your thumbnail?"

"No, about the thickness of my thumbnail."

"Right. I stand corrected."

Doc had recovered from all his tenseness. It was a way Boe had about him, slouched and ambling with his knob-headed walking stick, "like a wounded crane," as someone remarked. He was a friendly soul, the sort one could talk to.

"How about a Thirty-Eight?"

"About this thick. Just a very little bit less."

"It could have been a Thirty-Eight?"

"Yes, easy. A Thirty-Eight bottleneck has one hundred and eighty grains of bullet."

"How about a Thirty-Two?"

"Pistol? That's a rimfire. It wouldn't do much damage."

"How about a Thirty-Two rifle?"

"Now that's something else.. That's a Thirty-Two-Forty Ballard, also a Winchester. They have one hundred and seventy grains of lead and forty grains powder. That's about equal to a Forty-Four . . . a little more powder-to-bullet ratio."

"On the other hand it might be an old Spencer?"

"If you get into rifles, why, there's just no limit. You take a Fifty-Six caliber Spencer, it could be Fifty-Six-Forty-Six or Fifty-Six-Fifty-Six, and the old buffalo Sharps, no end to it."

"Are many of those guns around?"

"Oh, a lot of 'em, yes, sir!"

"Then, judging just by the wounds, and nothing else, it could have been anything from a Thirty-Two to a Fifty-Six caliber?"

"I'd rule out the Thirty-Two. It wouldn't do that much damage."

"Then the Thirty-Eight to the Fifty-Six?"

"That's right, only most people carry the Forty-Five."

"Especially Billy?"

"Well, naturally, *they* said it was Billy."

"Who said it was Billy?"

"Objection!" cried Wardrope on his feet in an instant.

Boe responded: "Oh, come. Let's not split hairs."

"I most certainly do not consider this splitting hairs. This kind of hearsay could be endless."

"I'm inclined to agree," said Judge Minough. "Mister Boe?"

"As hearsay, it has no value. However, it is incontrovertible that there has been a climate of opinion established that assumes my client to be guilty. I would like to know whence the reports, and how much they had to do with the examination."

"All right. You may answer the question, Mister Hingham."

"What was it?"

"*Who* said it was Billy?"

"I guess first it was Tom Putley. He rode in about noon and said

85

Gannaway had been killed by Billy Buttons. Then they brought Gannaway in. Avery Carns, Ewell Ethrington, Artie Shallock . . . there must have been fifteen fellows rode in with them. Avery Carns said it was Billy. What he said was that Billy had been looking for Gannaway, swore he was going to settle things with him one way or the other. Anyhow they run into each other out at Willow Creek. They were on that flat where the freight station used to stand. Gannaway yelled . . . 'No!' . . . and tossed up his arm, and Billy shot him."

"I object," said Wardrope. "Your Honor, this hearsay account is improper. Even though on surface it seems to favor the prosecution, the motives of the defense are perfectly clear. They hope to introduce this account in the hopes of blunting the edge of our true, eye-witness account soon to come. This is a very old trick, and a shabby one."

"Well, it's new to me," said Judge Minough. "Mister Boe, what are your motives?"

"My motives are to get down to the blunt truth by the shortest possible route. How about it, Doc? . . . when they told you all that about Billy, what did you think? Were you surprised he'd do it?"

"Why, yes, I. . . ."

"Objection."

"Sustained."

"However, you did assume it had taken place . . . substantially as described?"

"Objection!"

"No," said the judge, "this bears on his reading of the physical evidence. Answer."

"What was it, now?" asked Doc.

"You assumed it took place about as described, that is, shot once with a Forty-Five caliber pistol? You did believe it?"

"Yes, I believed it."

"Now, what if they had brought in the body and said . . . 'Here is John Gannaway, shot down by a Forty-Five-Sixty caliber Winchester rifle' . . . would you have believed that?"

"Yes, only I'd have been surprised."

"Why? You testified the bullets were much the same."

"Well, Billy wouldn't be shooting a Forty-Five-Sixty. If they'd said old Pat Brown had shot him with a Forty-Five Sixty, I would have believed it. Mainly the old buffalo hunters have those guns. But, in fact, I'd have been even more willing to think it was an old cannon like that than I would a Forty-Five, just the way it blasted through."

"Why'd you mention Pat Brown?"

"I don't know. I guess because he owns a Forty-Five-Sixty."

"Isn't there another reason?"

"No, I don't think so."

"Didn't Pat Brown warn Gannaway to stay away from Brown's Landing?"

"Objection. Attorney is attempting to plant something not in the evidence, and in no way connected with this case."

"All right," Boe went on, "what if you'd been told he was shot from ambush by parties unknown . . . would you have believed it?"

"Yes."

"From ambush . . . sixty yards off. Would you have believed *that?*"

"Sixty? I don't see why not."

"What if they'd have said there were two shots?"

"Well, one could have missed."

"Right. And on the other hand . . . bang, bang . . . both could have hit?"

"Well, there was just the one wound, straight through."

"How about two bullet holes, one from each side? Ever hear of a man being hit by a bullet that didn't emerge? That just ended up in the body?"

"Of course. They're always probing for bullets."

"Done your own share of it, hey, Doc?"

"I sure have!"

"What if they'd ridden in here from the Omaha, all those bosses and hired men, and said here's a man shot from ambush by a Forty-Five-Sixty and by a Thirty-Two pistol close up?"

"Well, I don't know about that."

"Couldn't the first bullet have gone straight through, and the second have entered the exit wound? You said yourself those wounds were big as your hand."

87

"Objection. Witness corrected that to 'big as a dollar.' "

Boe asked: "What kind of a dollar . . . trade dollar, gold dollar, Mexican dollar?"

"A silver dollar, but actually that was inside, where I ran my finger. I could put about three fingers in. On the outside where the flesh pulled away, it *was* the size of your hand. And on both sides."

"Let's take another possibility. Forget the rifle. Could he have been struck down by a Forty-Five fired from one side and subsequently by a small caliber, say Thirty-Two short, from the other?"

"Oh, I don't know. It would have to be more on the order of a Forty-One. A Forty-One short. I say that because they throw a big slug but not much powder. It's like getting hit by a club from close up, but they don't plow on through. Or, it might be a gun more on the order of a Wells Fargo type Colt shooting a Thirty-Eight short. You know, they put out a lot of double-action guns nowadays, a stepped-up Thirty-Two and the like, a Thirty-Two long, a Thirty-Two-Twenty centerfire, but you don't see local fellows carrying them."

"Who do you see carrying them?"

"Traveling men, detectives."

"Dudes?"

"Yes, dudes."

"Wealthy Eastern cattlemen?"

"Objection!"

Boe turned slowly and looked at Wardrope. "This trial seems to turn on guns. We have here in Doc Hingham a real authority on guns. It seems to me the more we learn about guns, and the more we learn about what particular guns could have caused those wounds, the better."

"Your intent is perfectly obvious. . . ."

"It does, Mister Boe," said the judge, "seem you are going rather far into the matter."

"Very well. Now, I would like to have you think very carefully. . . ."

"All right," said Doc, anchoring himself.

"If, instead of being told the victim was shot once and once only by a Forty-Five, you had been told he had been shot twice, and being confronted with two bullet holes, as you were . . . would you have

88

conducted your examination differently?"

"No, I don't see how."

"You said you'd probed plenty for bullets."

"Well, in the Army. . . ."

"But you didn't probe for these bullets?"

"No. There wasn't any."

"How do you know there wasn't any?"

Stopped cold, Doc looked around, open-eyed, and said: "I guess I didn't."

"So you would have probed?"

"Yes."

"So, for all you know, he's lying back there in Council Bluffs with those bullets in him right now?"

"I guess so."

"Witness excused."

"Redirect?" asked the judge.

Wardrope was already on his feet. "You didn't probe, and why didn't you probe? Because on the basis of the evidence laid out before you, there didn't seem to exist any chance of anything except a single open-and-out entrance and exit wound, right?"

Boe interjected: "Why doesn't the attorney ask the question without also supplying the answer?"

"Yes, Mister Wardrope," said the judge, "you can't supply the answer, or suggest it."

"Sorry, Your Honor, but the attorney's actions have left the witness confused."

"No, I'm not confused!" said Doc hotly. "It never occurred to me to probe because it never occurred to me to doubt their story. They were all there saying the same thing, and. . . ."

"Finished with the redirect!"

CHAPTER EIGHT

"The people call C. R. Brundage," said Wardrope.

"Hold on," said Boe. "What is all this the people call? The people call Doctor Hingham. The people call C. R. Brundage? What people? Those people?" He pointed to the spectators. "They didn't have anything to do with calling these witnesses."

"Oh, Your Honor, this is preposterous! How can the attorney object to this common and formal terminology . . . ?"

"I'll tell you how we can object. We can object because it was chosen by the prosecution specifically for effect. You want to make it seem that the people . . . all the people who planned this trial . . . all the good people of Ricketts County are on one side with poor Billy on the other, already adjudged the enemy of the people."

"It has been common to associate the prosecution's side with the people ever since the king of England was displaced in our republic by that government of the people, by the people, and for the people!" Wardrope leveled his finger. "Those are the people, Mister Boe!"

"Well, yes," said Judge Minough, "it is common in some jurisdictions to say the People versus John Doe and the People call so and so. In Michigan and New York, I believe, and in California. However here, although we do borrow heavily from the California codes, it has been common to say either the Territory versus John Doe or the United States versus John Doe, in that way differentiating between the specific laws under which the case is being tried, and which coat . . . or should I say robe? . . . your judge is wearing at the time. Why don't you say, Mister Wardrope . . . the prosecution calls or the Territory of Montana calls? That's how we generally do it."

Brundage, a small, middle-aged man, the town telegrapher and a photographer on the side, was still standing by his chair.

"You may take the witness stand," said Judge Minough. "The territory calls you."

Brundage testified that two photographs, enlarged to nine inches by twelve on egg albumen paper, were those of the victim. He had taken them by means of photographic flash powder between eleven and midnight on the thirteenth of June. They showed glaringly a human body naked to the waist. In one view his lips revealed the tips of his teeth in a macabre smile, not a pretty sight, and if the prosecution, in ordering such extreme enlargements, sought to inflame the jury to a feeling of outrage, it was a failure, because the effect was to dehumanize, to dissociate with life, movement, laughter, or anything that was the John Gannaway they knew.

"Cross examine."

"No questions," said Boe.

"The Territory of Montana calls Harvey Ferris."

Harvey Ferris was a furniture and lumber dealer and part-time undertaker. He testified that he had taken charge of the body after the inquest and shipped it away to Billings.

"Now, Mister Ferris," said Wardrope, "as an undertaker you have no doubt examined many bodies which were subject to bullet wounds."

Ferris did not answer, but it could be taken for assent.

"In your opinion, and based on your experience, how many times had the victim been shot?"

"I didn't examine the wounds."

Wardrope had expected much better from Ferris. He gave Stewart a glance, and Stewart, by a gesture, indicated his perplexity.

"Oh, come, surely you clothed the body?"

"No, I didn't clothe the body. I rolled it in blankets and put it in a plain, rough box and shipped it off to Billings to be embalmed. They were to send a suit of clothes and some other things of his along later . . . from the ranch. There was nothing here to dress him in. Nobody asked me to prepare the body. I do just what I'm asked to do."

"You might not have examined the wounds, but you certainly looked at them." When Ferris just sat there, Wardrope cried: "Well, how do you account for your testimony before the coroner's jury? I read there that you said. . . ."

Boe interrupted: "I object that testimony given before the coroner's jury is not admissible as evidence here. Anyway, we have already had an indication as to how that inquest was turned into a kangaroo court of foregone conclusion."

Wardrope resumed: "Did you look at the wounds? Did you at least glance at them?"

"I looked at them, but I didn't touch them."

"How many wounds were there?"

"Two."

"Was one under the left armpit?"

"I couldn't say exactly."

"Do you mean to say you had charge of that body and . . . ?"

"I didn't have charge of the body. I was just asked to ship it. That's different than having charge. If I'd had charge of the body, the first thing I'd have done was clean it up, and then I'd have been able to tell you about the wounds. They didn't want me meddling with a thing before the inquest, and afterward they gave me to understand that the Billings undertaker was to have charge. I filled a box with ice and laid him in it and covered him over with hay and blankets and shipped him away."

"How much were you paid, Mister Ferris?"

"Objection. This is a subtle denigration of Mister Ferris's character."

"What bearing does the fee have on this case, Mister Wardrope?" the judge inquired.

"This witness in his testimony has been far more reluctant after he learned the body was to be sent to Billings for embalming than before, when he appeared at the inquest."

"Mister Ferris, the attorney for the prosecution has made a very serious allegation anent your integrity," the judge addressed the witness. "How answer you?"

"As for my testimony at that inquest, I'll tell you this . . . nobody took it down. Harry Richards was supposed to take it down, but all he did was make some notes. Then he would come around afterward and ask . . . did you say this? . . . and didn't so-and-so say that? The record wasn't made until a couple of days afterward. As an undertaker . . . and I don't claim to be anything but a coffin maker . . . I was asked only to ship the body out. I don't mess around where I'm not wanted."

Attempting to show the proper contempt, Wardrope said: "I'm *through* with this witness."

"No questions," said Boe.

Sheriff Earl Hankey was called. He was very serious as he took the oath and sat down. Clyde could remember how he had sometimes come in the house and waited for Pa, hiding impatience, and had sat with his palms pressed together, squeezed between his thighs — that's how he sat now, and sidewise so as not to look toward Ma.

"You are the elected sheriff of Ricketts County?"

"Yes."

The questioning went on with apparent predictability, for Boe seemed to doze off, chin down, eyes closed until Wardrope said: "On or about the fifteenth of April did John Gannaway come to you and ask the protection of your office, saying he feared for his life?"

"Whether he did or not," interjected Boe, "the form in which that question was put is damnable."

"I agree with you," said Judge Minough. "This is a law officer who is perfectly able to describe whatever did or did not take place on a certain date."

"What took place," said Hankey, "was that I met John Gannaway on the street, and he stopped me to say thirty or forty head of his cattle were being held on the O X . . . that's Rooney's old Spider ranch on Paint Creek . . . Billy was a partner there . . . and what did I believe was my duty in the matter? I said my duty was plain, but he'd have to seek a warrant or make a formal complaint. Then the defendant's name came up, and he said any paper drawn here would be known to Pennecard, and, well . . ." — Hankey didn't know how to get out of saying it, and there among the spectators sat R. E. Pennecard, county recorder, listening — "what he said was that Missus Pennecard liked Billy pretty well, all the women did. . . ."

"Are those his exact words?" asked Boe.

Wardrope interjected: "If attorney has an objection . . . ?"

Judge Minough, moving things along, instructed: "Give the exact words."

"What he said exactly was . . . 'Every time Billy Buttons comes to town, Lyda Pennecard acts like a mare that's horsing.' " He looked at the judge and asked: "Should I say the rest of it?"

"Oh, yes," said Judge Minough, "in this place we deal with the bare bone of truth."

There was laughter.

"He said," Sheriff Hankey continued, " 'That woman of Rob's knows everything he does and will be right out to tell Billy if we draw up papers.' I said I wasn't sure of that. I'd heard things, but I discounted gossip, and he said . . . well, he *shouted,* the way he did when people argued with him . . . 'What in hell are you talking about? She was down in Billings last year laying up with him.' "

"Now, I *do* object to this!" said Boe, but he couldn't help looking amused. Several men laughed, but most of them remained quiet in deference to Pennecard who looked startled, shocked, incredulous. "Your Honor, we are trying this man for a matter set forth in the information, but now the prosecution strives to picture him as a cattle rustler and heaven knows what all."

"Mister Wardrope?"

"We endeavor to show by the very competent testimony of this county's ranking law officer that the victim was already, two months previous to the deed, given cause to be alarmed for his safety. There is the matter of motive. We allege homicide long planned, and with malice."

"Go ahead. But no wool gathering . . . *black* wool gathering. The object must not be the general denigration of the defendant. The object must lead directly to . . . be definitely applicable to the matter at trial."

"That's all there was to it," Hankey resumed. "Gannaway didn't push it any further, and a week or so later I saw him on the street, and he made a point of saying he intended to settle with Billy himself."

"What did he mean by that? What was your interpretation?"

"He didn't mean *settle* like shoot it out. He meant he was going to make it part of an agreement." He then told about the Buttons Reserve that Gannaway had leased from the government, but to which Mrs. Buttons refused to relinquish her claim of prior right. "He said . . . 'Billy thinks he can get away with murder because of the Reserve' . . . but he didn't mean murder like killing. He meant Billy thought he could get away claiming a lot of doubtful cattle

94

because he, John Gannaway, wouldn't dare rock the boat. He also said . . . 'I'm between the devil and the deep blue sea. Missus Buttons will balk on the deal if I take action, and Billy will steal me blind if I don't.' "

Wardrope asked: "On the evening of November tenth, last, were you called to the bar of the River House?"

"Yes, about seven o'clock. The McNeil kid came running over where I was having supper and said I'd better get to the River House because Billy and Gannaway were going to kill each other."

"And what did you ascertain?"

"They were drinking. They'd been Indian wrestling at the bar, and it seems that Gannaway had won, so Billy offered to throw him by Greco-Roman, and they'd torn each other's shirts to ribbons. They seemed to be laughing and having a good time. . . ."

"*Seemed* to?"

"Yes, well, I don't know how to describe it. It wasn't the actual words. You have to know Billy. One time Billy shot the weathervane off the top of the Mountdouglas House. That might have been high spirits, but he'd been having some trouble with R. L. Flescher who was the manager. He came around and paid for it afterward. Billy would always pay his damages. It was just when he got that extra considerate tone. . . ."

"I ask you directly for your interpretation of Mister Gannaway's statements to you . . . did he think William Buttons was stealing his cattle?"

"Yes, he did. But I'll say something else . . . Buttons thought Gannaway *owed* him cattle. It worked both ways. Billy . . . Mister Buttons . . . even got out a writ of attachment one time and tried to get me to execute it when I was deputy here for Chouteau County. It was signed by Judge Newby. It was really a writ of replevin. Well, I'd have served it, that was my job, but I couldn't execute it. It involved cattle grazing on the range. . . ."

At last Hankey got around to how he'd heard the news of the shooting, and here was a very strange thing — at about half past nine on the morning of the twelfth he was eating breakfast at the Chinese café, when Sam Seeley from the livery barn said a half-breed Indian by the name of Turcotte had ridden in early and reported that there'd been a shooting out on Willow Creek the evening before — a man by the name of Roberts had been killed. "Sam asked what I thought of the story, and I told him I didn't think much, because if he'd been shot the evening before, Turcotte would have had to ride all night."

"How had he got word of it?"

"I never found out, and I was never able to locate Turcotte to ask. It's still a mystery. The Indians do have ways of passing news that no white man has ever been able to understand. But it might have been just a false report, a coincidence. There was never a Roberts killed, that much is certain."

"When did the news reach you?"

"Tom Putley came in with it, like Mister Hingham testified. He said Billy Buttons had killed John Gannaway, and they were bringing in the body, so I saddled right up and rode out to meet them. I met them on those M Bar L flats about seven miles out. Carns and Ewell Ethrington in a buggy, Carns driving . . . Artie Shallock, Arvis Rapf, Bob Purdy, and Red MacLean on horseback . . . Paul Jarvis was driving a wagon. They had the body in the wagon. It was John Gannaway, of course, and he'd been shot."

"You made a thorough examination . . . when?"

"In town. I could see he'd been shot on the left side under the armpit, and the bullet had smashed right on through and come out, making a big break on the other side."

"They hadn't cleaned him up at all?"

"No. They said he was exactly as he fell. They hadn't got him to the ranch until after dark, and then they set out early. It's an all-day drive to town."

He told something about the examination and the arrangements for an inquest, and started to recount some reports that Billy had admitted to the shooting in a saloon at Brown's Landing, but Wardrope stopped him.

"I don't believe that's admissible. Did Mister Buttons make himself available for questioning?"

People laughed. The sheriff said: "No, he skinned out of the country."

"Your witness."

Boe remained seated which meant that the sheriff would have to turn to look at him. But the sheriff didn't turn. He sat doggedly with his face toward the jury, and Boe stayed where he was.

"Hello, Sheriff," Boe said.

The opening took everyone by surprise. Hankey shot him a glance, then his eyes returned to the old direction.

"I'm over here, Sheriff."

Hankey then turned his body to face the defense table, and he stared Billy right in the eye. Then he looked over at Ma for good measure, dipping his head in grave courtesy. He waited in tense attentiveness for Boe to proceed. Boe slowly got up, one limb at a time.

After consulting some notes, he said: "I see here where you say Billy skinned out of the country. How does a person skin out?"

"Well, that's just a term. I mean he left."

"If I left the room, would you say I'd skinned out?"

"No. . . ."

"Then it means something else. Will you be more specific?"

"Well, he ran out."

"Actually ran, on foot?"

"No. You know what I mean."

"Do you mean he escaped?"

"Yes, in a sense."

"Escape? I would like the exact descriptive word on the record."

"I guess it'll do. Left to avoid prosecution."

"To avoid prosecution presupposes knowledge. Did he know he had been indicted, or that a warrant was out?"

"Why, he couldn't help it."

"Was he informed? Given the particulars?"

"He must have known we'd be after him."

"Why?"

"Because, of course, he'd know a thing like what he'd done couldn't just pass. . . ."

"If you're assuming his guilt as an established fact, then this trial is a waste of time. *Do* you think it a waste of time, Sheriff?"

"I figure he'd know. The whole country knew. If any man ever knew what was going on, it was Billy Buttons."

"I'm sure that on sober appraisal that assumption of a general competence will seem insufficient."

"Well, he sure wasn't seen around town for a while!"

"Oh, come. That's not sufficient. Tell me, Sheriff, was Mister Buttons between the dates of December first and March first . . . *was* Mister Buttons seen around town?"

"No, I don't recall that he was."

"How about the month of April? Seen around town then?"

"No, he was gone some place."

"Then it wasn't unusual for him not to be seen for a month or two at a time?"

"No, he'd light out and go. God knows. . . ."

"Did you figure he was escaping then?"

"No, I didn't. . . ."

"But this time you did?"

"Yes, this time I did, because he couldn't help knowing. It was all anybody talked about. It was in the papers."

"You didn't inform him?"

"I didn't see him. If I. . . ."

"Didn't write him?"

"No. How could . . . ?"

"Send up any smoke signals?"

"No."

"Then you really can't say he left to avoid prosecution, or that his absence had anything to do with a homicide?"

"I went out to the Buttons' and told his mother. I informed her he was wanted, and that I'd give him a certain time to turn himself in."

"Was she hiding him?"

"I knew very well he'd come in there."

"*If* he was in the hills, hiding out. What if he was in . . . Idaho?"

"We knew he was around. We had reports. Everybody that hung around him, and kowtowed to him, weren't his friends. Lots of 'em would have liked to see him caught." Hankey gave Billy a look when he said it.

"The fact is, you haven't one specific, conclusive piece of evidence that he was in the area. He might have been in Butte or Helena. For all you *knew,* he might have been camping with the Indians. How about his previous arrests? You have arrested Billy before? Was he hard to catch?"

"I never arrested him before."

"No previous arrests?"

"I took a rifle away from him once."

"Did he put up a fight?"

"No, he was just having a high old time."

"How about warrants? Any previous warrants out for him?"

"There was a Wanted out for him one time. It came to the Chouteau County sheriff at Fort Benton."

"Tell us about it."

"It was from down in Wyoming. It was a federal warrant because it was across the territorial line. He was down in Jackson's Hole. It's always been an outlaw den. They're supposed to get stolen horses from all over the West. Billy was said to be a rep or something for this part of the country. They drive horses along the river and to the mining camps all the way from Dakota, even, and a lot of them end up in Jackson's Hole."

Judge Minough cleared his throat, causing the sheriff to pause. "Mister Boe?" But Boe indicated — let him talk, let's see the lengths he'll go in denigrating Billy.

"As I understand it, Billy had trouble with a fellow named Hodge Piper. This Piper was supposed to have killed three or four fellows one winter, and been a cannibal. He'd walk around with a sawed-off shotgun on a rope sling over his shoulder. He was a real burly fellow, black whiskered. He hung out down in the Gallatin for a while, but I never met him. He used to brag about never having had a bath and would say . . . 'If I can't shoot 'em out, I'll stink 'em out.' Well, Hodge was down in the Hole . . . he ran a sort of store and saloon . . . he had a wife who wasn't so old or bad-looking . . . and she was supposed to have fallen in love with Billy. But I also heard they had trouble over a horse. Anyhow, he was out to kill him . . . Hodge was out to kill Billy . . . and Billy knew it, and it was winter, the snow was about four feet deep, and Hodge had a long, doeskin overcoat on. He was just getting out of a sled when Billy was supposed to have come out the door and yelled at him. He tried to go for his shotgun, but Billy was too smart for that. There was deep snow, and the long, doeskin coat, but Billy was ready. He just pulled and shot him."

"Your Honor!"

"Mister Wardrope?"

"This is all improper questioning, very discursive. Surely we all want to get on with this trial."

Boe responded: "Is it the attorney's purpose to save time?"

"Yes. I don't believe this wandering into inadmissible fields. . . ."

"For what reason inadmissible? It's also something else, isn't it?"

"What does the attorney mean?"

"Isn't there a more serious and absolute term for this kind of testimony?"

"I already branded it as secondhand, or hearsay."

"How about forejudgment?"

"I was not aware that forejudgment, as you call. . . ."

"Prejudicial?" clarified Boe. "That means preconceived bias, or forejudgment. Isn't this the real reason you would like to stop the sheriff, because his testimony would tend to indicate a forejudgment, a preconceived bias, a prejudice in all matters relating to the accused, a willingness to believe the very worst? Observe what he has happily volunteered . . . Billy was running stolen horses . . . no proof . . . Billy moved in with a gang of rustlers . . . why did he? . . . because he wished to commit adultery with. . . ."

"But all this does seem to be rumor," said Judge Minough.

"I might argue for admissibility by saying it tends to prove, or cast light, on the matter in question. I quote the familiar . . . 'When offense is cumulative, consisting of successive acts, then evidence of those other acts are supportive of the charge, hence admissible.' "

"This is hardly evidence, Mister Boe," the judge said.

Boe addressed the witness: "Sheriff, what happened down there in Jackson Hole after Billy shot that poor, stinking Hodge Piper down?"

There was laughter, and the judge used his gavel.

"They divided up into factions. Then the Cattleman's Association went with a force of men from Uintah County to clean them out, but they were outnumbered and withdrew. The small ranchers were against them. You know how they are. . . ."

"Like over in our badlands?"

"I object," said Wardrope.

"Oh, all right," Boe conceded in the best of humor. "I withdraw the question. What about Billy? Whose side was he on? . . . big ranchers or small ranchers?"

"I never heard he was on any side. All I *knew* about was the warrant out for him."

"A warrant for *William Buttons?*"

"It was out for John Green, alias Belly Buttons."

There was laughter.

"*Belly* Buttons? I hope my client doesn't have to answer to such a derogatory sobriquet just to please the purposes of the prosecution! What do you think of Billy and how he acts toward women?"

"It's no concern of mine."

"But what do you think, Sheriff?"

"I think it's a disgrace on his family. It's not so bad when he goes down to Wyoming and gets in a mess like that, but here at home . . . well, I've seen tomcats that. . . ."

"What specifically?"

"If you want a specific instance, I'll tell you something I challenge anybody to contradict. He hangs around at Brown's Landing. Pat Brown has this one real pretty daughter. She's quarter Indian. Brown is married to a Cadotte girl who is a half-breed. They have a whole raft of kids. I don't know how many. Anyway, he had this daughter. Fellows used to go down there and flirt with her, and Pat would drive them off with a gun. But when Billy showed up, it was a different thing. Anything Billy wanted was all hunkey-dory with Pat. She wasn't any more'n sixteen. Well, he got her in a family way. He was in and out of there all the time and . . ." — he raised his voice when the spectators started to snicker at the off meaning of in and out — "of course, when her condition became obvious, Billy was gone. He was away off some place in Wyoming, or Portland, or at the silver mines. She married another fellow. His name was Griswold. He's a fellow about forty years old, has a herd of sheep on Freezout across the river. They went up to Judith on the steamboat and got married. Well, next spring, here comes Billy, riding back, acting like he was outraged that she'd been fickle with him! So what did she do but come back to the Landing and move in with Billy. Griswold didn't make a move to stand up for his rights. He retired from the scene, and Billy took right up where he'd left off. And that's how it's been, one season to the next. When Billy's there, he's number one. All he has to do is snap his fingers. Then, when it's good bye to Billy, she goes back to Griswold. Oh, don't get me wrong. If it's all right with

Brown, it's all right with me. They shack up like a pack of dogs down there. But it's a terrible way to treat his mother . . . one of the finest women. . . ."

"Your Honor," said Wardrope, "how long is this to go on?"

"You wouldn't want to hear chapters one to five in a romance and then just close the book, would you?" asked Judge Minough, looking with reproof at the witness. "I'd like to hear the rest of this. I have a couple of colleagues on the supreme bench of Montana who will be sorry they didn't hear this case."

"That's about all there was to it," said Hankey. "I was asked for an example of what Billy was like with women."

Boe queried: "I believe you frequently described him as a longtail tomcat?"

"I guess so."

"You didn't make that term up, did you?"

"No."

"Ever hear anybody else described as a longtail tomcat?"

"I suppose."

"What particular man, besides Billy, have you heard so described?"

"I don't know."

"How about John Gannaway? Isn't he really the one who was most often so described? In fact, haven't you heard it said that John Gannaway, and not Billy Buttons, was the longest-tailed tomcat in the country?"

No answer.

"Well, was he what you might describe as a vigorous man?"

"Yes, I guess. . . ."

"When he was bringing in some Percheron stallions a year ago, didn't the boys all remark it was like carrying coals to Newcastle to bring in any more stallions when John Gannaway was around?"

"I don't remember that."

"How about Gannaway's visits to Brown's Landing? He ever go down there?"

"I don't know."

"I think you do. I think you know very well he did. In fact, didn't you hear reports that he was driven away by Mister Brown for making illicit advances to his daughter? Ever hear that?"

"Yes, but I don't know it was true."

"You didn't investigate?"

"No."

"How about Billy's affair with Brown's daughter. Did you investigate that?"

"Not actually investigate."

"You didn't investigate either one, but you *believe* the tale about Billy, not the one about Gannaway?"

"Well, I heard it over and over about Billy, only once about Gannaway."

"Then, of course, Gannaway, being a family man . . . he *does* have a wife back in . . . ?"

"Objection. If Mister Boe is interested in establishing the facts of the victim's life, surely there is a more direct means."

"Sustained."

"Well, Sheriff, you certainly know all about Billy. Now, there are some things I would like to get straight concerning your own position. I mean, you were close to all the parties. By your testimony, you were deputy for this area when it was part of Chouteau County, right?"

"Yes."

"Then, when the new county was formed, you were a candidate for sheriff . . . elected by better than two to one?"

"I got two hundred and two votes. My opponents got one hundred and seventy-five among them. That was in the primary. We all filed as Democrats."

"No Republicans at all?"

"There used to be. Chouteau County used to go Republican. But all those cowboys from Texas kept coming in, and they're Democrats. Lots of people came over from the gold camps, and they were Democrats, too. They swarmed in after the war, from Missouri. Congressman Tom Foley, who you undoubtedly know, used to say that Montana was the western wing of Sterling Price's Army of the Confederacy."

Everybody laughed, including the judge.

"So any sensible man would run as a Democrat?"

"If he wanted to get elected. But I always been a Democrat. Illinois, but Democrat. I cast my first vote for the Little Giant,

Stephen A. Douglas, and would again."

"Who opposed you . . . as fellow Democrats?"

"Danner," he jerked his head at his undersheriff seated with a view of Billy, against the wall, "Mike Frisbee, and Norris Hadley."

"You ran as 'The People's Candidate,' right?"

"I guess so."

"Guess so? It's what your handbills read."

"It was sort of a slogan."

"How about Danner? What was his slogan?"

"I don't know as he had one. 'Experienced, vigorous. . . .' "

"Wasn't there another reason you called yourself 'The People's Candidate'?"

"Oh, I don't know."

"Didn't people refer to Mister Danner as 'The Company's Candidate'? And wasn't that why you called yourself 'The People's Candidate'?"

"Your Honor," said Wardrope.

But Judge Minough was interested in politics and waved him quiet. "Answer."

"I can't say as I remember just ex. . . ."

"You heard him called 'The Company's Candidate,' didn't you?"

"Yes."

"What company did they mean?"

"Why, Omaha Land and Cattle, I would. . . ."

"Why? Why would they call him that?"

"He worked for Omaha. That is, for their predecessors."

"As a matter of fact, he came up here from Wyoming, when he was under indictment for murder, and went to work as a range detective for the old Anglo . . . ?"

"Your Honor, I *do* object!" Wardrope was standing. In fact, since his previous objection, he had remained almost shoulder to shoulder with Boe in front of the witness. "This is entirely incompetent. If we are going to examine the qualifications of Mister Danner, if it has some bearing on this action, then let's proceed in a proper manner to that end."

"Mister Boe?"

"I'd like to determine just what this sheriff's office consists of, because we have seen its attitude toward my client right from the

104

outset. I'd like to determine the reason. If it is run in a fair and equitable manner, let's establish that. If it is, instead, run as sort of an adjunct, or department, of the big cattle corporations, let's determine that . . . and *why*. Specifically, I'd like to learn why Mister Danner, so-called range detective for Omaha, was chosen for under-sheriff, whether it was free choice, based on his qualifications, or whether he was rammed down this sheriff's throat."

Wardrope replied sharply: "The makeup of the sheriff's office has nothing to do with this charge."

"Well, we did allow the sheriff unusual liberty," said the judge. "He did, while here in the sash and brassard of his office, as one might say, have some tales to tell inimical to the accused, to say the least. But please expedite, Mister Boe. We can't indulge in the luxury of a week-long trial. Get to the heart of it."

"How about it?" Boe resumed. "Did Undersheriff Danner come here while under indictment in Wyoming?"

"I heard that, but if there was an indictment, it was quashed. He was a deputy sheriff down there and range detective for the Stockman's Association. He was involved in a hanging, and there was a big howl about it after it appeared in the Eastern papers. The charges were dropped."

"In fact, wasn't he charged with murder, and didn't all the witnesses mysteriously disappear?"

"You hear a hundred kinds of stories."

"You mean he was exonerated after an investigation? That's a *kind* of story. Did you hear that?"

"No, I never heard that."

"It just kind of blew over. Then he came here, and Montana got to keep Danner for its very own. Now, how did you happen to choose him as undersheriff . . . in other words, chief deputy?"

"Well, he was qualified. He wanted the job. He was runner-up in votes."

"Nothing else bent you toward him?"

"No, nothing much."

"You just weighed his qualifications and his human qualities, and decided he was the man for the job."

The sheriff was silent.

"Was he highly recommended?"

"Yes, he was recommended."

"By men of influence?"

He did not answer.

"Did one of those who recommended him happen to be Mister Ewell Ethrington?"

"Yes, he did. And several more."

"As a matter of fact, you had to name Danner undersheriff or you wouldn't have been sheriff, isn't that true?"

"I was elected sheriff."

"Yes, you were, you were elected sheriff of Ricketts County, a county never really formalized by the territorial legislature, and a county that the parent county . . . from which it was carved . . . never admitted to exist, and has not to this day. And if the big ranchers fulfilled a threat not to pay their county assessments, or had paid to the old county, you'd have been left a sheriff with no jurisdiction, isn't that true? In fact, that is exactly what would have happened . . . ?"

"I object!" Wardrope was violent in this. "I object, I object! This questioning, this tissue of suggestions, has no purpose except to impugn the nature of the sheriff's actions by making his office seem the fief of the large ranching interests. This matter of politics . . . what would have happened, if taxes had not been paid . . . all that is speculation."

"Yes, Mister Boe, confine yourself to specific acts of the witness . . . and further show that they relate directly to the charge."

"Sheriff Hankey, you testified that you paid a visit to Missus Walter Buttons on Arrow Creek, looking for the accused?"

"I did."

"Search the ranch?"

"No."

"Why?"

"I wanted him to give himself up. I called on Kate . . . Missus Buttons. I told her if she saw Billy, to talk him into it."

"For what reason?"

"Why, he was wanted for murder. I'm the sheriff."

"That wasn't the reason you gave her, though?"

"She was his mother. I tried to explain it would be better for him."

"Specifically what might happen if he didn't?"

"Well, it might keep him from getting shot, for one thing."

"By whom?"

"By whoever was after him."

"Didn't you name somebody specifically?"

"I might have named Danner."

"Didn't you say Danner would never bring him in alive?"

"I don't know that I did."

"Didn't you . . . look at me when you answer, Mister Hankey . . . didn't you say he'd shoot him down like a dog?"

"I might have."

"Didn't she censure you for naming a man like Danner as your undersheriff? And what did you answer?"

"It was a long time ago. I've forgotten just what was said."

"Didn't you say, specifically, that he was rammed down your throat by the big ranchers?"

"I object," said Wardrope. "This was ruled out before. . . ."

"Your Honor," replied Boe, "this is directly related to the charge. I will show, by the prosecution's own witnesses, that the sheriff's office had no intention of ever allowing the defendant to ride into its jail alive, that this trial was forced on it . . . and later I will show why."

"Go ahead."

"Sheriff! If I have to, I can call Missus Buttons to the stand later."

"Well, what I said, I guess, was that Danner wouldn't have been my free choice for undersheriff. I probably said he was rammed down my throat."

"By whom? You said rammed down your throat by. . . ."

"By the Big Dry Association. By the Omaha. I've forgotten."

"Your memory is improving. Go on. What did they threaten as an alternative to Danner's elevation?"

"They'd pay taxes to Chouteau County. They claimed I was elected by the rustlers, small ranchers, riffraff. That wasn't true. I intended to enforce the law impartially. If I hadn't named Danner, the runner-up in votes, there'd be no money for a sheriff, courthouse, anything."

"Didn't you plead for your job? I mean, at Buttons'?"

"No. How could I?"

"Didn't you say if Billy didn't give himself up, you'd get the blame? Didn't you say if he didn't show up in five days, you'd have to resign?"

"He didn't show up in five days, and I didn't resign."

"Didn't you say it?"

"I might have said it. I can't remember what was said, exactly. It was about the hardest thing I ever had to do, go out there. . . ."

"Now, what you hoped for was that Billy would be around the ranch? Stop me if I'm wrong. You hoped Missus Buttons would get him to come out of the barn, or out from under the bed, and you could take him in?"

"Yes, I had hoped he'd surrender."

"You also assured her that you were there on your own? In fact, you made quite a point of that?"

"Yes."

"In fact, though, if you'd have left with Billy, if he *had* come crawling from under the bed, you had a pretty good idea he'd never reach town alive, isn't that true?"

"No, it is *not* true. Nobody's ever taken a prisoner from me, or harmed one in my charge since I been. . . ."

"Sheriff Hankey! What road did you take after leaving the Buttons' ranch?"

"Why. . . ."

"You rode down what is known as the old Helena stage road?"

"Yes. Yes, I did."

"Is that the shortest road to town?"

"The point is. . . ."

"Answer the question. Is it, or isn't it, the shortest road?"

"No, but there's always water in. . . ."

"In the month of June you can water a great many places. You left Arrow Creek and rode eastward, taking your time, and darkness settled, and when you came down to that old, abandoned stage station in the bushes of Salty Creek, a man was waiting for you. You talked with that man. Who was he?"

Obviously shocked that he had this information, Hankey stared.

"Oh come, Sheriff. You must know who it was. The man is sitting right in this room."

"Yes. Danner was there. There was another fellow, too. A cowboy. It's not unusual for men to. . . ."

108

"Sheriff, if you had taken Billy Buttons prisoner, and disarmed him, and gone riding down the road with him, what route would you have taken?"

Hankey tried to explain there had been no prearrangement, but Boe said: "Just answer the question."

"Yes, Sheriff," confirmed Judge Minough, "answer the question."

"What route, Sheriff Hankey?"

"That route, I should imagine."

"Sheriff, did Missus Buttons tell you somebody had been hiding near her ranch house, waiting to ambush her son?"

"Yes, she said somebody was watching from the rimrocks."

"Did you go up to investigate?"

"No."

"Why didn't you go up to investigate?"

"I was all alone. I had to get back to Arlington."

"You *knew* who was hiding in the rimrocks, didn't you?"

"No. She told me about it. And somebody had shot her dog. They wanted to keep him quiet. It was guesswork. I didn't know beforehand, or afterward, either. In fact. . . ."

"Sheriff, you have made several references to being an old friend of the Buttons family. How long have you known them?"

"Why, I'd met W. B. down in Colorado as far back as . . . I guess it was 'Fifty-Nine. He went up to Idaho. He was at the Florence Diggings, and I met him again when he came over to the Beaverhead, that was the fall of Eighteen Sixty-Two. Billy, there, was a babe in arms. He was born on the way over from the Clearwater diggings to the Salmon. Old W. B. was my best friend."

"You followed him to this country in Eighteen Seventy-Two? He found you employment?"

"Yes, he did. He said . . . 'Come on over.' He drove his herd over here from the Smith, and had an Army contract, freighting. They had to use wagons to supply the Army when the river got too low, emergency stuff . . . it had to be hauled up from Utah. He had quite a thing going. He was a pretty big freighter at one time, and I was his wagon boss."

"You bought him out? . . . his freight business?"

"He wanted to go into ranching full time. I didn't exactly buy him out, though. He sold most of his stock. He was a great one for mules, and the Army was buying."

"How much capital did you have?"

"Not much."

"He staked you, didn't he?"

"He let me use some of his wagons and harness. I borrowed from the bank."

"The First Territorial Bank in Deer Lodge?"

"Yes."

"What did you have as security?"

"Nothing much."

"Isn't it a fact that W. B. Buttons co-signed the papers or you wouldn't have gotten a cent?"

"Yes, he did. And. . . ."

"And if you hadn't paid, they could have taken his ranch, stock, everything he owned?"

"I paid every cent. . . ."

"But they could have? He was taking quite a risk, wouldn't you say?"

"Yes."

"How much interest did he charge?"

"Nothing. The bank charged . . . oh, ten percent. But he didn't charge anything."

"That was quite an act of friendship, wasn't it?"

"I never denied it."

"That was away back in the old days when the shoe was on the other foot, right?"

"Your Honor!" objected Wardrope. "Where is this getting us? He's implying that some old friendship should in some manner influence this elected officer of the law in the present discharge of his duties."

"Mister Boe?"

"Your Honor, I sat here and listened while this witness with great impropriety, with no regard for the rules of evidence, set out to destroy the reputation of Billy Buttons. Even when he seemed to praise him, it was for something essentially lawless, or evil. This man has displayed the most phenomenal memory for every incident that might impugn the character of the defendant. His every act has been called forth in a manner that places it in an evil and baleful

110

light. Billy Buttons quarreled with John Gannaway. It turned out no words were spoken in anger. In fact, he was smiling. But he was smiling *in an evil way*. Anyone else would think that Billy was being friendly, but the Sheriff *knew* Billy Buttons. Then there's the matter of Jackson's Hole. Did the defendant happen in there because it was winter, and he was trying to survive? Was there any such assumption? No, he was there because he was a rustler. It was an outlaw den. Later, under cross-questioning, we find all were unsubstantiated rumors. But it was never admitted easily. It was like pulling teeth. This man is a prosecution witness. He's here to destroy the defendant. He is here to do in this court what his Company deputy was unable to do on the lonely road between the Buttons' Ranch and the Salty Creek station . ... to lead Billy into the gunsights. . . ."

"I object!"

"Acting as a Judas goat . . . !" Boe concluded.

"No, Boe! No more of that!" the sheriff remonstrated.

"I apologize to the court," Boe said. "I was carried away. Sheriff, if Billy Buttons were to be found guilty, would you hang him?"

"I was elected sheriff. I'll do my duty."

"You'd hang the son of your greatest benefactor?"

"Your Honor!" pleaded Wardrope. "This is outrageous. I can't stand by for this."

But Judge Minough was too interested to rule on the objection.

"You wouldn't resign?" Boe pressed.

"No, I never hung a man in my life, but I stood for sheriff of this county. . . ."

"Now, Sheriff, I want you to listen carefully. We'll assume there was a man who had a friend. The man was hard up, but the friend stuck to him through thick and thin. He received him like one of the family into his home, set him up in business, and without hope of possible gain, and at great financial peril, signed notes that rescued him from bankruptcy. . . ."

Boe went on to describe his hypothetical friend, right up to "tying a rope around the son's neck with his own fingers," whereupon Wardrope cried: "I object!"

Boe raised his voice and drove on: "Yes, he would put the rope around that son's neck with his own fingers. He would do that rather than resign his position of influence, gained through alliance with

111

the corporation. How would you describe such a man? What would you use to best convey your impression?"

Wardrope appealed: "Your Honor, this is an outrage!"

Judge Minough, who had let it go, who had sat placidly through the uproar of competing voices, now said: "Yes, Mister Boe, this would seem to overstep the bounds of the permissible example."

But Hankey wanted to answer. "I tell you! I'm *still* a friend! And I'm trying to do my duty."

"Your Honor," Boe said, "I have described a hypothetical case. If it is not applicable to the witness, let him point out wherein it is not. I will gladly stand corrected. I have asked his assessment of the man herein described. Can you think of a proper word to describe him, Sheriff?"

"No, I. . . ."

"How about ingrate?"

"Now that will cost you five dollars for contempt of this court, because you have overstepped the bounds," the judge ruled.

"In gold?"

"Gold will be satisfactory."

Boe took some coins from his vest, chose a small, five-dollar gold piece, and laid it on the table where Bunting was writing top speed, trying to catch up with the testimony. Still writing with his right hand, he took the gold piece, and slipped it under the transcript folder.

Judge Minough said: "Now, if this is to proceed. . . ."

Boe waved a hand. "I am finished with this witness," he said, looking at Sheriff Hankey as if he were carrion. With a handkerchief he wiped away perspiration, and then used it as if in ablution of his hands. "Yes, I . . . am . . . finished!"

CHAPTER NINE

"Your name?"

"Avery Carns."

"What is your business, Mister Carns?"

"Range boss for the Omaha Land and Cattle Company."

"And what are the duties of a range boss?"

"In charge of the stock, oversee the range, see to it we have a crew."

Carns was a powerful man, and he looked even more powerful than he was. About forty, he looked old as the rocky crags to Clyde, a stony-faced, hard, obdurate man. No one had ever opposed the small owners, the Badlanders — and the Buttons — more than Carns, but you never heard much against him, either. "He's tough, but he's fair," Ma often said. When the Association had its big meeting that summer, and it was proposed that the Buttons be dealt out of the roundup, treated as outlaws on account of Billy, Carns got up and said, no, it wouldn't do, membership was membership.

He was being asked about blooded beef and hadn't John Gannaway been the first to introduce such fine cattle north of the Yellowstone?

"No, the Judith did." Carns nodded at Major Morrison who sat with graceful forefinger over unlighted cigar, small finger glittering with a diamond solitaire, memory of his first wife. "They brought in English Rubies, also called the Devon Reds, some years before. Grazed them in fenced pasture at the mouth of the Judith. They have a regular show place down there."

"But Mister Gannaway pioneered the first blooded cattle on a large scale?"

"We brought in four thousand Herefords from the Swan River herd in Wyoming. Under our corporate reorganization it was so stipulated. More than a hundred and fifty people invested their money. Some of them their life savings, on the proposition that Hereford cattle be introduced, and for the purchase of lands for cropping and winter range. After what happened in the winter of 'Eighty-Six, it wasn't easy to get people to put money in Western beef."

"I'm sure we all realize the rôle played by you and your concern in the quick recovery of, and the introduction of, new methods on the northern range. Will you describe a Hereford?"

"Describe one? Oh, they're with white faces, white chests, and bellies."

"Always?"

"Practically one hundred percent."

"White-face cattle?"

"They call them that. It's the common term."

"That must be pretty distinctive? I mean, you'd hardly have to brand them?"

"We recognize our cattle, but they have to be branded according to the regulation, or they can't be marketed legally."

"If anybody else shows up with white-face cattle, you know pretty well where they came from?"

"We do."

"Has it happened?"

"Yes, it's happened."

"Tell us about it?"

"There's a fair size herd of white-faced calves on what we call the O X, or Spider brand. O with superimposed X . . . looks like a spider."

"Who are the proprietors of this brand?"

"The chief ones seem to be Art Rooney and Billy Buttons."

"I object," said Boe, who was ready. "We're not trying anyone for cattle stealing."

"This is only part of the sequence of events that led directly to the murder of John Gannaway, as we will show," Wardrope protested.

The judge said: "I'm going to allow the question. And now, Mister Boe, and Mister Wardrope, it looks like a long contest ahead. At the outset I had hoped we could get this to the jury in one day. It seems likely that two days will be required. But I tell you, we *will* get this to the jury in two days if it means grinding around the clock. I am going to allow the witnesses considerable latitude, and will ask that the attorneys refrain from arguing even though much testimony seems on the borderline as to propriety and admissibility. It works both ways. It may not be what you are used to back in the East, Mister Wardrope, or you, Mister Boe, in the big city, but the trial will be vastly expedited." To Carns he said: "Very well, tell us about that Spider Ranch."

"It's quite a hangout. It's a real old outfit. Once belonged to Rooney, Horn, and Glynn. Glynn and Horn both left years ago. Then other fellows came in from time to time. Most of them had their own registered brands. The Spider must have eight or nine on the books, and twice that number counting horse brands. I inquired at the brand inspection in Saint Paul, and most of the brands were in the name of Buttons. That's William Buttons, not the Buttons Ranch. Then I noticed a brand registered to a Belmont Hereford Ranches, Consolidated, with an address in Arlington. I knew of no such outfit, but later I had it checked in the Brand Book in Helena. It was there, and still a mystery, but then we found out that William Buttons had registered it with a certificate of fictitious name which reposed with the territorial secretary. You see, this was how he schemed things." Unlike the sheriff who had scarcely once looked at Billy, Carns looked straight at him every time he mentioned his name. "He went over there and hired a big lawyer. He retained T. Ford Donahue, the ex-governor, in this instance. It's easy to see that when a man like that draws up anything like a certificate of fictitious name, it will be regarded as legitimate. And it wasn't for any Spider Ranch, or Greasy Skillet, as we call it here! No, it was Belmont Hereford Ranches, Consolidated! You can see the thought behind it. The Belmont is a big gold mine near Helena, and there's a Belmont mine in Butte, and one down on the Mother Lode in California. It sounds like something! What if you went to court? A man like old Governor Donahue would get the case tried in Helena, or Butte, and over there nobody would know. Belmont Consolidated sounds just as big and legitimate as Omaha Land and Cattle. Buttons would show up, dressed like he is now, suit and tie . . . he'd look like a young banker, or insurance broker . . . nobody would believe he was a cattle rustler. You can't tell what a court might do."

The judge got to shaking his head and chuckling, and so did Boe. Bunting stopped writing and sat with a grin on his face. Then the judge looked over at Major Morrison, and Morrison laughed, and, when he did, so did Wardrope. Clyde laughed, too, but Ma turned on him, and he abruptly stopped.

The judge said: "Mister Carns, I must correct you. Judge Donahue is an old friend of mine, and he would be the first to protest the title of governor. I believe he took care of those duties one winter when Governor Potts was in the East." He was going to add something else and decided not to. "Proceed."

"What was Mister Gannaway's response when he heard the nature of Belmont Hereford Ranches, Consolidated?" asked Wardrope.

"He did what you did. He laughed about it, but he didn't think it was so funny, either. He knew what Billy had in mind."

"Did they have some Herefords?"

"Yes, and they were ours."

Boe waved for it to go on; he wasn't going to object.

"I'd have gone down there with a crew and cleaned those fellows out, but Gannaway said to wait. He said . . . 'Don't rock the boat.' He was trying to get hold of the Buttons Reserve. It was ours legally, government certification, rental and lease, but as Hankey was just saying, the Buttons had a claim. According to our lawyers, it couldn't stand up in court, but they might tie it up for years. We'd have had to sue to gain possession, and if there was one thing, the *only* thing in the world that scared John Gannaway, it was the idea of going to court. Well, our lawyer said. . . ."

"Your Honor, may I inquire who that lawyer was?" asked Boe.

"You may, but not at this time."

Everyone knew the lawyer to be Paul Stewart.

Carns went on: "He said Buttons would get a lot of sympathy, seeing they'd had possession for years. It's listed Buttons Reserve on a couple of maps, and Buttons Buttes nearby. It wouldn't mean a thing, actually, but when two people contradict each other and one can trot out a government map, well . . . of course, I mean nothing against courts. . . ."

"Good for you," said the judge.

"Also, the Army might not back us up if the Department of the

116

Interior got into it. If the Department of the Interior decided to hold it up. . . ."

"I don't think we need to go into the legal aspects," said Wardrope.

"On the contrary," said Boe, "Mister Carns is giving us a very good brief."

Laughter came from the jury and especially from Major Morrison, who had had his troubles with the Department of the Interior, with trip after trip to Washington, D. C., and thousands in lawyer's fees.

"Well, I'm just telling you what Gannaway said," Carns explained.

Wardrope asked: "You didn't like it, did you? Not going for them on the Spider?"

"No, I didn't like it. I was never a man for putting up with rustlers, maverickers, whatever you want to name them. I was always in favor of stopping it right away. You save a lot of trouble. You draw the line. We failed to draw the line about four years ago, and it led to vigilantes and hangings. I went through it once, and it taught me a lesson."

"Did you tell Gannaway that?"

"I made myself very plain. In fact, I let him understand it couldn't go much further, or they'd have to find a new range boss. He said to be patient just a little while. He promised me that they'd be cleaned out of there."

"What would be cleaned out . . . the cattle or the rustlers?"

"He meant the whole thing would be settled."

"How was it to be done?"

"It wasn't laid out."

"Any indication as to when?"

"He didn't spell it out."

"Well, this year . . . next year?"

"It was my understanding there'd be a shakedown before summer was over."

"But he didn't want to disturb the Reserve deal?"

"All he said was . . . 'Don't rock the boat.' "

"When we talked about this, you told me something of Billy Buttons specifically. His part in the negotiations. Can you recall what that was?"

117

"Well, Billy was supposed to talk the old lady . . . I'm sorry . . . his mother . . . into signing over the land. What he was supposed to do was tell her he'd seen a lawyer in Helena and found out they didn't have much of a case. He was supposed to get fifteen hundred dollars for that, and she was to get a thousand."

"Let's get this straight. Are you telling me that Billy Buttons was pocketing more than his mother?"

"That was my understanding. It was what Gannaway said."

"What did Gannaway think of that? I mean, wasn't this rather dishonest? . . . not only on Billy Buttons's part, but on his?"

"It's not my position to judge."

"Didn't he make any justification?"

"You don't know John Gannaway if you think he'd ever feel called on to justify anything or would have stood for my criticism. I knew my place, and I kept it. I didn't let him interfere with my job, and I didn't interfere with his. If you want to know, he seemed to think it was funny. One remark he made was . . . 'This is Billy's idea of a fifty-fifty split.' He said Missus Buttons wanted to get away and send her younger boy to college to be a doctor. He said . . . 'If Billy handles it, she'll get just about enough to make him into a horse doctor.' "

"Was the money ever paid?"

"Yes, it was. Billy rode over to the ranch one night, the home ranch on Big Piney . . . what everybody calls The Castle. He met there with John. Walt Marsh, my foreman, told me they were in the office. They didn't invite me, and I went to bed. A few weeks later, when no news was forthcoming, I asked John how things were going with the Reserve, and he said . . . 'It's all settled.' He got out a paper, a quitclaim on a special form, where it said for a thousand dollars and other good and valuable consideration, Missus Buttons, acting as heir of Walter E. Buttons, signed over in perpetuity all claim, and it was signed Kate Buttons and witnessed by a Weaver Gibson and David Young. I didn't know any Weaver Gibson, but I asked if that was Dave Young from Deep Coulée, and John said, yes, it was. I was suspicious because Dave Young had been crippled up with rheumatism, so what was he doing on Arrow Creek witnessing a signature? I asked . . . 'Is Missus Buttons's signature genuine?' Well, John said, he couldn't tell because her name wasn't on the election rolls, being a woman, but I said . . . 'Her signature is right here in this office.' She'd signed the roundup agreements, and we'd been made custodian of the books, so I looked, and there was no similarity. John still wouldn't believe it, so we went over to talk to Dave Young, and it turned out he hadn't actually witnessed the signature at all. He said Billy had come over one day with a paper and asked him to sign as witness, so he did it as a favor."

"What was Gannaway's reaction?"

"How would you feel if somebody had beaten you out of two thousand five hundred dollars? He called Billy every name he could lay his tongue to. He said Billy was trying to get back at him for a cattle drive three years ago."

"We've heard much of this . . . will you give us your version?"

"It's not *my* version. This is what happened. Gannaway wanted to bring some shorthorns up from Wyoming, so he hired Billy and a crew to take them across the Crow Indian Reserve. Billy was always in good with the Indians. And those rustlers in the Bull Mountains. All went fine till they got to Yellowstone. Billy wanted to hunt a good crossing. So he said. He left with his crew to scout around. Well, Gannaway waited for him, and he didn't come back . . . and he didn't come back . . . and it turned out Billy and his pals had ridden all the way into Billings and gone on a big toot. Gannaway sent a cowpuncher in for him, and he found Billy in a poker game. Naturally, when Gannaway got that piece of news, he pulled out. He drove across the river and right up through the Bulls and not one bit of trouble. A week or two after they got home, Billy came around and demanded his cut. The agreement was that Billy would get wages for the drive, but in addition he was to get half of all the cattle saved over normal loss by the short route. By way of Powder River they might have had a hundred or more fallen beefs on a dry year. That's on a herd of, say, twenty-five hundred. Actually, going across the Reserve and through the hills, they lost only about twelve cows and calves, and that included some given to the Indians. Hence, Billy figured he had thirty-seven head coming. But John was stubborn. He said Billy hadn't lived up to his agreement, and that was that. What Billy figured was he could run off a couple of cows here and a calf there, then, if he was hauled in, he could say it was part of those owing. Gannaway had signed a memorandum of agreement . . . he never denied that . . . but it was null and void because Billy never lived up to his end."

"I believe we've explored this sufficiently," said Judge Minough with his hunter's case watch open on the table.

"Now, Mister Carns, when it was learned the quitclaim was a forgery and what was . . . ?"

"Objection! If there is going to be a charge of forgery, I think we should stop right now and have a look at the signatures. Where is this document? Why hasn't it been produced? Let's bring it right in and lay it down on the table for all to see."

"Mister Wardrope?" queried the judge.

After some uncertainty at the prosecution table, it was Stewart who got to his feet. "Your Honor, we have not been able to locate it. We have no access to Mister Gannaway's papers. His estate is in something of a limbo. Letters in probate have been asked in the state of Iowa . . . but his heirs . . . well, Missus Gannaway has long been ill . . . there seems to be a conflicting last testament. I'm sorry about this."

"My client is sorry, too," said Boe. "It allows you to brand him a forger, while putting beyond reach the very instrument that could prove his innocence."

Wardrope responded: "We had no intention of introducing forgery at all, but this paper is part of the general dispute between Buttons and Gannaway, coming out not only here but in the sheriff's testimony. Your Honor granted certain liberties. . . ."

"Very well," said the judge. "I will take care of this matter when I instruct the jury. Proceed."

"When Mister Gannaway learned that the so-called quitclaim deed was most likely not a legal instrument . . . ?"

"Objection. Witness is being asked to testify as to the *fact* of its unlikelihood."

Wardrope laughed. "We wish to *oblige*. We certainly do not wish to imply anything underhanded on the part of the accused. When Gannaway learned what he did learn about the alleged quitclaim deed, what was his reaction?"

"He said . . . 'Don't mention this to anybody.' He said . . . 'This isn't going to cost the company one red cent.' He meant he would pay the loss out of his pocket, if there was one. He didn't want me to tell the Ethringtons about it. They had no trust in Billy, and he didn't want to be proved wrong. We went back to the ranch, and he didn't stop to sleep but had them hitch up a big red team, a favorite of his, and he set out again."

"What date was this?"

"We talked to Dave Young on the fourth of June, so this had to be the fifth. John was starting the last week of his life. He was killed on the eleventh. He was gone next morning, and I had to leave, too. I had to see Bodin, across the river, about cutting hay. The river was very high, and I was a whole extra day finding a boat to take me across. I got back home on the eighth. When I got there, John had just come back. He'd been gone four days. He looked all tired out. He was a big man, you know, about two five or two ten, but he looked as if he'd worn himself down to no more than one ninety. One side of his face was skinned and purplish. It wasn't really a bruise . . . it was more as if he'd scraped it against something. He was sitting in the bunkhouse, having coffee and bread, and old John Harnish, our cook, asked him . . . 'What's the other fellow look like?' It was a common, ordinary joke. Well, John went for Harnish as if to tear him to pieces."

"Physically?"

"No, just dressed him down verbally. Told him to mind his own affairs, or he'd find himself looking for another job, and so on. After a while he was sorry he'd lost his temper and said that he'd been in a runaway and been pitched out of the buggy . . . he said he'd been a day getting the team back. Well, you could see that the buggy had taken a beating. Later I asked if he'd talked to Billy? He wouldn't say whether he had or not. He had, though. He said . . . 'If Billy Buttons thinks he's got me where he wants me, he has a surprise in store. I'm going to cook his goose for good.' "

"What did he mean by that remark?"

"What he didn't mean was that he intended to shoot it out. John wouldn't even carry a gun. He meant to send Billy to the pen. I said he could get him for fraud, but he said, no, Billy would pay back the thousand dollars shown on the paper . . . that would leave him the fifteen hundred that had gone to him under the table. He said . . . 'That son-of-a-bitch thinks he's got me hoisted on my own petard, but it's not going to work out that way.' He said . . . 'I'm going to beat him at his own game.' "

"What did he mean?"

"He'd found out Billy had contracted to ship cattle on a certain boat . . . and which cattle he intended to ship. Herefords. They were ours. All that about being the issue of our bulls by his cows was untrue. They were Herefords, pure and entire. We knew it by reliable reports, but we'd have known it by the fact that he intended to ship them as stock cows, heifers, to a ranch in Dakota. He'd sold them, under the name of Belmont, Limited, as Herefords at a high price. Arrangements to ship had been made in Fort Benton . . . on the *Marietta*. Billy intended to load at Gravely Bar instead of Arlington to escape notice. It was John's intent to lie low until they were signed aboard. This would be under some name, acting for Belmont Hereford Ranches, Limited. Preferably Billy would sign, but if he didn't, John still had him. You see, Billy had registered himself as Belmont by that certificate of fictitious name. John said . . . 'I have him dead to rights.' He said . . . 'His certificate of fictitious name will jump up and bite him.' However, Billy found out about it at the last minute. John was on his way to spring the trap, and there was only one way to stop him. That's why John Gannaway is in his grave today."

"Objection," Boe said quietly. "The witness should just give his facts, and if the jury wishes to draw that conclusion, well and good."

"Attorney is right," said Judge Minough. "Witness is merely to give the facts. Any conclusions should be left to the jury."

"Now, all this happened after Mister Gannaway returned on June eighth?"

"Yes."

"When was the boat scheduled to arrive at Gravely Landing?"

"It wasn't scheduled. Those boats arrive when they get there. Actually he found out the morning of the eleventh that it would be there that night, to lay over and depart next morning."

"He learned this on the day of the murder?" Wardrope asked.

"Objection. An assistant United States attorney should be above that sort of thing."

"Yes, Mister Wardrope, no murder has been established."

"Will the court permit homicide?"

"It will not."

122

"Then the day Mister Gannaway died . . . it was the morning of that very day, Mister Carns?"

"And I object to that," said Boe. "Let the witness supply his own dates and schedules. Let him keep them straight. Attorney should not lay out the boundaries so witness can constrict his and his employer's movements thereto."

"Your Honor, this is getting preposterous. . . ."

"Let the witness furnish the dates," Judge Minough said.

Paul Stewart rose and sought a conference with Roman Wardrope, whereupon Wardrope said: "Your Honor, we withdraw the question." Then after more whispering: "May I defer briefly to my colleague?"

"Very well, Mister Stewart. You may address the bench, but not the witness."

"Your Honor, we foresaw that Mister Gannaway's movements on this final day would be very important, hence we have secured depositions from Mister Stearns and Mister Hakevart which we would like to offer the court at this time."

Boe looked at the depositions, each one page in length, and said: "Where are the witnesses? Are these men dead? Are they bedridden? Gone from the country?"

"Mister Stewart?" asked Judge Minough.

"They're at the ranch."

"If they're at the ranch, we can't cross-question them, can we?" said Boe.

Stewart was very upset. "That certainly is not the reason they were not produced here!"

"Give me the reason. I await the reason they are more essential elsewhere than here. What's more important than this trial?"

"This land is full of the lawless. Rustlers and thieves. Surely the testimony here today shows that."

"It shows the company would like us to believe that. So these depositions are sent in place of the witnesses because of the imminent danger of rustlers and thieves. Is this danger worse at this particular time than normally? If so, what has led you to that conclusion?"

"Your Honor, the Omaha Company is not on trial here. I do not represent them in this court. They. . . ."

Judge Minough interrupted: "You seem to speak for the Company in regards to the absence of these two witnesses. What danger, now

123

more than normal, prompts the decision to keep Messers Hakevart and Stearns away? It must needs be serious and real and, indeed, as attorney says, more compelling than this trial."

"For one thing, everyone is in town. What better time for the lawless to swoop down?"

"I must say, this speaks well of those present," replied the judge. "You are saying the lawful are within and the lawless without?"

"No." Then Stewart said: "Yes. To a degree." He was becoming more and more upset, and his colleague restless, standing on the verge of taking over. "These are essential men."

"Who are these men," asked Boe, "so essential they remain sequestered? Hakevart? Is he from this territory?"

"I can't see that has the least bearing. . . ."

"Is this essential man one of the gunmen brought in from New Mexico?"

"I protest! Is he to be maligned while not here. . . ."

"How much is he paid by the Company?" asked Boe directly of Carns in the witness chair.

"Ninety a month," he answered before Stewart could object.

"Stearns? The same?"

"Yes."

"That's nice cowboy pay. What's so special about them they get ninety a month?"

Whereupon Wardrope took charge: "The wages and expenses of the Omaha Company have no bearing on this trial. And I object to this improper cross-examination."

"You are trying to introduce signed statements in evidence when the signatories are readily available," said Boe. "I submit that the reason they are not available is to prevent a too close inquiry into their jobs and characters. Where are they from?"

"Hakevart's from New Mexico. . . ."

"What's the matter? Aren't our Montana gunmen good enough for you? How'd you happen to hear about them? Were they recommended? By whom? Ted Danner? Were these gunmen imported at the undersheriff's behest?"

Impatiently Judge Minough said: "Do you want a ruling on these depositions?"

"No, Your Honor," said Boe. "In themselves they amount to very

124

little. However, if I formally objected and was sustained, the jury would have every right to suppose there was something therein detrimental to my client. I do hope that, if the prosecution has any other irregular entries of this nature, they will offer them in private to Your Honor in chambers in the proper manner."

Bunting read the statements, almost identical, that Gannaway, considering himself in danger at the hands of William Buttons and/or others from the Spider Ranch, had asked them to accompany him on a journey starting June fifth during which he visited the Number Two Ranch, the Judith's Redrock Ranch, and the town of Arlington, arriving back at the Home Ranch at sundown, June eighth. They said they were followed on the final day by members of the Buttons gang, but the journey was otherwise uneventful except for a fall Gannaway had from his buggy, incurring minor injuries.

Boe asked: "Surely someone can at least verify this visit to town?"

Stewart replied: "Your Honor, that was one of the reasons this written and signed testimony was necessary. His visit was private, secret. Secrecy was necessary. He did not want the rustlers to be forewarned . . . the suspected rustlers. Messers Hakevart and Stearns waited outside of town. Mister Gannaway didn't confide in them."

Boe asked: "And no town person came forward?"

"No. We could only assume that whoever he saw felt endangered. Still feels so."

Boe asked: "What are we doing? Where are we? We were at the morning of the eleventh, and now it seems back at the eighth. What a tangled web we weave!"

Judge Minough said: "Well, yes, this has grown complex. I think we will consider the matter of the depositions at an end, as of now . . . though you may cross-examine later. Mister Wardrope, please resume."

Carns continued: "As I was saying, I don't know just when it took place. The night after John got back, he slept most of the day. Ewell Ethrington came along in the afternoon, and John got up. It all came out in the open . . . about the twenty-five hundred and all that. John'd been keeping that from Ewell. It turned out that John had had a talk with the undersheriff, and he had agreed to John's plan for nailing Billy for cattle theft. The only question was when would the *Marietta* get to Gravely Landing? However, that was

John's worry, not mine. I had my hands full. We had the roundup going, and there were reports that the Badlanders were staging a roundup, which was illegal. We had reports they'd threatened to shoot any of our reps on sight. You can see I had worse concerns than trying to catch Billy Buttons with forty head of stolen cattle. After his conversation with Ewell, I don't know Gannaway's movements . . . where he was between then and the eleventh. The night of the tenth I just happened to sleep at the ranch . . . the Number Two . . . instead of at Black Butte where we were branding. I was asleep, and John woke me up. He came in and stood by the bed. It was before dawn. We only get about five hours of darkness at that time of year. The stars were still out. It couldn't have been much later than three a.m. He hadn't been to bed at all. He seemed to be all excited. I knew something was up."

"What did he say to you?"

"I've forgotten. I was still half asleep. But he yelled . . . 'Get up, we got the damned son-of-a-bitch dead to rights.' "

"What did he mean?"

"Why, the defendant, Billy Buttons. He said . . . 'Get a crew together!' 'What do you mean, crew?' I asked. John said he meant half a dozen of the best men at the ranch. There was nobody much at the ranch. 'Where's Hap and Wes?' he asked."

"Those were . . . ?"

"Hap Stearns and Wesley Hakevart. I said they had gone out to Black Butte to help with the branding. He started raking me over the coals for that, saying why should we pay detective's wages to men doing a forty-a-month job? The only ones I could line up to ride along were Bob Purdy, who'd come in for something, and a cowboy named Rapf, who had broken his foot. He couldn't even get one boot on, but Gannaway said he was to come . . . he could earn himself a twenty-dollar gold piece. So we set out."

"You said Gannaway had arrived in a rig?"

"He left it and went horseback. He said the sheriff's office had been notified and would have men to meet us at the river. They were supposed to keep the boat from sailing."

"Wasn't there someone else?"

"Tell him who it was," prompted Boe.

"Oh, I can tell you, all right. I haven't forgotten a thing. Every move of that day is in my memory like cast iron. The somebody else was Louis Ethrington. He'd been in Chicago. He'd driven as far as Herendon's and put up there when it got dark. Then he got up about sunrise. It's only an hour-and-a-half drive, and he came up in his rig. He said he'd go along with us a ways, and then drive on over to Black Butte and look in at the branding."

"Proceed," encouraged Wardrope.

"We all went on together until about noon. It was very hot. It must have been as hot a day as we had all summer. Hot and bright. We came down across those alkali flats to where the old Camp Griffin road crosses Willow Creek. It was very hard to see, all that white glare, and all of a sudden Bob Purdy, who was out in the lead, wheeled around and came back. He said there were some fellows down on the flats, and he didn't like the looks of it. We rode on a while, and, sure enough, we could see three fellows down there, and one of them was Ace Carter. . . ."

"Who recognized Carter?" Wardrope asked.

"I did. Carter is tall, and there's a way he carries that crippled hand . . . with his shoulder around, and the hand always in front. Gannaway recognized him, too, and then he said one of the other fellows was the defendant. He was very annoyed. He said . . . 'Yes, the son-of-a-bitch is here, I wonder how he got wind of it?' The third man, we learned later, was Frenchy LaGrange."

"Was Mister Ethrington still with you?"

"No, as I said, he was going over to Black Butte. He was driving his rig and decided it was a better road by way of the old North-West Company sheep pens. The old road across the Willow is full of washouts. What started as wagon ruts have turned into gullies, some of them five feet deep. He heard the shooting and stopped, but, when there was nothing more, he drove on. He testified so at the inquest."

"All right. Now, Mister Ethrington had left your group, but the others saw men identified as Carter, Buttons, and LaGrange in the valley of Willow Creek? Did you conclude this was accidental?"

"No! I certainly didn't. And Gannaway didn't. He said . . . 'That dirty son-of-a-bitch has spies everywhere.' He said . . . 'Well, I still have him dead to rights.' He meant Billy didn't have to be present to sign the cattle aboard personally. The only thing was the under-sheriff and his men, with a warrant, were to meet us at Signal Rock.

That's just before the old road drops down through the badlands to Gravely Landing. We had to get there in time, or they might not act. Gannaway said he had to stall Billy off, and then ride down there. It was still about twelve miles."

"To Signal Rock or the river?"

"To Signal Rock."

"Now, how far were Billy Buttons and his companions when you saw them?"

"They were at least a quarter mile . . . and probably a little more."

"Sitting still?"

"No, they had spread out and were sort of drifting toward the crossing . . . down the valley. They were watching us every second."

"Could you have avoided them?"

"Yes, but I wasn't going to turn tail and be run off my own range. It never came into my mind. Or Gannaway's, you can be sure."

"But you said he intended to stall Billy off. What do you mean by that?"

"He wanted to talk to him . . . wanted to keep him quiet until he had him dead to rights by shipping those cattle."

"What did Gannaway do?"

"Rode down and talked to him."

"Alone?"

"Yes."

"Was he armed?"

"He had a carbine rifle in a saddle scabbard. He left that behind."

"Was there any communication with Buttons?"

"Yes, they wig-wagged. John made it understood he wanted to talk alone. He showed Billy the gun and handed it over to me, and Billy took a gun off and tossed it down on the ground."

"He didn't hand it to one of the others?"

"No, he tossed it on the ground. The other two were at some distance back."

"Then it was understood, by sight and signaling, that both were unarmed?"

"Yes, and that the extra men were to stay back."

"I see. Proceed."

"There were some old buildings where the freight station had been and big grassy flats, bare as a table. Billy rode over toward the

128

buildings, across the flats, east, away clear of the creek, and brush. He got where he wanted to be, just about to the old road, and stopped. So John rode down, too . . . down the hill. There are rims there . . . sandstone . . . with dirt banks beneath. It was quite a steep grade, but not very long."

"How far were you, at this time?"

"Well, naturally, we had to stay off beyond rifle range. Billy wouldn't ride down under our gun barrels, nor John under theirs. So we were about an eighth of a mile . . . a trifle more, say, three hundred and fifty yards. Rapf and Purdy stayed a little farther. We had some words about it. They'd been paid twenty dollars . . . or *promised* twenty dollars . . . just for the day's ride. But Purdy, in particular, was stubborn and refused to go any farther. He said . . . 'I haven't lost my buttons,' and made a joke out of it, but it was true, he was afraid of those fellows . . . while Rapf would do whatever he did. Anyway, I rode a short way, about halfway down the grade, down the steepest part, where I was pretty well out of range but could get in range in a hurry, and John rode the last, maybe three hundred and fifty yards, alone.

"Buttons was already there, as I said. He sat there perfectly cool, and John rode up. They didn't shake hands. The defendant sat with his hands sort of on the saddle horn, and every so often he seemed to be swishing at a fly. John did most of the talking. You couldn't hear, but you could tell. He always moved his head to give emphasis, and Billy just seemed to sit and look around. John kept moving his horse around so Billy would be forced to look at him. He was trying to convince him of something, that was plain. I'd about decided things were all right . . . there would be no trouble. It didn't seem so to Rapf and Purdy, either, because they decided to come on a little ways. Then all of a sudden the boss seemed to jump up in the saddle . . . as if he stood in the stirrups . . . and to give the bridle a twist. I took it he was disgusted and ready to ride off. Then I saw a puff of smoke. Billy had drawn a pistol and fired, but it was a second before the sound came. The boss had his arm up, like that. Left arm. He'd seen the gun and tossed his arm up, and that's what it was instead of twisting the bridle. And that was why the bullet hit him right under the armpit. He went off his horse. He didn't pitch off . . . he just seemed to slide off. He almost seemed to land on his feet. He seemed to take a step after he was on the ground. It was just the way he fell. He went down on his face. His horse ran off a little way and stood. The boss just lay there. You could see he must be dead . . . not a move . . . and all so slow . . . that was the thing of it. It seemed unreal. I couldn't believe it had happened. Then the horse started to graze. Not even the gunshot had been very loud. The heat seemed to deaden the sound. And Billy . . . he wasn't in any hurry to leave. Oh, he was cool! He turned and watched to see what we were going to do. I never saw anything so cold-blooded. Well, finally I stirred myself. I started to ride down and *zing!* It was a bullet. It whipped past through the grass. Somebody had shot at me. I heard the report right after. I saw it was LaGrange . . . who I later found out was LaGrange . . . he had a rifle. I think he'd aimed to scare me back, not hit me. Otherwise, he'd've had the elevation better. I pulled up in a hurry. I wasn't going to ride on them alone, and my two men weren't coming with me. They'd gone the other way. I didn't retreat, but I didn't ride any farther. Billy just took his sweet time and rode back the way he'd come. I could see there was no help for Gannaway. He was on his face, and you could see the flies buzzing over him" — Carns seemed called on to defend this — "well, you could . . . you can see those big, early June bulldog flies, greenish, brassy. They shine in the sun. It seemed so damned awful. The flies already drawn by the smell of blood. You know, I never saw a man killed before . . . for all the rough times I been through, here and in Nebraska?"

"There was just the one shot? By the defendant?"

"All I heard was one shot, but Purdy in his sworn statement said two. I think where Purdy was placed made him hear an echo. Rapf said he heard just the one. There was only the one puff of smoke. Then LaGrange shot with the rifle, but it was a while later."

Wardrope said: "Mister Rapf will testify. However, we have here a deposition from Mister Purdy who is out of the territory. Both will substantiate this testimony in all main regards, save for the question of one shot or two." He flourished the paper, and put it on his table again. "How long, total, between the time of the shot and when you reached the fallen man?"

"Well . . . two, maybe two-and-a-half minutes. He was dead."

"How did you determine this?"

"He just was. The bullet had gone through and torn out a hole

130

you could put your fist in. It must have gone through the heart. I turned him partly over. He was just dead. He wasn't breathing. His eyes were open. He had a dead look. Purdy and Rapf observed it, too. They followed along after me. I sent Purdy back to see if he could catch up with Louis Ethrington, but it turned out he couldn't . . . not soon . . . not until about four, that is . . . he didn't bring him back with the rig until four. We sat there with Gannaway. We didn't know what else to do."

"You didn't attempt to complete the mission? To contact the sheriff's men at Signal Rock?"

"No, perhaps we should have, but I didn't want to go off and leave John lying there. It seemed wrong. Then I knew Rapf was no good in a pinch. Billy and those two were all hard men. They'd killed once . . . *he'd* killed once . . . they wouldn't hesitate to do it again. I had no doubt they'd watch us, every move. We finally got the body down to the Omaha Number Two Ranch in the rig at about six . . . maybe closer seven. Then we started for town about sunup next morning, and the examinations and inquest were held as testified."

"Your witness," said Wardrope.

Boe, still seated, asked: "How was the range, Mister Carns?"

The question surprised him. "You mean the grass? Pretty fair."

"I see by the Billings paper you had a big, wet spring. It says here hay was being cut in the creek bottoms."

"Yes, we cut some hay."

"On Willow Creek?"

"Yes, on Willow."

"Was there water in the creek?"

"Yes, it ran pretty good. It ran at the lower crossing until August first."

"It says here the buffalo grass was knee deep. 'The best stand since the spring of 'Eighty-One.' "

"I don't know about buffalo grass. Newspaper fellows are always talking about buffalo grass. It's grama grass that gets knee high."

"How about brome grass?"

"Yes, and brome grass." He called it *broom* grass.

"Willows and cottonwoods in good leaf? Plenty of high buck-

131

brush? Cattails in the swampy places? Mint? Nettles?"

"What are you getting at, Mister Boe?" asked the judge. "I'd like to expedite."

"What I'm getting at is here was an ideal situation for ambush, and yet Billy Buttons rode right out in full view, to do an act that was certain to bring him before the bar. Now, wasn't that a fool trick? How about that, Mister Carns? Wasn't there ample place for ambush right there at the creek? Here's a man who, by prosecution testimony, was a marksman, who shot the weathercock off the cupola of the hotel, the Mountdouglas House. Surely he would have no trouble shooting down his man from the willows, cattails, box elders, high grama grass, sagebrush? Why do you suppose he didn't do it . . . if he was waiting there to kill John Gannaway as you would have us believe?"

"Objection. Witness should be cross-examined on the facts, not on his speculations."

"Oh, all right," said Boe, finally getting to his feet, though it caused pain. He leaned on the table until he could transfer his weight to the cane. All that seemed of more concern to him than the matter at hand. "Much of what we heard from the witness were speculations, suppositions, imputations which had nothing whatsoever to do with this case but were designed for the sole purpose of destroying the reputation of the defendant, but I'll not ask the witness to speculate, or conclude. I guess he's done enough of it."

"I'll tell you why I think he didn't . . ." — Carns went straight on, despite gestures from the judge and prosecutor to check him — "he couldn't resist the chance to swagger. He's had it in his system to get even with us for years. That's why he rustled those white-face calves and then held the land deal over our heads. Everything he did was set up to make us look beaten. He wanted to show the world he could kick us in the belly. Well, finally he went too far. He finally saw we had him dead to rights. John Gannaway hit it square on the nose when he said he'd hoisted himself on his own petard. The one way of saving himself was by killing the boss . . . but it had to be with a swagger. He had to be the great Billy Buttons that every god-damned Badlander, cattle rustler, horse. . . ."

"Mister Carns!" remonstrated the judge.

He stopped, but truculently held his position.

"You do believe, then," said Boe, "that my client has a free and open nature?"

Everyone laughed, and there was a general shifting of sweaty rearends to more comfortable positions. Boe was considerate, allowing them to finish and get set for the next question.

"Now, you bid good bye to Mister Ethrington at noon?"

"I didn't look at a watch, but Ethrington said later it was about eleven forty-five."

"From there, how long did it take you to reach Willow Creek?"

"I don't know. Half an hour."

"You testified that Louis Ethrington wasn't sure about hearing shots. He must have traveled quite a distance. Would you say it was as late as one p.m. when you reached the creek?"

"It could have been half after twelve."

"At what time were you to meet the undersheriff?"

"You'd have to ask him. It was set up between him and the deceased."

"All right, when would you have reached the appointed place . . . Signal Rock?" While Carns computed distances and pondered, Boe speculated: "What do you weigh, Mister Carns?"

"Hundred and eighty."

"You're no jockey, and it was a hot day, so let's not go galloping our ponies across the plains. When would you actually have made it?"

"We had to make it by eight o'clock at the latest, or we couldn't have gone down to the river. That's a very rough country. But that would be far too late. Gannaway wanted to make it by three or three-thirty."

"To Signal Rock by three-thirty?"

"Yes."

"Could you?"

"No, we'd have been late, but not very late."

"You'd only have been as far as Signal Rock, not to the river?"

"Yes."

"How much farther was it to the river?"

"Six or seven miles."

"Good road? Road to a steamboat landing?"

"No, it's the old freight road, but it hasn't been used much since

133

the big outfits moved here to Arlington. It's in bad shape."

"Not one you'd travel at a swift gallop?"

"No."

"Blind gullies? Spanish bayonet? Rattlesnakes?"

"Yes."

"Any truth to the report that a horse smells snakes?"

"There is. He'll put you right into the rocks. The gentler your horse, the worse he gets." It was the first he relented in his stony confrontation, but only for seconds.

"Mister Carns, will you look at this paper and tell us what it is?"

"A freight bill . . . Dakota-Far West Company."

"This is a signed bill of lading issued to the Baker Warehouse here in Arlington by the specified steamboat and company, the steamboat, *Marietta*, and the Dakota-Far West, date thereon shown. Will you read that date?"

"June eleventh."

"This current year?"

"Yes."

"In other words, the *Marietta* was here June eleventh, and not in Gravely Landing?"

"It was in Gravely Landing, too. It arrived early. That's why we were in a hurry."

"At what time would a steamboat have to leave Gravely Landing and still reach here . . . barring the chance it would run at night, which it didn't?"

"I don't know."

"The latest possible would be five p.m. That would put it here . . . a four-hour run . . . at nine. Just dark. As a matter of fact, the records show it touched the dock here at seven-thirty P.M., and made a fast run. Was there any way, Mister Carns, that you could have reached the Landing before the boat left?"

"Are there any verifications of these times and schedules?" asked Wardrope.

"Yes. I can furnish both witnesses and documents. But let the witness answer. If the boat left Gravely Landing at three-thirty, or even four, could you have possibly reached the Landing on time?"

They could see him silently figuring the times, but he made no answer.

"Then there was actually no need for Billy to commit murder to stop you from getting there?"

"He didn't know that," said the witness.

"You seem to be quite an authority on what Billy knew and what he didn't know . . . and what Mister Gannaway knew and didn't know . . . in view of the fact that he, by your own statement, was reticent and never really took anyone into his confidence. However, I'm not asking what might have been known, I'm questioning you as to facts. Just facts. This jury is perfectly able to put those facts together. I ask you again . . . and please answer yes or no . . . was there any need for Billy to commit murder in order to stop Mister Gannaway from getting to the boat?"

"Answer, please," said the judge.

"No!" Carns answered viciously.

"Do you know whether or not the cattle . . . the white-face cattle . . . in question were shipped?"

"I heard they were."

"And you heard correctly. I have here the manifests. There was no secret about this shipment. The cattle were shipped and sold in a perfectly straightforward manner, wouldn't you say?"

"I'd say Billy was bold as brass."

"Well, bold as brass. No secret of it. Did you or your employer make any move to stop that shipment downriver?"

"With all this happening. . . ."

"Did you, or didn't you?"

"Just answer," said the judge.

"No."

"Did you attempt to stop their sale, or otherwise recover what you have claimed was your property? Yes or no?"

"No."

"Do you just let people take your property without making a move to recover? Or was this a special case?"

"Once they're out of the territory, all you can do is seek to show by the brands. . . ."

"Are you saying it was a special case? Yes or no?"

"We never had a situation like this wherein. . . ."

"As a matter of fact, you didn't have a legal leg to stand on, isn't that true?"

"Objection. The legalities of this matter are not within the witness's range of competence."

"Oh, I think they are. I think he looked into it very competently and very shrewdly, and sought the advice of your colleague. But I'll withdraw the question, because the facts speak for themselves. Mister Carns, I'd like to talk about Hereford cattle. These are also called white-face cattle, right? Did you make the statement . . . 'If anybody here shows up with white-face cattle, we know where they came from'?"

"I might have."

"Well, do you subscribe to it? If anybody in this area turned up with white-face cattle, would you know where they came from?"

"Yes, pretty much."

"Where would they pretty much come from?"

"If they couldn't show they'd brought them in, I'd say they were ours."

"You also brought in some white-face bulls."

"Of course."

"In fact, white-face bulls are the only bulls you have?"

"That's true, as of now. We shipped our last old longhorn bull, so far as we know, two weeks ago."

Boe then questioned him in detail concerning the Omaha's range policies, particularly its practice of slaughtering stray range bulls, which Carns did not deny, and of claiming the white-face issue of other's stock, which Carns admitted. This consumed about ten minutes when, without warning, Boe asked: "How would you describe Mister Louis Ethrington? Is he the conservative, thoughtful type?"

Carns peered under his thick eyebrows to see whether Boe was serious.

"Careful?" Boe went on. "Thoughtful in plan, moderate in execution?"

The audience, including some of the jury, got to laughing because Louis Ethrington, reacting to being called an English dude, had early set out to prove he was more wild than the Wild West, never missing a chance to display his courage and pit himself against all comers as a horseman, a drinker, a hunter, and a womanizer, a severe problem to his elder brother, Ewell.

Boe said, evincing surprise: "I've never met Louis Ethrington, but gathered from the testimony that he was a very cautious and conservative young man."

"No, *I* never said anything like that."

"You described how he was hesitant to descend into Willow Creek with you, fearing washouts. Wasn't that the caution of a prudent man?"

Carns was hard-faced again, expecting a trick.

"Surely Mister Gannaway said why he was going down to the river? A man with any love of adventure could hardly have been kept home. This indicates the play-it-safe type, wouldn't you say?"

"I think he's calmed down considerably from what he was."

"By the way, how long had Mister Ethrington been in Chicago?"

Wardrope interjected: "Your Honor, we intend to put Mister Louis Ethrington on the stand, as Mister Boe can see by his list of witnesses. His questions can be determined by best testimony."

Boe rejoined: "Mister Ethrington may be first authority on how long he was in Chicago, or wherever he was, but Mister Carns is the authority on how long the ranch was without his presence. So let me put it that way . . . how long had he been gone?"

"Three weeks, maybe a little more."

"And he drove right up just as Mister Gannaway was leaving? That was quite a coincidence, wouldn't you say?"

Carns didn't answer.

"They must have been very glad to see each other. Was the meeting . . . cordial?"

"They shook hands."

"Did John tell Louis what he was about?"

"Not in my hearing."

"You seem in doubt. Didn't they share such important information?"

"I don't know anything about their private dealings. I always just took care of my own business."

"Well, good for you! This so-called quitclaim deed, that must have been your business because you described it at great length. I notice, however, the Ethringtons weren't likewise involved. Did Gannaway talk about *that* with Louis?"

"Not in my hearing."

"You know very well he didn't, because he wanted to keep the entire matter from Louis Ethrington's attention, and you said so."

"It was nothing underhanded, if that's what you're trying to make out. John Gannaway intended to pay the costs out of his own pocket if he couldn't make the quitclaim stand up."

"They didn't get along very well, did they?"

"They didn't fight and argue. They respected one another."

"Didn't you once say in the presence of witnesses that there wasn't room enough in the Omaha for the Ethrington brothers and John Gannaway both?"

His jaw set, Carns did not answer.

"Didn't you make such a statement, Mister Carns?"

"I might have."

"Why did Louis have it in for Gannaway?"

"I don't know that he did."

"Oh, come! Men right in this room have heard you remark on it."

"He thought John carried tales about him to his brother."

"To Ewell Ethrington?"

"Yes."

"Tales of what?"

Carns couldn't think of the right term.

"Escapades?"

"Yes, you could call it that."

"Can you give us a specific example of an escapade?"

"Well, one time Louis set fire to a hotel in Billings."

"That's hardly an *escapade*. That's arson, a felony."

"It was no felony."

"I'd be very glad to read you the law."

Angry, regretting he'd mentioned it, Carns responded: "There was a woman involved. A girl . . . a . . . one of the demimonde."

"All right, Louis was involved with a whore. What else?"

"Some other fellow had her in a hotel room. He lit some stuff on fire."

"Louis Ethrington set the hotel on fire, didn't he? That's what you said."

"He heaped some stuff outside their room and set it on fire. He waited for them to come out, and . . . I don't know. There were several stories. He paid for the damages. He got them to keep his

138

name out of the paper, but Ewell found out about it, and Louis blamed Gannaway. Gannaway had come in that night on the Limited, but he never told Ewell. He thought it was funny. He didn't carry tales. A thing like that is bound to get out. However, that was a long time ago. Louis has settled down a lot. It used to be all the Ethrington shares were held by their father in England. He visited here in 'Eighty-Four. Ewell is eight years older than Louis, and their father put him in charge. Then he died, and the shares were divided equally. Louis settled down when he got that responsibility.

"Could the Ethringtons, pooling their shares, outvote Gannaway?"

"There are a lot of other shareholders."

"But they're the big ones. Could *all the shareholders combined* outvote him?"

"Yes. By quite a margin. But Gannaway held shares for Sioux City Yards and the Dakota and Western. He had their proxies. Of course, he was also part owner of those companies."

"They could outvote him now?"

"The administrator will vote them . . . when named."

"But that will be months, or even years away?"

"I didn't say. . . ."

"It was a long, long time away when we wanted a look at that quitclaim deed. It's just as remote when it comes to voting Gannaway's shares against the Ethringtons. How about that, Mister Carns? Would you say the Ethrington brothers, and particularly Mister Louis Ethrington, who set fire to the hotel down in Billings, was more in control of the Omaha Land and Cattle Company before or after Mister Gannaway's death?"

"I object," said Wardrope. "The corporate affairs of the Company can only be remotely tangential to this case."

Boe rejoined: "Would learned attorney break those words down into smaller pieces?"

"Defense understands very well what I mean."

"Yes, Mister Boe," said the judge, "it does seem you are grazing in some rather remote fields. Do you have in mind something explicit to this charge of homicide?"

"Oh, I was just looking around for the people who would benefit most by Mister Gannaway's death. The prosecution has tried to show that Mister Buttons would so benefit, with what success I'm content to allow others to decide. So, what's sauce for the goose? Mister Carns, I ask you this . . . did Mister Gannaway not bring the Ethrington fortune, a very sizable one, consisting of pounds sterling, into the new corporation with the understanding . . . ?"

"I don't know anything about it," Carns broke in.

"These questions should be put to the principals, if to anyone," said Wardrope.

"You might wait until I've asked the question."

"It's getting very late," said Judge Minough. "Please hew to the line."

"Very well, hadn't Mister Gannaway promised to get hold of the Army Reserve lands provided the Ethringtons brought English capital into the corporation? And hadn't his failure to do so introduced severe displeasure, animosity, acerbity, and indignation into a formerly cordial relationship?" Boe raised his voice steadily to overcome Wardrope who was up and speaking: "Mister Carns, how would you characterize the relations between Louis Ethrington and John Gannaway on that specific last morning of the latter's life . . . as cordial, or just barely civil? Isn't it a fact that none of those apply, and that . . . ?"

"We have been into that. I did my job, and that was all I was interested in. They shook hands. I don't know what they talked about. They never partnered around together. There was quite a difference in their ages."

"Hadn't you heard it said, Mister Carns, that if Gannaway failed to get the Buttons Reserve, as promised, the Ethringtons would call a stockholders' meeting and vote him out of his number one spot in the corporation?"

"No."

"And wasn't that why Mister Gannaway secured the proxies heretofore specified? Hadn't you heard that reported, Mister Carns?"

"Are you asking whether I heard such stories, or whether they're true?"

"I asked you if you had heard such reports?"

"I heard lots of things, mostly untrue."

"The question can be answered yes or no."

Carns did not answer.

"Will the record please show that Mister Carns does not answer." Boe checked some notes, or appeared to, although when he could have taken them down was a mystery, because he was never seen writing. "So, we have Mister Louis Ethrington leaving the party half an hour's travel short of Willow Creek, giving as his excuse a fear that the roads . . . ?"

Wardrope said: "I object to the use of the word *excuse*. No excuse was required, and we have no indication that he needed an excuse. Use of the term excuse rather than reason is a derogation. . . ."

Boe took it up: "Giving as his *reason* a fear of washed-out roads? You said he turned in what direction?"

"East."

"Actually it was easterly, wasn't it?"

"I suppose."

"For how long was he in sight?"

"I don't know. Ten or fifteen minutes."

"After which he dropped from sight? He wasn't in view when you got to the rim overlooking Willow Creek, was he?"

"I don't know."

"Didn't you look for him? You were faced with an emergency . . . three men down on the creek bottoms and your two cowboys, Rapf and Purdy, showing very little disposition for a fight? Didn't you check to see whether a marksman and hunter of Louis Ethrington's skill could be summoned? It would seem only prudent."

Judge Minough said: "You will please answer, Mister Carns."

"Yes, I must have. Anyway, I recall he was gone from sight. How long, I don't know."

"Describe the nature of the land there."

"It's prairie."

"Flat?"

"Yes, fairly."

"Flat like a pool table, or rolling?"

"Rolling."

"Hills and draws?"

"Little bulges, and some draws."

"Draws and coulées?"

"Yes."

"Leading where?"

141

"Why, they wander. . . ."

"They're part of the drainage pattern. And right there the chief watercourse is Willow Creek. So they must perforce lead to Willow Creek. Right?"

"Yes."

"Now, in order to reach either the Black Butte Camp or Number Two Ranch, he had to cross Willow Creek, or follow along it?"

"Yes."

"So, when you lost sight of him, he must have followed a coulée to the creek?"

"I guess he must have."

"Where *did* he go . . . to the branding camp or the ranch?"

"To the ranch."

"How do you know? You didn't see him go to the ranch?"

"I object," said Wardrope. "If the defense wishes to determine Mister Ethrington's presence at the ranch, then he is the one who should. . . ."

"Overruled. Witness made a definite statement. We have a right to know what it is based on."

"Purdy said he found him at the ranch. They drove back in the rig."

"Might he have gone elsewhere first and then to the ranch?"

"Yes, but he couldn't have stayed very long, because Purdy set out right after the shooting, and that was where he caught up with him."

"That was when Louis Ethrington told you he heard shots?"

"Yes."

"How many?"

"He just said he heard shots."

"But he didn't investigate?"

"No."

"Did he say why?"

"He said he thought we might be shooting at a coyote, or something."

"Maybe he didn't want to meddle in Gannaway's affairs?"

"Where are we getting in all this?" Wardrope demanded.

"To the truth, I hope," said Boe. "Was he armed? If he didn't have a gun, it would explain his reluctance to investigate."

"He had a rifle in the buggy."

"Not only that, he also had a revolver, didn't he?"

"I don't know."

"He is fond of guns, isn't he? Fine, European calibers?"

"Yes."

"Quite a hunter?"

"Yes."

"Host for important guests from back East? Big hunting camps, wagons, cooks, tents? Photographer to take pictures of slaughtered game? Wagonloads of deer, elk, mountain sheep? Antelope? Hung them up by the tens and twenties, stacks and heaps of antelope, mountain sheep, blacktail deer, bears, elk? . . . carcasses smelling to high heaven? . . . but the photos didn't smell . . . hired hands were sent to bury the game?"

"Objection!" said Wardrope who had remained standing. "I must strongly object. . . ."

"What was it the boys used to call him?" Boe persisted. "Dead-Meat Louie? Ever hear him called that, Mister Carns?"

"Your Honor!"

"Get to the point, Mister Boe."

"Very well. So, Mister Louis Ethrington drove away. Good, old Dead-Meat Louie, with his rifle and his pistol . . . ?"

"I never said he carried a pistol."

"He drove away, over the edge of the coulée that wound down to Willow Creek, and that was the last you saw of him until late that afternoon. By the way . . . how *was* that descent to Willow Creek . . . the old freight road . . . could he have made it in his rig?"

"Yes, I suppose."

"Better or worse than the prairie sod and roadless coulée bottom?"

"I don't know."

"But he could have made it by the regular road?"

"Yes, I suppose he could."

"However, he decided to hunt his own route by way of the coulée? No road at all?"

There was no answer.

"How were the creek bottoms along there? All clear sailing? Or

143

was there brush? . . . cottonwoods, box elders, bullberries?"

"It's patchy."

"Bushes here and there?"

"Yes."

"I understand there's some sagebrush down there high as a man's shoulder?"

"Yes."

"Gee whiz! You know this is a shame? Do you realize if he had only turned *up* the creek, instead of down, he might have saved John's life?"

"I can't see how."

"Why, easy! He could have *showed* himself. Billy would have been too far outnumbered. Five men! Even if the bottoms were too rough for the rig, Louis Ethrington could have got out with his foreign rifle and walked. It's too bad . . . good, old Dead-Meat Louie, old eagle-eye, long-range, ten-wagonloads-of-venison Ethrington . . . he went and took the wrong turn just when he was needed. Well, that's life for you!"

"I object to this," said Wardrope. "Its whole tone to degrade, and its purpose is to cast suspicion. This is an obvious and contemptible last resort of a. . . ."

"I'll show you whether it's a last resort!" Boe returned in outrage. "Wait until I'm finished with these people . . . all of them . . . and you'll find whether it's a last resort, or no."

"We can do without all this Dead-Meat Louie business," said Judge Minough. "Proceed."

Boe was now a model of temperate reason: "I merely wanted to show he was an experienced hunter, and, although an Englishman, and an aristocratic one, not effete, in no way a tenderfoot to this land, and to inquire, having heard the shots, why he did not, in the light of his experience and his extraordinary interest in hunting wild game, *in this one instance,* not even turn back along the creek to investigate."

"Then Mister Ethrington and not Mister Carns is the one to interrogate," suggested the judge.

"Back to the shooting, then," said Boe. "You testified once it was an eighth of a mile, and again it was three-hundred-and-fifty yards, closer to a quarter of a mile . . . have you now decided how far away you actually were?"

144

"I never thought of it as yards, or part of a mile, but as to whether we were out of rifle range. My guess was . . . I think . . . three hundred to three hundred and fifty yards. At any event, we were close enough to see."

"I'm sure you saw what you wanted to see, Mister Carns . . . and none so blind as those who will not see, as Patrick Henry, our Revolutionary patriot, said."

Judge Minough interrupted: "It was *Matthew* Henry, the revolutionary Presbyterian divine, who said that, and we will strike the gratuitous remark."

There was laughter, appreciative of the judge's learning, and a crestfallen Boe appeared to have been put in his place.

"Your Honor," Boe now rejoined, "this witness has displayed the most remarkable eyesight, to see in the heat-glare of midday through the wavy distortion as from the top of a cookstove . . . where men and horse loom twenty feet tall, like plumes of flame! . . . to see yet with a *minute* exactness that revealed every movement of hand, and every flex of body, aye, even the smoke spurting from the muzzle of a gun, and I suggest that this requires an act of the spirit supplementary to the eyes."

"I didn't see every flex of his body," reproved Carns, "but I saw that man" — he pointed to Billy — "ride up to John Gannaway and shoot him down while he held his hand up for mercy. I saw that well enough."

"Yes, but by your own admission you were unable to recognize so familiar a figure as Frenchy LaGrange. I'm through with the witness."

Carns started to leave, but the judge stopped him.

"Just a moment." Looking sternly now at Wardrope, he said: "I hope the redirect will be short. The air in this room has become unbearable."

Wardrope, noticing that Major Morrison had sighed mightily, changed his mind. "No more questions, Your Honor."

"We stand in recess then until this evening," the judge ruled. "At seven o'clock. Seven on the dot. At which time I hope this trial may continue till its conclusion. It is still my fond hope, though perhaps not expectation, to instruct this jury before midnight. We can but try!"

CHAPTER TEN

"Oh, Billy, Billy!" said Ma, with her arms out, but Billy did not respond by coming over. He just stood and looked at her.

"Stop it, Ma," said Clyde.

"Billy, Billy!" Ma repeated, as if all were lost, and the Company testimony had condemned him for sure.

Clyde was on his feet. He wanted to get away, but the room was jammed with men pushing toward the door. He found himself squeezed against the railing. Paul Stewart was on the other side, not two feet away. He was so close Clyde could smell him, his serge coat, a whiff of old closet and sweat.

Disgustedly, Stewart was tossing books and papers into a black, leather satchel. "*Patrick* Henry, for God's sake! Such ignorance! And he supposedly a college-trained attorney!"

Wardrope, also preparing to leave, laughed cynically. "Oh, you miss the point! You don't tour with them the way I do. You should have heard them at the Slates trial when they got into Jeremiah, chapter and verse."

"The bench winning?"

"Oh, of course, of course," Wardrope said. "It's not so funny after a while. He isn't trying this case, so much as he is running for the Senate."

Clyde couldn't see why they'd be so sore at the judge. Even he could see the Company witnesses were saying just anything they liked, and in spite of that Wardrope had made five objections to Boe's one.

"It's all right, Missus Buttons," Boe said, comforting Ma. "There's no need to give up hope. We haven't had our innings yet."

Meanwhile, Billy was led from the room.

"Ah!" said Judge Minough, stepping outside into the fresh breath of the river.

146

"Does it smell like duck hunting tomorrow?" asked Major Morrison.

"I'm afraid we wait another dawning. There are two more prosecution witnesses listed, then the defense. He'll put Carter and LaGrange on. They won't take long. Blankenship is on the defense list. He's the undertaker from Billings. I understand he hasn't arrived. There's been no subpoena issued. Then there's Missus Buttons. Yes, he'll put her on the stand. It's all he can do. He has to do something. He may or may not put the defendant on. If he does, it'll be hard to limit cross-examination. Our esteemed government attorney is itching to tear him to shreds. Personally, I think that's what Boe wants. Go for him hard enough and they'll tend to side with the home boy against the city stranger. If so, we'll be here all tomorrow, and maybe tomorrow night."

"Well, I won't be influenced by such considerations one way or the other," said the major. "I'm rather enjoying this, discomfort notwithstanding. I've never been on a jury before, except a coroner's jury and court martial. There's a privilege and a pleasure in a man's doing his citizen's duty. The ducks can wait."

When Major Morrison saw Ma Buttons walking with her younger son past the last sidewalks of the business district, he sent Sam Brown, his Negro coachman, with the first rig he could borrow to give her a ride.

"You're very kind," said Ma. "Tell the major, thank you, but I'm almost there. I'm staying right down there at Missus Hemphill's."

"Yes, ma'am," replied the coachman. "If there's anything I can do, ma'am, he said particular to let you know I was at your beck and call."

"That was real nice of Major Morrison," Ma said.

"Yeah," said Clyde, when the coachman turned back, but he didn't think it was so nice. In his judgment Major Morrison was just trying to gentle the vengeance he was about to wreak on Billy.

"Aren't you coming in?" Ma asked him at Maud's gate.

"No, I need some air."

"Oh, dear, why doesn't Billy just make a clean breast of everything?" she said, stopping there. "Oh, dear God, when is this travail going to end?"

147

"Maybe he *is* making a clean breast of everything. We haven't heard one word of Billy's side."

"If he thinks any lawyer will get him off, he's very much mistaken. No lawyer can get him off. Why, oh, why doesn't he make a clean breast of it?"

Clyde expected to find the jail full, but he could see only Deputy Wall and Billy. Billy was lying on his back on his cot, hat over his eyes, and hands folded back of his head, and Pete Wall stood in the outer office.

"Hello, Clyde," said Billy. "Ma give up on me and go home? Or is she going to stick around for the hanging?"

"I left her at Maud's. Major Morrison sent his nigger coachman for her with a buggy."

"The major did that? Things must look worse for me than I thought. Did she get in and ride?"

"No, we were almost there."

"She would have?"

"Yeah."

Billy lit a cigar and filled the air over him with smoke. It was wrapped in tin foil with stars stamped on it, and he gave that to Clyde. Tin foil was supposed to be worth a dollar a pound. "I wish Ma wouldn't stay over at Maud's. I wish you'd get her in the buggy and take her back to the ranch. It's very unpleasant having to sit there with your mother listening while you're branded a cold-blooded killer, a thief, and a forger. Those sons-of-bitches. Did she say anything?"

"No."

"Nothing?"

"Nothing much."

"Well, she's thinking plenty, you can bet. Did she think I forged that deed?"

"She says she'll testify that she asked you to sign her name if it'll do any good."

"She's not going to testify."

"Yes, she is."

"Like hell she is!" cried Billy, sitting up.

"I heard 'em say she was on the list of defense witnesses."

He laughed and said: "Well . . . aw, to hell with it. Don't ever get wound up with the law. If I had it to do over again, I'd head for the Athabasca . . . or the Pampas."

Clyde couldn't stand it any longer, because he knew it would be no use. "They won't believe a word you say, or that Ace or Frenchy say." He quieted down because Pete Wall had his head turned to listen. "Your only chance is to bust out of here," he said right close to Billy's ear.

"Now, stop that. No more of that talk. I mean it. We're going to clear the family name. God, I'm hungry. Do you know I haven't had a bite since this morning?"

"The Chinaman will be here presently," said Pete.

"You know what I'd like? A great big quart of cold beer. But I'm not going to. I'd have to piss, and I wouldn't want to interrupt the trial."

"They could set you over a knothole," said Pete.

"No, I'm not going to drink a drop till it's over. When the trial's over, I'm going off on the damnedest whangdoodle this camp ever saw. They'll have to reshingle it when I get through. I'm not eating but a very little, either. Maybe I'll eat an apple. An apple and a cup of tea. The hungrier you are, the smarter you are. Just like a winter wolf. Get too much food in you and your mind slows down. My mind's not going to slow down, not tonight, and not tomorrow. Clyde, boy, I'm going to be smart as an old wolf in February."

Pete Wall was now at the front window: "You might want to keep that lawyer of yours in apples, too, because it looked to me like he was headed for the saloon."

"Time will tell," said Billy. "Tomorrow at midnight all will be known."

Judge Minough had a very pleasant repast at the Denman Chamberlains' The Cottonwoods — the six-room mansion standing on a rise above the river. There were fifteen at dinner, a spirited company dominated by the ladies — Mrs. Chamberlain, forty-five but still pretty, Mrs. Morrison and her two daughters, the elder most visibly nubile under her summer voile, the two rather plain Chamberlain girls, and Mrs. Gute, Mrs. Fairchild, and young Mrs. Flondel. The repast was excellent — salad and lemonade, served on the wide,

149

screened porch, then a roast-chicken dinner inside on white linen, followed by wines and cigars. Minough appeared princely in the chair of honor, acceding to the honorary title of "Senator" — all but a foregone conclusion.

Time slipped away in pleasant conversation, so it was dark, an hour past the "seven on the dot" specified, and the courtroom already warm from its long-waiting crowd when the judge briskly entered. He glanced with a rueful smile at the coal-oil lamps, three of them on let-down wires from the ceiling.

"No electric fluid here," someone said.

"Well, this is an old-fashioned court," said the judge. "We'll just find our way by the old-fashioned light. It's the light of *truth* we're looking for . . . Mister Bunting? . . . Boe? . . . Stewart? . . . Wardrope? Jury all present? Call your next witness."

Wardrope said: "The Territory calls Arvis Rapf."

CHAPTER ELEVEN

"What's your business, Mister Rapf?"

"Business?"

"Cowboy?"

"Yes, a cowboy."

"How long have you been a cowboy?"

"It's all I ever been."

"Just stepped from the cradle onto a horse?"

"Just about."

"Where all have you cowboyed?"

"Kansas, the Indian Nations, Wyoming, and here."

"Never out of a job? I mean, stay at work pretty steady?"

"Yes, I never been on the bum. I sometimes ride the grubline a little."

"How much of the time would you say you were employed? Half the time? Three-fourths?"

"Most of the time. Nine-tenths. Never been a year when I didn't winter on a job, or have a grubstake."

"Ride the roundup? Ever miss a roundup?"

"No, I've always worked at roundup time."

"Read the brands?"

"Yes. I know all the brands."

"But can you read them from pretty far off?"

"Yes."

"That's important, isn't it? . . . good eyesight for brands? Dusty old brands away out across the coulée? How far off could you read the brand on a cow?"

"It all depends. If it was one of those big brands like the Wing W, I'd know it from, well, three or four hundred yards."

"Then you didn't have any trouble seeing what happened at that distance on the noon hour of June eleventh, last?"

"No, I saw all right."

"Tell us about it?"

Rapf said he had been laid up with a broken foot. He couldn't walk on it, but he could ride, and, when Gannaway woke him up, he was willing to do what he could. He heard it was an emergency. He wasn't sure what, but he had an idea they were out after rustlers. It would be just the chance for a bunch of Badlanders to swoop down and drive off any cattle that had been missed because just about everybody that was able to stand up or ride a horse was over at Black Butte for the branding. Rapf started in well enough, straightforward and confident, but the longer he talked, the more nervous he became, saying things he hadn't intended and having to go back to correct himself, and he bent farther and farther forward, arms between his knees, his voice without substance.

"You'll have to speak louder," said Judge Minough.

"Here, have a drink of water," suggested Wardrope.

Rapf's hand shook so, he could not get it to his lips. His legs were drenched, and he looked at Billy for the first time.

"You don't need to worry about the defendant," said Wardrope sternly. "You tell the truth. The. . . ."

"Objection. That violates the first rules of courtroom decency," said Boe. "My client is most anxious that the witness tell the truth, the whole, unvarnished truth."

"Yes, Mister Wardrope," said the judge, "we'll dispense with any more of that."

"I apologize. I merely wished to put the witness at his ease. He is not used to testifying, and it makes him nervous that the defendant is listening. At what time did you reach Willow Creek?"

"About noon. There wasn't a bit of shadow."

"What happened?"

"We stopped. They was a little up ahead. . . ."

"Who?"

"Carns and Gannaway. Gannaway seemed pretty mad. He wasn't talking to me. He was talking to the boss. To Carns. He said something about *him* being down there. He meant Billy Buttons, I guess. I looked, and I could see him. He was riding out real slow on a sorrel horse. It was a sorrel, all white under the flanks. . . ."

"Just a minute. Is this man, this rider, in the courtroom?"

"Yes."

"Will you point him out?"

"Him," he whispered.

"Louder."

"Him!"

"May the record show witness indicated the defendant, William Buttons?"

"Mister Bunting?" the judged queried.

Bunting nodded, writing.

"Did you see anyone else?"

"Yes. Two."

"With Mister Buttons?"

"Yes."

"Did you recognize them?"

"Not right off, but I did later. One was Ace Carter, and the other was Frenchy LaGrange. I could tell Ace by his arm, the way he carries it. And Frenchy always wears a black hat, pulled down, like an Indian."

"I see. It took a little time, but you recognized all three?"

"Yes."

"This was a matter of posture and movement as well as their actual features?"

"Yes."

Boe interrupted: "Why doesn't the attorney sit in the chair and be comfortable while he is furnishing testimony for the witness to agree with?"

"Your Honor, this sarcasm. . . ."

"Allow the *witness* to furnish the facts," the judge ruled. "Proceed."

"I wished only to render the facts *explicit*," Wardrope persisted.

"You should not employ descriptive sentences or postulations that could prompt the witness," Boe advised.

"The witness is not an educated man, and his severely limited vocabulary should not militate against. . . ."

"I've found that most cowboys make themselves understood very well and are not lacking in a vocabulary, much more of a descriptive

153

color than his Harvard cousin," the judge instructed. "Now, *do as I say!*"

"I beg the court's sufferance. Mister Rapf, will you tell us in your own words what you saw?"

"I didn't know what was going on. Gannaway and Carns were having some sort of a word tussle. They were both down the hill a little. I didn't want to snoop in something not my business. That's why I stayed where I was, not because I was afraid of Billy or the others. Carns was out of range, too, except maybe from one of them new express rifles. Anyhow, Gannaway rode down toward the old freight station and met with Billy. They just sat there. I didn't dream there was anything wrong. Then I thought Gannaway was turning to ride back, but instead of that there was a shot. It took about two seconds for the sound to come."

"Did you see the gun?"

"Yes, I saw it. A six-shooter. I saw the smoke come out of it. It might not have been smoke. But I saw *something* before the sound came. Then the bang came. It was the first I knew Gannaway'd been shot."

"And then?"

"He fell off his horse. The horse wheeled, and he sort of pitched off, shoulder first. I knew he was dead."

"How did you know he was dead?"

"He didn't put his arms out like a live man would. He just went head and shoulder first."

"Right side or left?"

"Right side."

"And Buttons?"

"He just . . . nothing. Just seemed cool as could be."

"Did he examine the fallen man?"

"Not especially. He just turned his horse, seemed to look at us more'n anything."

"How long?"

"Half a minute. It might have seemed longer than it was."

"Mister Rapf!" Wardrope shouted.

He looked startled.

Pointing to the defendant, Wardrope asked: "And is that the man you saw fire the shot and then coolly ride away?"

154

"Yes, that's him."

"Your witness."

"How's your foot?" asked Boe without getting up.

"My foot?"

"Yes, you were suffering from a broken foot."

"Oh, it's all right."

"Can we see where the bones knit?"

"What?"

"Will you please remove your boot and sock? I'd like to have the jury see where the bones have knit."

"Your Honor, I see no purpose in this," said Wardrope.

"Then you and your witnesses shouldn't have introduced the matter of the broken foot. Can we see it?"

"Remove your boot," instructed the judge.

Rapf did, and his sock, revealing a very white-skinned foot, and toes which he wiggled around.

"Who set the bone?"

"Set it?"

"Yes, who set it? I'd like to congratulate the doctor."

"I didn't have a doctor. I just wrapped some tight bandages around it."

"No medicine? No pain killer? Liniment?"

"Just vinegar and sagebrush. It's a poultice."

"Why, that's remarkable! Did you ever see a bone knit as well as that without being set?"

"I guess it wasn't broken very bad."

"I guess not. I guess it wasn't broken at all. In fact, you were a liar in regard to the broken foot, weren't you?"

"No. I couldn't put my weight down. . . ."

"There was one part of your body you could put your weight down on, though. You could put it down on that portion that is situated between your two hips. You didn't have any trouble putting your weight down there while the other fellows were over at Black Butte, wrestling calves and burning brands on them."

"Your Honor, this is sheer abuse," said Wardrope.

Judge Minough peered at the witness without too much concern, but Boe responded in anger.

"Let's see how much of this abuse is warranted! You testified

155

you were a cowboy, and a valuable one. . . ."

"I don't believe that term was ever used," said Wardrope.

"He testified how steadily he worked which was implicit to the same thing. You were in Wyoming before you came here, Mister Rapf. How long did you work in Wyoming?"

"Three years."

"How many outfits did you work for?"

"I'd have to count up."

"In other words, you can't remember right off?"

"No, not right off."

"So many you can't recall? Did they line up and bid for your services? Or were you always getting fired?"

"No. I never got fired. I. . . ."

"You quit several times."

"Yes, I quit and. . . ."

"You found out they were going to fire you, so you pulled your saddle off the wagon. Isn't that how you quit?"

"No. . . ."

"How about the Signal Butte Company? Didn't the boss say . . . 'You're fired,' and didn't you tell him . . . 'No, I quit ten minutes ago'?"

"Well, yes, I guess I said that."

"And the truth is, nobody would hire you down there, so you came up here? You quit the Combo, too, didn't you?"

"Yes, I drew my pay. I heard they were looking for more men up on the Goosebill."

"You went to work for Bob Sams on the Marias River, didn't you? What name did you use?"

"Oh, I just told them my name was Smith. Tom Smith."

"Why?"

"I don't know."

"Afraid they'd find out you were a loafer? Afraid your reputation would follow you?"

"No," he said, very uncomfortable. "I just said my name was Smith. It was a spur of the moment thing."

"If you'd had more time, you'd have thought of something better?"

"Well. . . ."

156

"And traveled farther?"

Rapf sat curling his naked toes and looking at Boe.

"You'd have done what Purdy did? . . . get out of the country?"

No answer.

"Get a raise in wages? Goosebill pay more than the Omaha?"

"Answer the question," ordered Judge Minough. "You know whether you were paid more, less, or the same."

"Less. I got thirty there, forty here."

"Just like it better on the Goosebill?"

"Yes, I guess so."

"Better climate?"

"No. I just like it better."

"Ten dollars a month better?"

No answer.

"How'd you happen to leave that place you liked so well and come back to testify?"

"I'd already testified at the inquest. They told me I had to come over and testify here."

"Willingly? Were you glad to do it?"

"Well, yes."

"They came after you, isn't that a fact? In spite of your going over there and changing your name, they found you and went over after you. They told you they had everything you'd said down in black and white, and, if you didn't return and give testimony, they'd . . . ?"

Wardrope objected and was overruled.

"Didn't they have it all written down?"

"Yes."

"And didn't you protest that some was not as you recalled it?"

"I just didn't remember saying some of it."

"But you signed it?"

"Yes."

"Didn't they say you'd sign it, or you'd go to jail for perjury? Didn't you claim you weren't under oath at the inquest, and didn't they tell you the oath was *understood?* Then didn't they tell you that your testimony here at this trial had to match that statement . . . the statement containing things you didn't remember? . . . or otherwise you'd be prosecuted? Now, who was it came and brought you back

157

from the Goosebill and told you that?"

"Danner and Stewart."

"The undersheriff and this lawyer?"

"Uhn-huh."

"But if everything went right, and Billy Buttons was convicted, what then? Were you offered a reward?"

"No, they said I could go where I liked, and nothing would happen to me."

"Didn't they offer you a sum of money?"

"Just for the pay I missed. I had to leave my job."

"Now, I want this straight. They offered you the amount that would make up for pay lost leaving the Goosebill Ranch?"

"Well, that is . . . yeah. That's about how they said it."

"Again, how much were you making at the Goosebill?"

"Thirty a month."

"How much did Stewart and Danner offer you?"

"Two hundred dollars."

"A month?" asked Boe, pretending astonishment.

"No, lump sum."

"Then they paid you for nine months' lost time?"

"I was getting thirty and found, grub, a place to stay. Now I don't. I'm out of a job and winter coming on. I'll probably be on the town till next spring roundup."

"On the other hand, you had to *work* on the Goosebill, and here you just lie around on the town? . . . loaf and testify? I guess testifying is about the best job you ever had? Cowboying ain't shucks to testifying, is it, Mister Rapf?"

"I do most strongly object to these imputations," said Wardrope.

"Oh, very well. Question withdrawn . . . imputations regretted. I certainly would not wish to demean Mister Rapf's standing in the community. So, back to June eleventh . . . what happened that morning when Mister Gannaway awoke you and said . . . 'Come along?' Did you hop right out of bed and strap a gun on?"

"Well, I had to have a crutch. No matter what anybody says, I couldn't walk. I had to one-foot. . . ."

"Strap a gun on?"

"Well, no. I didn't own a gun."

"Didn't own one?"

"I had one, and I sold it."

"How'd you happen to sell it?"

"It was broken."

Boe laughed and turned away, shaking his head, and everybody else laughed, too. Even Major Morrison laughed. The judge laughed. Clyde laughed. But Billy didn't laugh. His face was serious. He was certainly a different Billy from what Clyde had ever seen before.

Boe said: "So there you were with your broken foot. What good would you be unarmed? Did you think you'd scare 'em to death . . . those Badlanders?"

"No, the cook lent me his gun."

"Pistol?"

"Yeah."

"It must have been a very long-range pistol to carry from where you were . . . where you placed yourself on reaching Willow Creek?"

"He said to stay back."

"Who said to stay back? Mister Carns testified differently."

"Gannaway. He wanted to see Billy alone."

"On the other hand, Mister Carns testified this morning that he wanted you to come closer, and you refused." Boe looked at some papers. "He said . . . 'I called them some hard names, but they refused to come farther.' Then, quote . . . 'Haven't lost any Buttons lately.' Now, all these things can't be true. Carns testifies you were cowardly. You testify you didn't want to snoop. Next you say Gannaway sent you back. Will you clear this up?"

Rapf didn't know what to answer. Wardrope sought to rescue him by saying: "Your Honor, Mister Carns never said the witness was cowardly."

Boe replied: "The entire tenor of his testimony was implicit to cowardice, and I will ask the clerk to read that testimony if it is required."

Judge Minough said: "I hardly think that is necessary. We remember very well Mister Carns's resentment of the witness's action. Could you think of a predicate nominative less obtrect than cowardly? Cowardly does smack of the invective."

"I'll forget the word entirely, but Mister Carns says the witness refused to advance down the road with him to give Gannaway proper backing. The witness has not one but *two* other stories. I'd like to know which is true."

"I guess a little of both," said Rapf.

"All three tended to restrain you?"

"Yeah, I guess so."

"You stayed back because you hadn't lost any Buttons . . . because you didn't want to snoop . . . and, besides, Gannaway told you it was what he wanted?"

"Yeah."

"Would you say, Mister Rapf, that *each* kept you back its own distance? Would not having lost any Buttons have kept you back three hundred yards? And not wanting to snoop two hundred? And your broken foot, say, three hundred more? Now, if you get all those added together, you must have been far away?"

"Well, no. Naturally if I was back where I wouldn't hear the argument, I was out of range."

"Two birds with one stone?"

"Yes."

"Now, Mister Rapf, you testified as to how far you could read a brand on a steer. We were all much persuaded by the sharpness of your eyesight. Is that also true of your hearing? I mean, are all of your senses good . . . unimpaired? Do you hear all right?"

"Yes. Fine."

"Then that would call for a greater retreat, wouldn't it? How far back would it be necessary for you to remain in order not to overhear the argument between Mister Carns and Mister Gannaway, which admittedly did not concern you?"

"Oh, I don't know."

"You know everything else, quick! . . . like that. Come, Mister Rapf. All you have to do is tell the truth. Just the facts. How far from Carns and Gannaway were you so you'd be sure not to hear them? . . . arguing, remember . . . how far? From here to the door? But those at the door easily hear us, and we do not lift our voices. So it had to be farther. Here to the street? The far side of the street?"

"It's hard to tell. If I was out there, I could. . . ."

"We're not out there, Mister Rapf. We're in here, and I want you within reason to tell just about how far you stayed back when Carns

160

and Gannaway were arguing so you wouldn't hear them?"

"Not quite from here across the street. More like from here to the middle of the street."

"That's about, say, one hundred feet. Gannaway then rode down the road alone, and *that*, according to testimony, was when Carns wanted you to advance, and you refused?"

Rapf was silent.

"The road descends in two pitches, right?"

"Yes."

"Where did Gannaway stop?"

"Just at the foot of the steep pitch, on a little sort of step."

"How far would you say that was?"

"Well, more'n the length of this room."

"This is a sixty-foot room, or slightly more?"

"This building is ninety foot to the inch," said a voice from the audience, "because I helped build it. This room measures seventy-eight, then you add the twelve-foot storage rooms. You can prove it by counting rafters. It's got fifty-nine rafters at eighteen-inch centers."

Instead of rapping him to silence, or having him ejected from the room, Judge Minough, after a look of surprise, did some figuring. "You seem to be off one rafter or one foot six."

"No, sir! The front and back are the ends of the building. They're the king truss. The end rafters are two-by-twelves, sway braced. This is a very strong building."

Laying aside his pencil, the judge said: "This court defers to superior knowledge when it encounters it. Proceed."

For the first time, Boe showed annoyance, but he hid it by turning and consulting his notes. "Very well, we have now, by adding these together, placed you at least one hundred and sixty feet farther back than Mister Carns, but in spite of that you seem to have seen fully as much as he did? You saw Billy draw a gun and smoke puff from it?"

"No, I didn't actually see him draw. Well, I saw him move, and the gunsmoke, but I didn't realize what it was until some time later when the shot reached me."

"How much later? It must have been quite a while?"

"Yes."

161

"How long would you say? One second? Two seconds? You already stated, I believe, 'a couple of seconds,' but that could have been only a figure of speech. I now call on you to be more exact. I will ask you to imagine yourself back on those rimrocks overlooking Willow Creek on that hot, June noontime. I want you to close your eyes and think about it, just the way everything was. I'll bet you've done that a hundred times?"

"Yes. I thought about it."

"Right! Now, I am holding my watch. I ask others do the same. Ready? Eyes closed, Mister Rapf? Imagine yourself there. I'll call out . . . 'Movement!' Then, when you hear the actual shot, you are to say . . . 'Bang!' I'll say . . . 'Movement!' You're to say . . . 'Bang!' All ready?"

"Yes," said Rapf, very tensely leaning, eyes closed.

"Very well. Ready. Imagine you're there . . . *Movement!*"

Rapf seemed to be counting, and he weaved slightly to and fro in the immensity of his concentration.

"Bang!"

"Good! Excellent! It was just about two-and-one-quarter seconds. Are you sure it took that long, Mister Rapf?"

"Yes, it was quite a while."

"Do you know how far sound travels in a second?"

"No."

"Sound travels at a rate of one thousand twenty-nine feet per second, or slightly faster, depending on the heat of the day. By your demonstration, we can see that you were not a quarter to an eighth of a mile distant, as previously estimated, but from two thousand two hundred and fifty-eight to perhaps twenty-six hundred feet, or half a mile, give or take a couple hundred paces. I can see now why the prosecution made such a point of your eyesight, and your ability to read one of those dusty brands from away off across the coulée. Now, by the distance actually demonstrated, do you mean to sit here and tell us that you really did see all those things with such a minute exactitude? . . . and with the heat rising like waves off a pancake griddle?"

"I saw what I saw. It was no half a mile away. Maybe I guessed the time too long. It might have been only a second. It might have seemed longer."

"What does gunsmoke look like?"

"Well . . . smoke."

"Pretty distinctive? You say it was gunsmoke, and yet a while ago you testified you didn't know what it was."

"I never said that."

"You said you saw *something* . . . but you didn't realize what it was until you heard the shot?"

"Yes, but then I knew it was gunsmoke."

"Knew it *was,* or what it must have been?"

"Well, must have been."

"Then what you saw might have been any flying thing in the air?"

"No, I could see it came from Billy."

"It was between Billy and Mister Gannaway?"

"Yes."

"But, on the other hand, it could have been blood, fragments, bits of shirt from a bullet passing through. If it was just *something,* as you testify, it could have been that, couldn't it? And when you heard the gunshot, more than two seconds later, you knew it *must* have been gunsmoke? Isn't that possible?"

"I don't know."

"Right! You don't know."

"And no matter what you say, I wasn't half a mile away."

"It was not what I said, Mister Rapf, but what your memory proved. How about it? Would you like another test?"

Wardrope interrupted: "Your Honor, these so-called tests aren't proving anything."

"Then you should have objected before," returned Boe. "I explained carefully what the test would consist of. Defense objects only after the test made suspect, indeed *demonstrated* the miscreant nature of this entire testimony."

"Nevertheless, objection is sustained," ruled the judge. "A repeat demonstration would add nothing. It could hardly add to the witness's judgment. Proceed."

"I believe the credibility of his testimony, if it can be called that, has been pretty well established, and hence any further questioning a waste of the court's time," said Boe and sat down.

"How far were you away?" asked Wardrope.

"Like I said, well, upwards of a quarter mile. No farther."

"Was it, or wasn't it, too far for you to see what took place, and I want the truth!?"

"I'm tellin' the truth. I saw what I saw."

"No more redirect."

"Witness excused. You're all finished," said the judge when he still sat there.

Rapf got up and limped away, one foot bare, carrying a boot and sock.

"Your Honor," said Wardrope, "we have been unable to locate the second cowboy witness, Mister Robert Purdy. We wish, therefore, to introduce into evidence a statement, signed by him before witnesses, and ask that it be read to the court."

"Mister Boe?"

"May I read it first?"

He had difficulty under the oil lamps turning the statement one way and the other, five pages of it.

"This is very good!" commented Boe when he had read it. "May I ask who actually authored the prose of this flawlessly grammatical disquisition?"

He waited while the prosecution table was poised in silence. At last Paul Stewart got to his feet. "Your Honor, the witness gave this by word of mouth, and it may be that I corrected some of the grammar."

"You substituted one word for another? You changed things here and there?" asked Boe.

"Only for purposes of clarity. The witness, however, read it over, every word, before affixing his signature."

"He was willing to sign what you wrote even though it was in certain aspects different than what he said?"

"Your Honor, this is a *true* statement," Stewart protested.

"Unless," said Judge Minough, "defense wishes to challenge the authenticity of signature, and hence of document, it will be accepted in evidence . . . for what it is worth. Jury realizes, of course, that such statements *in absentia* are poor second best to the actual verbal testimony. In this instance, defense has a perfectly good reason to ask why the witness was not produced. If he left this jurisdiction, one would inquire why? Was he unwilling to face cross-examination? And what real effort was made to bring him back? All these imponderables diminish the force of this statement. But it is accepted with these reservations. Clerk will now read it."

Rapidly and with clear enunciation but with no vocal coloring whatsoever, Bunting read the statement which point by point corroborated Rapf's testimony.

"It would be interesting," drawled Boe, "whether this man, too, managed to slow the speed of sound down to, say, five hundred feet per second."

"Objection!" cried Wardrope, hair-triggered.

Judge Minough said: "Yes, for heaven's sake, Mister Boe, you know better than to interject such comments."

"It can serve as the cross-examination I have been denied."

CHAPTER TWELVE

"The prosecution calls Louis Ethrington."

"Your Honor," said Thomas F. Boe, "I do not see the name on my list of witnesses."

Paul Stewart responded: "We were uncertain up till the last minute whether Mister Ethrington could be located. He is a very busy man, deeply involved in the management of the Omaha Company . . . this being the very busiest time of year, the affairs have been left in upset after. . . ."

Boe interrupted him: "It troubles me, I must say, that this trial has been made second in importance to corporate convenience all down the line. All these men" — he indicated the spectators rather than the jury — "have businesses or ranching interests. It's their busy time of year, too, but they are here . . . and in the interests of justice. With these men the public good came first."

"It came first with Mister Ethrington, too, Mister Boe!" Stewart declaimed.

"But not to the extent of getting him down on the dotted line!"

"Where is the witness?" Judge Minough asked impatiently.

Ethrington had apparently been waiting in the coolness of the back stairs. A black, silk kerchief was still wrapped around his throat, and he carried his hat in his hand. The lights seemed bright to him. He stopped and blinked as the oath was administered. "I do," he said, and sat down. He was still young, though slightly gone to fat, good-looking in a way, but hardly the image of an English adventurer in the Far West.

Guided by Wardrope's concise questioning, Ethrington gave his version of the fatal day, adding little that was new. He had heard some shots — two or three, he had not been certain. He had stopped his rig to listen before driving on.

"Did it occur to you to investigate?" asked Wardrope.

"Yes."

"But you decided against it. Will you say why?"

"I heard only two shots. One I wasn't too sure of at the time, and then one a while later. It seemed to me that any trouble . . . a real shoot-out . . . would call for more. I didn't seriously consider any trouble. It might be a wolf or coyote. That's generally the case."

He then told of driving on to the ranch where he had only arrived and was washing up when summoned with news of the killing. He changed teams and returned, followed by another rig, driven by Ike Thrift, the Association detective, who had also just arrived at the ranch. Actually the body was carried back in Thrift's wagon, not Ethrington's. Ethrington described its condition.

"Considerable point has been made here of your fame as a game hunter," Wardrope continued with a smile. "From your knowledge of guns and loads, what was your conclusion as to the wound?"

"I didn't even try to examine it. I don't mind saying the whole thing was quite a shock to me. But I assumed it resulted from a single, heavy bullet fired from quite close, passing through with some expansion."

"Thank you. Your witness."

Boe took his time. "So you're an expert in ballistics?"

"I didn't say that."

"No, but you did not correct the attorney when he made flattering tribute to your knowledge of guns and loads. How did you get the nickname 'Dead-Meat Louie'?"

"Your Honor!" said Wardrope, poised and waiting. "I demand a certain measure of courtesy for this witness. After all, he is one of the leading men of this territory."

"I couldn't very well say . . . 'Your Lordship, are you also known as Dead-Meat Louie?' It would sound foolish."

There was laughter which was met with the judge's gavel, after which the judge said: "I'm certain Mister Ethrington, after his years in the West, qualifies for the rough-and-tumble of this courtroom."

"Well?" asked Boe, returning his glance to the witness.

"It's the first I ever heard it. I don't know why, or if, they called me that."

"Would you hazard the guess that you were one of the biggest killers of game this area has ever seen?"

"No. I like to hunt. Not so much of late years."

"Given up your old ways? How about setting fire to whore-houses?"

"Your Honor, this is wasting the court's time," protested Wardrope.

"Prosecution's own witness saw fit to bring up the matter of arson in relation to this man," Boe responded. "It's not my fault that it was volunteered by the prosecution. We have heard the hearsay report, now let's hear it . . . *viva voce,* in the first magnitude."

"It wasn't a whorehouse as you put it . . . ," said Ethrington, and then he clamped down on his feelings. "There was a hotel fire. . . ."

"There *was?* You set it, didn't you?"

"Yes, I set it. It wasn't an attempt to burn anything down. . . ."

"Just a joke?"

"Yes. It was a foolish trick."

"A divertissement?"

"I'd been drinking."

"Paid for the damage?"

"Yes."

"Kept it out of the papers."

"Yes, I . . . kept it out."

"How? How'd you manage to keep it out?"

Wardrope showed his displeasure in various ways, standing, walking, thrusting his hands deeply into his pockets and jingling coins, but he made no further futile attempts to save Ethrington.

"Well, I asked if I could buy an ad in the space where he . . . the editor . . . would set it up in."

"That's one of the advantages of having money?"

No answer.

"Of all the people who might have seen that news item, who did you fancy seeing it the least?"

"Frankly, my brother."

"The item wasn't run. He learned of it nevertheless?"

"Oh, he found out," said Louis ruefully.

"Who told him?"

"I don't know. Those things always get known."

"I think you know very well who told him."

"He could have found out from a dozen sources!"

"Yes, but he didn't. He found out from John Gannaway."

Silence.

"Didn't he?"

"I don't know."

"You thought so at the time. What did you call John Gannaway on that occasion?"

"I don't remember. It was a long time ago."

"You named him by some suitable epithet, or what you considered a suitable epithet, one which you remember, and I want you to tell this court what it was."

"What I said was he was the lowest thing an Irishman could be, which was an informer. But I was sorry afterward. We were good friends. We got on all. . . ."

"Did you call him that to his face?"

Ethrington didn't want to say it. "No."

"Just behind his back?"

"I said it to somebody. . . ."

"Behind his back you said John Gannaway was the lowest thing an Irishman could be? Now, how would you describe your more recent relations with Mister Gannaway? Business-like? Cordial? Ardent? Cool? Is there a word there which fits?"

"Business-like. Friendly."

"You were trying to gather proxies that would outvote him at the annual shareholders meeting, weren't you?"

"Objection. This is immaterial. The presumptive inside affairs of the Omaha Company, had the victim lived, have nothing whatsoever. . . ."

Boe addressed Wardrope: "The business affairs of Mister Gannaway had very much to do with the defendant a little while ago, and, in fact, you yourself introduced a matter of quitclaim deed and land reserve, failure of which, by the imputation of your witness. . . ."

"Now, now," said Judge Minough, "I'm going to allow the answer, but get to the heart of it."

"Yes, we were in a contest for control. Nearly all corporations are in. . . ."

"The yes will do. We just want the facts, not the interpretations.

If we give this court the facts, that's all that will be necessary. How'd it turn out?"

"Well, he died."

"Get the proxies?"

"The meeting has not been held."

"Things stack up pretty good? Ethringtons are right in the saddle?"

Ethrington didn't answer, and Boe unexpectedly signed that he was through.

"Any redirect?" asked the judge.

After a whispered conversation with Stewart, Wardrope said: "Your Honor, the prosecution rests."

"Then that's all for tonight," said Judge Minough. "I urge you all to repair to your quarters, for we will have another hard day before us. We convene here again at seven A.M. Yes, *seven A.M.!* . . . with, at this date, the sun thirty-eight minutes above the horizon."

When they got outside, Ma started right in on Clyde and where was he going to sleep? "No," she said, "I'm not going to have you sleeping in that Square Deal barn. You come with me. Maud will be glad to fix you a bed on the floor."

Clyde had to get away, off by himself. He couldn't stand it any longer. He had to breathe the cold air and get all the sticky smell of the courtroom off him. So he just left Ma at Maud's and walked. He walked in the dark along the river under the big cottonwoods with their ghostly autumn leaves rustling to where some old warehouses had been carried high, wrecked by the flood. He walked to where Arlington was an island blaze of electric light, rendered small in the immensity of night hills, the great river moving along, with its deep sound. The river was there and always would be, and over it, cheap and temporary, was the town, voices, and slammed doors, a fiddle and a cornet, that last coming probably from Nell Gwynne's, a parlor house where an orchestra was brought in for busy times, also girls to add spice to the two or three drab regulars. Then a wind came up, sharp as a blade, cutting right through him, so, shivering, hat down and kerchief across his chest, Clyde got back into the shelter of the buildings, and he walked down Main Street.

Fewer were outside than he expected. He stopped at the drug

store. He could smell vanilla. He could see the goose-neck, copper fountain, signs for cherry-lemon phosphate and River Queen Root Beer. He had very nearly four dollars distributed through his pockets, but some fellows and girls were at the counter, making him feel big-footed and awkward.

"Hello, Clyde." It was Harry Wilson from the Lost Wagon Ranch. "Is your Ma all right?"

"Yeah, she's all right."

"Well, it's bound to be hard on her . . . hearing all that stuff."

Clyde didn't know what to answer.

"Well, it's always darkest before the dawn," said Harry.

Then Clyde was in the shadow of a rain barrel by the Drover's Hotel when three men walked from the door. One was Cal Reims, who was on the jury, another a rancher named Creighton Sallows, and the third was a big, red-faced man named Bundy.

When Bundy started across the street and also out of earshot, Reims said: "I'm duty bound as a juror not to talk about the case, but as an old friend I'll tell you I think that god-damned lawyer should have pleaded him guilty. I suppose he feels he has to earn his money."

They were talking about Billy. Clyde flattened himself closer than ever, straining to hear.

"It'd save money for everybody concerned," rejoined Creighton Sallows.

"Not only that, it's for his own good. He might have made a trade and got off with life imprisonment. He shot that man. He's admitted it far and wide. He bragged about it. We all know that."

Sallows said something about an appeal. Reims said that it was unknown for the judges sitting in Helena on the supreme court to overrule one of their own members and grant a new trial in a criminal case. When they stepped down from the sidewalk, Sallows said, in his opinion, letting Morrison on the jury was the "preëminent folly . . . just a lawyer showing off. . . ." Their voices trailed.

Oh God! — they were going to hang Billy. Clyde had heard a juror actually say so. *How long*, he wondered, *between a verdict and the actual hanging? Two or three weeks? Three or four months, allowing for the appeal? But the time would come. What will I do?* he thought. *Where will I go?* He couldn't just run away. He couldn't leave Ma. *But what? Stay at the ranch and wait for word? Would Uncle Earl ride out and say Billy was dead? Would he come out with the body?* Would they have to come in and claim the body when it was cut down, and have a funeral? Was the family supposed to attend a hanging? No — they would go to town and wait for word at Maud Hemphill's. No matter how it ran through his mind, it was horrible. Yet he knew as certainly as there was earth under his boots that it would come to pass. Even as he walked through the dark, the minutes were shortening to that unthinkable time.

CHAPTER THIRTEEN

"Court will come to order," said Judge Minough. "Those who alleged a tardy gavel at our last session, will note we recapture three precious minutes today." There was laughter. He waited a while. With a stirring and standing, way was made for Mrs. Buttons who came in with a beefy, truculent-looking boy of about sixteen, the youngest of the Buttons tribe, the boy whom Major Morrison had remarked was ambitious to attend medical college in Indiana, a fairly hopeless project, judging from his appearance. When she was seated, and the boy cross-legged on the floor, no place being vacated for him, the judge asked: "Is the defense ready with its first witness?"

Thomas F. Boe had made no motion for dismissal. It would have seemed preposterous under the circumstances, and Boe was an uncommonly good lawyer. He knew just how to try a case before one of these rude frontier juries, much better than Wardrope who was continually objecting to improper statements by witnesses, and closing off things the jurors wanted to hear, making them think the prosecution had something to hide. Boe made his rights known but denied the spectators nothing. There he sat, in the cool that still pervaded the room, with an old shawl around him, looking like a dissolute, beardless Abraham Lincoln.

"Defense calls Henry Froelich," said Boe.

Froelich was a cooper and stave pipe-maker, a very heavy-shouldered German with a longhorn mustache. Although he had served on the coroner's jury, and had signed a finding that Gannaway had come to his death at the hand of William Buttons, here he was, testifying in an accent thick as warm schmaltz. "*Ja,* I saw tree vounds in dot man's chest. Dot fellow hat been shod up sometings terrible!" He indicated how he had put four fingers in the wounds. "I don' know who vood shood him up like dot, but it was terrible!"

"Let me ask you this . . . would it have been possible for *one* six shooter, fired *once,* to have caused those terrible wounds?"

"Vell, I don' know. He was really shod up."

"Was he shot up on one side more than the other?"

"*Ja.* Right side."

"You say there were three wounds. That means of necessity one on one side and two on the other."

"*Ja.*"

"Which side had the two?"

"This side. Ride side."

"Was the right side the one you could put your whole hand in, or just two fingers in?"

Wardrope was poised like a sprinter: "Objection!"

"For what reason, Mister Wardrope?" asked Judge Minough, still placid in the cool of the morning.

"Defense attorney is rearranging the testimony. He is organizing it for the witness."

"Vell," mimicked Judge Minough, "this vitness don' speak English so goot. Ja?" He looked at Froelich.

There was laughter. "Ja," said Froelich, laughing also.

Boe repeated the question, and Froelich said: "Vell, on von side I put these fingers in." He held up four. "I coot feel proken pones. Dis odder two finger I stik in not so good, odder side."

"How about the right side, the one with the two wounds? Both big enough to stick four fingers in?"

"No, dot second von was about like so."

"One finger?"

"*Ja.*"

"Your witness," said Boe.

"Well, that's moving right along!" said Judge Minough. "I guess you can speak this language better than you thought you could, Henry."

"Ho, ho, ho, ho!" laughed Froelich.

Wardrope smiled tolerantly, but he gave Froelich a good, stiff cross-examination, reminding him — as Boe quickly lodged objection — that he had signed something different while serving on the coroner's jury the night of June twelfth. Wardrope then explained the difference between entrance and exit wounds, the meaning of the word *exit,* how bullets of large mass expanded, or mushroomed, with

174

consequent splintering, both of bullet and of bone, and asking that his observations be reappraised with that in mind, but all he could get was: "Vell, I don't know about dot. He was shod all up."

"Why did you sign that coroner's jury finding?" asked Boe, not bothering to stand.

"Vell, everybody signed dot thing."

Oh, well, Boe gestured, as if it was of no consequence. "No redirect."

"This has been a redirect, and an improper one!" cried Wardrope. "Defense asked the question I was *prevented* from asking."

"It was improper for you," said Boe, "but not for us."

"It is highly *improper* that the defense objects to my question, and then asks the same question himself," Wardrope pleaded.

"Yes, Mister Boe, you're flirting with another five-dollar fine. Excused, Mister Froelich. You may step down. Call your next witness."

"The defense calls A. T. Blankenship."

Blankenship, the Billings undertaker, a small, compact man with a very pink face, and wire-rimmed, half spectacles, took the oath and sat down.

"I'm an undertaker and embalmer," he said, in answer to Boe's query. "Seventeen years."

"In addition to practicing your profession for that period I believe you have served diverse times as coroner?"

"Yes, here and in Dakota."

"For a total time of . . . ?"

"Four years full time, but often in emergency. Too often to count."

"In that time, Dakota being what it is, I would suppose you examined a number of bodies that had suffered gunshot wounds?"

Everyone laughed at the "Dakota being what it is . . ." but escaped the admonishing gavel of Judge Minough who could be seen smiling in his collar. But Blankenship saw nothing funny about it.

"Yes, quite a number."

"Many of them victims of the six-shooter, Forty-Four or Forty-Five caliber?"

"The Forty-Five Colt seemed, there as here, to have been a favorite weapon."

"Men felled by one bullet?"

175

"There might be several wounds, but one of them had to be the fatal one, if that's what is meant by *felled*."

"Of course. Ever see a single six-shooter bullet that did quite this much chest damage?"

"I . . . no, I don't recall that I have. Still a Forty-Five Colt can kill you, if it hits you almost anywhere. Even an arm or leg. Severe artery and vein damage. A doctor has to ligate in a hurry, or amputate. But in answer to what you seem to be asking . . . no . . . a Forty-Five doesn't generally go all the way through the chest. It depends on whether the bullet keeps its direction. As a rule, it glances."

"If it hits something . . . a bone for instance?"

"Yes, generally a bone."

"How is a human body most likely to stop a bullet . . . preventing through passage?"

"This way, and up."

"Will the clerk please note witness is indicating the side, under the ribs, and up. Is that a true description?"

"Yes, the bullet travels up. It sometimes glances off the clavicle, away over here."

"Ever see a Forty-Five Colt go all the way through in that direction?"

"Not that I recall."

"How about a rifle? Say, one of these modern express rifles like the dude hunters are bringing in?"

"Objection," said Wardrope. "Mister Blankenship is not testifying as an arms expert."

Boe replied: "He very well *is* testifying as an arms expert . . . a former coroner who has seen the action of various pistol and rifle loads on the human body."

"Overruled."

"In answer to your question, I don't know. Those guns are about Thirty caliber, and have velocities as high as twenty-five hundred feet per second. My guess is they'd go through, all right, but they might not cause so much damage."

"*Might* not. But again, with all that power, might they cause more?"

"Yes. But I don't know exactly what guns you're talking about. Whether they use the new brass-jacketed bullets."

"When you saw the body, what did you think had caused the wounds?"

"Objection!" said Wardrope. "The term *wounds* implies there were two wounds and two bullets."

Boe responded: "There was at least one wound on each side of the body. Prosecution's witness has already referred to entrance wound and exit wound. One and one makes two and takes the plural."

"*Wound* in the dictionary is a separation of flesh caused by a foreign body in which bleeding or suppuration results. If this wound is continuous through the body . . . !"

"Mister Wardrope," the judge intervened, "will you allow this questioning to proceed?"

"Exception, Your Honor. I take most vigorous exception to this entire line of questioning which implies so much more than the specifics warrant. I ask that the witness testify as to facts."

"Exception noted. Do you have that down, Mister Clerk?" Bunting, writing, gestured that he did, or would shortly. Minough looked sternly at the U. S. attorney and said: "Now, why don't you sit down, take the weight off your shoes, Mister Wardrope, and allow me to conduct this trial? You'll have your innings, never fear."

Boe resumed: "When you first looked at the body, what sort of a gun did you assume had caused this wound or wounds?"

"A Forty-Five Colt. A six-shooter."

Boe looked surprised. "A Forty-Five six-shooter! This seems hardly compatible with what you were saying a moment ago. Did you also believe that in this instance the big Forty-Five slug of lead had pierced all the way, and the hard way?"

"Yes."

"Will you tell us what led to that conclusion?"

"I read about it in the paper. The news had come by telegraph."

"The newspaper said what?"

"That Gannaway'd been shot by Mister Buttons with a six-shooter."

"And you believed it?"

"I didn't have any reason not to."

"Later on, though, you had a reason?"

"Yes."

"Will you tell us about it?"

"They wanted me to embalm the body, so I had to remove the lungs and viscera. There was considerable damaged flesh, and it had started to mortify. Well, a bullet dropped out."

"A Forty-Five bullet?"

"No. I thought at first it was a strung-out buckshot. A big Number Two, or what they call a Triple-Ought back East. However, I could tell it never had been round. It was a bullet, or half a bullet."

"Half? Why not the quarter of a bullet, the tenth of a bullet?"

"As a rule, they break off about half and half unless they're real high velocity, and then it would have some remains of a jacket. Or else, if a lower velocity, it would be a brittle lead. Bullets that shatter almost always have a lot of antimony in the alloy which hardens the lead but makes it brittle. This was the regular soft lead, what they call Number One Blue Ductile in the stores."

"How about those bullets that shear off slivers?"

"They do that on rocks but not in the body. In the body, passing through flesh, they almost always mushroom if they break. They turn inside on themselves and then part just about in the middle."

"So what caliber would you say this bullet was?"

"I didn't think much about it at the time, but then one day I was at the drug store and happened to find it in my jacket, so I had Davis weigh it on his apothecary scale. It weighed forty-two grains."

"Any gun you know of shoot a bullet that small?"

"A target rifle, maybe . . . a Twenty-Five caliber. The only common gun that came to mind was a Thirty-Two short rimfire."

"That's a revolver?"

"Yes, or one of those little pistols the ladies carry in their muffs."

"But you said it looked like *half* a bullet."

"Yes, and in that case it could have been a coyote gun . . . a Twenty-Five Express. They shoot about eighty-five grains of lead."

"So then what did you think of that news account . . . all about how Billy Buttons had shot him down, *bang!* . . . with one blast of a Forty-Five?"

"I thought they'd made a mistake some place along the line."

"It didn't square with the facts as you found them? It didn't match the evidence?"

"Not as I saw it."

"You still thought Billy had shot him, though?"

"Yes. I just thought there was more than one gun involved."

"You believed he'd shot him from one side, and some one of his pals had shot him from the other? Did something like that occur to you?"

"Yes."

"They had him guilty as . . . ?"

"Objection," said Wardrope. "Attorney is formulating and suggesting."

"I withdraw the question. When you found what you did find, what occurred to you?"

"I thought he'd been shot twice, once from each side."

"Is that your opinion now? Based directly on the evidence which you yourself found, do you believe Mister Gannaway was shot once, or more than once?"

"More than once."

"By different caliber guns?"

"Yes."

"From different directions?"

"Yes."

"Thank you. Your witness."

Wardrope needed some time to think, so he conducted a whispered conference with Paul Stewart.

"Mister Wardrope, do you intend to cross-examine?" asked Judge Minough.

"Yes. How much does a Forty-Five caliber bullet weigh, Mister Blankenship?"

"Three hundred grains."

"That's quite a bullet! Forty-two grains is about one-seventh of that, isn't it?"

"Why, yes, approximately."

"Forty-two grains taken away would still leave how much bullet?"

"Forty-two minus . . . oh, two hundred and fifty eight grains."

"Do many guns fire that much lead? . . . other than the Forty-Five Colt?"

"Not many, some old-time rifles."

"You made a distinction between a bullet shattering and a bullet shearing. You say a soft-lead bullet is more likely to shear, and a

179

hard alloy more likely to shatter. Which is the common Colt Forty-Five bullet? . . . hard or soft lead?"

"Soft lead, but I didn't distinguish between shearing and shattering, as you say. I said a bullet is likely to shear off small parts of itself on rocks, but to mushroom and part in the body."

"And shear on bone? Hence this soft, ductile six-shooter lead was likely to do just what you said it would. Now, Mister. . . ."

"Let him answer. Would it be likely?" asked Boe.

"Not in my opinion."

"Where is this bullet?" cried Wardrope. "The one you found?"

"I laid it down somewhere."

"You couldn't have thought it very important or you would have saved it for this trial!"

"No, I didn't give it too much thought. Not until I read more about the case, and then I couldn't find where I'd put it."

"I certainly can't agree that this court would give any weight to an exhibit that a former, long-experienced coroner thinks no more of than that."

Boe said: "Maybe you can find it wrapped up in that quitclaim deed you have talked so much about."

This brought laughter.

"Your Honor . . . !" Wardrope protested.

"Just finish the cross-examination," said the judge.

"I am finished with the cross examination."

"Call your next witness," the judge instructed.

"The defense calls Amos Carter, better known as Ace Carter."

"Ace Carter, take the stand."

"Do you solemnly swear . . . ?"

180

CHAPTER FOURTEEN

Ace Carter had to lift his right hand — the deformed one with its withered wrist and three-elongated fingers. He had a habit of always carrying that hand near his belt, walking or riding, but now everybody had a good look at it.

"What business are you in, Mister Carter?" asked Thomas F. Boe.

"I'm a cowboy."

"I believe you have ranching interests?"

"I own a share in the O X."

"You're a business partner of the defendant?"

"Yes."

"Where were you on the night of June ten?"

"I was down at Lolly Springs where we have a line cabin. We have to keep close watch on our stock because, if they stray over on the big corporation range, they seem to disappear." Everybody glanced at Major Morrison, who gave no sign, his face perfectly handsome and immobile. For his part, Ace Carter was just as composed — two men of unflinching nerve. "We had Clint Stabler there, riding line. We try to look in on him every week or so. Fellow we had there last year quit after somebody took a shot at him. We never did find out who did it for sure. . . ."

Boe interrupted: "You say you were with Stabler at Lolly Springs line cabin on the night of June tenth? What happened?"

"We turned in about dark, and around midnight or some later, the dog raised a howl. Clint has a shepherd dog. It was Billy . . . the defendant. He rode up, and the dog barked at him."

"It appears that on that night of the tenth there were a great many men abroad, riding across the land . . . Gannaway, Ethrington, and now Mister Buttons?"

"Objection. Such a comment is highly improper."

"Yes, Mister Boe, you can save those correlations for your

argument," said Judge Minough.

"I was going to inquire into the cause of this strange noctambulation, thinking perhaps Mister Carter could enlighten us."

"Without the comments, then."

"Can you, Mister Carter?"

"No."

"Billy Buttons never explained? Not a word?"

"He said something. I knew he was looking for Gannaway. It was the first I'd seen him since . . . well, it had been a month at the very least. I figured they had another of their deals going."

"Still it was a strange time to be out riding, wasn't it? Would you say so from your experiences with him?"

"With most people, but not Billy. He gets in moods. He'll ride all night out in the long lonesome."

"Was that what he was doing on the night of the tenth? . . . just drifting across the long lonesome?"

"I don't think so, but we didn't ask for an explanation."

"I see. He arrived, and then what?"

"He came in and sat down."

"Light a candle?"

"No, he just sat down by the table. There wasn't any door. I mean, nothing you could close . . . only a doorway you could hang a blanket over. It was open, and he just sat there. He was there when I went back to sleep, but when I woke up at daylight, he was outside."

"The approximate time?"

"Four a.m., or a little past. The sun wasn't up yet."

"Do you think he'd slept at all?"

"I don't think so."

"What was his appearance? Was he high-strung? Nervous? Heavy-eyed? What?"

"Something was troubling him, you could tell that. He couldn't keep his mind still. You'd say something, and he might not hear you."

"But you, as one of his best friends, didn't inquire?"

"No. If he wants to tell you, he will."

"Did he say *anything?*"

"Oh, yes. He joked and said . . . 'I thought you were going

182

to sleep all day.' But something was gnawing on him. Then he said . . . 'Come on, let's go.' "

"Did he say where?"

"No."

"Did he say it to you and Stabler, or . . . ?"

"Just me."

"Proceed."

"We headed out east. I expected he'd be going to Gravely Landing. I knew he was going to ship his cattle."

"Wait a minute. You say *his* cattle. Didn't you own a share?"

"Not in Belmont. That was his."

"You still didn't ask where he was going?"

"No."

"What's wrong, afraid of him?" asked Boe cuttingly.

"No, I'm not afraid of him!" Ace talked as though Billy were in the next county and not sitting about three steps away. "And I'm not out to change his nature, either. I take people as they are."

It was not flattering. He was not quite saying that Billy was true blue. There was a tiny mounting of tension in the air, everyone felt it, as if all were not well between Ace and his old partner. Perhaps it had been the sharp note of Boe's question, which was not that of a lawyer with a friendly witness. But Ace was going on, dealing out the facts.

"We rode to Gromley's where Frenchy LaGrange was waiting."

"What is this Gromley's?"

"It's a ranch, but nobody lives there now."

"Where is it situated, in relation to Willow Creek?"

"North about four miles . . . on Bone Coulée."

"Did you know Mister LaGrange would be there . . . at Gromley's?"

"I didn't, but Billy did. He was there watching for Gannaway. Frenchy told me later on."

"Did he tell you why?"

"Objection," said Wardrope. "This is second hand . . . third hand. Both Mister LaGrange and Mister Buttons are here in court. Mister LaGrange is next on the list of witnesses."

"Let's get on with this," said the judge. "Answer."

"He said it was because of the cattle. He said . . . he told Frenchy they were part of a deal."

"You met LaGrange at Gromley's. Then what?"

"Billy asked him if he'd seen anything, and Frenchy said . . . 'Not a thing.' So Billy said . . . 'Let's head over to Squawtit.' " There was laughter and a glare from the judge. "That's a little butte where you have a good view of Willow Creek. At about eight o'clock we were on the butte, and we waited there. We were thirsty, but Billy wouldn't let us go down for a drink. We stayed until about eleven o'clock, and saw some riders and a rig. He said it was them, so we rode around to the creek bottoms. We followed a coulée down, and got to Willow Creek about half or three quarters of a mile west of the road."

"After keeping hidden on this jaunt, did Billy make any further attempt to hide?"

"No, once we were in the bottoms, he sat in plain sight."

"How soon did they arrive?"

"We watered and sat around for about twenty minutes."

"See any more of the rig?"

"No, it disappeared. I never knew what happened until here at the trial . . . yesterday. I never heard that it even came up at the inquest."

"Did you watch for it? . . . for the rig?"

"Yes. We kept watch. Naturally it looked suspicious. For all we knew, he might . . . whoever he was . . . be lying up on the rims with a rifle. Some of those new high-priced guns will shoot a long way."

"But you didn't know who it was?"

"No, only he was driving a rig. It shone pretty good, so I thought it was probably one of the bosses."

"Then what happened?"

"Billy said . . . 'I'll see if he'll talk to me.' He rode out by himself and gave an Indian sign, like this." Ace showed him, using his good arm. "After a while, maybe five minutes, Gannaway rode down by himself and met Billy on a grassy spot, out from the brush, about a hundred paces from the old corrals and tumbled-down cabin."

"Did they seem to be having an argument?"

"You couldn't tell. Gannaway had a way of sawbitting his horse. He was a very cruel rider. But he did that all the time. Frenchy said

184

. . . 'I guess everything's all right.' He saw Billy coming back. I did, too. Then all of a sudden Billy wheeled around, and *bang!*"

"Billy shot him?" asked Boe.

"No."

"You said he wheeled around and *bang!*"

"Yes, but at that distance . . . it took a while for the sound to reach us. Billy heard it a full second or more before we did. He wheeled when he heard it, and it looked to us like he'd wheeled *before*. I thought he'd turned and shot. But on second thought I could see it was impossible. Then I thought for a breath or two Billy had been shot. I mean, just the way he moved. But then I saw Gannaway's horse on the run and him not on it."

"You saw nobody fire a shot?"

"No."

"Could it have been Billy?"

"I don't see how."

"You heard Mister Carns testify yesterday that he saw smoke come from Billy's pistol."

Ace nodded.

"Did you see anything like that?"

"No."

"Too far away?"

"Not only that, it was the sun. The heat rose off those bottoms like from the top of a cookstove. It made things look thirty feet high."

"In our previous conversation, though, you stated you did come to believe Billy had shot him?"

"Well, he was the only one close enough. So, that's true, I said to him . . . 'Did you shoot him?' Well, he looked shocked. I guess it was the first he even thought he was suspected. 'No, I didn't do it!' he said. Then he said . . . 'Here, if you don't believe me, smell of my gun.' "

"Had it been freshly fired?"

"I don't know."

"Didn't you smell of the gun?"

"No. It would be like asking for proof of his word."

"We heard testimony that both men made a point of taking off their guns before proceeding to the parley."

"I didn't see it. It could have happened. I didn't watch too close when Billy was on his way over. I would have if I'd dreamed what would happen. . . . what he would be accused of. As far as that goes, about him drawing a pistol, like somebody said, well, he never carried a pistol when he was riding. Sure, he generally had one, but he kept it in a saddlebag, and if he needed a gun in a hurry, why, he'd just bend over and get out his rifle."

"Did he have a rifle?"

"Yes, he did. He had one in his saddle scabbard."

"Then he was armed when he rode over?"

"He was. He had the rifle in his scabbard."

"But you'd have seen him pull the rifle? That would have been hard to miss?"

"Yes, a man has to swing away over. He'd have to put it away, too."

"If Billy didn't shoot, who did? He must have had some explanation."

"He said Gannaway had shot himself."

It was so unexpected and ridiculous that several laughed.

"Did you believe him?"

"Yes."

"Still believe him?"

"No."

"What caused you to stop believing him?"

"Things I heard later."

"Then you're no longer willing to take Billy's word for it?"

"I just think he was mistaken. He'd turned and was riding away. He assumed he'd shot himself."

"But didn't you go investigate? When you saw he was down, didn't you go help him?"

"Not with those fellows on the rims."

"Afraid of them?"

"I wasn't looking for trouble."

"So he rode up and told you Gannaway had shot himself? Intentionally? Was it accidental?"

"He didn't explain."

"What did he say . . . *exactly?*"

"He said exactly . . . 'He shot himself.' "

"So with that, the three of you rode away?"

"Yes."

"Your witness."

Wardrope could hardly contain his eagerness.

"Mister Carter, you testified that the heat made vision very difficult. To quote, it was 'like seeing across a hot cookstove.' Yet you testified that you could see Mister Gannaway sawbitting his horse."

"Did I say that?"

"Indeed, you did. Your very words."

"I think you're mistaken because I didn't *see* him sawbitting."

Boe inquired: "Why not have the clerk read the testimony?"

"So be it," said Judge Minough.

It took some time. "He was a cruel rider," read Bunting. "He had a way of sawbitting his horse."

"Very well, how could you tell he was sawbitting if you didn't *see* him?"

"That was how it looked. He had a habit of doing it. When something made him mad, he'd sawbit 'em till their mouths bled."

"I think you've repaired that bit testimony quite enough, Mister Carter. Tell us again what you saw next?"

"I saw Billy headed back."

"You had no trouble making out his face rather than the back of his head through that terrible cookstove heat? . . . heat waves rising and making objects seem twenty feet tall?"

"I know, but you can always tell which way a man is riding."

And so it went.

A noon heat had settled in the courtroom. The next witness, Phillipe J. "Frenchy" LaGrange was entertaining for his accent and obvious alarm at finding himself on the witness stand. He had been at the Sixty-Six Ranch the day before the shooting, looking for horses, when Billy Buttons appeared and said to come along, so he did. He had camped that night at Gromley's where Billy told him to keep watch, and he was still there, having seen nothing, when Billy returned next morning in company with Ace Carter. From there his was a general corroboration of everything Carter had said, and interest waned. His testimony had one dramatic moment, and it was about all anybody remembered.

"Are you a citizen of this country?" Wardrope asked, seeking to call attention to his French-Indian blood, probably Canadian, and perhaps discredit him.

"No," said LaGrange.

"Do you intend to become a citizen?"

"No."

"Why not? Do you like the old country better?"

"Yes," said Frenchy, "I theenk so. I like heem ol' country pretty good."

"What are you going to do? . . . get hold of some of our money so you can take it back there?"

"Sure, sure, yah," Frenchy indicated.

At this damning point, however, Judge Minough interrupted: "By the way, Mister LaGrange, where *is* your old country?"

"Upper Michigan."

Everybody laughed at this, even Billy, the first break in his respectful seriousness since the trial opened.

CHAPTER FIFTEEN

"The defense now calls Missus William T. Buttons."

Everyone was looking at her, so Ma got to her feet. A railing separated her from the trial area. It had been fastened from wall to wall as a temporary barrier. There was no gate, and the men crossed by merely stepping over it. She did not know what to do, and after a few seconds Luke Kilpatrick hurried to lower it by pulling the wall spikes out.

"Just a moment," said Thomas Boe. "The defense calls Missus *William T. Buttons.*"

"Ma!" said Clyde. "It ain't you."

She did not seem to comprehend. She was the only Missus Buttons she had ever heard of.

Alf Bunting called out: "Missus William T. Buttons! Is Missus William T. Buttons in sound of my voice?"

"What are they talkin' about?" Ma demanded.

"It's somebody else!" said the clerk.

There was a commotion of making way near the door. The stairs and entry were packed with men. Someone, trod on, very plainly said: "Son-of-a-bitch!" Clyde could see Pete Wall, taller than anyone else, trying to make a path, also Deputy Sam Dolson. Between them, as they inched forward, the top of a woman's head was visible. She was quite small. Her hat with folded dove wings came barely to the middle of Pete's arm.

"Can the witness be brought in the back way?" asked Judge Minough.

It was too late for that. She was finally making her way. She seemed girlish in size, very slimly corseted, garbed in a pearl-colored woman's traveling suit. She waited for a moment at the railing. Finally it was let down. Boe stepped forward gallantly, bowed, and gave her his hand. She was veiled, but the outlines of her face could

189

be seen. She was staring at Billy. Billy was on his feet. She seemed about to go to him, but Boe checked any such display. Firmly but kindly he escorted her to the witness chair. He whispered to her, and she lifted the veil.

She was in her twenties, maybe as much as twenty-five, but there was a girlish quality in her face. She was light-complexioned, reddish-haired, with a sprinkle of freckles across her forehead. She had a plain little face, snub nose, a wide space between her front teeth, but there was something very attractive about her. She was wistful and appealing. It was partly how she sat there, so small, hands folded, head tilted slightly, assailable and frightened.

"Is everything all right?" asked Judge Minough. "Can we have a glass of water? The ice water."

"Thank you," she said with obviously genuine gratitude.

"No hurry about this," the judge said to his nephew, the clerk, who was up with Bible in hand. "We can wait for a moment."

"I'm all right," the witness said.

She was sworn, and Boe, puttering so the audience would have time to look at her and get its whispering done, finally cleared his throat and said: "You are Missus William T. Buttons?"

"Yes," she said in a scarcely audible voice.

"You are the wife of this man, William, better known as Billy Buttons?"

"Yes."

"You'll have to speak a little louder, if you please," said Judge Minough.

"Yes," she said strongly.

"Your Honor!" cried Wardrope, who had been in a frenzied conversation with his colleague. "What is going on here? We had no warning that this woman would appear, or that Mister Buttons even had a wife."

"Her name is on the list of witnesses," said Boe, "and the list was presented to you yesterday morning."

"The name Missus W. T. Buttons is on the list, so naturally we assumed it was Missus Buttons, the mother. It was our understanding that she would testify anent the document, the quitclaim deed, perhaps even rebut the evidence of forgery. Instead, we have been presented this young woman, unknown to us, an obvious trick, a ruse to deny us a proper preparation."

"The only W. T. Buttons is the defendant. He is the only W. T. Buttons charged in this case, or connected with this case, and for all I know the only W. T. Buttons in the territory. It is not the fault of the defense if the prosecutor mistook Missus W. *T.* Buttons for her mother-in-law, wife of Walter *B.* Buttons, deceased. Missus Buttons, senior, goes by the name of Missus Kate Buttons, as is common with a widow. Objection without substance."

"Yes, I must agree," said Judge Minough. "In fact, you yourself have several times referred to the elder Missus Buttons as Missus Kate Buttons, never as Missus W. T. or Missus W. B. Buttons. Proceed."

"What was your maiden name, Missus Buttons?"

"Carmody. Mary Margaret Carmody."

"And your girlhood home?"

She was very nervous. "Pekin. Pekin, Illinois."

The judge said: "Now, just take your time. Don't be alarmed by us rough-and-ready Westerners."

She smiled gratefully and said more strongly: "Pekin, Illinois. It's south of. . . ."

"We know where Pekin is," said Judge Minough. "Or should. Were you born there?"

"Yes. No! No, I was born south of there, at Dilman. That's a little crossroads farm town. My father was a storekeeper. We moved to Pekin when I was about five." The judge encouraged her to this detail, nodding his head, and she became more sure of herself as she told how she had attended grammar and two-year Latin school in Pekin, and later the teacher's training course in Springfield. On graduation she taught primary grades at Lovington where her uncle was on the school board.

There was general laughter at that, and the judge said: "Ah, yes, yes! It always helps to have an uncle on the school board."

She seemed taken aback, as if she had spoken improperly, but the judge reassured her. "There, there, now! You go right ahead, and don't let this levity disturb you. Tell your story in your own words."

Boe said: "I believe in our previous conversation you told me

191

you were one year in Lovington, and then journeyed to a new position?"

"Yes."

"Where was that?"

"In Omaha, Nebraska."

"How old were you at that time?"

"Nineteen."

"Wasn't that a long journey alone for a girl of nineteen?"

"I had an aunt in Omaha. Her husband worked for the Chicago, Rock Island, and Pacific Railroad."

Everyone called it just the Rock Island, and it seemed very sweet that she called it by its full name; it was girlish and appealing that she would so fully designate it, as if fearing to deviate from the truth in even the smallest particular. Clyde, watching the jury, could see they were taken by her. They probably felt very sympathetic that she'd been victimized into marrying a man like Billy Buttons, Billy, the dashing cowboy who had dazzled and carried off the little small-town girl from Illinois. But Major Morrison was not taken in. He was not impressed, not one bit carried along. He never took his eyes off her. He was leaning forward a trifle, and his eyes were like gimlets. She evidently felt his gaze because she turned, her little handkerchief still clutched in her hands, and looked straight into his face, a very direct and simple glance, and then she turned away.

Boe said sharply: "I don't believe you actually taught in Omaha?"

"No, I had diphtheria and was a long while getting well. Afterward Auntie . . . my aunt . . . wouldn't hear of me teaching, but I taught piano."

"I believe one of the places you taught was at the Valley Home, across the river in Council Bluffs?"

"Yes."

"What was the nature of Valley Home?"

"It was a place where people with nervous sicknesses could stay. It was something like a school . . . only for grown people."

"It was in common parlance what people call. . . ."

"An asylum."

"You taught there? In an asylum?"

"I visited there and taught piano to some of the guests. They didn't call them inmates. Nothing like that."

192

"Of course. It was no Bedlam. No one was chained in the cellar. In fact, most of the guests were wealthy, isn't that true?"

"Yes."

"Was there someone there whose name is prominent in these proceedings?"

She looked puzzled. She had a sweet way of puckering her brow and pressing her lips together.

Boe continued: "I'm sorry. You haven't heard the proceedings. Would the name of John J. Gannaway mean anything anent the Valley Home?"

"Oh, yes! Missus John J. Gannaway was a guest."

"Was Missus Gannaway one of your pupils?"

"She liked to hear me play. The headmaster said it did her a great deal of good. She sometimes got very nervous. She would cry, and nobody could comfort her, but music helped."

"Did you talk to her?"

"Oh, yes!"

"Did she mention her family?"

"Yes. She said her sons came to visit her."

"Her husband?"

"No."

"He never came? The headquarters of his cattle company was located in Omaha, only a few miles away. Surely he came to visit her on one of his frequent trips to that city?"

"No. She said. . . ."

"I object to this," said Wardrope. "This has no bearing. Surely the defense does not propose that Mister Gannaway's neglect of his wife, if true, justifies his homicide."

"Mister Boe?" inquired the judge.

"Having heard Missus Buttons's full story, I have the advantage, but I can assure the court the story is coherent, and Missus Buttons's chance friendship and sympathy with this poor, unfortunate woman is a logical part of the whole." To Mrs. Buttons he stated: "You may tell us what Missus Gannaway said."

"She just said that he never came to see her."

"You left Council Bluffs . . . when?"

"The next year."

"Had you secured another teaching position?"

"I went to Denver. I taught piano and drawing at Missus Fillett's."

"That's a seminary?"

"She called it a boarding school. About half the girls lived on the premises, the rest went nights to their homes in Denver."

"You had no aunt or uncle *there?*"

"No, I lived on the premises."

"You met the defendant . . . your husband . . . in Denver?"

"Yes."

"How did that happen?"

"I played piano for glee club at Denver College. He was there, visiting. His brother planned to become a doctor, he said. He was looking into the possibility of sending him there for the one-year Latin and science preparatory course. They have a very good record for getting their graduates admission into the medical schools, even Johns Hopkins and the University of Michigan." She smiled for the first time. "I thought he was one of the professors. I thought he was young Professor Soles who taught Biology."

Billy, she said, had taken her to the theater . . . later for carriage rides as spring showed in the new buds along Cherry Creek. He asked her to marry him. She promised to consider it. She came to realize she was in love with him. They corresponded, and she met him again at Fort Sanders, Wyoming, where she had gone as a guest to the Deems' home, parents of a pupil. Their troth was plighted there, in the spring. Billy then left while she returned to Denver. Thence she went home to Illinois where she hoped their marriage might take place, but her family was upset by her decision to marry a Westerner, whom they thought were godless savages, so she came West again, meeting Billy at Bridger Station, and there they were married.

"When was this?" asked Boe.

"May the second."

"May second this past spring?"

"Yes."

"Proceed."

"We took the train in Ogden. We saw the Great Salt Lake, and then we went north to Butte City. Billy . . . my husband . . . promised to take me on a honeymoon to Yellowstone Park, to the Hot Springs Hotel. But we found it was not yet open. Instead, he took me to Alhambra."

194

Judge Minough interrupted to say: "Yes, yes. And many more would be well advised to visit that famous spa." He seemed to forget he was trying a murder case and proceeded to describe the Alhambra Springs, which had a temperature of one hundred and seventy-eight degrees, Fahrenheit, and were charged with beneficial sodium and sulphur gasses. "A godsend for those afflicted with rheumatic disorders as well as" — and he laughed — "what the newspapers like to call 'a vaporous purgative of the elite dipsomania.' "

When she looked puzzled, Boe explained: "What the distinguished judge means is that Alhambra is favored by some of our most prominent mining, cattle, and financial figures after overindulging in spiritous liquors . . . but a spa of unblemished respectability."

"Yes, indeed," said the judge.

"Now, Missus Buttons," Boe resumed, "I believe you found at Alhambra someone whose name was very familiar."

"Just the name. I didn't meet him."

"And that name?"

"John J. Gannaway."

"He was staying there?"

"I happened to see his name on the register. There were names for a month back on facing pages. I asked if he might possibly be the same John Gannaway whose wife was in Council Bluffs? The clerk said he had registered from Arlington. Later I asked my husband and learned he was the same man."

"What else did your husband say?"

"That he was an old friend."

"An old *friend?* Was he in any way derisive? . . . or ironic?"

"No. He just said he was an old friend and business associate. He said . . . 'We've had many quarrels in the past,' but he laughed. It was as if he meant it cemented their friendship. In fact, he said . . . 'Our friendship has been annealed in the furnace.' I remember, because I didn't know exactly what *annealed* meant. Then he said . . . 'It's been forged in some hellish fires.' "

"Did these remarks make you believe he was fond of Mister Gannaway?"

"Yes."

"Do you still believe he was . . . as of that time?"

"Yes."

"But Mister Gannaway had already departed?"

"Yes. I learned later he was at Deer Lodge where he had ranching interests."

"You met him, though?"

"A week later in Helena. We were at the Capital Hotel, in the dining room, and Mister Gannaway insisted we come to his table. He was alone. I somehow had the idea he was waiting for us. He said . . . 'I have some business matters to talk over with your husband, but they can wait.' He said he wouldn't tire me with them. He was very cordial."

"Now, answer this frankly, no false modesty. He was attracted to you, wasn't he?"

"He seemed to be. He was very complimentary."

"Only that?"

"He kept looking at me, and looking. But. . . ." She was at a loss for the right word.

"Circumspect?" supplied Boe.

"Yes."

"Did you mention knowing his wife?"

"Yes."

"And his response?"

"He seemed almost . . . grateful. He was, well, he wept. That is, he wiped tears from his eyes."

"Yet he seldom visited her, and by Missus Gannaway's description those few visits were cruel experiences, isn't that so?"

"Yes."

"Did you consider him hypocritical?"

"No! I felt very sorry for him. And I was surprised."

"Why?"

"Billy . . . my husband . . . had prepared me for someone, well, cruel. No, not exactly. . . . more hard and unfeeling. 'A diamond in the rough' was how he put it."

Boe then offered a deposition from Walker Andrews, manager of the Capital Hotel attesting to the dates at which Mr. and Mrs. William Buttons were registered, and copies of the *Helena Herald* for late May with separate items, three in number, one reporting the presence of Mr. and Mrs. William Buttons, and two that mentioned John Gannaway being in the city.

"Mister Wardrope? Do you wish to address the bench?" asked the judge.

"Your Honor. I certainly cannot challenge . . . repeat, *cannot* challenge . . . any of this, lacking any warning or opportunity for preparation. But I must rise again to protest this departure from the agreed compass of the trial. This sudden surprise, this . . . I suspect *ambush* . . . carefully laid to spring at the final moment, presenting an entire new climate, set of conditions, background, and, I would suppose, set of motivations. . . ."

"We have already gone into this," said the judge calmly. "Surely you can't maintain the defendant kept his marital status a secret when here it is implicit in the *Herald*, the official newspaper of record in this territory? Also the hotel registry? If you have no objection, as distinguished from protest, these exhibits will be accepted. Will you read them, Mister Bunting, and pass them on to the jury?"

During all this the witness sat very quietly. There was something touching in her patience, in the obvious girlish trust with which she had placed herself in the court's hands. It brought out the best in them — all except for Roman Wardrope, the U. S. attorney, who paced and stamped for a time, wheezing in anger or its simulation, outraged against tricks and shady practice, before resuming his chair. Even Paul Stewart seemed to realize his onslaught was a mistake. It was aimed at Boe — Wardrope had repeatedly jabbed his finger at him as he spoke — but all eyes were on the girl.

"Did you see Mister Gannaway only the once?" Boe resumed his questioning.

"No, several occasions."

"Will you describe the chief of these?"

"Well, the *chief* one was when he invited us to dinner . . . evening dinner at the San Francisco Chop House. It was a Chinese café. He had ordered a Chinese dinner. We had Canton duck, and other things."

"Was it quite an impressive dinner? I mean, what of the preparations? Did you have the impression he was a man of importance? Or were you as his guests just ordinary customers? How were you received?"

"Oh! You could see he was a man of great importance. The Chinese were very anxious to please."

"Will you describe that dinner?"

"They put screens around the table. We were screened off from the other customers, but there was a place where the waiters could slide through. We had an aperitif, and wine. Chinese wine. It was very sweet and strong. The room seemed a trifle warm, and I wasn't used to drinking. I'm afraid I lost track of things for a while. Then one of the waiters came and told my husband someone wanted to see him. After he left, Mister Gannaway reached over and took hold of my hand."

"And you were alone with him?"

"Yes."

"In what manner did he do this? As a father? After all, he was old enough to *be* your father?"

"He said that. He said he wanted me to feel toward him like a father. He said he felt protective toward me, and toward Billy, that there had always been a closeness between him and Billy, in spite of their quarrels."

"What was your reaction? Did you welcome this fatherly affection?"

"I was afraid. I was just, somehow, terrified. There was something about his hand . . . it was so heavy . . . and *warm* . . . dry and very *warm*. I can't describe it. I had an uncontrollable fear of him."

"And yet people were just beyond the screen, the waiters, customers, other women? . . . and your husband, I would suppose, within calling?"

"Yes, it was unreasoning, but it was how I felt. It might have been the strange food, and the perfumed wine, when I wasn't used to drinking. It was only the third glass of liquor I'd had in my life."

"Your husband must have known this. He knew you weren't accustomed to wine. Why did he allow you to drink it?"

"He said one of these days, as a rancher's wife, I'd be moving in the best circles in the territory. He said all the upper crust drank wine. Mister Gannaway agreed. He said . . . 'Indeed, yes, your husband has a bright future.' Then they drank their wine, and so I drank mine."

"Now, back to Mister Gannaway. You were left alone with him, and he took hold of your hand. Did you let him know that his attentions were repellent to you?"

"Oh, no! I tried not to. After all, he was my husband's friend. And I knew they had a very important business deal in the offing. It was a very important agreement as far as my husband was concerned."

"Then you allowed his hand to rest on yours while he told of his fatherly concern for you and your husband?"

"Yes, until I could decently gèt away. Then Mister Buttons came back."

"Did anything else happen?"

"No, we ate, and Mister Gannaway took us for a carriage ride. We looked at the fireworks. It was an observance of some sort by the masons. There were drill teams there from Butte and Virginia City."

Judge Minough said: "I believe it was one of the several Memorial Days."

"Did you see him again?" asked Boe.

"Next day. We were waiting for the coach."

"To what destination?"

"We weren't quite sure. That is, we were going home" — she obviously meant their new home — "but it was a little uncertain where we would stay. My husband thought we could camp out for a while. He said he could get a tent. The weather was beautiful. Or he said we might fix up a house on the ranch . . . the O X, where he was partner. He didn't want to visit his mother before he took me there. She didn't even know he was married."

"Hadn't he written?"

"No. He said he wasn't much for writing. He said . . . 'Oh, she always thinks the worst of me.' That was all he'd say when I asked him. I thought he should have written, and I would have included a note, too. Mister Gannaway must have had some inkling because when he came around, while we were waiting for the stage, he said he hoped. we'd be comfortable. Then Billy said something, about camping out, I think, and he said . . . 'Good Lord, man, think of this girl you married.' He said something about the spring storms, and that the Omaha had several houses empty and waiting. I recall specifically that he said . . . 'The lodge is yours for the asking.' "

"Had you ever heard of *the lodge* before?"

"No. I'd never even heard of the Omaha . . . the Omaha Land

and Cattle Company. Missus Gannaway had always spoken of a ranch called The Northwestern, and my husband always spoke of the Company."

"Did you ask about it . . . the lodge?"

"My husband told me later that it was a place that the old English company had built on Camp Creek, near the mountains, the Big Pineys, where the dudes could fish for trout and go hunting. Its real name was Ivanhoe Lodge. He said nobody was there at that time of year, generally . . . only a wrangler or two, maybe, and a Chinese cook and caretaker. He said there would always be the Chinese cook because he raised a vegetable garden for ranch use."

"What was your feeling about this? Did you want to accept the invitation?"

"No."

"Did you tell your husband that?"

"Yes, I did."

"And what was his response?"

"He said I might get plenty tired of living in a tent, or a dirt-floor cabin. He said . . . 'Any old port in a storm.' Then he said . . . 'Believe me, this is quite a port, storm or not.' "

"But you didn't tell him your real reason?"

"No."

"Why not?"

"I didn't want to cause trouble between old friends. And so much hinged on the business deal they were closing . . . so much for Billy, and for his family. Then, I thought it might only be a notion I had . . . my fear of Mister Gannaway."

"You went to Ivanhoe Lodge, then? Will you tell about that trip?"

"We left by stage and crossed the mountains by way of Diamond City. I became ill, so we stopped over at a ranch on . . . I think . . . a stream called Camas River. The names were all new to me. The country was so strange . . . and huge."

"I believe," said Judge Minough, "where you stopped was the Huntzinger Ranch on Camas Creek, a fork of the Smith."

"Yes. A very fine, tall, gray-haired woman helped me. I slept there, and I felt better next day, so we went on."

"By stage?" asked Boe.

"No, the stage had gone. There wouldn't be another for days. It's not a regular run. My husband hired a rig and some camping gear. He had friends. Everyone there knew him. His family were real pioneers. They told me his father had represented the Smith River district in the territorial legislature when Virginia City was still the capital."

"Now, Missus Buttons, to retrace our steps a bit, you say you returned to your home in Illinois before marrying your husband. Why?"

"I wanted to tell them . . . to announce my engagement."

"But you didn't get married at your home. Were your people against your marrying Mister Buttons?"

"They didn't even know him. . . ."

"But were they?"

"Yes."

"For what reason given?"

"All I had was his photograph. He was dressed as a cowboy. He had on boots, and his big hat was on his knee, lariat rope in his hands, and a pistol on. I guess it was a very poor choice of portrait. They didn't want me to marry just a cowboy. I told them. . . ."

"Apparently their arguments were not too convincing. You returned on the train, alone, and married him? I gathered a modest wedding?"

"Yes."

"It wouldn't seem to me that your description of your visit to Alhambra and Helena were typical of a wife whose husband is *just* a cowboy."

"No . . . ," she said uncertainly.

"Can you elucidate? Was your husband better known . . . did he move in better circles than you expected?"

"Yes. I don't know what I expected. He seemed to be well known . . . liked . . . and respected."

"And his prospects . . . ranching . . . were they . . . or did they seem better or worse than he had led you to believe?"

"Better. He said I had to be ready for real primitive conditions. He said we might be years working to get a start."

"Now, you paused at the ranch on Camas Creek, and your husband borrowed a rig and camp gear. Will you describe the remainder of your trip?"

"We crossed a bridge. The river was very high. Then we traveled all morning across a prairie. Then there were foothills, pines and spruces, and we followed a creek for miles and miles into a steep valley, a cañon. It became steeper and steeper. We climbed finally to the top of the mountains. It was a mountain pass. It was frightening, but beautiful. It would take your breath away. We camped in a little meadow where there were dozens of springs . . . spongy moss . . . mountain tops all around. It was so cold you could see your breath. Then next morning we went around one of the mountains. We traveled for hours almost at timberline, and dropped down a winding, frightening road, and finally we came to a town . . . a post office and store. There was a man named Simmons. I don't know exactly where we'd gone. We crossed a river. It was very high and roily. . . ."

"I believe that was the Judith River," supplied the judge. "Did you cross two heavy streams that morning, or one?"

"Two."

"Then the first one was the Judith, and the second was Ross's Fork of that same stream. And truly, at that season, swirling torrents to dismay the most impetuous. Your pardon. Proceed."

"I think we traveled to the northwest. The sun slanted across my face all morning. Then we looked almost directly into the sun that afternoon. We crossed a big, wide valley. The grass was beautiful . . . and the wildflowers. It took us almost the whole day, but then we came to foothills again, and there were mountains on the south. We crossed one creek after another, all running down from the mountains."

Judge Minough amplified her testimony: "That was the Judith Range, and the valley was the famed Judith Basin, still a favorite of trappers when I first came to this land. Your route was the old Carroll Road to Helena. And Captain Clifton's Army road, ere it was called that."

"We camped at a ranch, I think it was Arrow Creek."

"I believe it was Armel's Creek," said the judge. "That would be the historic Armel's Station. Were there some organpipe rocks nearby?"

She puckered her brow to remember. "Yes, there were."

"Your circuit judge is not famed as an explorer, but we do get around! Proceed."

"We set out again very early. There wasn't a road. We drove over the prairie. We seemed to go around the base of the mountains, the slopes, and into the foothills. There were little knobs of rock with pines, but all out and away was the prairie. Oh, the prairie just seemed to reach forever! We could see the breaks of the river. I never saw such an expanse, even in Wyoming. My husband said we were getting into the home range."

"Do you recall any specific landmarks?" asked Boe.

"He pointed out the Buttons Buttes, I recall that. They were, oh, very far away. I remember he pointed out the place where the Buttons home ranch lay, but it was too far off. By late afternoon it looked like a sea . . . all purple and red. Buttons Buttes were like islands in the sea."

"But you didn't drive to that pioneer home ranch?"

"No, he turned into the hills. I think he called them the Piney Hills. They seemed to be an eastern continuation of the mountains."

"The Judith Mountains?"

"Yes, the Judiths. He mentioned the Snowy Range, and the Judith Range of the Rockies."

"They aren't the Rockies," clarified Judge Minough. "These are outlier ranges in the plains. So it's not a fair comparison with Colorado. You should see our Rockies . . . the Lewis Range, the Beartooth, and the mighty Pintlar."

"These were beautiful. The hills and the pines! Then we came on a road that led down into a deep, little cañon. It went back and forth across a stream. The stream was clear as glass, and, every time we crossed, the trout darted away by tens and dozens."

"Yes, yes," said Judge Minough, "those would probably be the cutthroat, or Montana native trout, the speckled trout. They prefer the very cold mountain streams even more than the famous rainbow."

"Then the cañon opened up. There was a very green meadow and some beautiful log buildings. I asked where we were, and he said he had decided to accept Mister Gannaway's invitation. We were at the lodge . . . Ivanhoe Lodge."

"Was Mister Gannaway there?"

"No. A Chinaman had a little house nearby. He was taking care of it. It was spotless. Everything was log, inside and out. There were huge rooms with fireplaces . . . even the bedrooms had fireplaces.

The mantels were hewed pine. There were Navajo rugs on the floors. As I said, everything was spotless. And there wasn't a fly or a mosquito. The flies and mosquitoes had sometimes driven us almost crazy, but all the windows were screened. It seemed like a dream come true." Suddenly her voice changed. She drew herself up as one awakening to a terrible memory. "But it turned to a nightmare!"

Clyde, sitting on the floor, cross-legged by Ma's knee, felt a shudder, and he knew he wasn't the only one. It had passed through the whole room — surprise, and the realization that the girl must have experienced something terrible. For a space of seconds it was so quiet he could hear the voices from outside, through the open windows, the men down on the street who had been unable to get in.

CHAPTER SIXTEEN

"Now," Thomas Boe said quietly, "I realize this will be very difficult for you. I caution you to proceed event by event, in order as to time. With as simple language as you can command, you must state the plain facts. Just remember that everyone here, the court and the spectators, all wish to hear the truth. Simple, plain words are the most dignified."

"Yes," she whispered.

"Perhaps a drop of our *aqua pura?*" suggested the judge.

"Thank you."

After she was provided a glass of water by the bailiff, Boe asked: "You spent the night at Ivanhoe Lodge?"

"Yes."

"Did the Chinaman . . . his name was Loo Sing, I believe . . . did the Chinaman prepare your supper?"

"No, I did. But he brought some food. My husband caught trout in the creek. The Chinaman brought us some eggs next morning."

"He lived in a separate house?"

"Yes."

"How far was his house from the lodge? . . . from the main house?"

"About a hundred steps. He lived in a tiny house with a porch. It was hidden beyond an evergreen hedge."

"Now, in the event you wanted something . . . soap or bed linen . . . how would you summon him?"

"There was a bell, and a little bell tower. You could ring from the kitchen. A rope came down through the ceiling."

"And he would hear it inside his house? What if you called to him? . . . by voice?"

"No, you had to ring the bell."

"Did you try summoning him by voice?"

"No."

"Then how can you be sure?"

"He said he only came for the bell. He said . . . 'No yell, only bell.' My husband thought it was amusing. He said Gannaway and the dudes might not want him snooping around, so those were his orders."

"In other words, he wasn't to get too curious about what happened in the lodge with its parade of Eastern visitors, heretofore described?"

"Objection. The Eastern visitors of the lodge hardly concern this case."

"If Missus Buttons's visit to the lodge pertains to this case," said Judge Minough, "then the conduct of the lone caretaker might also, and the reasons that are predestinate thereto. Proceed."

"My husband said that Mister Gannaway told him Louis Ethrington had the Chinaman trained. . . ."

"Objection. Are we to content ourselves with hearsay when one of the originating parties of this alleged conversation is himself sitting right here before us?"

The judge stared at Wardrope. "It is not hearsay within the meaning of that term when one is party to the conversation."

"I beg pardon of the learned bench, but hearsay implies that which one hears but is not within one's direct knowledge."

"Hearsay in regard to evidence consists of that which one has heard others say, or commonly said. Now, this lodge was a place of known repute, its conduct general knowledge, and 'in matters of custom or general matters or repute the courts admit of this evidence' . . . Blackstone."

"Your Honor, I deem my objection valid in that, if Mister Billy Buttons had any information concerning the instructions and practices at the lodge, then it could be stated by him, first hand. If he has such appurtenant information, let them put him on the stand instead of weaseling it forth in this underhanded manner."

"You know very well the defendant cannot be asked to take the stand, nor shall defense be denied the opportunity to bring out the pertinent facts therefore, a procedure that would penalize him for exercising his constitutional privilege."

Boe responded: "We have every intention of placing Mister Buttons on the stand, and I'll let the prosecution ask him anything it pleases. Now, Missus Buttons, what was this about Louis Ethrington having the Chinaman trained?"

Wardrope again objected: "Mister Ethrington is present, or can be brought before the court shortly. If this concerns any training specified by him, then he is the one to ask."

"I withdraw the question. I ask, instead, how were the numerous corporate owners, from the East and from England, said to have the Chinaman trained?"

"Not to break in on the orgies. He said . . . my husband said . . . Mister Ethrington brought out his Eastern friends in the fall, and there was a great deal of drinking."

"Were you worried staying there?"

"No."

"Behind those log walls of massive ponderosa pine, mortised together like unto a fortress? How long were you and your husband there, alone?"

"Two days. Mister Gannaway came on the third day."

"Two whole days? Not counting the first which was almost gone?"

"No. We had been there three nights."

"At what time did Mister Gannaway arrive?"

"In the morning . . . about ten o'clock."

"Did he expect to find you there?"

"Yes. I think he knew."

"Was he pleased?"

"Oh, yes. He seemed very cordial."

"How did he arrive? Horseback? Carriage?"

"Carriage. Team and buggy."

"Same old diamond in the rough as he'd been in Helena?"

"Yes. He was very . . . effusive."

"Tell us about it . . . what he said . . . did?"

"He gave Loo Sing . . . well, a real tongue-lashing for not preparing the meals. He said he should have given us some fresh meat. That he had ducks and chickens he could have butchered."

"I believe he threatened some unusual punishment, didn't he?"

"Yes, he said he'd hang him up by his queue if he didn't mind his ways."

"And what was Mister Loo Sing's response?"

"He kept talking back in Chinese. He threatened to quit."

"But he didn't?"

"No, he stayed in his house and refused to come out, and I prepared dinner."

"Noontime dinner?"

"It was closer to one o'clock."

"And then?"

"I took a nap. I knew my husband and Mister Gannaway had something they wished to discuss. When I got up, it was about four-thirty, and they were down by the bridge, arguing. I could tell they were arguing by how Mister Gannaway strode around . . . and my husband who always has a very, oh, a *very* casual manner in such times. It was . . . well, hard to describe."

She glanced at Billy, and their eyes met. It was one of the few times she had allowed herself to do this, whereupon Billy smiled in a rueful way, and in sudden upset she seemed to blush.

"We all recognize mannerisms . . . subtle mannerisms, particularly in those we love," said Boe. "Would you say they were quarreling?"

"No! Nothing like that, only heated. It was as if each thought himself right and hence was unwilling to give a point. After a while they seemed to go on to something else. . . ."

"Having settled the question?"

"Or just leaving it. As if to say . . . 'Well, we'll settle it later.' That was the attitude. Finally they saw me and walked back to the house."

"Did Mister Gannaway stay the night?"

"He left, after dark. It seemed very dangerous, but he laughed and said it wasn't dangerous as by day."

"Did he explain that?"

"No, but my husband did after he was gone."

"And what was his interpretation of that remark?"

"He said he was having trouble with the Eastern powers. He meant he'd be safer by night."

"And why? Didn't you ask why?"

"Yes, I did, and my husband said . . . 'Because they can't see to aim.' "

208

"Did that frighten you?"

"No, I thought he was joking."

"Did he explain who those Eastern powers might be?"

"I do object to this," said Wardrope. "I do most vehemently object to the defense taking some chance, joking remark said to be made by the deceased and interpreting it in a manner which would imply cabals, conspiracies, and bloody ambush."

"Mister Boe?" queried the judge.

"We merely wished to place the remark regarding potential danger, a danger that Mister Gannaway *said* he felt, in its proper context. After all, the prosecution put much this same question to the sheriff."

"Very well, now we're all even. Proceed."

"So Mister Gannaway departed. Did your husband say what their discussion had been about?"

"It was something about cattle. I didn't understand a thing about it. He said . . . that is, Mister Gannaway said . . . that Ethrington was making a lot of trouble."

"There are two Mister Ethringtons. Did he distinguish?"

"No, I just recall the name Ethrington."

Wardrope interrupted: "These purported statements of the deceased in regard to his partners in the Omaha Company cannot be proved and are introduced only to cast a cloud of suspicion."

"On the other hand," said Judge Minough, "the jury knows all the principals better than we, and will protect us in this matter, I am sure. Proceed."

"Did Mister Gannaway visit you again?"

"He came back next morning."

"Was it a social call?"

"He said he had to see my husband. They talked privately a while and then Billy . . . I mean, my husband . . . said he would have to leave for a while. He said he would be back by evening."

"No explanation, even to his wife?"

"It was business. I guessed that my husband had been gone too long . . . from his ranching interests. I felt at fault for that. He should have been here taking care of his affairs instead of honeymooning me at the hot springs."

"Did he indicate such resentment?"

"Oh, no! Anyway, I didn't want to inquire into things I wouldn't understand."

"Then you were left alone. When did they return?"

"Billy came back that evening. He seemed very tired and upset. He said somebody . . . I've forgotten the name . . . was making trouble. He said . . . 'We may have to go to the county seat.' I didn't want to inquire. Next morning he got up at dawn or even before. He told me to go back to sleep . . . that he'd be back in the afternoon. Well, he didn't get back in the afternoon, but Mister Gannaway came and said Billy had to visit the Spider. I asked what the Spider was? He said . . . 'Oh, that's a ranch he shouldn't be involved in.' He spent some time catching and hitching a fresh team. There were quite a number of horses in the pasture. They were beautiful horses, but they seemed very wild. He had a hard time handling them. He wanted me to take a drive with him. I said, no, but he laughed at me, pretending to think I was afraid of the team. . . ."

"Were you?"

"No. I could see how he mastered them. But I didn't think it was proper to ride with him."

"Then he departed without you?"

"Not right away. He kept delaying."

"Was loathe to leave?"

"He seemed to be."

"His reason?"

"He said he was concerned for Billy . . . why he didn't return."

"He left finally . . . when?"

"About six o'clock. He said he was going to look for my husband. He made me promise to lock the house . . . I mean that night . . . as soon as it got dark. It had shutters that could be fastened. It was built like a fortress. He said the shutters were to lock the saddle tramps out when it was left empty in the winter. There were three doors, all very heavy, and heavy wooden bars. Then he showed me where the guns were. He unlocked the case. They were locked in a rack behind heavy strap iron. Everything in the lodge was just simply massive. It must have cost a small fortune to build. He said I could use the guns for my protection. I told him I'd never fired a gun in my life . . . I wouldn't know how. They were rifles . . . hunting guns. Some were very heavy with peculiar curlicued things on the stocks. . . ."

"I believe," interpolated Judge Minough, "those were target pieces with shoulder brackets. Twin triggers, no doubt? The one was for haring the other."

"He wanted me to take what he called a Damascus gun."

"Now, that was a fowling piece with Damascus barrels, probably from Belgium," the judge expatiated. "It's what we commonly call a shotgun."

"I wouldn't touch them. I was afraid one might explode."

"Yes, yes, yes," said the judge.

"He tried to make me take a small pistol. I wouldn't touch it, so he put it in a drawer. He bolted some of the shutters himself."

"Surely," Boe asked, "he offered some explanation . . . why he thought you were in danger?"

"He said I *wouldn't* be in danger. He said that several times. He said he wanted me to feel secure."

"But was the net result of all this a feeling that you were, indeed, in danger?"

"Yes. It worried me the more I thought of it. Then my husband didn't come home. I watched until dark. I was sick from worry. I was sure he would send word, if he could. It wasn't like him. It grew dark, and I lit the lamp. I kept listening and listening. It was just terribly quiet. Then there would come tiny sounds . . . birds . . . or the packrats under the floor. But he didn't come. At last I barred the doors and went to bed."

"Did you make certain that every window and every door was secure?"

"Mister Gannaway said most of them were already secure. He had barred most of them."

"I see. Then you fastened the rest?"

"Yes."

"And retired for the night. Did you leave a light burning?"

"No."

"You didn't?"

"I was afraid of fire."

"It must have been very dark, that massive house with even the moonlight shuttered out."

"Yes."

"Proceed."

"I lay awake for a long time, but finally I went to sleep. I didn't think I'd get a wink of sleep all night. I was too taut and nervous, but I did, and, when I went to sleep, it was a very deep sleep. I was just dead to the world."

"And then . . . ?"

"Then something woke me."

With sudden lowering of her voice, the fear of it could be felt across the room, and for the moment scarcely anyone breathed. Even Major Morrison, who had become restive and seemed to lose the taste of his cold cigar, grew tense, and watched her narrowly — waiting.

She said: "There wasn't a sound, but I knew someone was in the room."

"No one knocked?"

"No. I just *knew*. I knew someone was there . . . in the dark."

"In your room?"

"Yes. In the dark. Right beside me."

"Beside you?"

"Right by the bed! I . . . I couldn't breathe . . . I . . . I. . . ."

"Be calm, now." Boe limped, using his cane, and poured a glass of water. "Take this."

"No. Just let me go ahead." She pushed the glass away, spilling a few drops of the water. "I thought . . . 'It's Billy! It's my husband!' I wanted it to be. I thought . . . 'Yes, he's come in without me hearing him. He's found some way to open the door.' I said . . . '*Billy? Billy?*' "

"Calmly, Missus Buttons," Boe counseled.

"Then a man spoke. It was John Gannaway's voice! He was standing right there, in the dark. He was in the room. He spoke my name."

"What name? What did he call you?"

"My first name. 'Mary!' he said. Then he said . . . 'Don't be frightened. It's John.' And he said . . . 'Everything is all right.' I don't know what I said. I must have asked him how he got in, because I remember that he said . . . 'The door was unlocked.' He said . . . 'Are you all right?' I don't know what more . . . my heart was beating so. Then I could hear him moving in the dark. I could smell him . . . feel him . . . yes, actually feel him, in the dark, the smell of tobacco

212

and his clothes . . . I don't know how to describe it. I started to scream. I must have because he shouted . . . 'Stop that!' Then he said . . . 'Mary! You have to be calm.' He said . . . 'I have some very serious news for you.' Strange, but that calmed me. That is, I came to my senses. I got command of myself. My ears rang, I was so frightened . . . but it was a new kind of fright. I was frightened for my husband. I thought . . . 'Something has happened to Billy!' "

"Did you ask him that?"

"What?"

"Did you ask . . . 'Has something happened to Billy?' "

"I don't know. I remember he came close and sat down. He sat on the edge of the bed. He got hold of my hand and said . . . 'You'll have to be brave. There's been an accident.' He changed it and said . . . 'There's been trouble.' I cried out . . . 'For God's sake, what happened to my husband?' Then he said . . . 'Missus Buttons, your husband is dead.' "

"He said your husband was *dead?* He used that word?"

"Yes! He said . . . 'Your husband is dead.' He said . . . 'There was some shooting.' And . . . 'I'm not sure, but I believe his own men from the Spider Ranch ambushed him.' I said . . . 'No, no, he isn't. It can't be!' But he held me by the wrist. He forced me to stay where I was."

"And that was . . . ?"

"Sitting . . . in bed. He kept saying . . . 'You'll have to be brave. You'll have to be a brave girl.' And . . . 'We'll bring these men to justice, but I know that can't comfort you now.' Then he said something about me being a poor, lone girl in a strange land. He said . . . 'Don't be afraid. I won't let anything happen to you. I'll take care of you like my own little girl.' He kept talking, wanting me to lean my head on his breast. He said . . . 'Here, just go ahead and cry. Don't hold back, go ahead and cry.' I did cry, for a while. I don't know. I don't know how long I sat there, trying to realize what had happened. I tried to accustom myself to the idea that Billy was dead, that I'd never, never see him again."

"You didn't doubt Mister Gannaway?"

"Not for an instant. Why should I?"

"Of course. Proceed."

By Boe's stern tone, all knew the most difficult part was coming.

"I wanted to get up. I said . . . 'Go in the other room and light the lamp.' He said . . . 'No, just lie back and rest a moment.' I insisted that he light the lamp. He said he would, provided I would lie down. So I did lie back. I heard him stirring around in the room. I didn't realize what he was doing, but he was . . . was. . . ."

"Missus Buttons," Boe said gently, "you must inform this court simply, truthfully, and directly . . . what happened?"

"He was removing his clothes. I didn't realize it. I didn't have the slightest idea, but suddenly he lay down in the bed beside me. . . ."

"Was he unclothed?"

She sat with her eyes closed, fists clenched.

"Missus Buttons! Was he nude?"

"Yes!"

"You were wearing a nightgown?"

"Yes."

"Of what nature?"

"A long, cotton flannel nightgown."

"You knew he was nude despite that garment?"

"Yes."

"Did you touch him?"

"Yes! I tried to keep him away."

"Where did you touch him?"

"The abdomen. Chest. I don't know. . . ."

"But still he might not have been *completely* nude. Nude is a definitive term. It means no clothes whatsoever."

"I touched him in other places."

"All right. What next?"

"He grabbed me. I couldn't escape. He laid on me, and his weight trapped me against the bed. It was a huge, soft bed, and I couldn't get away. I had a hard time even breathing. I struggled and struggled."

"Did he speak?"

"He kept saying he wanted to take care of me, over and over. He said he would protect me, to put my faith in him. And he kept saying . . . 'Please, please.' And . . . 'Let me love you.' "

"Proceed."

"I fought him. I clawed him. I must have, because later my

214

fingernails were torn and bloody."

"The nails of which hand were torn?"

"Both, but my right hand the more."

"During all this time, was he wrestling with you? Where were *his* hands?"

"He was pulling my nightgown up. All the time I fought him, he grasped me, lifting me, holding me against him and pulling up my nightgown."

"And how far up did he pull the nightgown?"

"I don't know. Around my waist. When he got it around my waist. . . ."

"Did you have anything else on? You were naked under the nightgown?"

"Yes."

"And when he pulled your nightgown to your waist, you were naked from the waist down?"

"Yes."

"Do you remember what his words to you were at that juncture? Did he threaten you?"

"No. He kept saying . . . 'Please!' And . . . 'Oh, God, lie still.' "

"Did you so comply?"

"No!"

"Did you submit?" cried Boe ruthlessly, ramming a finger at her. "Did you then submit to his strength and entreaties?"

"No! I got free of him as far as getting my feet to the floor."

"How could you possibly do that?" Boe cried witheringly. "You would have us believe that you, a small woman, and he . . . how much do you weigh?"

"What?"

"How much do you weigh?"

"One hundred and ten pounds."

"And he, twice that, or nearly so. Powerful, massive, impassioned . . . ?"

"It's true, anyway. I got free of him. He let me go for a moment, and I escaped from him."

"And why, if he was impassioned, as you say, would he let go of you for even a moment?"

"Because he was. . . ." She buried her face in her hands.

Boe pulled her hands away and cried: "Stop that! You must go on. You must recite these facts."

"Mister Boe!" Judge Minough reproved. "The witness should be allowed time to compose herself."

"Your Honor, we might as well get the ordeal of this telling over and done with. Missus Buttons! Finish what you were telling! Why did he let you go?"

"He had to let go of me. He had to use his hands."

"For what purpose? Were you aware of his male organ? At this time did you feel his erect muscle of Priapus striking against you?"

"Yes!"

"Was it out of control, swinging with ponderous weight, engorged with blood, its hot tip striking you? Is it not true that this you recoiled from in terror? Then freed, or half freed, while he tried to guide it on its final plunge, was it not *then* you escaped?"

"Yes!"

"You got out of bed?"

"Yes."

"You stated your feet were on the floor. Were you standing free?"

"No. He grabbed me by the nightgown. I tried to escape by slipping it over my head."

"That would have left you naked."

"I wanted to get away!"

Savagely Boe said: "Go on! Tell the rest as it happened!"

"I tried to escape by slipping the nightgown over my head. . . ."

"Yes . . . !"

"But he dragged me back."

"How?"

"By the nightgown!" she cried.

"Where was the nightgown? Was it like a garrote around your throat?"

"Yes!"

"Dragged you back to where?"

"The bed."

"Like a great, raging, lusting animal, he dragged you backward, and you fell on the bed."

"Yes."

"You were on your back on the bed? You were naked from your

216

breasts to the tips of your toes?"

"Yes."

"Proceed."

"I don't know. Everything went black. He was choking me."

"For how long did everything go black?"

"I don't know."

"When you regained consciousness, what was happening?"

"He was on top of me."

"Only that?"

"He was raping me."

"Did you then still attempt to free yourself?"

"I don't know."

"Were you helpless?"

"Yes."

"He was lying on you, his massive weight was between your parted legs?"

"Yes!" she cried.

"He also had you clutched under the small of your back?"

"Yes!"

"And with ungovernable thrusts he was accomplishing his animal design?"

"Yes."

"Then what?"

"I must have lost consciousness again. I don't remember."

"When you did regain consciousness?"

"He was lying on top of me, snoring!"

"Snoring?"

"He was lying on me making loud noises in his throat, nostrils. He was making terrible, ugly sounds. He seemed to be snoring and slobbering. It seemed loud because he was snoring and slobbering against my ear."

"He was then recovering from his bestial exertions?"

"Yes."

Boe turned away. He indicated by his manner that the worst of the ordeal was over. Clyde, who had listened in shock, looked now at Billy. Had he known? He couldn't tell. Billy was leaning forward, hands gripping his knees, but his eyes were closed. His teeth seemed to be clenched; he did not seem to be breathing.

Boe resumed: "Now, Gannaway was still mounted on you, between your legs?"

"Yes."

"You were then helpless until he chose to let you go."

"Yes. I was very weak. I wanted to die."

"When at last did he arise from your ravaged body?"

"I don't know."

"Was it on the order of five minutes? Fifteen minutes? An hour?"

"Ten minutes. A quarter of an hour. I must have fallen unconscious again. I realized he was gone."

"From the house?"

"I didn't know then, but he was only in the other room. I got up and found my nightgown."

"It was around your throat."

"No, it wasn't. He must have taken it off me. I found it tossed across a chair."

"It was dark, remember?"

"No, there was a light. It came from a lamp in the other room. Then he heard me and came in. He was cleaning some cuts on his face. He was holding a towel to his cheek."

"Which cheek?"

"His right cheek."

"When he came in, were you out of bed?"

"Yes."

"Standing?"

"Yes."

"You now had put on your nightgown?"

"I was trying to. He took it away from me. He said . . . 'You don't need this.' "

"Did you struggle with him?"

"No."

"Not to retain your nightgown?"

"No."

"Why?"

"I just couldn't. I felt ready to collapse. I had to hold to something . . . a chair . . . to keep from falling to the floor."

"Was he clothed?"

"No."

218

"He was still naked?"

"Yes."

"Then you were both naked."

"Yes."

"Proceed."

"He forced me to lie on the bed."

"Again? His lust had not yet been satisfied?"

"No."

"Did you struggle?"

"No. Oh, I don't know. I don't know what I did."

"Did he immediately mount you once more?"

"No, I don't think so. He laid on me, but he didn't . . . didn't. . . ."

"Yes." Boe turned and walked away, speaking bitterly. "He must needs now wait on his great bollix. He must now needs wait for that organ of lust to become engorged and heavy. Now, on this second occasion, would struggling, indeed, have done you any good? How did he lie on you? In what manner were you? Your back was to the bed?"

"Yes."

"Your legs were parted, and his hulking, brute form was at rest between them?"

"Yes."

"And his hands?"

"They were under my back. His hands clutched my, my. . . ."

"Your buttocks?"

"Yes."

"You were then helpless. Did he speak to you?"

"Yes. He kept talking in my ear. I can still recall the sound of his voice. It was so close. And the feel of his breath. He slobbered on my ear. The side of my head was wet with his spit. He kept licking my ear and biting it."

"You let him do all this?"

"Yes."

"Why?"

"I wanted to be dead. I prayed I would die. It was all I wanted, just to die. My whole world had come to nightmare. I felt as if I had visited hell. Yes, *hell!*" she cried. "Do I *have* to talk about it any more?"

219

"Yes, Mister Boe," said the Judge. "This little woman has. . . ."

"I am almost through, Your Honor. Did he, after holding you in this position, again obtain erection?"

"Yes."

"And how many times again before morning?"

"I don't know. When I woke, when I became conscious, it was like becoming aware after a fever. . . ."

"We understand."

"When I came awake, I was in bed alone. I got up. . . ."

"And put on your nightgown?"

"No. I had it on. I didn't remember putting it on. I thought for just a moment it was all a nightmare. I remembered him saying my husband was dead. Oh, I hoped . . . 'Let it be a terrible dream. *All* a dream.' But I was bruised. My wrists and arms were red and purplish. My lips were swollen. It wasn't a dream. I thought . . . 'Oh, why didn't I die, too?' "

"Where was Mister Gannaway?"

"He was in the kitchen. He came in and spoke to me."

"He was still unclothed?"

"No. He was dressed."

"And what was his manner?"

"He asked me to forgive him."

"He was contrite?"

"He said he had acted like a beast. I didn't answer him. I couldn't bear to talk to him, look at him. Suddenly he started to shout at me. He said . . . 'Damn it,' . . . do I have to repeat exactly?"

"You do! *Exactly!*"

"He said . . . 'Damn it, what is a man to do?' He said, 'You are the most beautiful girl I ever saw. How much can a man stand?' He said something about having a 'crazy wife.' Then he mentioned being a Catholic and divorce being impossible. 'I wouldn't be such a brute as to divorce her.' He said . . . 'I don't get any credit for that. Oh no,' he said, 'not from my own family.' He said something about his boys hating him. Then he said . . . 'I saw you, and my desire was more than any man could stand.' He said . . . 'I had hoped you would accept my help. I would do anything for you, love you like my own wife. I'd even divorce my wife, even though divorce is a sin and would send me to everlasting fire.' "

220

"He changed his mind about divorcing his wife?"

"I don't know. I'm telling you what he said."

"Did you answer him?"

"No. I asked him to go away. I begged him to leave."

"And then?"

"He left, and came back with a gun in his hand. It was the small pistol he'd made me put in the drawer."

"It was still in the drawer? Did he get it from the drawer?"

"I don't know. He got it somewhere. I *think* it was the same pistol. He handed it to me. That is, he tried to make me take it. He said . . . 'Here, go ahead and shoot.' I wouldn't touch it. I didn't want to kill him. I only wanted him to leave. I just never wanted to see him again."

"And then?"

"He put it down on the table and stepped back, pulling his shirt apart. 'Shoot, if that's what you would like. Kill me, if that is what I deserve.' "

"And you? Did you pick up that pistol?"

"No."

"What were your feelings at that moment?"

"I don't know. I just wanted him to leave."

"But didn't you hate and loathe him? Didn't you wish him dead?"

"I didn't care. I didn't care whether he lived or died. He was part of a terrible dream."

"After he offered his breast to you for vengeance . . . ?"

"He begged me to sit with him and have coffee. He said he wanted to make amends. He said he wanted me to be his little girl-wife."

"He used that term?"

"Yes."

"Did you join him in coffee?"

"No. I went in the bedroom and closed the door."

"And bolted it?"

"There was no bolt on the door."

"And there . . . ?"

"I lay down and cried. I cried and cried."

"For what reason? I mean, because you had been violated or because of your husband?"

221

"Oh, *everything*. All my hope had gone. I just wanted to die."

"But finally you arose and faced the realities?"

"Yes. He came in and talked to me. He stood in the door, and stood in the door, and finally he said he had to leave, but that he would come back. He kept asking me to forgive him. He said all his life would have that single purpose, to so act that I would forgive him. And finally he left."

"Did you see him ride . . . or drive away?"

"No. When I got up at about mid-morning, I was alone."

"Aside from the Chinese."

"Yes."

"Where was this well-trained, non-snooping celestial?"

"At his house. He stayed there."

"Inside his house?"

"I guess so."

"Was that unusual? I mean, although he might not come on orders, except to the bell, he had some ducks and chickens . . . he cared for them . . . he worked in his vegetable garden?"

"Yes."

"But on this morning, he did not show himself?"

"No."

Wardrope, long dissatisfied with the tactics, stirred himself. "It would be interesting at this point, Your Honor, to examine who is testifying at this time? Is it the witness, or Mister Boe? I am reminded that attorney for defense has repeatedly raised objections on this point himself, and I am surprised he usurps such liberties when so strict in his demands on others. This a most alert witness, one commanding the language in a way which would seem to preclude all this prompting, supplemental or definitive words, and yet we hear long, dissertative interpolations by Mister Boe requiring only a verifying yes or no."

While Wardrope spoke at some length, the judge's attention was diverted. Ike Thrift, the range detective who had been badged as a temporary deputy, came in the rear door to whisper something to the sheriff, who in turn relayed the information to the judge. The judge, leaning far over, heard him and looked back toward the door, now closed. Indicating yes, yes, and yes again, he resumed his seat. By then Wardrope had finished.

"Oh," he said. "Yes. Quite valid. Allow the witness her own expression. Proceed."

Again people bent forward for the testimony, but Clyde wanted to know who had come in the back door. He suspected some trick and kept his eyes open. He sat as high as he was able, senses alert. This time Thrift had left the door, carefully, one-quarter open. Then he caught a scent of perfume, and he knew. It was Mrs. Morrison, the new wife. At first he thought of Mrs. Morrison and her daughters, but the perfume was cloyed with other smells. Mrs. Elrod Smith and Mrs. Dr. Adams came to mind, women from the High Point section of town. Word had reached them, and they'd rushed over, to revel in the dirt, enjoy a poor woman's shame. It was low and despicable. Yet he had always heard that those high-toned women were the very worst kind. Billy had said so. He wondered if the major knew they were there. He looked over at him, and *he* was looking at Clyde! His eyes were boring right into him! He knew they were there, and he knew that Clyde knew it also. The major looked at him for one terrible instant, and then without really moving his eyes he looked on and beyond, through him and over him, as if he were an inanimate object.

"About what time was this?"

"About ten."

"You remained alone until . . . ?"

"Until it was night. I sat by myself until long after dark. It must have been midnight. I didn't know what to do."

"Did you eat? Did the Chinaman finally show himself?"

"I couldn't eat anything. I saw him sometimes peeping through the hedge. He didn't come in. I couldn't swallow a bite. I was shocked, in a dream. I couldn't think."

"Very well. With Mister Wardrope's sufferance, let me set the scene. You were sitting there, at midnight . . . ?"

"I had decided to go to bed."

"Unclothed?"

"No. I had my shoes off. The light was on. Then I heard someone."

"Who did you think it was? Did you assume it to be . . . ?"

"I don't know. I just . . . don't know. I got up. Someone came in."

"The doors were unlocked?"

"Yes. It just didn't occur to me . . . I don't know. . . ."

"Yes, you heard someone and you got up?"

"I went to the bedroom door. I could see across the big main room to the kitchen. I could see the kitchen floor. It opened, and Billy came in."

"Your husband?"

"Yes. He came in. I couldn't believe it. I thought it was a dream. This will sound . . . crazy. I looked at the bed, actually expecting, fearing. . . ."

"That you would be lying there?"

"Yes."

"That you were dead also?"

"Yes."

"I'm sure such dismembered thoughts have come to many of us at times of great anguish, of shock, of desolation. And then . . . ?"

"I must have lost control of my senses, because he kept saying . . . 'Don't cry!' 'I'm all right,' he kept saying. Finally he carried me to a chair and held me in his lap, and I got control of myself."

"And what had happened? What had delayed him?"

"He said they'd tried to kill him."

"Who'd tried to kill him?"

"He didn't know. He had been riding along . . . this is what I gathered . . . riding to keep an appointment. . . ."

"With whom?"

"With someone from the Omaha. With someone . . . it had been arranged by Gannaway. I couldn't get it sorted out. I was too upset. Anyway, someone had shot at him, and he'd been forced to get behind some rocks. He mentioned some rocks, and again an old dry wash. He lost his horse. He said he didn't dare move until dark because they were waiting."

"Who was waiting?"

"*They* . . . the men. He never identified them. He said . . . 'They thought they killed me, but they didn't have the nerve to come and make sure. Then night came, and he began on foot."

"Where did this take place?"

"He said it was at Big Alkali. The place didn't mean anything to me. It could have been north, south, east, or west."

"I'm sure it means something to the residents present. Did he start back to the lodge?"

"He said he walked all night."

"By his description, what would you say his would-be killers were doing at this time?"

"This is pure speculation," interjected Wardrope. "It is this witness' speculation concerning someone else's speculation."

"Your Honor," said Boe, "I was attempting to show the logic of events. If Gannaway had arranged the ambush, as his assumption of Billy's death would indicate, then the testimony as to when the news would reach him, and when he would respond, in this instance by visiting the lodge, bearing the tidings to Missus Buttons, gaining entrance by stealthy means, offering sympathy and protection, and then either by design or passionate impulse forcibly and lasciviously fondle, strip, and rape the witness *is* germane."

"You may question the witness as to any direct statements made to her by the defendant," the judge ruled. "Any correlations should wait for your summation."

"Missus Buttons, relying on the information your husband offered as to his whereabouts the previous night, where was he at that moment when John J. Gannaway, after having choked you to unconsciousness with your nightgown, was mounted on you in the act of forceful copulation?"

"At *that* moment?"

"Yes, where was he at that time, as nearly as you can ascertain?"

"He was walking. He walked all night. He told me where he went, but the places were all strange to me. He retrieved his horse at a small ranch, then he came home."

"Home?"

"To the lodge."

"In this time your attacker raped you at least twice more, then got up, dressed, asked for forgiveness, offered a pistol and his breast for vengeance, and finally rode away, and was gone the entire day? You were then alone, at night, and your husband entered? The time was . . . ?"

"I don't know. It was past midnight."

"Did you tell your husband what had happened to you?"

"Yes. But. . . ."

"But what, Missus Buttons?"

"Not right away! I couldn't bring myself to . . . I was so glad to see him alive."

"When did you tell him?"

"Next morning."

"As a matter of fact, you even then did not tell him of your own free inspiration? I mean, didn't he first make a discovery?"

"He saw blood on the sheets. They weren't sheets, but what are called sheet blankets."

"We know what they are. Thin, cotton flannel, gray blankets."

"Yes."

"And whose blood was this?"

"I don't know. I hadn't noticed it before."

"You could have told him you had a nosebleed, or it was your functional time of the month? Did not such an excuse occur to you?"

"No. I didn't want to lie. I knew I had to tell him. I knew he was still in danger. He didn't know who tried to kill him. *But I did!* I mean, who had sent them . . . and why. It had been John Gannaway. He had told me Billy was dead. He thought he *was* dead. He thought he was telling me the truth. I'm certain of that. The truth had to come out!"

"You may have a moment to compose yourself, Missus Buttons," said Judge Minough.

"So I told him everything! I showed him how my nightgown had been torn."

"And what was his response?"

"He couldn't believe me. He said Gannaway wouldn't do such a thing. He said I'd had a nightmare and imagined it. He said . . . 'I could tell you were feverish last night.' He said I had been sick and out of my mind. I swore it had happened. Then I wept and fell on the bed, and he kept trying to calm me down. 'Get your wits about you,' he kept saying. He tried to make me drink some whiskey. I wouldn't. I couldn't. Then I remembered about the gun. I told him about . . . I told him where Gannaway had been standing when he said to shoot him. But he wouldn't believe it. He said I was victim of hysteria."

"Did he mean the term *hysteria?*"

"Yes."

226

"Do you know whether he meant it in the medical sense, or the common?"

"I don't know."

"Hysteria is a diagnostic complaint of women. It reveals itself in fits, convulsions, anesthesia, visions, delusions. This was his meaning when he used the word? And not, as it frequently meant, uncontrolled laughter?"

"Yes."

"When he saw the pistol . . . ?"

"The pistol wasn't there. I had to hunt for it. It was in the locked case."

"Did you have the key?"

"No."

"Then how did you get it?"

"I didn't. I showed it to him."

"Did you finally convince your husband of the terrible facts?"

"I asked him how, if Gannaway hadn't been here, and he'd been decent and noble like he thought, how had he known, or thought he knew, that Billy'd been shot?"

"So then he *did* believe you?"

"Yes, he had to."

"If you had told him the night before, at the time he walked in, if you had then thrown yourself on the floor in front of him with word that his friend had violated you, then do you think he would more readily have believed you?"

"I don't know. Yes. Yes, I suppose so."

"We are very nearly at the end of your ordeal, Missus Buttons. I will be very brief. Did you remain long at the lodge next day?"

"No, we left in the rig. He drove all day."

"In what direction?"

"As we had come . . . but more southerly. Billy said we could keep going and get to the Three Forks. Finally we stopped at a ranch. They were friends. He left me with Missus Perch and her children. Sarah Perch. They called it Rocky Ford post office. He said it was on the old stage road."

"*Left* you there?"

"Yes. I didn't want to go back. He said he had to go back."

"Had to? For what stated reason?"

227

"He said he wanted to get at the truth of everything."

"Was he more specific?"

"I begged him not to do anything . . . not to . . . shoot anyone. He promised me. He said . . . 'If nobody shoots at me, I won't shoot at them.' That was his promise. He held both of my hands and promised it. I believed him. I knew he would keep his word."

"Did he mention Gannaway?"

"Not by name. He said . . . 'Either he'll leave the country, or we'll leave it. It won't be big enough for the two of us!' "

"Yes." Boe spun and leveled a finger. "He said . . . 'The country won't be big enough for the two of us'?"

"Yes."

"Then didn't he thus indicate he intended, if thwarted, to *kill* Mister Gannaway?"

"No!"

"But one of them would have to go. Either Gannaway would be gone, or he would be gone? There is no other interpretation. Did he indicate he would leave the country if Gannaway refused?"

"Yes."

"He would take you away?"

"Yes."

"Where?"

"He mentioned Washington state. He talked about Coeur d'Alene. Then he talked about Alaska. He said Alaska was a good country, still wild and unspoiled. He asked if I would be willing to suffer such frontier hardship. I told him I would. I'd go anywhere with him."

"Leave his ranching interests . . . everything?"

"Yes. Unless Mister Gannaway left."

"Unless *Gannaway* left?" Boe asked incredulously.

"Yes."

"Do you mean to sit there and tell this court, Missus Buttons, that he actually thought Gannaway would leave this country, his business and his property, at anything like a request, or a moral demand? . . . and that he convinced you of that possibility?"

"If you had been guilty of such an act, wouldn't *you?* What man wouldn't who had a spark of *decency?*"

"But Gannaway refused. He refused, and Billy shot him down."

"No! He didn't!"

228

"Whether he did or not, is what this jury is going to decide. When did he next see you at this Rocky Ford post office? . . . at this Perch Ranch? What date?"

"It was the fourteenth."

"Three days after he shot Gannaway!"

"Yes." She realized what she had said and cried: "No! He didn't shoot Gannaway."

"You lied to me, and he lied to me. All this is a tissue of lies. You came to me with this tale of rape in the hopes you could save your husband from the gallows."

He said it! He said Billy had lied to him! Oh, God, thought Clyde, *his lawyer has turned against him!*

"I didn't! I didn't come to you with a lie!" she cried.

"You lied to me then, and you lied to me today. Now, I want the truth."

"I've told you the truth!"

"He *murdered* John Gannaway!" Boe thundered, rapping his cane on table. "Murder! Murder!"

"No! He didn't! John Gannaway asked him to kill him."

"*Asked* him?" cried Boe derisively.

"Yes, asked him! He bared his chest to Billy and said shoot, just as he had said it to me."

"This was far different! This was between men. This is man to man, men of the West. One does not ask another to shoot him, a man whose wife he has violated!"

"I'm just telling you what he said. He said Gannaway denied everything. He said . . . 'If you doubt me, draw your pistol and shoot.' But Billy called him a yellow dog. He said he was vile and low. He said there was nothing on earth lower than a man who would do what he had done, and then look his friend in the eye and lie afterward. He said he wanted him to know that *he* knew him for what he was. Then he told him to leave the country and never come back, to have that much decency, and he turned and rode off. My husband turned and rode off! Gannaway called to him once, but he didn't turn, and then he heard the report of a gun. He turned and saw Mister Gannaway fall off his horse."

"Did he then go back?"

"No."

"Not even to see whether the man was dead?"

"No."

"Didn't you regard this as callous and cruel?"

"I think shooting himself was the only decent thing left for Mister Gannaway to do!" she said with her head high.

"Did your husband suspect he would be accused of murder?"

"I mentioned it. I said . . . 'They'll accuse *you*.' But he said . . . 'No, there were three witnesses on the bluff, and maybe a fourth.'"

"Maybe a fourth?"

"Yes."

"Did he say who the fourth could possibly be?"

"He'd seen someone in a buggy."

"As a matter of fact, there were five and perhaps six witnesses?" She looked blank.

"Didn't he mention Mister Carter and Mister LaGrange?"

"No. Not as witnesses."

Boe's tone and manner had changed. Apparently he believed her, after all. "How long did you stay on at Rocky Ford?"

"We left next day. He didn't want to go back to the scene . . . or to Arlington, or the home ranch. He said he wanted Gannaway to be buried and forgotten. That was how he said it. The whole thing had shocked him terribly, although he tried to pretend that it hadn't. We left and drove to Three Forks. He made arrangements to have the rig sent back to Camas Creek. Then we rode by train to Butte and got a room at the Montana Hotel. That's where he found out for the first time that Mister Gannaway was really dead, and that he was being accused of murder."

"By what means did he learn it?"

"He read it in a newspaper."

"What was his first reaction? To hide? To run? To avoid the law?"

"No. The account was so ridiculous. It was so far different from what happened, he hardly credited it at all. He said the editor must have made it up."

"He had signed his name on the hotel register? Buttons is not a common name. It would surely be recognized?" She did not answer. "Surely he must have felt in some jeopardy?"

"No. We were there two days. Finally he decided I should go back to Wyoming. Actually I went to Denver."

"*You* went . . . not your husband?"

"He sent me away. He said he wanted to see what substance there was to the allegations."

"Did he use those words?"

"No. Words to that effect. He said it must be a mistake. He didn't believe he would actually be charged."

"Then he did not yet know of the so-called coroner-grand jury findings?"

"I don't know."

"When did you hear from him?"

"I telegraphed when I arrived, and he telegraphed in return."

"Where did you address your telegram?"

"To Helena."

"Did he then, or ever, ask you to return and give testimony?"

"No."

"Was it your idea to return?"

"No. It was yours."

"Had your husband, previous to your arrival here, told anyone of your rape by Mister Gannaway?"

"No. I'm certain . . . no."

"You volunteered the information yourself?"

"Yes."

"To whom?"

"To you."

"To Mister Buttons's attorney. Please refer to me in that manner."

"To Mister Buttons's attorney."

"Where?"

"In your . . . in the offices of Hubbard and Boe, Helena."

"How did you happen to visit these law offices?"

"I was summoned by letter."

"What name was signed to the letter?"

"Thomas F. Boe, Attorney-at-Law."

"Had this attorney any previous factual knowledge of that carnal night in Ivanhoe Lodge? Did he know you had been raped?"

"I don't know. No. He suspected much had been untold."

"Had Mister Buttons informed him?"

"No."

"What did the attorney tell you in his letter?"

231

"That Mister Buttons was to stand trial, and he wanted me at my husband's side."

"You have recounted these terrible experiences how many times?"

"Three . . . no, four times."

"Four?"

"To my husband, to you, to your law partner . . . I mean to Mister Hubbard, and here."

"Why twice to attorneys?"

"Mister Buttons' attorney wanted to be positive that my account was true in every particular."

"What did your husband tell you before you left for Wyoming and Colorado anent this matter? This terrible experience?"

"He said he would rather be hanged by the neck by a Company sheriff than subject me to such shame on the witness stand."

"But you broke your word? Is your word not to be trusted?"

"No, it is!"

"You, indeed, told and retold of this experience?"

"I never promised. I didn't give my word. I knew, if he was accused, all the truth would have to come out."

"Your witness."

232

CHAPTER SEVENTEEN

"Missus Buttons." The tone of the assistant U. S. attorney was kind, but stern. There was no doubt at all he intended to call this young woman to account, however much it pained him to do so. "You stated that you took teachers' training and then left for employment in the West. How old were you?"

"I taught school one year. I was nineteen when I left for Omaha."

"Yet you left alone?"

"Yes."

"And after some time in Omaha, you traveled on to Denver . . . again alone?"

"Yes."

"Wasn't that a bit unusual . . . a young woman, scarcely more than a girl . . . single, traveling across the land . . . alone?"

"I had relatives in. . . ."

"Objection!" said Boe. "This is a statistical matter having to do with the traveling habits of the public."

"I withdraw the question," Wardrope amended, "and ask this woman whether people were surprised when they met a girl of her tender years, and innocence, taking off all by herself, unchaperoned, by public conveyance?"

"Objection! Attorney's use of such terms as *tender years* and *innocence* and his entire manner and inflection have no purpose than to degrade the witness, imply she was an adventuress, a nineteen-year-old spy of the Confederacy, a Madame Mustache on her way to deal faro under the layered cigar smoke of the gaming dens of Denver, lurid city of sin on Cherry Creek."

There was laughter met by the judge's gavel.

Angry, Wardrope spun toward Boe and cried: "Very well, it is not I who first used the pejorative *adventuress*. I call this court to note it was the defense who chose that term." He breathed indignation and faced the witness with newly fortified determination. "Missus Buttons, traveling across the West alone and unaccompanied, were you ever accosted by strange men?"

"Yes."

"Did these men sometimes sit with you?"

"Yes."

"Did they ask you to dine with them?"

"Yes."

"Did you on occasion accept?"

"Yes."

"And soon they were no longer strangers?"

She indicated that she did not know how to answer.

"Restate the question," suggested Judge Minough.

"How long, on average, would you say it took you to get acquainted with these men?"

"I don't know. . . ."

"Well, was it ten minutes, an hour, an evening?"

"A girl does not get acquainted with strangers in the way your question would imply."

The defense and prosecution wrangled over the meaning and pejorative nature of *get acquainted*, and Wardrope burst forth to face the witness: "You did, though, meet men on trains and accept their favors?"

"I dined with one man. The conductor said he was a man of good character. The conductor was an old family friend. My uncle worked for the railroad and. . . ."

"Missus Buttons in those years while on your own, a thousand miles from parental supervision, in those towns along the Union Pacific and Rock Island railways, how many times would you say you were sequestered in private quarters with men? Quick, now! Just a guess."

"Well . . . never."

"Never?"

"Unless you mean behind the curtains and potted plants of restaurant booths."

"And at night in carriages?"

"Yes."

234

"Yes, how many times?"

"I don't know. . . ."

"Five or six? Ten? Twenty? A hundred?"

"Five or six."

"Did these men ever hold your hand?"

"Yes."

"Did one ever touch the skin of your arm?"

"Yes."

"Did these men ever drop a glove, and, fumbling for it, touch your ankle? Did one ever run his hand up your leg? Speak fairly! You are under oath. Did any of these men run his hand up the inside of your leg? . . . and did you struggle and scream for help? Did you scream, Missus Buttons?"

"No."

"No, you did not scream, and why not?"

"It didn't happen."

"None of it happened? You admitted to having been alone in carriages with men. What you are really saying is that it didn't happen in that exact manner." He spoke, walking away, then he turned suddenly and said: "You first met John Gannaway in Council Bluffs, didn't you? Will you give us the details of that first accidental meeting?"

She was surprised and sat staring at him. For just a moment she seemed on the point of recollecting such a meeting, and her eyes sought out Boe. Wardrope quickly placed himself between them.

"No!" he said. "Answer by yourself. Just tell us the facts. Isn't it true that you met him? . . . he wanted to know about his wife? . . . you were alone together?"

"I'd heard of him from Missus Gannaway. . . ."

"And you met him?"

"Yes."

"Where, under what circumstances?" cried Wardrope triumphantly.

"I already told you. I met him in Helena."

"You have just said you met him in Council Bluffs and were alone there together?"

"No," she said, troubled, "you asked if I had met Mister

Gannaway and was alone with him, and I said yes. I meant in Helena. . . ."

"This was sequel to my question if you had not in matter of truth met him long before in Council Bluffs and were alone in his company there?"

"Oh. No, I recognized the name on the hotel book in Alhambra and met him in Helena."

"You have changed your mind?"

"No!"

Like a fighter, boring in for the championship, shaking off blows, he waged on: "If you want it in Helena, very well, have it in Helena . . . you at last found yourself alone with John Gannaway. Knee to knee and face to face, the Gannaway who had so long piqued your fancy! Yes, you finally sequestered with him in that Chinese restaurant with its exotic smells and foods, its strange and heady Oriental wines. And what happened then, Missus Buttons? Did he then not ask of his wife, and for your assurance and comfort? And when he laid his hand on yours, did you not feel a bond between you? Looking back now, did he not need you, and did you not respond to that need? Did you not feel a flush of power and satisfaction that you, a woman, had such influence over John Gannaway, big John Gannaway? Did you not secretly revel in the knowledge that you, a woman, held him in thrall as your husband never could? Looking back now, won't you admit that you encouraged that man to follow you, encouraged that lonely man to believe that an even greater comfort could be secured in the warm and lascivious luxury of your bed?"

She stared at him, shaking her head in a shocked manner.

"Missus Buttons, when you were left alone in that private booth, and he took your hand, how did you let him know his touch was repellent to you?"

"I took my hand away, and. . . ."

"Did you cry out? Call a waiter? Ask the screens be removed?"

"No, I. . . ."

"In fact, you didn't do anything to truly discourage him. Then you met him again, according to your testimony. Was he to suppose his feeling was unrequited? And when you came to this county, where did you go? To the Buttons' ranch? . . . to the so-called Spider or

236

any of the other ranches your husband has interests in? Did you? Answer, will you?"

"No."

"But you went to the lodge . . . Ivanhoe Lodge . . . heroic name, emblem of romance. You went there, that secluded nest of luxury, fortress of pleasure? When you went there, was he to suppose his attentions would be ill received? In fact, you, by your every act, encouraged him?"

"No, I did not."

"This jury will be judge of that! Missus Buttons, why did you leave the door open that night?"

"I locked both doors. The outside doors. Everything was locked."

"How are we to think he got in? Did he simply pass like a spirit through the walls?"

"I don't know how he got in. There was some way he knew about."

"Now, come now! Think back. Did you not that night leave a door open for your husband?"

"No."

"How did you think he would get in?"

"Knock."

"I believe John Gannaway walked through a door left unbolted! Then you would have us to believe he prefixed his seduction with news that your husband was dead?"

"Objection. Witness testified rape, not seduction."

"Doesn't the news of a husband's death seem to you a preposterous prelude to lovemaking?" Wardrope demanded.

She did not answer.

"You testified he strangled you with your nightgown?"

"Yes."

"And when you regained consciousness, the act was being performed?"

"Yes."

"But after that, there was no need in further struggling, so you allowed the act to be performed again and again?"

"I wanted to die. I just prayed to be dead."

"Missus Buttons, when were you married?"

"I. . . ." She seemed at a loss.

237

"All women know the date of their weddings."

"I already said when it was."

"Say it again. Have you forgotten already? No, don't look at your lawyer . . . look at me."

"May second, this spring."

"Do you have any proof of that marriage?"

Boe asked: "Does Missus Wardrope carry proof of *her* marriage around with her?"

"Missus Wardrope is not testifying at a murder trial! Your Honor, I object to this sniping."

"Yes, Mister Boe. Please express any objections in the proper manner. However, when you say *proof,* Mister Wardrope, do you mean documentary exhibit? . . . and on that score, are married couples to be in personal possession of such proof? . . . the lack of which is to be considered evidence of concubinage? Out here in the territories many marriages are performed without a scrap of documentation . . . perfectly legal. At all events, the burden of proof of concubinage would rest with the accuser."

"Your Honor, concubinage has nothing to do with this. According to this witness, she has been Billy Buttons's wife for half a year, and yet no breath or hint of it was ever heard. Now, as witness was obviously in contact with attorney, is it not reasonable to expect that documentary proof be ready at hand?"

"You should have approached the bench with this. Yes, Mister Boe? We'll let the jury hear you, too."

"I would point out we supplied documentary proof in the form of a deposition from the hotel manager in Helena. They there lived as man and wife. This has been found by our courts to be good and sufficient proof of the married state. The matter came up in Judge Garryman's court in Butte only this past winter. Is the prosecution suggesting that this marriage was part of a complex plot? . . . laid out so far in advance? If he has such information, I wonder why it was not part of his case against the accused?"

"It is quite obvious why it was not part of the case!" cried Wardrope in anger. "It was because this witness, this woman, Missus Buttons . . . if, indeed, so she proves to be . . . was smuggled in under a subterfuge . . . yes, sir, I repeat a duplicitous subterfuge. . . ."

"Well, those are the worst kind," remarked Boe.

"In spite of your snideries, yes, the worst, most contemptible kind ... knowing full well that this trial must hew to a rigid time schedule, leaving not even a single day to investigate. Oh, it was clever! Missus William T. Buttons? It was a ruse! And every person in this room recognizes it as a ruse. It was the ruse of a defense, grasping at straws when confronted with a case which on plain evidence was hopeless." He turned and addressed the witness. "Your husband's attorney has seen fit to deride any idea that your marriage, or purported marriage, could be part of a complex plot laid far in advance. Seeing he has chosen to introduce this matter, let us pursue it. You testified that you were already acquainted with Missus Gannaway. Subsequently you traveled to Denver, Colorado, where you chanced to meet Billy Buttons. In your conversations with Billy, the name Gannaway`... ?"

"Your Honor, I ask that the prosecution be courteous enough to refer to the defendant as Mister Buttons, or as the defendant, not by the patronym, Billy."

Judge Minough said: "I hardly believe patronym is the correct word. Patronym derives from the Latin *patronymicus,* of or pertaining to the father, not, as you apparently intend, patronizing, showing condescension."

"The defense defers to the bench's preëminence in the Latin syntax, praxis, and perspicuity."

"The term *praxis* is hardly applicable to a single term, but nonetheless the bench is flattered by attorney's tribute." All around the room people looked at one another, agreeing that the judge truly outclassed them all, and Minough smiled benignly. "But *praxis* and *syntaxis* aside, Mister Wardrope, will you amend?"

"The witness herself has referred to the defendant time and again as Billy. Prosecution had no desire to demean, or patronize. Missus Buttons, in your early conversations with *Mister* Buttons, the defendant, the name Gannaway was mentioned, is this not true?"

She protested: "No!" and said, "No," again, but Wardrope forged on.

"Hence, when he mentioned that name, John Gannaway, did it not then clang in your recollections like a brazen bell? Did you not then recall having met his wife? Now, whose idea was it that this chance acquaintance of yours might be put to good account? Was it Mister Buttons's? Did he suggest you accompany him to Montana,

239

knowing well that Mister Gannaway, a victim of rheumatism, frequented the Alhambra spa for the hot sulphur baths every spring? And failing to meet him there, was it, indeed, mere chance that sent you to the territorial capital a short twenty miles distant?"

"We were going to Yellowstone Park. It was not yet open. We then started for Helena and stopped off at the hot springs. . . ."

"How better insinuate yourself than through an acquaintance with his afflicted wife? What better entry into a lonely man's confidence? An ardent man, yes! . . . a man long denied the comforts of the connubial bed. You knew that, didn't you? You knew that and William T. Buttons knew it! Was it your plan, Missus Buttons? Or was it Mister Buttons's plan? . . . to use Mister Gannaway's loneliness and his affection as a thrall to draw him into a compromising situation? Was he to make advances to you in the Chinese restaurant? Was that why Mister Buttons so conveniently was called away, leaving you alone? And was then the husband to discover you in that public place and hold over your victim the threat of blackmail? Did it fail? And then was the scene moved to Ivanhoe Lodge? Was it timed for your husband to burst in on you at the concupiscent moment with witnesses at his beck and call, if not actually at his side? Was that *the* plan? Yes, in bald language what the city people call the badger game! . . . wasn't that . . . ?"

"Here it is!" she cried.

He stopped. The witness, who had for some time been hunting through a large, flat, needlepoint bag, had found a paper which she held up. "I think this is what you wanted."

"Answer the question!" shouted Wardrope.

"Just a moment," said Judge Minough. "What do you have to show the court?" It was a stiff paper, about six inches by eight, folded across the middle. He took it. "Oh, yes! Indeed. This is a certification of marriage performed. *'In sanctum matrimonium.'* 'William Tyler Buttons.' 'Mary Margaret Carmody.' Imprint of the Cross of Malta. Or is this the Cross *Fleury?* Signed . . . 'Thomas V. Power, S. J.' So, you were married by a Jesuit father." He seemed very pleased. "Penmanship! All but a lost art! Calligraphy! Deserving of the word. Would you observe this fine example of the secretary's hand! Who, indeed, inscribes like the Irish? *In sanctum matrimonium,*" — relishing the Latin words, he continued on his own — "*momento etiam*

240

domine famularumque tuarum. Ah yes, the Roman tongue . . . its rolling magnificence . . . dead language, indeed! Alive. Immortal. *Semper vivat!* Mister Boe, do you offer this marriage certificate . . . *certificatum in sanctum matrimonium* . . . from the hand of the witness in evidence?"

"I want it back," she said, "eventually."

"Of course, and I'm sure it can be arranged," assured the judge. "The attorneys and jury can view it, and a copy inscribed by the clerk. Do you have any objections, Mister Wardrope?"

Wardrope, with a tight rein on his temper, examined it at some length. Clearing a hoarseness from his voice, he finally commented: "There is no way the validity of this paper can be determined without reference to the church records."

"Church records, indeed," said the judge. "This is a Jesuit . . . the Society of Jesus. The Jesuits are soldiers of Christ. These men merely tighten their cinctures and go to the ends of the earth. Their cathedral is the starry firmament, and their churchly pews the logs of the forest. In Wyoming the Jesuits have missionary status, unless I am mistaken, and, unless I am further mistaken, this church . . . I see the certificate specifies no town, only Uintah County, W. T. . . . wherein the priest, the book, and the Eucharist may be. We are not back in Ohio now, Mister Prosecutor! This is still the Wild West, and unless my memory fails, Uintah County still the untamed land . . . land of the winds, and of the untamed Arapaho."

"Exception."

The judge looked at him for a second as if applying it to the land of the Arapaho. "Oh, yes. Exception to admitting document as evidence is noted."

"I don't object to admitting the document, I object to any and all attribution as to its validity. Whether it is, or whether it is not, genuine. We should hold such ascription interpel. I do not object to its being entered as exhibit, provided its certitude be held *onus probandi.*"

"*Onus probandi* nothing! If disproved, the weight must fall on the opposition. Ever since I commenced the practice of law in this territory, certifications of the Catholic church have been accepted on a level not exceeded by those bearing the seal of public office. If there is something about this which substances the attribution of

241

forgery, the court would like to hear it."

"All I maintain is that the coincidence of all this is too neat, too pat, and I say it smells to high heaven. Why, even the manner by which that paper was produced, the pretense of frantic search. . . ."

Boe interrupted: "I object to this untempered attack on the witness. If the prosecution has any evidence of forgery, let it be brought out in a regular and, if possible, a gentlemanly manner."

Wardrope finally lost his temper. He had simulated a towering outrage on several occasions during the trial, but this was the real thing. He turned pale and was caught in a fit of trembling. Losing the power of speech, he jabbed a finger in Boe's direction once, twice, three times, but *bang!* fell the gavel, and Judge Minough said: "I really think we've come to a point where we should recess, if only for a few minutes. Mister Wardrope . . . ?"

"Your Honor, I deeply resent. . . ." But he stopped for the right terms.

"Yes. Well, we've all grown hot and tired. It is now almost three o'clock. We have been here continually since almost seven this morning. I had hoped we might recess and come back for the final arguments. We seem to have reached some brink of endurance. Gentlemen, gentlemen . . . our tempers are all frayed. Are you nearly finished with the witness?"

"I am finished with that witness, Your Honor," said Wardrope scathingly.

"Do you have anything on redirect?"

Boe looked at the young woman and said: "You *are* really his wife, aren't you?"

"Yes."

"No further questions."

"We stand in recess until four P.M." Minough stood, as did everyone, relieved to get off the hot chairs. "At which time we will drive straight through to a conclusion. This case will be given to the jury before we again leave tonight."

"Oh, dear, dear!" said Ma. "It was awful. We'll never be able to hold our heads up in this country again."

But Clyde came right back at her: "It was no disgrace on us! It was a disgrace on *them*."

"Keep quiet. You're not old enough to know about such matters.

Oh, dear. Oh, dear, dear, dear! It was filthy. Dirty, dirty . . . and everybody listening. They should have cleared the courtroom."

"Ma, let's go. People can hear you."

"What if they can? You watch your manners!" But she lowered her voice. "Why would he go and marry without even telling his own mother?"

"He was going to tell you."

"A Catholic! Why would he get himself mixed up with a Roman Catholic?"

Ye gods, thought Clyde, *what was the difference?* But Ma was an old-fashioned, complete-immersion Baptist. One time — it was a long time ago — when Billy was about seventeen, they all had taken the steamboat to Fort Benton for the revival, conducted by a Baptist minister, a famous speaker who had been all over the world. The meetings had been held for three days, afternoon and night, in a tent, and they all had gone the first afternoon, but somewhere along the line Billy had slipped out. What he had done had been to crawl out under the tent on his hands and knees. Pa had been mad enough to horsewhip him. He had said it was no way to treat his mother, the woman who had gone down on the mattress and suffered to give him birth! But Pa had found excuses not to go again himself. Ma had taken Clyde, however, and on the final afternoon, when all the converts had been taken out to the river, he had been with them. He had on a long white dress and stood up to his hindend in water. He could still remember how the dress drifted up, floating, and the river tickled his naked backside, wobbling his testicles around, and he was enjoying it, not realizing what was taking place, when the preacher had grabbed him from behind and dipped him right under the water. "You're saved!" Ma had cried, weeping for joy and holding his face against her, when he got to the bank, still coughing and blowing that muddy Missouri River water. "No matter what happens, you are saved in the blessed blood of Jesus Christ because you've been washed in the waters of Jordan." But the one she really had wanted baptized was Billy. She'd hoped and prayed he'd be saved. If he'd just be immersed, it would make all the difference. She had tried every way she could to get him to do it. She had come around to the subject a dozen times, but he had just laughed and made jokes, and, when Clyde was baptized, he wouldn't even come to watch.

He'd promised to, and Ma had dreamed that maybe at the last minute he would go ahead and *do* it! He'd just cast Philistinism to the winds and say: "All right, I'm game for anything." Because he really was drawn toward it. His impiety was only a pose. "He'll be here!" she had said to Pa. "I just know it." But Pa had been so sure. "Don't get your hopes up," he had said. And, of course, he had been right. Billy had taken up with a lot of cheapjacks and gamblers, fellows like Speedy Wallinder and Tom Allen from the horse auction, and on the very day of the baptisms he had left with them for Helena where they were going to race a half-cold, blooded mare named Sily Main in the free-for-all stakes. "Don't worry about him," Pa had told her. "He'll get his gut filled with that bunch and learn a lesson." But Ma had from that moment started giving up on Billy, and more and more fastened her hopes on Clyde. "Surely the Lord will let me save *one*," she had said. "One out of twelve isn't asking too much, do you think?" It was about that time she'd set her heart on his being a doctor.

CHAPTER EIGHTEEN

"The defense calls William T. Buttons," said Thomas F. Boe.

Bunting administered the oath.

"I do," said Billy, raising his right hand.

Boe began: "You are William T. 'Billy' Buttons?"

"Yes."

"Born at Salmon City, Idaho, Eighteen Sixty-Two?"

"No, at Leesburg, near Salmon City."

"Very well, Leesburg, Idaho Territory, Eighteen Sixty-Two . . . carried thence by covered wagon over the Big Hole Pass to Beaverhead, Montana Territory that same year, a babe in arms . . . residence at Rattlesnake, otherwise known as Argenta City, Eighteen Sixty-Two and Eighteen Sixty-Three and thence to the Deer Lodge Valley, Eighteen Sixty-Four . . . the Smith River via Diamond City, that being your home until Eighteen Seventy-Two when you came to the Willow and Arrow Creek ranges which has since been your home?"

"Yes."

Billy was very attentive, straight and alert, listening to every word to make sure it was exactly correct. For just a moment his eyes rested on Ma, but he never let his eyes stray to rest on any other person. He was particularly careful not to look at the jury.

"You are the husband of Missus Buttons, just preceding you to the witness chair, *née* Mary Margaret Carmody?"

"I am."

"You did not have to take the witness stand . . . you could not have been required to testify . . . you understand that?"

"Yes."

"You willingly did so, just as you willingly surrendered to this court, although no particular effort was made to bring you in although openly residing in southwestern Montana Territory . . . ?"

"I object. The details of Mister Buttons's incarceration are not at issue here."

"Overruled. If defendant saw fit to co-operate with this court, he should get credit for it. Our courts can do with all the co-operation they can get. But ask specific questions, please," instructed Judge Minough.

"Were you brought here shackled?"

"No."

"Were you brought here at all?"

"No."

"Were you captured?"

"No."

"Were you hiding out?"

"No."

"How did you manage to avoid the search?"

"There was no search that I knew about."

"You were wanted. A warrant was issued."

No answer.

"Such search was not detectable where you were?"

"No."

"Where was that?"

"Butte City . . . Helena."

"You lived there openly?"

"Yes."

"You came from Butte to Helena . . . how?"

"By train."

"Without fear of apprehension?"

"It didn't occur to me." He added: "I wasn't sure then there was a warrant out."

"No Wanted posters? No offer of a five-hundred dollar reward?"

"No. None in that part of the country."

"Did you assume you were wanted?"

"Yes."

"Why?"

"I read the newspapers. I knew I was being blamed."

"Were the news accounts accurate?"

"No. Most of them didn't even have my name right."

246

"Why did you go from Butte City to Helena on the train?"

"To see you."

"That was how long? . . . total elapsed time . . . since Mister Gannaway's death?"

"Three weeks."

"Where was your wife?"

"As she testified . . . she went back to Denver."

"Did you intend that she should come here to testify?"

"No."

"When did you first know she was going to testify?"

"This morning."

"Not when you saw the list of witnesses?"

"No. I saw it said Missus Buttons, but thought it was Ma."

Boe walked to his table and balanced himself on his cane while looking through some papers. Then he turned and said across the distance: "Mister Buttons, did you shoot, or otherwise cause the death, of John J. Gannaway?"

All expected the positive answer, no, but it did not come, and for a breathless few seconds, as Billy pondered, there was a tenseness similar to the hair-stiffening magnetism before lightning — that he was about to say yes, that he was guilty.

"I don't know."

"You *don't know?* Are you telling me that you have a faulty memory . . . a blank spot of memory . . . of that day's events?"

"No. I don't know if I *caused* his death. That is, maybe I caused him to shoot himself. I accused him of. . . ."

"Of raping your wife?"

"Yes. I told him I knew everything that had happened. I accused him of ambushing me so he could return to . . . be with my wife."

"You accused him of that, face to face, on that fatal day?"

"Yes."

"And what said he?"

"He denied it."

"Then?"

"I said he was a liar. I said he was a defiler of women."

"I want your exact words."

"I've forgotten my exact words, but I told him he was a defiler

247

of women. I said he was a yellow dog and not fit to live."

"Not fit to live! A prelude to shooting him!"

"No. I didn't shoot him. I turned and rode away. I said . . . 'Go ahead and shoot me, John, that will make it complete.' I meant the way he'd treated me, an old friend."

"Did you expect him to shoot you in the back?"

"I didn't think much about it. I didn't care. I was at the point where I didn't care what happened."

"And then?"

"I heard a gunshot."

"From where?"

"From the direction of John Gannaway."

"Did you look around?"

"Yes."

"Tell the court what you saw."

"I saw his horse running and Gannaway falling to the ground."

"Did you go over to him?"

"No."

"What did you do?"

"I kept riding away."

"Weren't you interested in whether he was dead or not?"

"I didn't care. I didn't care whether he lived or died."

"Mister Buttons, do you sit there and ask us to believe that you rode all that distance to face him and yet didn't care whether he lived or died?"

"Yes."

"Why did you do it, not caring whether he lived or died?"

"I wanted to make him look me in the face and admit what he'd done. I wanted to let him know that he'd have to leave the country, or I'd have to."

"The prosecution may question," said Boe abruptly, and sat down.

Roman Wardrope stood and pondered, while holding the lapels of his black, silk-faced, court coat. It had now become his awesome duty to bring this defendant by his own word to the hangman's noose, an obligation that saddened him, that prompted him to a moment of reflection, a steeling, a honing of the sword of justice, to do what had to be done for the good of society, resolutely, aye, even ruthlessly, pity left behind.

"Mister Buttons." Billy waited alert, intent, looking Wardrope in the eyes. "Mister Buttons, I see by my notes that you are quite a traveler."

He waited.

"How many times were you to Colorado and/or Wyoming last spring?"

"Total?"

"Yes."

"Two."

"Missus W. T. Buttons, *née* Mary Margaret Carmody, and you seem to be at odds on that point. Her testimony indicated it was more. She had you meeting her twice in Wyoming . . . once in Cheyenne, once in Bridger, and at least one time in Denver."

Billy did not answer.

Wardrope went on: "Which of these occasions slipped your memory?"

"None."

"But there are three, and you said two. Will you explain this discrepancy?"

"You said last *spring*. I was in Denver during the winter."

Stung, Wardrope cried: "But this woman who presents herself as your wife. . . ."

"I object to that," said Boe.

"Yes, Mister Wardrope," said the judge.

"But the previous witness gave us quite an engaging account of your carriage ride on Cherry Creek that spring. The word *spring* was specifically used."

"It was spring weather. Spring comes early to Denver. It was March. I think it was about March twelfth. I recall her wondering if it would be green for Saint Patrick's Day. She's Irish. Spring on the calendar was the twenty-first of March."

"It happens that spring commences on the twentieth of March this year and every year, but we won't split hairs. Let us say in that season between winter and summer, you were three times in Colorado or southern Wyoming?"

"Yes."

"How long does the journey take?"

"To where?"

"To Denver."

"It all depends."

"Oh, come. You know what the conveyances are, the schedules. You should be an authority."

Thoughtful and detailed, Billy said, if he happened to be at his ranch, it was closer to Denver via Confederate Gulch and Helena, but a person starting from Arlington could save at least half a day via Billings or Livingston, both by the western route. If one were to go east to Minneapolis on the N. P., thence by the C. M. & S. P. to Council Bluffs, and on the U. P. to Cheyenne, it might be possible to make Denver in four days. From Helena it was necessary to take the N. P. to Garrison Junction over Mullan Pass, then change to the Montana Union as far as Butte, the Utah and Northern to Ogden, then the U. P. up over the range to Bridger, Cheyenne, and Denver, a shorter distance, but the Utah and Northern was very slow. Five days, if you were lucky, and in the winter it might take a week from Butte to Ogden alone. The quickest way in good weather was to get off the N. P. at Miles City and take the stage to Deadwood in the Black Hills, a day's journey, then the Black Hills and Western Railroad down to the U. P. in Nebraska. If a man was lucky making connections, he could leave Billings and be in Cheyenne in as little as forty-eight hours.

Wardrope moved impatiently, hesitating to cut this short because it was plain Billy was being followed with interest.

"The trouble is," said Judge Minough, "a man gets down in Dakota and starts looking for a railroad, and he may find out it runs nowhere but through some promoter's prospectus."

There was laughter. It was plain, however, that Billy's way of getting to Cheyenne in the phenomenal time of forty-eight hours was one of the most interesting facts that had come out during the trial.

Wardrope asked: "We take note that the defendant is most knowing in the ways of traveling in a hurry." He squared around. "Mister Buttons, the Deadwood route aside, isn't it true a journey by rail, or any means, to, say, Rawlins, Wyoming, requires at least four days?"

"Yes."

"And Denver?"

"Four days, five days. You leave Rawlins for Cheyenne at three twenty-five in the morning and get to Cheyenne at three in the afternoon. Denver, on the Denver and Pacific . . . about eight that night."

"And that's *one* way! Down and back requires how long?"

Billy had a habit of giving quite a bit of thought to even the most obvious question, and Wardrope, wishing to hit him rapid-fire, became nervous.

"Come, Mister Buttons! That requires no great concentration."

But Billy was not to be rushed. "It would be from eight to ten days."

"If you jumped on the train and came straight back . . . eight or ten days?"

"Yes."

"Then your three journeys to Wyoming and Colorado took at least how long, travel time alone?"

"Upwards of thirty days."

"Upwards of a solid month, on the train. I say, Mister Buttons, that must set some sort of record for a cowboy?"

Billy waited.

"And time to court your girl, inspect schools, attend theater, get married, sleep, eat? Play any cards when you were down there?"

He thought for a while. "Yes."

"Got in quite a bit of gambling, too?"

"No."

"You said you played cards."

"But you said quite a bit of gambling. The answer to that. . . ."

"So, in addition to the month you spent on trains and coaches, would it be fair to estimate an equal amount of time was spent in your various activities at the ends-of-line?"

"No."

Wardrope drove straight on. "Yet, you also had time to be seen here, at your home ranch, riding around the country, arranging land deeds, herding cattle. In fact, you were here so much that nobody suspected you had even been gone?"

"Objection. There has been no testimony that would justify the attorney's assumption that nobody suspected the witness was gone."

"Withdrawn. Mister Buttons, I'm a little perplexed, and I'm sure

251

others are, as to just how you managed to get all this peregrinating in. These peregrinations" — he smiled — "of what I may call a crepuscular nature, are most . . . ?"

"Objection. The use of the word crepuscular *denigrates* the witness. Let attorney show by admissible means that his peregrinations were predominantly crepuscular."

"It was merely a light remark, Your Honor. I'm sure his peregrinations had to be daylit, crepuscular, and nocturnal all three, and *that,* Mister Boe, was implicit in his testimony!"

Judge Minough said: "Prosecution specifies that crepuscular in the present sense does not mean *shady?* Is that correct? Proceed."

"How did you manage to get all this peregrinating in?"

"I don't know what the word means."

"Well, let's get down to specifics. That first trip to Denver . . . when did you leave? What route? Let's have the details?"

Billy drew something from his pants pockets and studied it, cupped in his hands. He started to answer, and Wardrope cut him off.

"What's that you have?"

"Notes. It's a small notebook. I have all the dates."

"Of what?"

"Everything. All the dates and places."

"Indeed! Do you always keep records like that?"

"No."

"But for this, you've come prepared?"

"Yes, my lawyer" — he nodded to Boe — "told me you'd ask me for dates and places. He said I'd better spend some time remembering back where I'd been, as exactly as possible. He said I'd have to account for every minute of my time or the prosecution would catch me up on it. I didn't have much else to do the last few weeks, so I sat down with a calendar and figured where I was every day. I don't think I could remember exactly without the notes. There's six months to account for, all up till the day I rode in here and asked to stand trial. That's a total of one hundred and eighty days. I haven't that kind of a memory. My lawyer said I had to be absolutely sure of every fact."

Wardrope turned his back. With a tolerant smile for such coaching and rehearsal, a preparation indicative of guilt, he let Billy run on.

252

He seemed actually amused, but Clyde noticed that his hand, when he reached for a paper on his desk, seemed thick and numb. He couldn't take hold. He gave up and rested his hand on the table, flat, resolute, his jaw set, but it was only a posture, just a front. It seemed to Clyde he was seeing him naked, that the veil had been stripped away, and he was no match for Billy. Yes, despite his education and official presumptions, Billy was smarter than he was, and Wardrope knew it! Still he had to wage on with the cross-examination. He had entered the lists. There was no retreat.

"Never mind those notes. Just look me in the eye . . . ?"

"Objection," stated Boe. "Witness should not be denied recourse to any reasonable means of furnishing an exactly truthful testimony."

"And I object to a prepared and written script . . . ," Wardrope responded.

"Does the United States attorney, or any man in this room, possess such a memory that he is able to provide the exact dates and times of his comings and goings for the past six months?" Boe inquired.

"I say only a liar would require notes!" Wardrope replied.

Judge Minough banged the gavel. "I'm going to assume that was not said. Strike that last remark. I realize we are far into a hot and trying day. Tempers will suffer. Let us show our Spartan . . ." — with a smile — "at least our *Roman* fortitudes in this hour? Proceed."

Attorney Roman Wardrope assumed a posture of bearing up under inequity, glad to do so, willing, more than willing, to give the guilty all measure of advantage, aye, to the scale of seven times seven. "Billy," he said, introducing a light and familiar tone. "Correction . . . Mister Buttons . . . do you have in your notes the date on which you drew up that quitclaim deed on the so-called Buttons Reserve?"

With usual careful thought Billy finally answered: "No."

"But you did draw up, or cause to have drawn up, such a paper?"

"No."

"You are familiar with such a paper?"

"Yes."

"Give the details, please?"

"Last winter . . . I think it must have been about December tenth . . . I met John Gannaway here in town. We talked about it. Mister

253

Stewart can tell you about it. He drew it up."

"My colleague?"

"Yes."

Paul Stewart shifted uncomfortably under Wardrope's stare.

Boe said: "Would the assistant U. S. attorney like to put his colleague on the stand so he can clear up the matter?"

Ignoring him, Wardrope addressed Judge Minough: "Your Honor, as you know, we had very little time to prepare this case." He then turned toward the witness. "Mister Buttons, seeing you and your attorney are little handicapped in this regard, perhaps you could tell us the details of that agreement?"

"It was just a form of quitclaim deed to the Buttons Reserve. The Omaha Cattle Company averred itself to be the lessor from the Army . . . Mister Stewart's words. He said for that reason, being already the legal proprietor, it could not purchase anyone else's claim or right . . . its position being that none other existed." He kept looking to Stewart for verification, but the associate for the prosecution looked stonily ahead. "Paul said that a quitclaim was a means of quieting title."

"Did you, for this instrument, receive in hand certain moneys?"

"Yes."

"In what amount?"

"Five hundred dollars at that time. Later I was paid another thousand. Fifteen hundred, total."

"We have had testimony it was considerably more."

"No, the total was fifteen hundred."

"At any rate, you will admit that the amount specified on the face of the document . . . ?"

Boe interjected: "Objection. The witness admits nothing . . . *admits* is a calumniative word . . . *admits* has an implied inculpation . . . it bears the slur of one caught cheating . . . it is pejorative. I am surprised that a man of Mister Wardrope's stature would try to sneak it in."

"Yes, Mister Wardrope," said the judge, "*admit* is hardly fair."

"Well, we're inquiring into some pretty shady dealings."

"And no more of that, either."

"Was the amount you received the amount shown on the document?"

"No."

"What *was* the amount shown?"

"It said five hundred dollars and other good and valuable considerations."

"What were these *considerations?*"

"Old claims, debts, obligations . . . we wanted to start with a clean slate."

"But they weren't set forth explicitly?"

"No."

"Was it not strange that a businessman such as Mister Gannaway would fail to be more explicit?"

Billy did not answer.

"Enlighten us, please?"

Boe interjected: "Is attorney inquiring as to Mister Gannaway's character, or of businessmen in general?"

"I am attempting to explain the motives understood, or implied, behind this agreement!"

Judge Minough said: "I believe the questions should be addressed to separate points of fact."

Billy said: "The quitclaim was just something for him to show the Ethringtons. John wanted proof the Reserve was all clear, but he didn't want them to know that more than five hundred dollars was involved. He had Mister Stewart draw it up. Then he left the office . . . Stewart's office . . . and went next door to the express counter and wrote in 'and other good and valuable consideration.' He said . . . 'Anything Stewart finds out will get to the Ethringtons in two days.' I'm sorry, Paul, but he thought you were leagued against him. He. . . ."

"Don't address Mister Stewart," Wardrope demanded, "address me!"

"I wanted Mister Stewart to know what it was. We had a verbal agreement supplemental to the deed. John was to pay me the one thousand dollars out of his pocket."

"A total of fifteen hundred, one thousand of which was under the table? That's what you would have us believe about this man no longer able to defend himself?"

Billy looked sad — pensive and sad.

"And how much of this purported fifteen hundred dollars did your mother receive?"

"None."

"You kept it all yourself?"

"She never signed the deed. I gave the paper back to John Gannaway unsigned . . . and the money."

"We have testimony that it *was* signed, whether by your mother or . . . ?"

"No. She never signed it. I had it witnessed, but I never took her the paper."

"Why?"

"I decided it might not be a good deal for her. I got to thinking our claim on the Reserve must be pretty good, or John wouldn't put up that much money."

"So, what happened to the money?"

"As I said, I returned it to Mister Gannaway."

"Do you have in your possession a receipt attesting to that?"

"No."

"You just handed over fifteen hundred dollars without a scratch?"

"Yes."

"And he paid you a thousand of that fifteen hundred without receipt?"

"Yes."

"Are you asking me to believe he trusted you, whereas he did not trust his partners?"

"No, I'm just giving the facts."

"Now, I'm going to present you with the *true* facts! The truth is this . . . you received that money on consideration you secure your mother's signature, but that signature was not forthcoming. She refused to sign for a mere five hundred dollars, with your keeping the lion's share, diverting it to your own use. And thereupon you *forged* the name Kate Buttons to that paper, delivering it back to the purchaser, and he, learning the *truth,* confronted you with the demand that restitution be made, that you return the money, which in fact was the sum of twenty-five hundred dollars, a sum you no longer possessed, having squandered it on journeys to Colorado and else-

256

where, living the fancy life, taking excursions on the Denver and Rio Grande in parlor cars, driving women by carriage along Cherry Creek, entertaining at fine restaurants on white linen, battening on champagne and *foie gras* . . . that *is* the truth, Mister Buttons . . . and when Mister Gannaway set forth an ultimatum that the full sum had to be returned by such-and-such a time, with the alternative of arrest and the disclosure of your perfidy to your mother . . . *then* you acted in desperation, first to ship stolen cattle, and, when that failed, when all else failed, when only prison lay before you, you then waylaid Mister Gannaway and shot him down, seeking to silence him forever?"

"Is that a question?" asked Boe, "or closing argument for the prosecution?"

"I'm asking the defendant to say whether, indeed, that is not true?"

"No," said Billy, "it's not."

"Who signed your mother's name?"

"I don't know. I didn't know anybody did until I heard Carns testify yesterday. If we had the deed here and could look. . . ."

Judge Minough, who wanted to hurry things to a conclusion, cut in: "Really, Mister Wardrope, we can hardly discuss either the deed or the signatures intelligently without having it here for examination."

"The defendant admits to having secured the signature of a witness in a highly irregular, aye, fraudulent manner. If he did that with one signature, then how are we to believe that he did otherwise with another? Why . . . ?"

"Alas, this practice is all too common, and as much the fault of the legal profession as the signatories," the judge offered by way of explanation. "The current legal forms and contractual procedures were, after all, designed to the uses of the populated lands where witnesses were more readily available, not for these vast spaces, these solitudes. Hence, we pay lip service, cut corners . . . we honor the form and the ideal, but it is, nonetheless, true that few Notaries Public demand that all signatories appear before them, as stated on the forms."

"Mister Buttons, what is the train fare from here to Colorado?" cried Wardrope.

"Well . . . ," — Billy was taken by surprise — "I guess . . . oh, about sixty dollars."

"Round trip?"

"No, one way. A Pullman berth costs five dollars extra."

"And the dining car? You do eat on the diner?"

"Yes. If there is one. The Harvey Houses are. . . ."

"You like to travel in the first class? . . . in *style?*"

"I don't like to be a cheapskate. Yes, I like to go first class. As for going. . . ."

"The Pullman Palace?"

"Well, on the N. P. and U. P. But these north-south lines. . . ."

"Then would you say a journey to and from Colorado would cost you at least a hundred and thirty dollars?"

Billy was not to be rushed. He did some mental computing while Wardrope moved impatiently. "Yes . . . about that."

"Three trips would cost you at least three hundred and ninety dollars . . . shall we say four hundred? . . . tips for the porters, *et cetera?*"

"No. I. . . ."

"More? Or less?"

"More. I figured it cost me more than five hundred dollars, trains and Pullmans alone."

"And your hotels? Where did you stay in Denver? At the Windsor?"

"Yes."

Wardrope acted surprised. "Isn't that a little expensive?"

"Not too," said Billy. "You can get an inside room at a real good hotel for about standard rate at a second class hotel."

"Well, from a much-traveled man, we'll remember that!"

The trouble with Billy, as far as Wardrope was concerned, was he always had information that people got interested in, especially, it seemed, on the subject of travel. Clyde could see how everybody had perked up, wanting to hear how they could stay at the Windsor cheaply. Billy must have realized that, too, because he went on.

"The beds are all the same, six-dollar room or two-dollar room. I've stayed at the Windsor for a dollar six bits . . . a dollar seventy-five."

"I know what six bits is!"

"You get to use the lobby and everything else just the same as if you paid out six dollars. A man only uses his room to sleep in, anyway."

"I wouldn't have thought a few dollars one way or the other would make much difference . . . five hundred dollars, trains and Pullmans alone! Then the additional expenses! Hacks, restaurants, excursions. How much would you say your total expenses would be traveling . . . one thousand dollars?"

"No, but almost. I figured about nine hundred and seventy-five."

"In other words, just about what Gannaway paid over?"

"No, he paid over five hundred and twenty-five more, but I gave it all back."

"Then where did you get that kind of money, Mister Buttons . . . more than is earned by an able-bodied man in a year?"

"I run cattle and horses. I've been running an estray auction the last two years. It makes a small profit over and above expenses. I've shipped cattle twice this year, once on the N. P. and once on the river. I have a quarter interest in the Rock Lily lead-silver mine over in the Castle Mountain district. We have nineteen claims and two mill sites. This year we put it out on option and bond to the Butte North Ridge Mining Company. They let the option lapse and forfeited the bond, twelve hundred dollars, after six months. My share was three hundred, and left the mine netting me one hundred and sixty as of this time. Every little bit helps. This has been a costly year for me. I don't believe in going in debt."

For years Billy had joked about his silver mine and compared it to the one in Bill Nye's lecture that had the ore running ninety-nine percent "pyrite of poverty." He was always being dunned fifty dollars for giant powder and fuse, or hauling over a ton of flour, beans, raisins, and salt pork. The two partners operating the mine were named Harley and Able, and Billy called it the Hardly Able Mining Company. However, there was nothing funny about that eleven hundred dollars from a big outfit like Butte North Ridge.

Wardrope, though, seemed to think the mine was just a spur-of-the-moment idea. He smiled and then spun around to say: "Mister Buttons, when your wife told you that she had been raped by John Gannaway, what was your reaction?"

It was no use trying to take Billy off guard because he always gave thought to every answer.

"Shock. I couldn't believe it."

"Didn't he have quite a reputation with women? Didn't he chase the lace, as the saying goes?"

"No . . . not particularly."

"Oh, come, Mister Buttons. Didn't the two of you once stage what you called a roundup of all the red-light houses in Helena?"

"No. I have no memory of it."

"Didn't the two of you brag about it one night right across the street at the Mountdouglas House? Didn't you refer to it as the Buttons-Gannaway heifer roundup association?"

"Not that I remember."

"But you were in Helena, having a gay time?"

"We had a few drinks."

"Did you chase the lace?"

"We visited some parlorhouses."

"You visited prostitutes with John Gannaway, and then you introduced him to your wife?"

"Several years had passed."

"You did visit parlorhouses, and you did introduce him to your wife?"

"No. I didn't introduce him."

"Your memory of the event is at variance with your wife's. She testified you introduced him."

"He came to our table. He said . . . 'I'm John Gannaway.' He introduced himself."

"Did you not say . . . 'Missus Buttons, this is John Gannaway'?"

"Yes, I guess I did."

"Then you did introduce him! Tell me, weren't you worried, considering his reputation? Yet you dined with him, threw your bride into his company, visited his lonely hunting lodge, and went away, leaving her alone there?"

"I didn't plan to be ambushed, left for dead, so he could come back and rape her."

"Just answer."

"Will you repeat the question?"

And so it went. At last Wardrope tried a new tack. He became friendly. He smiled and had a drink of water.

"Can I buy you one?"

But Billy did not respond. He had no intention of letting Wardrope be anything except the enemy.

"Mister Buttons, you said a while ago that you experienced shock when your wife told you your so-called friend had raped her?"

"Yes."

"Then you said you couldn't believe it. Those were your words?"

"Yes."

"You couldn't *believe* it? Did you think she was lying?"

"No."

"But you couldn't believe her?"

"Lying is a pejorative word," said Boe.

"Well, you supply a word for someone not telling the truth."

"It has already been testified that the defendant believed his bride to be distraught and mistaken," Boe offered.

"But you saw blood on the sheet blankets, and then you believed her?" Wardrope demanded.

"Yes."

"What was your reaction? Blinding rage?"

"No. I was just . . . stunned."

"Oh, come. You haven't stayed alive all along the frontier being *stunned*. You're the man who shot it out with Hodge Piper right in his rustlers' lair in Jackson Hole!"

Billy did not answer.

"Now, wasn't your first action to strap on your gun and ride forth?"

"No. I didn't leave for an hour."

"But then you strapped on your gun and rode forth?"

"No."

"You left. Did you leave unarmed?"

"No, but I never ride with a gun strapped on."

"What if you need it in a hurry?"

"You can't shoot riding."

"I'm sure the old cavalrymen present will be surprised to hear that."

"I couldn't. No accuracy. I don't think many horses would stand for it."

261

"Where do you carry your gun when riding?"

"I have my rifle in a scabbard. Down . . . about here. Right side."

"How about your pistol? You carry a pistol, don't you?"

"Yes. Generally. I carry it in a saddlebag."

"Did you carry both when you set out from Ivanhoe?"

"Yes."

"Where did you secure these guns? Had you carried them to Denver and back?"

"No, I'd taken the pistol. I'd left the rifle in Helena."

"How about ammunition? Plenty of ammunition?"

"Yes."

"How much?"

"Half a box."

"For each gun?"

"No, half a box, total."

"For which gun?"

"Both."

"But one was a six shooter, and you said the other was a rifle."

"That's right."

"There seems to be an inconsistency?"

Billy didn't answer.

"You didn't intend to use your rifle ammunition in your pistol, and *vice versa?*"

"Yes, they were both Forty-Four caliber, a Forty-Four-Forty Winchester . . . same cartridge fits."

"Why did you carry two guns?"

"The rifle shoots farther."

"With the identical cartridge?"

"Yes."

"Same powder load?"

"Yes."

"How can it do that?"

"The rifle has a longer barrel."

"Oh, come! That's illogical engineering. The rifle barrel would impede through greater friction."

"No, it shoots farther."

Wardrope turned, smiling, apparently thinking he had caught the witness in an inconsistency, although hardly a man in the room did

262

not know it was true — the longer barrel had the greater range.

"You set out well equipped?"

Billy didn't answer.

"Do you generally set out equipped for close- and long-range shooting, both?"

"Yes."

"Ready for trouble?"

No comment.

"You set out to hunt down Gannaway . . . where did you go?"

"I rode to our Sixty-Six ranch, then to the Castle."

"The Castle?"

"The Omaha. It used to be the Northwestern Home Ranch."

"Isn't that the ranch from which Mister Gannaway set out on his last, fatal ride?"

"According to the testimony, yes."

Hiding his annoyance, Wardrope inquired: "Well, there certainly has been no previous testimony hinting at this visit! What did you do . . . lie low and spy on the ranch?"

"No, I rode up and asked for Gannaway."

"Asked whom?"

"The cook."

"Weren't you worried, riding right up, openly, after the attack against your life previously recounted?"

"No."

"That seems strange, Mister Buttons. Can you explain your boldness?"

"They'd be too smart to shoot me down in their own ranch yard."

"Can you give any evidence of this visit?"

"The cook will verify it. Len Halter."

"When you didn't find Mister Gannaway . . . ?"

"I rode off."

"What time was this?"

"Early afternoon."

"Day before the shooting?"

"Yes."

"Where next?"

"To Gromley's, and Lolly Springs."

"How far . . . total?"

263

"About twelve miles."

"Was that the line cabin previously specified?"

"Yes."

"The testimony indicated you reached it in the early morning . . . past midnight?"

He waited. Billy did not reply.

"It took you all that time? Twelve hours?"

"Yes."

"Why did it take so long?"

"I rested a while . . . let my horse graze. I'd been traveling steady."

"And it took you all that time? . . . until early morning?"

"Yes."

"Then you left in the morning with two trusted friends?"

"With Mister Carter."

"How about Mister LaGrange? He seems to be unaccounted for?"

"No, I found him at the Sixty-Six."

"You asked him to go with you?"

"Yes."

"Then you weren't alone when you visited the Omaha?"

"Yes. I left him back along the road."

"Why?"

"My business with Gannaway seemed private."

"Now, Mister Buttons . . . back to the events of the day before. I must say, I am surprised your attorney did not see fit to bring out in full detail the attempt which was, according to Missus Buttons, made on your life? I give you that opportunity now?"

Billy started out, very detailed, telling how he had set out with Gannaway, horseback and Gannaway driving a buggy, to inspect fence communal between the Omaha and the Flying R, part of the O X in which Billy had an interest when Wardrope cut in.

"We can safely skip all that. I would like to hear about the so-called attack?"

"It was about an hour later. I'd parted from Gannaway near the Chalk Faces on the Paint Creek road and crossed over a divide to Sixteen Mile Coulée. I was following the old Buttons freight road when, all of a sudden, the mare I was riding made a move, and I knew something was wrong. I knew there were some horses upwind,

264

which was more or less to the northeast. There was a little outcropping just ahead of me, and a small gully. I intended to ride on until I got there, and once I was out of sight, investigate."

"Wasn't that a bit unusual? You weren't a fugitive?"

"No, but I had a brother shot from ambush about eight miles from there, and a thing like that makes you cautious."

"Go on."

"I never made it. I saw some bushes move. There was somebody about a hundred steps away, just over the rim of the coulée. I didn't stop to think. I went off the side of my horse, leaving the reins tied. I always use a jam loop on the saddle horn, anyway, and I wanted the mare to run and cause a diversion. I think it saved my life. Somebody shot. There were *two* shots, and one of them, I later found out, nicked the horn. From the angle it came, it would have got me right here, and through to here."

"Let the record show," said Judge Minough, "that the witness indicates bullet would have entered at the umbilicus at a course which would pass through the spine."

"I was left without a gun. I wasn't carrying a pistol, only a rifle, and it was in a boot under the saddle. The mare ran, and the last I saw her that day, she was going over a little hill rise with stirrups flopping. There was a little draw and some rocks. I ran for a way and lay down. I expected them to come looking for me to finish me off, but, of course, they didn't know I was unarmed. For that matter, they didn't know I was alive. So I stayed down, figuring they were waiting. I knew somebody was there. If there were three, two could be waiting and the other gone for help. Anyway, I didn't move for the rest of the afternoon or evening. Finally it got dark, and I struck out on foot. My mare . . . she was an Omaha horse, but she had an old Roman V brand, so I figured she'd been foaled on the old Hess Range . . . a mare will generally head for her old home. Luckily I found her next morning on what's now the McCoy place, about a mile above the Little Sage Creek sinks. I managed to catch her and went back to Ivanhoe. I was worried about my wife."

"This is a good story, but really, you can offer not one iota of proof that the attack was ever made."

Boe interjected: "Objection. A preknowledge of the attack

265

was implicit in information carried from Gannaway to Missus Buttons."

"Can you offer any physical proof or impartial testimony that any such attack took place?"

"No."

"Nobody saw it? Nobody heard the shots? Surely somebody saw you walk to this McCoy place?"

"It's a homestead. Owen McCoy and Charlie Stroud live there, but they work around at different outfits. June is the branding season."

"Still, it's a shame nobody in all the broad land had the slightest suspicion the attack took place?"

"Well, that's a precaution they took."

"Mister Buttons, you say you lay there until night? How long was that?"

"A long time. About five hours."

"You laid there for five hours?"

"Approximately. It might have been longer."

"Were they waiting for you?"

"I don't know."

"If they were intent on killing you, and if you had no gun, why did they not make some move to hunt you out?"

"They didn't know I was unarmed."

"Then they could have had no association with Mister Gannaway. He knew you were not carrying a pistol, and by your own testimony your gun was still in the saddle boot?"

"They couldn't see that. The horse ran off and was gone. They figured they'd got me, all right, but they didn't dare come over to make sure. So they waited around. I thought at first there were three. Now I'm certain there were only two. One of them pulled out to tell Gannaway the job had been done. The other stayed on watch to make sure. He left just about sundown."

Boe interjected: "If prosecution would really like to know what lay behind the reluctance of these men to investigate their handiwork, we will be glad to call the culprits to the stand. One of them is sitting right in this room."

"Objection!" snapped Wardrope. "Your Honor, this is unconscionable!"

"Yes, Mister Boe," declared the judge, "any more interruptions of this kind and you'll be paying another fine, and one that will tax you to the utmost."

But everybody was looking around. Clyde was looking around, and there were about six fellows, starting with Ted Danner, that it could have been.

Wardrope resumed. "Mister Buttons, you have testified that you wished to *face* Mister Gannaway. Only that? Not challenge him? Not shoot him down? No! Even though his sins against you were on the order of seven times seven, though he had *allegedly* raped your wife, and made an attempt through unseen parties to shoot you down from ambush, you . . . ?"

Boe said: "Objection. Is this a question? Or an argument?"

"Yes, Mister Wardrope," said the judge. "Your time for such organized presentations will come."

"Very well. I ask this, direct and to the point . . . how was it that in all this broad land you knew exactly where to wait for Gannaway? How did you know he would that day be at the crossing of Willow Creek?".

"I didn't know it."

"Merely chance? A one in a hundred chance?"

"Not one in a hundred. More like one in three, one in five."

"How in the world do you come up with that figure?"

"There are three main roads in that part of the country. We could see two of them from the top of a little butte. Ace . . . Mister Carter . . . already testified we watched from there. If we hadn't seen them that morning, I'd probably have headed for Black Butte where they were branding."

"Oh, come, Mister Buttons. You were trying to get a shipment of disputed white-face cattle out of the country by steamboat? Didn't you know a posse was out to stop you?"

"No."

"The fact is, you were preoccupied that day with the shipment and nothing else? Isn't that so? Too late you learned that the cat was out of the bag? It had been discovered what you were up to . . . but the die was cast . . . there was no way you could stop the shipment? Mister Buttons, didn't you know that a warrant had been issued for your arrest?"

"Objection," said Boe. "Testimony indicates no actual warrant was issued."

"And Mister Buttons," Wardrope pursued relentlessly, "in that extremity, with the trap actually closing on you, and the penitentiary opening to receive you, was it not *cattle* instead of rape that caused you to intercept John Gannaway at Willow Creek?"

"No."

"You have to speak more loudly," said Judge Minough.

"No," Billy said in a firm voice. "No, it was *not* cattle. I faced John for the rape of my wife."

"Did you not try to make a deal in regards to those cattle, and in regards to the forged document, the quitclaim deed, and, when John Gannaway refused, when he said, no, that you would have to take your medicine, is not that when you drew a pistol and shot him down? . . . *shot* him down unarmed, while his arm was lifted for mercy? That is really how it happened, wasn't it, Mister Buttons?"

"No."

"Didn't you, in fact, bring the woman and deliberately throw her in Gannaway's path, not once but many times? Did you not bring her to lure that man, in Helena and later in the luxury of the hunting lodge? Did you not absent yourself from Gannaway that day and lie in wait, hoping to surprise him by bursting in on their adulterous bed? But didn't something go wrong . . . there being *no adulterous bed?* Isn't that the way it really was?"

"I object to this," said Boe. "This is not proper cross-examination."

"Overruled," stated the judge.

"Isn't that so, Mister Buttons? Wasn't this all designed to divert Mister Gannaway from your depredations, the cattle you'd stolen, the money you had taken from him through forgery? Weren't all the chickens coming home to roost, and wasn't this complicated plan devised to rescue you in a final, grand swashbuckle? And when it failed, when it all fell in ruins, didn't you then decide, coldly, not in anger, and as a last resort, to murder John Gannaway?"

Billy waited.

"Well?" cried Wardrope.

"No. There was nothing like that. I'd never dream of playing John for a fool . . . nor. . . ."

268

"In bitter frustration, you shot him down! I'm through with the witness."

Wardrope sat now, breathing through his nostrils, his face shining from sweat. It took him a while to recover from outrage, apparently genuine. Paul Stewart looked over and nodded an assurance. *You tore him to pieces,* the nod seemed to say, but Wardrope was too overwrought to acknowledge it.

"Any redirect?" the judge asked.

Boe stood and said: "Was your wife brought here in any way to lure, entice, or compromise Mister Gannaway, or any man?"

"No."

"Your Honor, the defense rests."

Is that all? thought Clyde. He wanted to jump to his feet and cry: *Wait, wait!* Was there to be no surprise witness who had seen the killer — the *real* killer — Louis Ethrington, slinking back along the bottoms of Willow Creek, long-range rifle in hand to fire the fatal shots? But it was all over. They would have to decide Billy's fate on this, and on this only!

"We will recess for twenty minutes. I would like to see the attorneys in chambers. The jury may repair outside by the back stairs, but no farther. They are to remain in easy call. I admonish the spectators to keep their seats, except those spectators who wish to leave and do not wish to return. . . ."

Only a few among the spectators left. The judge, lawyers, and jury went out the back way, either down the stairs or into one of the rooms. Billy remained seated, and the deputies. Billy's wife sat in the very corner of the court area, erect and attentive, buttoned tight in her traveling suit, the little dove-wing hat on her head. Bunting, the clerk, remained, writing, blotting, writing, and it was so quiet the scratch of his pen was the main sound in the room. The sun had swung around and now shone in from the southwest, reflecting from a warehouse roof against the ceiling with a yellow glow.

Earl Hankey came in the back way, and he walked over to ask Ma if she wanted to retire for a while, but she shook her head, hardly glancing at him.

And the time dragged on, and on. . . .

CHAPTER NINETEEN

"I don't think we'll need the lamps," said Judge Minough. "Will you be able to see, Mister Bunting?" Pete Wall was carrying in two, big-bellied, three-wick, coal-oil lamps by their chains. "Just set them down. We may be finished here before they're needed. This land is blessed with the longest twilights in the world. Now, the attorneys have agreed to limit their closing arguments to thirty minutes each. Mister Wardrope . . . do you and Mister Stewart both wish to speak? I then ask that each limit himself to fifteen minutes, or a mutually accretive or decretive part thereof, whichever penultimate and whichever final to inverse the proportional span of the other. Now, as for the orders of speaking, which first, last . . . there are several ways of doing this, but for clarity and celerity I have found that, if the prosecution speaks first, it may then present its full summary of the case and at the same time its main plea for conviction. The defense will then answer in full time. The prosecution then rebuts, but with the addition of nothing new or of basic summary nature. In fairness, if it did, then the defense would deserve another chance, and so we might go on *ad infinitum*. There is never an absolute fairness in allotting these times. Mister Stewart, I believe you wish to address the jury first?"

Stewart was nervous, with a tendency to stumble in putting his material in order. He retraced himself time after time, but for all that he gave a good account of himself. It helped that he knew he was no orator, so he didn't try to be. He merely put forth a good, logical, common-sense resumé of the case, with emphasis on what was important and had been based on eye-witness accounts. He then pointed out that Mrs. Buttons's testimony regarding the rape had not altered the essential charges, because, even if true, and Billy, the aggrieved husband, had been thereby motivated to homicide, two full days had intervened. The blind passion of the heated moment could hardly be extended over such a period. On the contrary, the defendant's actions, as outlined and attested to by himself and his friends, bespoke coolness, and meticulous planning. Therefore, nothing had been done in the heat of the moment. Rather, against a background of enmity across the years, Billy Buttons, realizing that his forgery and his thefts were at last, inevitably, to bring him to the bar to his day of reckoning, had attempted to burst forth by a single, desperate act — the elimination of the one man who had brought about his downfall.

This was his state of mind when he rode, unerringly, to intercept the path of Mr. Gannaway, on his way to apprehend him in the shipment of stolen cattle. It was the only possible explanation that fit the facts. There he found Mister Gannaway unarmed. Undoubtedly he had hoped to make what followed look like a fair gun fight and even self-defense. Thwarted in this, driven by the hopelessness of his cause, seeing prison as inevitable, this man, this roving and errant son of the plains to whom the prison cell would be a worse fate than death, had, failing in his arguments to win more time from Gannaway, drawn his gun and without mercy pulled the trigger. It was all attested to by witnesses, not only by the three on the hill, but not even denied in essential particulars by Buttons's own friends in the valley bottom. So it was proved beyond any reasonable, commonsense doubt, and however much one's sympathy might be stirred by the young woman's story, it was not truly germane to the case. Under the law, he was not privileged, therefore, to act. "And make no mistake about it, the law must be obeyed, especially in this frontier land, or it will be a bad day for all of us!"

Paul Stewart sat down, and Wardrope shook his hand. It had been a good performance.

Boe laid a watch on the edge of the table. "It is my understanding that I take my entire thirty minutes now, Mister Wardrope's being left five minutes . . . rather closer to four-and-one-half minutes . . . by his colleague." He said this in a manner that precluded an answer from the bench while taking a while to get his weight adjusted between cane and table. Then, although time was ticking away, he looked far off, and he kept looking for so long that Judge Minough seemed at the point of speaking to him, but finally he shook free of his preoccupation and started to speak, and did it in a florid, old-fashioned way.

"Your Honor, gentlemen of the jury, of the court, citizens of Ricketts County, my peers," — a thoughtful pause — "I come here a stranger from another land. From Montana, yes, but a Montana across the mountains, from a land of forest and mines, and I look with awe upon the vastness of these prairies. I look about me and feel small and humble. Tomorrow we will be a new state, and a new state of what immensity! . . . an empire of endless grass, of orchards and grain, of timber, silver, copper, and gold. Of rivers whose harnessed power will turn the dynamos of a mighty industry. We are the land of the future, and you, gentlemen of the jury . . . of a very *select* jury, are chosen men of such esteem that, as Judge Minough so aptly stated, the customary challenges for cause, for bias, for prejudice, for anything but a fair and equitable open-mindedness is unthinkable. You are the men who have built this land, wrested it from nature and the wild Indians, managed its rivers with boats of steam, conquered its distances with roads, and in less than a generation have transformed it from the land of the buffalo to the range of some of the finest cattle on the face of the world. But I am a stranger, from the land beyond the hills, and it is not my conceit to come here and lecture you on the difference between right and wrong, and on the stern and necessary application of justice. Your own Mister Stewart . . . Paul Stewart . . . county prosecutor . . . has delivered to you what I must concede was a masterly resumé of the broad outlines of this case. So now all eyes look to me. Who is this stranger? . . . who this man with his cane and his peculiar mannerisms? Who is this man from across the mountains, one day here, another gone? . . . gone like the winds that stirred the dusts of yesteryear . . . this man who comes today and leaves tomorrow . . . leaves his triumph or despair. Time will heal . . . time, time." He seemed to be speaking to himself, thoughts turned inward, to have lost himself in a moment of reverie, living with old tragedies, the ancient ironies of truths learned too late.

"Time," he continued, "the sad comforter. Time that knits up the ravell'd sleeve of care . . . 'Brief candle . . .' '" — he stood and looked out across the room, to the windows — " 'a moment's halt, a momentary taste . . . of being, from the well amid the waste . . .' and what matters? How will it be with Thomas F. Boe, lawyer? Where will he be tomorrow? Gone, new fields, new scenes, new cases, defeats, triumphs . . . .will he close from his mind the fate of Billy Buttons? . . . even though he be condemned to lie so early cold and low within his grave? . . . the six feet of earth that is finally all our heritage? Tomorrow, and tomorrow . . . how many of us will there be breathing God's air and seeing His light twenty-five years hence? . . . or fifty? Soon or late, gone, all gone. What matters it then? One cries out, isn't there some small thing to cling to? What of right and truth? Oh God, that it were possible for one short hour to see."

Boe's voice had dropped by degrees, with excellent articulation but lower and lower, carrying his listeners along with him until the room was tense and poised as a set trap, hair-triggered, scarcely a breath being drawn so as not to miss one word — because it was what they had come for. They would have come, anyway, to see the trial, but Boe had wide fame. They had all heard of cases apparently hopeless won, always *won*, and his oratory, like the oratory of Senator Roscoe Conkling or Robert C. Ingersoll, was to be heard, and recollected, and recounted to interested listeners to their dying day.

"A hair, perhaps, divides the false and true," he continued, "and time will wash away the pain. And so it will be with you here amid your pursuits, and I across the towering mountains. John Gannaway and Billy Buttons, old friends, strangely united in the twilight world of death." He smiled with sad irony, a knife cutting his florid utterance, and said directly to Ralph Richardson, rancher from the Little Teton, who sat in the front row of the jury: "Of course, it might be a little more painful and harder to forget for the girl, little Mary Carmody, who learned to teach school and came West, the *golden* West, so full of the sunlit morning of hope . . . little Mary Carmody who met and married a young man anxious to retrieve and rebuild his father's frontier ranch, who said yes in her vows, and went with him hand in hand to this country . . . ah, what hope seemed to shine around her then! Little did she suspect . . . that girl . . . what lay ahead of her . . . how her trust was to be rewarded. Raped, violated, stripped gown from flesh in a night of lust, nightmare of terror, ending . . . where? . . . in justice? . . . justice of a husband strung to a hangman's tree? Yes, that could be justice," he went on, walking away. "Well, if that is where the fact of this tragic case takes us, then we must harden our hearts to her sorrow. Anyhow, she'll be far away . . . far, far off with her tragedy and heartache . . . out of sight, out of mind, and we'll never have to think of her again . . . or almost never again . . . only perhaps at night when we are falling off to sleep, then perhaps the memory of her sweet, tear-stained face will come to us, but for only a moment, like a ghost of the past."

He looked at the watch. But the time was ample, he indicated, for the few simple truths he had to say. Now, speaking in a singularly flat voice, in a series of statements, Boe enumerated the several motives put forth "as though, if one shoe didn't fit, try on another" — the *forged* signature which had never been produced, the so-called *stolen* cattle for which a hot pursuit was supposedly staged, hills teeming with posses and deputies . . . not one of them ever was seen, however . . . certainly not at the point of shipment. "Why all these alarms and excursions with no attempt at arrest, no formal complaints, no warrants issued? One must ask, were there, indeed, any stolen cattle at all? If so, the receiver of this livestock is a matter of record. All one has to do is examine the manifests, the bills of lading. Why has no move been made to recover? Is the Omaha Company such an easy mark? So I say, lacking any attempt to recover, one is forced to conclude there is no theft. A tissue of suspicious and unsubstantiated claims, it was trotted out here to explain a charge of homicide . . . to supply a *motive*. As a matter of fact," Boe said very quietly, "every man here knows deep in his heart that both cattle and deed were merely stages in the game of feint and parry that Buttons and Gannaway had engaged in for, lo, these many seasons. Suddenly, however, it assumes nonpareil importance. It becomes not the cause for some Indian wrestling contest, but for homicide. You are asked not to think that a man would sally forth because his wife had been raped. No, no . . . you are to think he does so because of some chronic dispute concerning thirty-seven-and-a-half head of cattle. Then if, in spite of all arguments, you *do* insist on believing that a husband *might* be moved to action by the forcible taking of his wife in lust, you must not believe that any overpowering sense of anger would persist. Oh, no, not for as long as two days . . . not for forty-eight hours." He looked over at Wardrope and said: "How long, Mister Prosecutor, do you propose a man should harbor anger over the rape of his wife? Will you tell me? Give us a figure. How about thirty-six hours? No? Twenty-four hours? Would he be justified in anger for one entire day?" Wardrope refused to respond and looked unflinchingly at papers on his desk. "I hear no answer. Of course not. Nobody could stand here and say what is the normal response from a man whose wife has been ravaged. Some men would sneak away and not respond at all. Is this our ideal of a good citizen? Well, I understand that the prosecution is faced with a dilemma. It does not wish to say a man should normally accept the rape of his wife in a calm and rational manner, yet any admission of a rage precluding such rational judgment would render inapplicable its charge, for we know, and the judge will tell you later, that it is not possible under the law for one of inflamed and impaired judgment to commit a first degree of homicide."

Boe said, very well, he would make it easy for the prosecution. "We do not claim the shooting followed a derangement of emotions, or a continuing rage for the rape of the defendant's wife. We don't claim it, because it didn't happen. Gannaway did not fall at the hand of Mister Buttons. To tell how he did fall, at whose hand, would be exceeding my prerogative as the defense attorney. It is not my duty to solve this mystery and bring before you the guilty party, or parties. That is the province of the law officers of this country, and of the prosecution. It is they, not I, who must charge with crime, and then prove that charge beyond any reasonable doubt. Obviously there is *much doubt*. They have not even come close to proving it . . . or anything."

He was not hurried. He looked at his watch. "Fifteen minutes," he said to Judge Minough, who dipped his head. "Witnesses, exhibits, logic . . . ," he said, apparently to little point. Then, still taking his time, almost introspectively, he mentioned that it had occurred to him to call the defendant's mother to the stand, but then, what weight would be given a mother who might naturally be expected to speak out for her son? — even a good, Christian, pioneer woman who would always speak either the truth or not at all, because what was true and what was not true often depended on who looked at it. That was why two witnesses could tell almost diametrically opposite stories and neither be lying. It was merely a fact that people looked not only with their eyes but with their hopes. Alas, even mothers, foremen of ranches, owners, lawyers, merchants, cowboys. "It applies to Kate Buttons. It applies to Avery Carns, too. It applies to Ace Carter, and it applies to Arvis Rapf." He named over the witnesses and asked which could view this matter impartially, uncolored by hope, fear, jealousy, self-interest? However, very little testimony was wholly useless. It always told something. For instance, all the witnesses that day at Willow Creek agreed on a number of points. That in itself was remarkable, considering the distance, which all agreed was beyond rifle range. "It was only when, out of rifle range . . . and think of how far that is! . . . out of rifle range, on that cloudless, heat-distorting noon, that their eyesight became more than remarkable. It makes one wonder. Yes, wonder, and ask . . . 'Is this what they saw? Or what they wanted to see? . . . and after days and months of thinking, came to *believe* they saw?' "

He turned the watch slightly, thoughtfully. With time ticking down like the sands of Billy's life running away, he was not hurried. "The eyes of eagles! Eyesight miraculous! One of the witnesses even saw smoke and bits of burned powder flying from the gun muzzle and made comments as to anger, which could only mean he saw the expressions on the faces, and at a distance he was later to show by lapse of time was in the range of half a mile. But, let's be honest. Lawyers play on this failing of the sincere but ever-zealous witness and draw him out to ridiculous extremes. I was guilty of that. The distance of the witnesses on the rimrocks was not half a mile. It was not an eighth of a mile, either. Both are extremes. It was, *in fact,* a quarter of a mile. This can be shown by inspecting the maps of Captain Logan's survey of Eighteen Seventy-Four when the Army laid out the alternate route, the so-called Cow Island Road to Canada. The crossings were contoured at ten-foot intervals, and it is easy to tell by the descriptions of the witnesses" — he had a map which he picked up and tossed back — "exactly where they had placed themselves, which was, in fact, about a quarter mile, a few feet closer in the case of Mister Carns, a few farther in. . . ."

"Your Honor!" broke in Wardrope, outraged and shocked, "is attorney introducing an exhibit as evidence at this late juncture?"

"Oh, no!" assured Boe. "I am not introducing a map. Why should I? Coals to Newcastle? I feel safe in saying not a man on the jury but is familiar with that very spot, that notable crossing of the freight road, and knows very well the distance. Maps would be a waste of time. But by the way, in regard to distances, if you will look out of the window, across the river, to those cottonwood trees, you *will* have a fair idea of the distance separating those witnesses from the scene of the tragedy."

He offered it as just sort of a casual observation, but everybody looked. They got up to see, welcoming the relief from hot chairs and stiffness, the jury no less than the audience. The room was growing dim, but a brightness still hung on the river, and along the clay faces of distant bluffs. Ducks were flying along the river.

"The river here is six hundred feet wide, a trifle more because it's a natural bay. The Missouri is a remarkable six hundred feet wide for more than a hundred miles from Little Sandy to old Fort Union at the mouth of the Yellowstone, as anyone who has to drive cattle across well knows. But call this five hundred feet, one-ninth of a mile. Add the distance to the docks, one and one-half survey city blocks . . . this townsite *was* surveyed . . . a total of about twelve hundred and fifty feet, or lacking only seventy feet of a quarter mile. The trees on the far bank would put it just about a quarter mile away. Take an average gun . . . the Army Springfield Forty-Five-Seventy. It has a velocity of twelve hundred and sixty feet per second, average load. The distance is about right with witness Rapf's testimony. He had it at two seconds, but I think one second was about right. He was *trying* too hard. Common sense should rule in these matters. As for what would be out of range, the Springfield is targeted pointblank for two hundred and seventy-five feet. That means it's sighted to shoot two inches high, the drop at two hundred and seventy-five feet being two inches. The drop at six hundred feet is twelve inches, less the two mentioned, or ten inches total, and at nine hundred feet, thirty-two inches, less two, or twenty-nine inches. The top elevation of the Springfield rear sight is for twelve hundred feet, which must be considered its extreme range. Hence out of range would be right here for an Army rifle. Some of the new, high-speed express rifles will shoot farther. You see how it holds up to reason. However, whether you could actually *see* what was happening over there . . . well, that depends. I'll leave that up to you. You could see men over there, but actual hand movements, drawing of weapons, shooting, flying powder, well . . . use your common sense."

Wardrope cried: "This introduction of statistics, distances, maps . . . I rise to object. It is irregular and unfair."

"You will point out the manner of the unfairness, then, when it is your turn to speak, which will be shortly," ruled Judge Minough. "Proceed."

Boe then said the findings of the only two expert witnesses, Mr. Blankenship and Doc Hingham, showed that the homicide, if such it was, could not have happened in the way described. "It was the belief of Mister Blankenship, on observing the body, that there were two separate wounds, not one. He came to this conclusion by personal examination overriding what purported to be a true account of the shooting which appeared in the newspapers. Mister Blankenship then performed what to all practical purposes was an autopsy. This was in no way an attempt to determine the cause of death. He had been requested to embalm the body before its transportation east by express train. You all heard him recount how he had to remove trachea and lungs. You all sat here and heard him testify that in all his experience he knew of not one instance in which a Forty-Four or Forty-Five caliber pistol bullet had actually passed *from side to side* through the most impenetrable part of the human frame, the upper chest. A rifle bullet, yes. A brass-bound, high-speed, new type hunting bullet, yes. But not the blunt, slow-traveling slug from a cowboy six-shooter. Then, to make that remote chance even smaller, Mister Blankenship *found a bullet*. Questioned most closely by the defense, and the prosecution, Mister Blankenship discounted any possibility it could have been a small shaving of a heavy pistol bullet. No, it was, by his observation and long experience, *half* of a rifle bullet, and he postulated a Twenty-Five caliber express, one of the new, light, sporting or small-game pieces. Will the clerk please read his exact testimony, commencing with my question . . . 'You said it looked like half a bullet?' "

Bunting, alerted, opened his book and read: "Mister Boe: 'But you said it looked like half a bullet?' Blankenship: 'Yes, in that case a coyote gun, Twenty-Five express, which shoots about eighty-five grains of lead.' Mister Boe: 'So now what think you of the news account of Billy Buttons's shooting down, *bang,* one blast from a Forty-Five?' Mister Blankenship: 'I don't know.' Mister Boe: 'Did it square with facts as you found them? Did it match evidence?' Mister Blankenship: 'Not as I saw it.' Mister Boe: 'You believed he'd shot him from one side, and one of his pals shot him from the other? Did that occur to you?' Blankenship: Objections. Deleted.

Mister Boe: 'When you found what you did find, what occurred to you?' Mister Blankenship: 'I thought he had been shot twice, once from each side.' Mister Boe: 'Is that your opinion now?' Affirmative sign. Mister Boe: 'Based strictly on the evidence which you yourself found, do you believe that Mister Gannaway was shot once or more than once?' Mister Blankenship: 'More than once.' Mister Boe: 'By different caliber guns?' 'Yes.' 'From different directions?' 'Yes.' "

"Thank you, Mister Bunting. My time grows short. I have but four minutes remaining. Remember these were the words of Alben Blankenship, embalmer and experienced coroner. He had read the newspaper accounts, knew what had happened at the inquest, yet in spite of those advertisements of guilt, he came not to believe the single-bullet theory. According to Mister Blankenship, the victim had to be shot at least twice, once from each side. This squares with the testimony of Doc Hingham, U. S. Army, retired, practical surgeon, whose *first* assumption was two separate wounds, or barring that, the massive power of a rifle bullet. Now *his* testimony, Mister Bunting . . . ?"

Bunting was ready. "Mister Boe: 'If they had brought in a body, saying, quote . . . "Here is John Gannaway, shot down by a Forty-Five-Sixty Winchester rifle," would you have believed it?' Hingham: 'Yes, in fact, I'd have been more ready to believe it that way . . . blasted hole all way through.' Boe: 'What if you'd been told he was shot from ambush?' Answer: 'Yes.' Question: 'From ambush sixty yards off, would you have believed it?' Answer: 'Yes.' "

"Thank you. Will you now read the final portion of his testimony?"

"Hingham: 'It' — the death weapon — 'might have been something on the order of a Wells Fargo type Colt. They put out a lot of double-action guns nowadays in steamed-up Thirty-Two longs, Thirty-Two centerfire, but you don't see local fellows carrying them.' Mister Boe: 'Whom do you see carrying them?' Answer: 'Traveling men, detectives.' Mister Boe: Question and answer deleted. Mister Boe: "If, instead of being told he had been shot not once but twice, and being confronted by two bullet holes, would you have conducted your examination differently?' Mister Hingham: 'No.' Mister Boe: 'You said you had probed often for bullets.' Answer: 'In the Army.' Boe: 'But you didn't probe for these bullets?' Hingham: 'No, wasn't any.' Boe: 'How do you know?' Hingham: 'I guess I didn't.' Boe: 'So *now* would you have probed?' Hingham: 'Yes.' Boe: 'As far as you know, he's lying back there, Council Bluffs, with those bullets in him now?' Hingham: 'I guess so.' "

"Thank you, Mister Bunting. And now you see what kind of evidence the grand jury's finding was based on. One is inclined to ask why? Why was no thorough investigation conducted? Was it an accident, a series of blunders? Or did this sort of investigation suit some larger purpose? One is inclined to ask an even more serious question. Was this a means of killing two birds with one stone? On this score, why, after the indictment, was no real, serious attempt made to apprehend the defendant? Why was it necessary for him to ride in on his own and to all intents and purposes *demand* this trial?" Boe smiled. "Oh, yes, everyone here has heard how this county was combed by sheriff and posse, rope in hand . . . or should I say *undersheriff* and posse, rope in hand? It was common knowledge that a watch was kept twenty-four hours a day and night on the bluff above his mother's ranch with instructions to shoot on sight. Yet, no fugitive warrants in Idaho and Wyoming. No, not even to the sheriffs of nearby counties. The message was clear . . . stay away from the old home range and all will be well. Mister Buttons was able to live openly in Butte, register in hotels, ride the train to Helena. Well might he doubt that he was charged at all! And why shouldn't he doubt it? If a murderer, would he shoot a man down in cold blood before three unfriendly witnesses? If a cold-blooded murder, as claimed, why not from ambush? There was plenty of brush in which to hide. Why, as this case is presented, William Buttons would need to be not only a murderer, but crazy . . . or stupid. Is this the Billy Buttons you know? Nothing holds water here. The eye-witness testimony does not square with the physical facts. I have proved beyond any reasonable doubt that this killing did not take place as set forth by the prosecution. This charge and all connected with it are rotten with error . . . or reek of conspiracy."

He wanted to go on in that vein, but the watch stopped him. He picked it up and closed the case. "My time ticks to a close. You are fearless men. You are men of the West. I know deep in my soul you will act with justice. In the teeth of the powers that 'seek to rule this land,' you will find without fear or favor. You will find this man not guilty. Not guilty. Not guilty!"

"Mister Wardrope," said Judge Minough, "you will now have your final, brief time."

Wardrope smiled wanly and remarked: "I might say that my colleague's watch seems as errant as his logic, as he has taken not thirty minutes, but thirty-eight . . . but no matter. Now, just to bury the defense's contentions. First, as far as its contention that Billy was let go free as a bird as long as he stayed beyond the mountains but was to be shot dead on sight if he returned to this jurisdiction, well, one can only observe that he sits there safely . . . that he sat through all the weeks of his incarceration safely. No attempt was made on his life. And, as for his public movements in Butte and Helena, the people of this region do not need to be reminded how little the citizens of the mining towns, gorged with wealth and arrogance, care for the affairs of the eastern ranges. We know well enough how they thumb their noses at us. Your representatives and councilmen have only to attend the territorial legislature to sample the cavalier treatment *they* mete out, arrogantly reminding them that a single mile of bare-blasted mountainside on Butte Hill produces more wealth in copper than all the cattle ranges east of the Continental Divide, and more silver in a season than all the steamboat traffic of the Missouri since the days of the fur trade. And for that reason, we are of little account. But I am surprised to hear it flagrantly used as an argument that this whole prairie country is, therefore, guilty because an indicted person walks free."

He let it sink in and made a display of taking his watch out, putting it back again. "We are required by the defense to suppose that the distance from certain rimrocks was too far to observe two men on horseback, and see one man shooting the other down in cold blood. He would have you look across the river at certain points, implying, without a shred of proof, that such was the distance separating witnesses from the action on Willow Creek. He referred to what he said was a survey map, but no such exhibit appeared at the proper time. This is pretense and subreption. The act was *seen* . . . it was seen by three witnesses . . . seen and exactly described . . . all in agreement. Now, as for the so-called bullet which appeared in Billings on the embalming table . . . this was most obviously and most certainly a small fragment of the heavy bullet which tore at pointblank range through the victim's breast. Never was the smallest scrap of evidence presented that it was anything else.

"So, these are the three points on which the defense asks an acquittal. They are without substance. I tell you, if this man is not guilty, then there never was guilt anywhere. Your duty is plain."

Wardrope then seemed, in that final minute, to think of something else. "You were told that only an idiot, a crazy man, would ride openly before witnesses and commit this deed. I say that it lies in the character of this man. It is typical of him." He looked at Billy, shaking his head in bitter sadness. "For isn't he the one who rode openly into this city and shot the weathervane off the Mountdouglas House? A study in arrogance! Challenge to authority! Observe his past history, how every safeguard, legal and of common custom, he has usurped and derogated to his own uses, turned against its true intent. The very brands of cattle, adopted as safeguard against thieves, he subverts by gathering to his own registry in numbers beyond counting. Without a hair, hide, or acre he puts the stamp of authority on grandiose-sounding corporations! The very pure-bred cattle brought to this land partially as a safeguard against thieves . . . distinctive in white-face markings . . . he subverts. Openly, a challenge. Why, *of course* he rides openly on trains, registers in hotels, and at last cannot resist the final swagger and arrogance of riding down the very main street of this city, and strolling with an aplomb that was nothing less than a sneer into your sheriff's office to say . . . 'Hello, I hear you been looking for me!'

"So this is all in character, and all of a piece. This is Billy Buttons from his head to his toes, from his hat right down to the ground. This is the Billy Buttons you know so well. To shoot down your leading citizen . . . like a dog before witnesses. And then rub it in! How? By seeking to divert you with a so-called rape. A tale more shocking than the murder, and hence designed to render murder to the second class. Men! Men of Arlington! Murder is not of the second class! Men of Ricketts County! The question is this. Are you going to let him get away with it? Because, if he does, what will become of this land? Good God, men, what will become of all of us?"

He stood with his watch for a moment, put it in his pocket with finality, and sat down.

It was quite a speech. It rocked Clyde and left him dizzy. It left him shocked and sick. From the heights of certitude on listening to Boe, he was plunged in hopelessness. Then, after a while, he heard Judge Minough.

"Now, there were many things said here which constitute improper evidence, which I must admonish you to disregard, or give very light weight. For example. . . ."

It had grown dark, and the lamps were burning. The crowd grew restless, and Judge Minough stopped for quiet. He was talking about the "young woman's testimony" and "the unwritten law."

"And so I must tell you that there is no such thing as 'the unwritten law.' Hence, dramatic and shocking as the events described by Missus Buttons, defendant would be without justification in seeking recourse to arms or violence. Had he entered while the asserated attack was in progress, then he might have been justified to act in such a manner as to protect his hearth and spouse, but after the fact he must needs rely on the due course of law, either the criminal or the civil procedures, as the case may be. Hence, I admonish you to disregard the testimony of Missus Buttons as affording any shade of justification should you decide the homicide did take place as alleged, although you may regard it as motive. Now we will take up that evidence after the fact, the state of the body, wounds, morbid exhibits, expert testimony. Primarily you must decide whether this evidence, which is real evidence, and not in any way less in weight than that offered *vive voce* . . . and certainly not less than those signed depositions already mentioned, testimony offered *de bene esse* . . . whether this renders illogical or in the realm of improbability the eye-witness accounts. . . ."

His voice went on, sentence on sentence in slow enunciation, tearing down everything that might help Billy and giving weight to that which condemned, and Clyde shut his ears to him.

The judge stopped finally. He sat waiting while the clerk finished writing and did some scratchings and blottings. The light was poor under the hanging lamps, but at last Bunting nodded that he was through.

"You will select a foreman upon being closed away," resumed Judge Minough. "Major," he said to Morrison, "you will be temporary chairman to effect that arrangement, and to lead this group, without communication with others, to the Mountdouglas House. A supper will be served, and a room will be provided for your deliberations. It is my hope that with due regard for all, with courtesy to those with divergent views, but without stubbornness in untenable positions, you will reach a firm and speedy verdict. I will anticipate that verdict before my bedtime."

He stood, and everyone stood. With some stumbling, long cramped from sitting, the jury followed Undersheriff Danner to the rear stairs. Billy left with Deputies Wall and Dolson. The crowd still remained, held by Judge Minough, and waited, and waited. He gestured to the sheriff. Earl Hankey came over and said: "Kate. You can come out this way."

"No, I'm all right."

However, the judge nodded at her, so she let Hankey take her through the barricade to the court area and down the back stairs. After a few seconds, Clyde followed.

"I'll find a buggy," said Hankey.

"Where's Billy?" Ma asked. "I want to see my son."

"No, Kate. He's not *at* the jail."

"Where is he? What have you done with my son?" She pulled away from his restraining hand and demanded: "What have you done with him?"

"Now, Kate. He's all right. It's for his own safety as much as anything."

"What are you going to do to my son?"

"All isn't lost by any means. He had a good defense. You have to keep up hope."

Clyde wanted to push the sheriff away and ask who did he think he was, acting like a *friend* when he'd done everything in his power to make sure Billy was convicted?

Hankey said: "Stay with your mother. I'll see if I can find a buggy."

Not a rig in town was hitched, so they walked to Maud Hemphill's where Maud, Jane Volkman, Mrs. Froelich, the Crowleys, and Miss Mary Lively were all waiting, anxious to provide reassurance and prove what real friends were for.

"I'll come back for you in plenty of time if I hear anything," said the sheriff. "Eat something and lie down and rest."

"Oh, dear," said Ma. "I couldn't swallow a bite. I just want to lie down a while."

They all went tiptoeing around while Ma rested, and were very kind to Clyde. Harry Wilson, whom he had always liked, came and tried to make conversation about other things, but the facts bore down until they seemed to be pressing the breath out of him. Clyde made an excuse of going out back to the privy, but he walked around it. It was too dark outside. He'd never be able to hit the hole. He went on, into the willow trees, leaves mostly gone, and urinated. He drained the brine off his pickle, as Billy used to say. God! He wanted to break down and bawl, thinking how Billy had said it, with his smile. Nobody ever had a smile like poor Billy. Then he circled back around town to the Square Deal. He had an idea he'd like to sit there with the horses, friendly creatures from familiar times. He didn't want anybody to notice him, but he scarcely got inside the shed when Square-Deal Hackersmith came poking around saying: "Buttons? Hey, Buttons!"

"Yeah?"

"I took care of your team. Say, I notice that big bay gelding with the shoulder scar is here."

It was old Fiddles, the horse Billy rode into town when he surrendered.

"Who brought him here?" asked Clyde.

"Beats me. I thought you'd know."

"No."

"Well, say nothing about it. I guess they figured he'd need something to ride out on when they found him not guilty."

"Think he's got a chance?" asked Clyde, sounding offhand and manly.

"*Of course* he's got a chance! Why, acquittal's the only verdict possible after what happened to that woman. There's not a man on that jury but would have done the same. Major Morrison, or anybody. Mark my words, Billy will walk out a free man."

But Major Morrison was the reason Billy didn't have a chance. Morrison would line up with the Omaha sure, and there wasn't a man on the jury who would go up against the major when he came down for conviction.

Clyde didn't go look at the horse. He'd have needed a lantern, and he didn't want to give anything away. He stood in the dark, wondering if the sheriff had got wind that something was afoot and that's why they'd moved Billy to a secret place. If so, he might be able to find out where. He might see Earl Hankey, or Danner, or gangling, tall Pete Wall going there. It would be a tip-off, and he could pass the word on to Ace Carter or Long Tom Cooper. They were Billy's friends through thick and thin, and, if they hadn't brought Fiddles around, they knew who had. Fiddles was Billy's favorite horse. He was a real long horse, which meant he might not travel so fast, but he could go for a long, long time. Put Billy on Fiddles and head him into the badlands, and they'd play hell ever catching up with him, because he traveled that country like a night wolf. He knew it like the back of his hand. It was his native soil.

Clyde walked down an alley. It occurred to him he might be able to see just about everything from a roof, but they were all too steep, or they had false fronts like walls that couldn't be seen over, or they were next to higher buildings from which he might be seen. Then, there was always somebody around, doors opening and closing.

After wandering all over town, and no sign of sunset left in the sky, he sat down with his back against a log wall where a cabin had been burned out a long time before. The logs were very thick. They had absorbed the heat of the day and were still warm at his back. He shivered, and his teeth chattered, but finally he managed to close out the chill, and he waited and waited. He waited until finally he got to wondering if it was midnight, and, if so, they'd probably put the jury to bed, so he got up and went around to the street where he could see the clock in the jeweler's window, but it was only a quarter past ten.

He walked slowly, killing time. It was cold, and he wondered whether to go back to his old place, or the barn for a jacket, when he heard excited voices — and running bootheels along a sidewalk.

"There they come! They're leaving the hotel!"

Oh God, they had reached a verdict.

CHAPTER TWENTY

Clyde stood where he was. He didn't know what to do. He wanted to hide, or run — do anything except listen to Billy's fate. *I'll have to get Ma,* he thought. Yes, they expected him to.

He cut around behind the hotel and through empty lots with big sage growing in them, but, when he got about halfway to Maud's, a buggy passed by. He realized it was Earl Hankey with Ma beside him. The sheriff had been forewarned that the jury was done, and gone after her.

Clyde ran after the buggy and tried to see the sheriff's face. He tried to catch something in his manner, or a word or two that would tell him what the verdict was, but there was no hint. The sheriff sat rather stiffly and drove, and Ma sat just as rigidly. They didn't seem to be exchanging a word.

Clyde followed the buggy to the rear of the courtroom where all was bright from an electric post light. The jury was just climbing the stairs, and some had stopped. Jurors Spear, Casey, Sauer, and Stefling were still outside. They weren't saying anything; they seemed very sober, serious. They could look down on Ma in the buggy, or they *could* have looked down. They gave her only a glance, maybe, then looked away. With Earl Hankey holding her by the elbow, she found the iron buggy step, kept her skirts clear, and made it to the ground. Then they climbed the stairs back of the disappearing jurymen.

Clyde stood all alone. The stairs were empty. Then he started up, and Ted Danner confronted him. He was guarding the back, posted just inside the door, and he had a sawed-off shotgun. There he stood, evil and sallow, with his drooping mustache, and he didn't move.

"I got to go inside."

"Go around in front."

"I'm with *her*."

"Get away from here. Get away from these stairs. Go around in front."

"I'm with *her*."

"Get away from here. Get away from these stairs. Go around in front."

Was it possible he didn't recognize him? — didn't even know who he was? Clyde retreated back to the ground, and Ike Thrift, range detective for the Association, was watching him, and he also had a sawed-off shotgun. Mace Kuykendall came walking up: even *he* was wearing a badge, and he was weighted with two pistols and a rifle. They were out in force, taking no chance on any break after the verdict was passed. Clyde thought for a second Thrift was going to stop him, but he just stood and watched, and he got out of their sight by going around the building to the front sidewalk. There was no possible way of getting inside the courtroom. The best he could do was climb the stairs to where about twenty men jammed the landing and the top several steps.

I've got to get in, he told himself, but he couldn't. It was impossible. He had to wait there, nobody knowing who he was. From the stairs he could see the ceiling and the lamps. When he got just a little higher and on tiptoes, he could see the top of Judge Minough's head. The judge was seated behind his desk on the little platform, but he hadn't called the court to order. Finally he did, and the crowd quieted. The sounds slowly died, and he could hear the judge's voice, but the words didn't come through.

Somebody on the step ahead of him said: "Yes, they have. They've come to a verdict."

"Mister Foreman, will you read the verdict?" he heard the judge say.

It was coming. Major Morrison was giving the verdict. Clyde could not hear it for the beating of his own heart, but above him, and halfway through the door, Sam Tibbs let out a yell — *"Ya-hoo!"* — and turned with his face contorted and staring.

He was a friend of Billy's and partner at the Spider, and from the depths Clyde's heart sprang up.

"What is it?" they were yelling from below.

"Not guilty! They found him not guilty!"

Clyde let the crowd carry and buffet him. He was dizzy with

elation and relief. He wanted to laugh and cheer and run capering down the street. Everybody seemed elated at the verdict. He couldn't believe his ears. They were whooping and laughing and slapping one another on the back! Somebody fired a pistol in the air. The country was not lined up against Billy, after all. Only the great and powerful — and not even all of those.

All of a sudden a terrible thought came to Clyde. What if he had heard wrong? Or had been told wrong? What if the verdict was *guilty?* It frightened him, so he stopped abruptly in the middle of the street. He started back toward the courtroom

"What was the verdict?" he asked the first man he saw.

"Not guilty. Wait, aren't you the Buttons kid?"

"Yeah."

"Say, you're cool about it!"

"Aw, hell," said Clyde, making his voice careless, "I knew how it would go. He was innocent. They couldn't find it any other way."

At last the crowd thinned out, and Clyde was able to get upstairs to the courtroom. Billy was standing there, a free man.

"Come here, kid!" said Billy and brought him right in through all the noisy well-wishers. "This is my brother, Clyde, who stuck with me through thick and thin!"

Ma was off to one side with Earl Hankey. Judge Minough was at the back door, arguing with Cal Reims and Major Morrison. Then Wardrope joined in. Wardrope kept emphasizing with sharp jerks of a free hand, the other holding the big, square portfolio. After a while the major stopped him, laughing, gentling his feelings with pats on the arm.

"There, there, now," he seemed to be saying. "Time will help you see it differently."

Finally Wardrope came back and shook hands with Boe, and they left together, following Minough, Reims, Morrison, Bunting, and Stewart down the rear stairs. There was not the slightest interest in Billy. He seemed to have lost all importance.

At last Billy and Ma got together. He didn't want her too close so she could grab hold and slobber over him.

"It's all right, Ma. Look, I'm hale and hearty. Nothing happened to me."

"It's not all right if it didn't teach you anything. Oh, I pray God this taught you a lesson."

"You got it all wrong. They're the ones ought to be taught a lesson. I'm not guilty. I was falsely accused. What have I got to feel sorry for?"

"You've been given a second chance! You had ought get down on your knees and thank Almighty God."

But Billy only laughed, and winked at Clyde.

"You take care of her, will you? Ma, listen, I'll see you after while. I got to pick up some things of mine, and see the lawyer. You go on back to Maud's, and I'll see you later."

She didn't want to let go of him, but she finally had to, and then she just stood there, and stood there.

"Come on, Ma," said Clyde, "everybody's going."

"Where's that wife of his, if she cares so much for him? Why ain't she here?" And while going down the stairs, Ma asked: "Why didn't he ever bring her around?"

"He was in jail."

"Then *she* should have come around. It was her righten duty."

Harry Wilson was waiting with the sheriff's buggy.

"Ain't you coming?" Ma asked Clyde.

Harry said: "He's been a real good boy. You let him go, now, and see the sights."

"At this hour . . . this lurid hour between night and morning?"

"It's not even twelve o'clock," Harry Wilson said.

"Oh, dear. I don't want *him* to go chasing after false gods."

"You don't have to worry about Clyde," Harry said, casting a wink. "That lad's got good stuff in him."

Clyde was left by himself. In a couple of minutes Billy came down the front stairs, surrounded by friends, most of whom had their guns on. They weren't supposed to carry them in the courtroom, but they sure as sin *had* them. Clyde could tell by the way they had their coats and jackets buttoned, and hitched their bodies around. They weren't taking any chances on a sudden ambush right there in the street, that was certain. Clyde stayed back, and Billy never noticed him. They were going some place to celebrate, and that didn't include him. He wasn't old enough. Besides, Billy had said to take care of Ma.

They walked straight over to the Mountdouglas House, best hotel in town, not taking a back seat for anybody. They went inside, and Clyde watched for a long time, wondering if they had ended up at the bar, or where? Finally he decided to walk around and see what else was going on. He walked all the way to the docks, where, well away from the saloons, stood the Grand, a two-story building that was a whorehouse. There was an orchestra playing, and he could hear men and women laughing, but he didn't stay very long for fear somebody would see him and think he was trying to peek inside. He walked back along the other side of the street and saw the drug store had closed. If it hadn't, he'd have gone in for a soda. Then, all of a sudden, he got the wild notion to go over to the barber shop for a haircut and shave, but, when he got there, the barber was just sweeping up. Clyde had a lot of long hair on his cheeks and under his jawbone that he trimmed off with Ma's shears, but he'd never shaved. Every time he said something about shaving, old Tom, or whoever was around, would say: "Why don't you put some milk on it and have the cat lick it off?" So he decided not to go in, the barber shop getting swept out and all.

He stalled around and stalled around, and once, just for the hell of it, he yelled: *"Ya-hoo!"* and heard his voice echo. He yelled: *"Ya-hoo!"* again, and it came back as plain as anything from the bluffs across the river. *"Yip-ee! Yip-ee!"* yelled Clyde. What he wished he could do was cut loose, really cut loose and raise a little hell, but he wasn't quite old enough.

He was just standing there, wondering what he ought to do — he didn't want to go to Maud's, or to the barn to bed — when Ted Danner slouched from the Elkhorn Saloon and stood looking at him. Clyde wasn't afraid of him because there were too many people just inside, and somebody had hitched up and was leaving, late as it was, in a wagon. Still, it gave him a bad turn, and he felt as if his insides would fall out, because Danner might have guessed how the lawyer found out about his meeting the sheriff at the old R & O stage station. If he ever guessed, he'd wait his chance and shoot Clyde down like a dog.

Clyde walked off. He went inside the Green Front Saloon because it was right there, handy. Nobody paid any attention to him. He went over and watched the games for a while. They were playing poker, and there was a faro game being run by two strangers. One of them sat on a stool and kept tabs on all the cards on an abacus, and the other one worked the box. Clyde put down two bits on the eight, but it lost. He didn't want them to think it bothered him, so he put down another quarter, and after a while he lost that, too.

"Well, I guess it ain't my night," he said. He kept thinking what a damned fool he was to be taken for fifty cents, just as if he had thrown it in the river.

Clyde started for the door.

"How's your mother?" asked R. V. Blackwood who had a ranch over on the Musselshell.

"She's all right. I was just going over there."

They went outside together.

"Give her my regards," said Blackwood. "Tell her I'm glad for her . . . how it worked out."

Clyde said he would and walked for a while, but he didn't want to be out in the dark lonesome with his back toward Danner. He couldn't get over the feeling he had, so he went in the Mountdouglas in hopes of seeing Billy.

The lobby was L-shaped with hardwood, mosaic floors and a desk of polished marble, like a tombstone. There were brass posts at each end of the desk, with frosted globes, and new electric fixtures on brass chains from the ceiling. There were big, leather, padded chairs and divans, and palms in green tubs. A fountain and stone tank where fish had lived was dry and coated with limy crust. Clyde didn't know where to turn. There were seven or eight men, sitting and talking, but nobody looked at him.

Finally somebody asked him: "Looking for your brother?"

"Yeah."

"Upstairs one flight and turn to your right. They're in the old Steamboat Club."

When the Mountdouglas was built, and Arlington was to be a city with ice plants and the largest beef-packing houses northwest of Sioux City, the Steamboat was a private club with its own bar, restaurant, card rooms, and bedrooms.

Clyde followed directions and came to a double door. Nobody answered his knock, so he went in. He was in a small room with hats and coats hung around, tossed over settees. Somebody was playing

292

a piano. Through an archway he could see a room teeming with people. Old Arnold Pease was playing the piano. He was little and dried up, no bigger than a jockey, and he played with his head turned to one side and an eye closed because of the cigarette in his mouth. Amid whooping and brawling, a fight seemed ready to break out. Leo Grimes was seated on the floor, cross-legged, and Rocky Cartot was trying to show how he could hold him helpless with one hand, but Leo wouldn't assume the right position. A Negro in a white coat was behind a bar about four feet long, and there were women somewhere. Clyde could hear their high-pitched laughter. There was no sign of Billy.

"Well, look what the cat drug in!"

It was Kid Nehf. He got hold of Clyde's arm and pulled him to the bar.

"Hey, what you drinkin'?"

Clyde didn't know what to say. The Negro looked at him.

"Guess he can't figure you out, George. What's the matter, ain't you ever been served by a nigger before?"

"Take yo' time," said the Negro.

"Give him a bolt of that real old Kentucky lightning right out of the oak."

"How yo' like yo' whiskey, suh?"

"Straight!" said Nehf. "Why, this man is a Buttons!"

Clyde had had whiskey only with hot water and sugar for the croup, and even the smell of it made him want to throw up. However, when he took the glass in his hand, Long Tom Cooper came over and stopped him.

"Use your brains, Nehf," Long Tom said, pronouncing it *Neef*.

"He's grown up!" Nehf protested. "You're a man now, aren't you, Clyde?"

Long Tom said: "Clyde has his ma to look out for. Billy's orders. Do you have any pop back there?"

"Yas, suh! I got sarsaparilla."

While drinking sarsaparilla from a beer mug, Clyde looked around to see who all were there. Most of the bunch from the Spider were on hand, and Oscar Friedahl who'd been playing cards with Billy in jail, Pat McGraw, the bartender who'd been challenged from the jury, Tom Bush who was supposed to be on the slope from the law, and about a dozen more. Lots of the men were all dressed up as Clyde had never seen them before, in white shirts or white-striped shirts, boiled collars, and neckties. The women were at the far side of the room, two of them, one fat and one skinny. The skinny one was terribly painted. The fellows were having a merry time with them, and every few seconds the fat one would let out a laugh like a whinny. She'd go *"E-e-e!"* as if somebody had goosed her from behind. The skinny one just stood and puffed on a cigarette. Clyde had heard about such women, and he suspected they were whores.

"You son-of-a-bitch, you been cut," the fat girl was saying to Pat McGraw. "You ain't got any nuts at all. You ain't got a pecker, even. All you got is a little wee-wee piece of skin to hold out of your pants when you go pee-pee. You never been circumcised because, if you had, you'd have just a hole in your belly. *E-e-e!"*

Clyde had never heard a woman talk like that. Old Bertha Griesbach swore like a man, but she never talked that way. Yet the men were roaring with laughter.

"What do you think of *her?"* asked Kid Nehf, to which Clyde managed a laugh.

"You're just jealous because I got a new girl," said Pat McGraw.

"E-e-e!" she whinnied. "You ain't got a girl. All you got is a board with a knot hole in it. *E-e-he-he-he!"*

"Shut up, Annabelle," said Long Tom cheerfully.

"Shut up yourself, you son-of-a-bitch."

After a while, Long Tom motioned for Clyde to follow him into another room, not so large, or light, or full of tobacco smoke. There sat Boe with a woman on his lap. She had her arms around him, and they seemed to be in a very intimate conversation. Clyde did not recall having ever seen her before. Art Rooney was standing with Ace Carter. Both nodded to him, and continued their conversation. Things were much more quiet and well behaved than in the first room.

"Where's Billy?" asked Art.

"He's around," answered Ace.

"Hello, young fellow," said Boe.

"Hello, darling," said the girl on his lap.

Then he heard another woman's voice, very familiar. "Why, it's the cute little brother!"

He didn't know what to say. It was Billy's wife. Clyde stood looking at her. She had come into the room so close to him he could smell her perfume — an unnerving, warm odor. It gave Clyde a jelly feeling. She smiled, and she looked different than at the trial. She was the same woman, but she wasn't. She was more vivid. She had a quality of carmine and glitter, but not from paint or jewels. Clyde realized that she no longer had the gap between her front teeth. Her teeth were perfect. She did not take her eyes off him. She never touched him, but he was aware of her.

"What's the name? Clyde? *Is* it Clyde?"

He managed to answer, strangely short of breath: "Yeah, Clyde."

"Oh, that's nice. Clyde. I'm Francie. Oh, don't pay any attention to what they called me *there*." She meant at the trial. "My friends call me Francie."

Billy came in. There he stood, smiling. He still wore his collar and tie, but he had shed his coat, and his shirtsleeves were pulled up by arm bands. He had been drinking. Billy never got drunk. Sometimes he'd *act* drunk and then get over it in a hurry, when he needed to, but even a few drinks would show itself in his heightened color and the shine of his eyes.

"What are you drinkin', there?" He took the mug from Clyde and tasted it. "Christ!"

"It's all right. It's what I wanted."

"What is it? Cough medicine?"

Clyde started to answer sarsaparilla but was ashamed to. "I have to go back and see Ma. I don't want her smelling liquor on my breath."

"Of course, you don't," said Francie. "Here, let me give you some of this."

"I hope you know what you're doing," said Long Tom.

She poured a wine glass of bubbly liquid. It looked greenish in one light and slightly yellowish in another.

"That'll fix you up," said Billy. "That's Mumms Champagne. You're really living it high class now. It's what us Buttons were really born for, given our just share of luck."

Clyde drank it straight down because Francie was watching him, smiling and encouraging him, and it raised lightnings in his stomach.

295

"I'll give you one more, but don't drink it down like that," Francie said.

"Well, I needed something," Clyde said.

"He's just in off the range," Billy remarked. "And riding herd on Ma! *Jeez!* I'd rather ride herd on a rangy, old buffalo than our ma!"

"He's a good boy! You *are*," Francie assured him. "You're a good, good boy. It must have been very, very hard on you . . . just sitting there, not knowing what was going to happen."

"He's not the only one. How about me?" asked Billy.

"I don't worry about you. You had it all coming to you." Francie looked gently at Clyde. "What a good boy. Come over here. Let me take hold of you."

"Go ahead," encouraged Billy. "It's all in the family."

"Oh, you keep quiet. Don't you pay any attention to him," Francie insisted.

"Show her your muscles, Clyde."

Clyde didn't know what to do. He still couldn't figure it all out. He hadn't seen her smoking when she came into the room, but now, as she came up very close to him and took hold of his arm, he could smell the tobacco on her breath. It implied she was one of *those* women, but he rejected the thought. She was certainly nothing like those two in the other room, loud, painted, and vile. She was perfumed, but she was scrubbed and clean under it. The strange complexities of odors baffled him — perfume, liquor, cigarettes, and clean skin. And, oh God! how it stirred him when he felt her hands on his arm, and, when she turned, he could feel her body under her dress. He knew it was sliding along perfectly free under the silk. It was all she had on, just the dress! Long and modest enough, but no corset underneath. He could actually feel her breast pressing against his arm. She slowly pressed it toward him while saying: "Oh, what a nice boy. You didn't tell me I was going to have such a nice little brother."

"You keep that up," said Billy, "and you're likely to have more on your hands than you bargained for."

"Don't you pay any attention to him. You're not afraid of me, are you?"

"No," Clyde said, but he got free. He was all in a sweat of embarrassment from the awareness that everyone was looking at him.

Boe was smiling in a rather placid and philosophical way, and the girl on his lap had sat up to watch with real interest.

"Go ahead, Clyde," said Billy.

Go ahead, what? he felt like asking, but didn't. Above all, he didn't want them laughing at him, thinking he was a kid.

"You stay out of this," said Francie. "Now, come along with me."

Clyde didn't know what to do. Everybody was grinning and looking at him. He was still gripping the champagne, and Francie was leading him with an irresistible pressure, not strong as a man would be strong, but irresistible.

"You look out for him," said Billy. "He's wild as a two-year-old stallion. He's never been halter-broke."

"Oh, you keep quiet. We're just going to get acquainted."

The girl in Boe's lap said: "You better take a bullet to hold in your teeth, Francie!"

"Just you shut up. Don't you pay the *least* attention, Clyde. Oh, you smell so nice. And you're so strong."

With these words, and the steady strength of her arm, with that breast now under his armpit, Clyde let Francie coax him through a door. She closed the door, and they were in a bedroom, lit by a coal oil lamp rather than harsh electric bulbs. He saw the bed had been rumpled and pulled back together and knew she'd been in there with Billy. He stood, trying to get his bearings, and, before he realized what she was about, she reached right down inside his pants and grabbed hold of him. She grabbed him by the genital. It was hard as a rock. It had been poking out like a hammer handle, and he'd been forced to lean farther and farther forward with his hindend back so it wouldn't show.

"Hey!" he said, pawing to get her away. "Wait a minute!"

But, instead, she started working at him with both hands. She had his testicles in one hand and his penis in the other.

"Leave me alone!"

"Why, Clyde?"

"I know what I want to do. I don't need anybody. . . ."

"Clyde. Come on and lie down. Just lie down."

He fended her off.

"Come and sit down. Just sit beside me. Don't run away."

"I'm not running."

"Do you think I'm a bad, bad woman?"

"No."

"Then sit down and just talk to me."

He sat uncomfortably on the side of the bed. He thought she was going to sit beside him and talk for a while, just sit quiet while he got his bearings, but she started running her palms around under his shirt. She stroked his chest and blew under his ear.

"What nice hair."

"Too long," muttered Clyde. "Should have got a haircut."

"No, it's nice and thick. I've seen *girls* who would pay a lot of money for such hair. It's so curly."

"You and Billy ain't even *married?*"

"Why, how you talk! You saw the certificate."

"Who are you? You admit your name isn't even Mary Mar . . . ?"

"Oh, they just call me Francie. It's a nickname. Why Clyde, what are you saying? Do you think I'm a bad, bad woman? Be a good boy now and take off your clothes. Just undress and lie back. I want you to like me. It's what Billy wants you to do."

She let go of his head and lay back on the bed. She kicked off her slippers and pulled her dress away up and lay with her legs spread out. She wore stockings with fancy garters, but all the way from her knees to her belly button, she was completely bare. There it was, that place he'd thought so much about, and speculated about in his imagination, and he never imagined it would be awesome in size. He mind shot back to one time in the bunkhouse at home when old Tom Shipley, with his usual filthy talk, had been telling about some woman in a whorehouse where he'd been. "She looked just like she'd been hit by a meat axe," old Tom had said. Clyde remembered that. Despite her being such a slim and delicate woman, it was huge. It was big as a cow's. And his own erection had vanished. It was just gone. His penis was limp and dribbly. Oh God, how he wanted to escape!

"Clyde," she said alluringly. Then she realized he was on his way to the door and cried out: "Oh, you god-damned fool! You sanctimonious, overgrown whelp. You big cow turd. Who do you think you are?"

"I ain't taking any of Billy's leavings!" he cried defensively, stopping.

"Oh." She said it in a certain, final manner, and sat up.

At least it was an explanation she could accept. She stood and smoothed her clothes in front of a mirror. She found a box of cigarettes, lit one. Leaning over the lamp chimney, there was a glinting hardness about her, especially the lines at the corners of her mouth. She didn't look old. In fact, she didn't look so old as she had in the courtroom. She was young and old at the same time. She was only about five or six years older than Clyde, but he knew he'd never in a hundred years have the worldliness she did. He busied himself buttoning up his pants and tucking in his shirt.

The cigarette was rolled in brown paper and had a smell like a cigar. It came from a box with a picture of mosques and camels with powdery gold speckles. The smoke was heavier than a cigar, and on second whiff absolutely different than a cigar, and he wondered if it was one of the cigarettes he'd read about in the magazines with Turkish tobacco cured in tincture of opium. When the light from the oil lamp hit her from beneath, there was a glinting hardness about her.

"You got a girl out in the hills?" she asked.

"Yeah," said Clyde, seizing on that explanation.

"Being true to her?"

"I guess so," he muttered. "I'm beat out. I ain't in the mood."

"How about a cigarette?"

"Yeah."

He sat around with the cigarette in his fingers, not wanting to smoke it too much for fear it might make him sick, but willing to have a certain amount of time go by. He didn't want to come charging out as though she'd scared him.

"What about Gannaway?" he asked. "Wasn't there any truth in that?"

"What he did to me? You don't think I'd lie to the court, do you?"

"Well . . . ?"

"I know better than perjure a story for the court, sonny."

"Yeah, that's what I figured in the first place."

"You're smarter than you let on. Did you think I came here to rope that big bully-boy into what we call a contretemps? Do you think Billy got me here to set him up?"

"No, I don't think it, and I never thought it."

"Billy wouldn't wipe his feet on a deal like that. Let me tell you this. Anything Gannaway got was good enough for him. He drove his wife crazy. Even his own sons wouldn't come out here for his body. They left it to the freight handlers, but they'd view the body to see if there's money in the pockets. Otherwise, they wouldn't bother so much as to arch their piss into his coffin. If Billy died, there wouldn't be room in this town for the people that'd march to his funeral. Let me tell you, I'd go to the end of the world for that brother of yours. He was the best man in the courtroom today, and don't you forget it. You may end up being a famous doctor. I hope you do, but you'll have to travel a long road before you're ever the man your brother is."

Clyde was impressed. He couldn't help but be.

She said, changing her tone: "What's your little sweetheart's name?"

He didn't know what to answer. He really didn't have a girl, but he let on he did, and the only one he could think of was Bob Wallin's daughter, Lillian, but Bob was out in the other room, so he said: "Lois."

"How old is she?"

"Oh . . . I don't know."

"Make a guess."

"Fifteen."

"Fifteen? I was fifteen when I ran away from home. I didn't get along with my mother. I ran away with a brakeman on the railroad. I got on a passenger coach one night, and he just hauled me free. He promised to marry me, but it turned out he already had a wife. I told him I was knocked up. I only wanted to squeeze him into providing a little more money, but Jesus Christ! You know, he fell between two cars of the Western Flyer and was cut in half? I never did know whether his foot slipped or whether he took the easy way out. The dispatcher knew all about us and came around and said he'd been cut in half at the waist and which half did I want? He thought it was one hell of a joke. He said I ought to take the top half, because it was the bottom half that was the cause of his trouble. He was playing with a woman in Decatur, too. He was red-haired and freckled. I never saw anybody so freckled. He had a brakeman's cap with a patent leather bill, and he used to perch it on top of that mop of hair.

300

He always had a smile. He was no good, and he got what he deserved, but, if he walked through that door today, I'd forgive him. Life's a funny thing. You do things, and then you hunt for the reasons afterward. Just live it one minute at a time. Don't you forget that, Clyde. Try to lay it out too far ahead, and life will have some bad surprises for you."

"'Yeah," said Clyde. "That's the way it goes."

She was being considerate. He knew she was talking for time to pass so he could go back and make it seem logical that he'd given her the old prod, so he could be a man among men, a stud among the stallions, as the saying went.

"I let his wife have both halves. I even frisked the room for his stuff. I gave her his stickpin and an alligator suitcase . . . all except his watch which he was having repaired. Those railroad men will have half their fortune tied up in a watch. He had a seventeen-jewel Hampden with an engine engraved on it. I had to dig down for the jeweler's bill, so she didn't get that. I sold it for enough to go to Chicago. I knew a man there who'd been a friend of my father's. He got me a job playing piano in a theater. It wasn't a theater, exactly. It was a big parlor house where a lot of girls brought their squires . . . three-story place called Chapprick's, named after a political boss. It was really famous. Operators rented the saloon concession, gambling concession, food, even hat check and prize ring, boxing, roosters. Everything was leased out. It made a mint of money. It was the sort of place the silk-hat crowd came to when they wanted to slum. They even had opium, and some of the biggest muck-a-mucks from the Lake Front came there to have a pipe. I mean, I didn't have to go between the sheets if I didn't want to. The madame, Belle Britling . . . everybody called her Aunt Belle . . . she'd show up with twenty thousand dollars' worth of diamonds hanging on her. She took a liking to me. She'd introduce me to men and let me do what I liked. I wouldn't say they were love matches. There weren't any brakemen, you understand. But I could choose, and the men brought me gifts. Don't be shocked, Clyde. A girl out by herself doesn't have much choice. Not like a man. I went to live with one man for six months, and three months with another. Finally I went out West to Colorado. I was in Leadville. I helped run a theater, and lost everything in the big fire, then I went down to Black Hawk, and Denver, and all around.

I was in San Francisco. I was there a week, turned around, and went back. I didn't like the fog. I ended up in Council Bluffs. There were two girls there, sisters. They'd been at Aunt Belle's. You've heard of the LaValleys? Paulette and Mitzi? They were from New Orleans. They started the Majestic, and it became famous. They used to say it had seven levels like the seven levels of hell. But that was only talk. It was a very nice place. It had the main theater, bar, and restaurant, and the parlors, which were on the second floor, the crystal ballroom on the third, and the gentlemen's *Soirée* through a private passage in the next building. Gambling was illegal, so, if the main place was raided, nobody could be apprehended next door. That was an added protection for the *gentlemen*. The LaValleys separated out the lower class and the upper crust. If you made it to the *Soirée*, it really *meant* something. We entertained senators, railroad presidents, millionaires, European nobility. If you were a banker, you could go to the *Soirée* without the least risk of meeting your teller, because he'd never get past the second floor. The Major Morrisons never ran the slightest risk of meeting one of their cowboys, or some walloper who'd come along on the cattle train."

Her laugh came in a musical derision when she saw his expression. "Didn't Billy tell you I was an old friend of Major Morrison's?"

His slack jaw and stare were the answer. But things were dawning on him — why the major had been accepted on the jury.

"Oh, yes. I played the piano for him in that very *Soirée*. Oh, it was an ultra private occasion when Major Morrison came. We were forewarned, and everything had to be very discreet. No vulgarity tolerated. The group was small, but very select. No vulgar language, you understand. That was not to imply a rein on the libidinous art. No, little boy. The tastes of some of those *patricians* would be enough to shock the boys down at the roundhouse. They asked for things never dreamed of by a brakeman or a conductor. I wouldn't even tell you about it. Well." — she patted his arm — "now, now! This isn't to *imply*. No. The major was a gentleman. The LaValleys presented me as a niece, from down the river. Oh, he didn't believe a word of it. He knew very well . . . and I told him the truth. He kept coming back, bringing me gifts, then he presented a very lavish gratuity to the place . . . almost like buying me . . . and he took me to Chicago. He promised to marry me. We went everywhere together. The most beautiful hotels and resorts. He was no piker, I'll say that for him. He used to write to me from out West. I never kept the letters. He didn't sign them. It was so transparent. I could see through him like a pane of glass, smart as he was. Man of the world. That son-of-a-bitch. One day . . . he'd taken me to Saratoga, New York . . . and I woke up, and there was five hundred dollars, lying on the bed, and I knew he was gone for good. Back in Chicago I read where he'd married the widow of Colonel So-And-So who had been over at Fort Kehoe. He'd been visiting her in Vermont and sleeping with me between times in Saratoga. He has political hopes. He wants to be governor. I'd hardly do for first lady, would I? There I'd be in the receiving line at the governor's palace, and some mining man would remember me from the Palace Theater in Leadville."

"Did he know about you and Billy?"

"He never dreamed I was nearer than Chicago, honey. Oh, you should have seen . . . well, you *did* see his expression when I walked in and sat down in the witness chair. He was all ready to put the rope around poor Billy's neck. He couldn't believe his luck in being on the jury. He must have thought Boe was a damned fool. Poor Maj! He always suffered from a sour stomach. He used to wake up in the morning with a gutful of vinegar. Well, he had that expression . . . that all-of-a-sudden-sour-stomach-expression. He watched me sit down in that chair, and I could see it coming up on him. He looked sort of greenish."

She laughed gaily. "And he with his new high-toned wife and her two high-assed daughters right on the ground. Here, in camp! Why, she even sneaked in back while the trial was on. I knew some women came in, and I guessed. That made it perfect. Could you plan it more perfectly? Of course, it wasn't *planned.*"

She patted Clyde on the head. "Boe said there was every chance the major would be here. . . ."

"He had to be here to answer the Lively-Wilson lawsuit."

"Why, the sons-of-bitches! So that's how they knew he'd be here! Anyway, Billy didn't know he'd get on the jury."

"Yes, he did! He had them put Walter Cole on the venire and balance him off with the major. It'd make it look more impartial, and they could have both been challenged by the lawyers. I heard 'em say so. Earl Hankey was willing. He jumped at the chance. He's

303

the sheriff. And R. E. Pennecard, he's the recorder. . . ." Clyde decided not to say any more about Pennecard, and how crazy Lyda Pennecard was about Billy, though she was thirty-five years old at the very least.

"Why, the son-of-a-gun! Billy did that! I thought it was plain accident. Anyway, you can't say Billy isn't ready to take a chance. He'd ride up and spit in the face of God or the devil. It's just that he's smarter."

"He never shot Gannaway at all, and they proved he didn't. They proved he couldn't have done it, and so somebody else had to do it. Louis Ethrington did it. He's the only one that could possibly have done it."

"Why, yes," Francie said, regarding Clyde. "I'm not implying anything against Billy. We all know very well he came down here and took his chances, and that wasn't the act of a guilty man. No, Clyde, it most certainly was not! I think you should be very, very proud of your brother."

She put out her cigarette and said: "Come along."

"How'd you make out?" asked Billy when they emerged.

"All right," said Clyde.

"What do you think of my brother?" Billy asked Francie.

"Say, you better look to your laurels. He's a real man."

"I don't know that I like this," said Billy with mock chagrin. "I don't mind standing aside, but I don't want to be put completely in the shade."

"It wasn't nothin'," muttered Clyde.

"Oh, God!" said Francie. "I'd hate to be around when there *was* something."

"Clyde, you're a regular stallion. You're a real, genuine Buttons."

"No, it wasn't anything. She's just shootin' her gab."

But Billy and Long Tom and Ace were all laughing, because they thought Clyde was being modest.

"Look at him blush!" said Ace.

"I tell you, it wasn't anything!" Clyde cried in anger.

"Don't let them tease you," said Francie. "They're just jealous. They don't like the new competition they have to contend with."

"Leave me alone," said Clyde. "Is there anything more to drink around here?"

304

"Yes, where's that nigger man?" Billy asked aloud. "Sam, bring this fellow a stiff one."

"Oh, *cripes!*" cried Francie. "Don't say that word in front of me!"

And the fellows walked around, just laughing their heads off.

CHAPTER TWENTY-ONE

Later Billy said to Clyde on the quiet: "She's a good woman. She'd swim the river for me."

"Yeah."

"Did she tell you about the major?"

"Yeah."

"That lordly prick! He's one of our prominent citizens! Did you see him take his seat in the jury box? He couldn't believe it. He was ready to swing me on a rope, Clyde."

"I know."

"That son-of-a-bitch."

"Yeah."

"I wouldn't say anything against their mothers, but they're sons-of-bitches. They're a bunch of self-constituted sons-of-bitches. But we taught 'em a lesson. Morrison, Arbogast, those Englishmen, and all the killing, kneeling, buckling, ass-hole bastards that crawl and take their orders. Our dear old Uncle Earl for one. Do you know I loathe him more than I do a snake like Danner?"

"Yeah," said Clyde. "He's out there. He's hanging around."

"They won't get me in the back like they did Walt. Oh, god damn their righteous souls. I'd like to see them sink away into the ground, like carrion. This was a great country once. I can remember it when Pa first drove in here. Grama grass was so long it scraped the bottom of the wagon. You could sit and hear the team comb their legs through it. Look at it now. They took 'er all, Clyde! They harvested the grass. They turned it into beef and sold it. All for the dirty dollar. Those Eastern corporations. One little patch they didn't have. The Reserve. So they had to have that, too. I suppose they'll end up with it. You know Ma. But the country will turn on them. They had a taste of it in 'Eighty-Six. Wait till we get about three of those winters back to back. It happened in the old trapper days, and it will happen again.

306

Pat Brown will tell you. I'd like to see the wolves take over and pick the bones of their last fat-assed cow. I'd like to see the buffalo come back. And they will. I often wondered how the longhorns will fare when that day comes. By God, they'd battle the buffalo! And the wild horses. They're here to stay. They're my kind of livestock. Us Buttons, we showed 'em. Didn't we, Clyde? We gave 'em a lesson they won't forget. Them and their piss-assed county attorney, judge, jury, and their cow-turd sheriff. We picked up their chosen weapons, and we cut their balls off, brother."

"Yeah," said Clyde.

"They were all ready to ram it into me. Oh, they were ready to give me a rough ass holing. They were all ready to give it to me with the bark on."

"Ha, ha!"

"Oh, Christ, but Uncle Earl felt sorry that he was going to have to hang me."

Nerved by liquor, Clyde asked: "You didn't shoot Gannaway, did you?"

"Let me tell you what happened. I had an agreement with big John. It was very important for him to clear title to the Reserve. I said all right. Ma was set on sending you off to be a doctor. I'd work on her, and he promised to look the other way while I got those white-face cattle shipped out of the country. That way, we'd both be in the clear. Well, fine and dandy. It was all set. But then, somehow, I had a hunch. It was just a sort of a feeling down in my spine. I sent Grover into town to smell around, and by God if Ted Danner wasn't gathering a crew of more or less ten fellows like Hadley, Stearns, Ike Thrift, of course, A. K. Allen, that fellow they call Beanwhistle. Word of it was all around the saloons because they needed booze to build up their dutch courage, so Grover lit right out and told me. John had me living *de loox* in his hunting lodge! He really had things set up! I rode over and told old Solly Gordon to keep watch of the road to Gravely. Sure enough, here came the posse, but they stopped at the edge of the breaks. They camped where the road goes past the caves and the picture writing. They laid to, and Solly could see the flash of their field glasses. He got on that pinto horse of his and almost run him to death getting word to me. He didn't know whether they were waiting for me or for John Gannaway. It had to be Gannaway, because I was supposed to be in cold storage at the lodge. Once those cattle were consigned to the boat, he had me, and Art Rooney, too. Well, there was only one way to stop it, and that's what I did. I watched for him to come along, and he came on schedule."

"But you didn't shoot him?"

"The hell I didn't! You should have heard him. 'Good old Billy! We've been friends for donkey's years, Billy.' That son-of-a-bitch. I told him . . . 'Here I am. Settle it like a man.' 'I haven't got a gun, Billy. You wouldn't shoot an unarmed man, Billy.' I said . . . 'John, the hell I wouldn't.' And I shot him. I shot that son-of-a-bitch. I shot him right in front of his chosen audience. And now I've run it down their throats. I've rammed it up their hypocritical asses."

Clyde couldn't believe what he was hearing. "But how about Louis Ethrington? Didn't he shoot him from down the crick?"

Billy didn't bother to answer.

"Gannaway did have a gun, didn't he? He carried a hide-out gun?"

Billy regarded Clyde with narrow amusement. "Now, what if he did, or what if he hadn't? The main thing is, I had to get him before he got me."

"You wouldn't shoot down an unarmed man."

With withering, thin-lipped contempt, Billy said: "Stop talking like a kid. Why wouldn't I? He set up to whipsaw me. He chose to do that." Then he got to laughing at the expression on Clyde's face and laid an arm around his shoulder. "Don't take it so much to heart. This ain't one of Ma's books by Sir Walter Scott. Let me tell you about something. One time down in Silver City, Idaho, a fellow they called Short Stack had a faro concession in one of the joints. A gambler I knew named Bob Suffrige was bucking this game pretty steady, and it got late, and he kept betting the same numbers over and over, the same way. Well, this dealer, Short Stack, ran in a cold deck on him, but Bob got wise and coppered all his bets . . . that is, he changed them over to lose instead of win, and Short Stack wanted to pull the deck. . . ."

He went on telling about Short Stack and Suffrige, but Clyde couldn't keep his mind on it, and he didn't know where the story ended, except the moral was when you ring in a cold deck, you've got to pay them out when you're caught with them.

"But how about the other bullet, the one the undertaker found?

308

And the rifle? They practically proved there was a rifle."

"Yes, you're absolutely right. How do I know what they did after I was gone?"

"How'd you know he didn't have a gun? I'll bet he had a hide-out gun. He might have had a bulldog pistol under the saddle skirts."

"Right! You're absolutely right. A man needs a fresh view every so often."

A great many things happened, and Clyde was caught in the current of them. He seemed to be carried along, buffeted, spun around. Bits and pieces of events seemed to fly past, laughter and voices, piano music, and he got to dancing with one of the girls. After a while he found a place to sit down.

"How do you feel?" asked Long Tom.

"I'm all right now. I got sort of dizzy."

"You're not used to all that booze. How much did you have?"

Clyde couldn't remember whether it was three or four drinks.

"Do you want to go outside?"

"No, where's Billy?"

"He's right here."

It seemed to Clyde that something had happened. Somebody had come for Billy, and he'd left with them. But then Clyde saw him talking to Ace Carter. He looked different. He no longer had on his suit. He was wearing his serge pants, but he had shed the coat for a sheepskin-lined jacket, and his pointed shoes for riding boots. Up high, around his waist, he had strapped a belt and six-shooter. He seemed to be cold sober — *ice-cold* sober.

"What's wrong?" Clyde asked Billy.

"How do you feel?"

"I'm all right. What's going on?"

"I think they're cooking up some trouble for me."

"Huh?"

"They're out to kill me. The big interests. They have Danner out in the alley."

Somebody had come with news. It had been Grover Nelson. Kid Nehf, Frenchy LaGrange, and Cromley all got to talking to Billy. They seemed to be in a steamed-up hurry, but Billy wasn't in a hurry.

"Hey, I haven't any tobacco."

"We'll get you some," said Ace.

"Here, he can have mine," said Nehf.

"No, get him some at the counter. Go down and do it. For Christ's sake, don't tell 'em who it's for."

"I got that much sense."

Billy said: "Now, Clyde, I have to get out of town for a while. See to it Ma's all right. Take care of her. I'll probably be back in a couple of weeks, but in case I'm not, you'll have to . . . listen, don't let her get swindled out of the ranch. Make 'em lay it on the barrelhead. Listen. . . ."

"I am!"

"Don't do a single thing unless you see a lawyer. Go down to Billings and talk to O'Donnell. In case of any dispute just remember that possession is nine points of the law, and that's Eastern law. It's ninety-nine points out here."

"All right."

"Don't sign anything, and don't let her. Do this . . . tell 'em it's part of the estate. Say it's Pa's, and they can't clear it without everybody's signatures. Just say they have to have *my* signature. It's not so, but it'll stop 'em. As long as you set tight, you can hold onto the Reserve forever. You do that, Clyde, because Ma will let 'em gyp her out of it."

Clyde had never heard the word *gyp* before, but he got the idea.

"Where you going?"

"I don't know. I have an idea I'd like to go up in Canada, along the coast, or Alaska. There's the country! You'd never count all the bays and inlets . . . and the forests . . . mountains. They just stretch off to the end of the world. Hidden valleys where you can't believe what grows in 'em. Cabbages that big because they get twenty to twenty-two hours of sunlight in the summertime. It's a gold country. Why, it's Bannack and Lost Chance Gulch all over again. Ten or a hundred times as big. And those rivers! . . . they come boiling down out of the wilderness. Nobody knows where they come from. Full of salmon and trout. God! What a country. It's like Montana was when Pa first drove into it. Before the Eastern sons-of-bitches took over. The hog-all sons-of-bitches."

"You ain't even figuring on coming back!" Clyde said desperately.

"Oh, the hell I'm not. Why, you'll be doctoring some day, sitting in your office, and in I'll walk smelling of fish."

"Come on, Billy!" said Ace. "You better get going."

"All right." Billy grabbed Clyde's hand. "Good bye, Buttons."

Clyde had never shaken hands with Billy before, at least not that direct, face-to-face way, man to man.

"Good bye, Billy. Don't take any Chinese money." For some reason, it just came to his mind, and Clyde said it.

"Same to you. And be a good doctor. There ought to be somebody in the family amounts to something."

He walked off, so easy and graceful, and passed from sight through the front room, and down the stairs, and Clyde knew it was the last time he was ever going to see him.

"All right, boys, let's sing a little song," said Long Tom. "Let's whoop it up a little. We want 'em to think we still got a whingding going."

To the banging piano they sang raucously:

> The old gray mare she
> Pooped on the whippletree
> Pooped on the whippletree
> Pooped on the whippletree

Most of them made the sound of farting instead of saying "pooped" and vied with one another in the noise of the blast, louder and louder:

> Many long years ago. . . .
> Many long years ago. . . .
> And that's where the cook
> Got yeast for the sourdough
> Many long years ago.

Ace Carter came in and asked for quiet. All stopped save for two or three — and old Arnold Pease, half deaf, at the piano.

"Stop, damn it!"

"What is it?" Long Tom asked.

"I heard a shot."

One man, very drunk, sang on, and rather than try to stop him, they pushed him from the room, to the hall, down the stairs. The lobby had a brownish light from coal-oil lamps, the dynamo having shut down. It was dark outside, and only a few places had lamps burning. It was so black one could hardly see the steps down from the hotel porch, and Clyde had to feel by sliding his feet.

"Nobody could *see* to shoot," Ace said

"Those bastards were all out with shotguns," Grover Nelson remarked.

"It's down back of the Baker Mercantile," said Kid Nehf.

"What would Billy be doing there?" Ace asked.

"Well," — Grover said with uneasy laughter — "Danner was there."

"That's right," agreed Ace. "They figured Billy would be going for his horse."

Long Tom said: "What a damned fool trick. Why didn't he leave well enough alone? Things might have blown over."

Grover Nelson said with another laugh: "I guess he wanted to burn his bridges behind him."

Long Tom kept muttering and cursing under his breath. "It was all so god damned useless. Why couldn't he lie low for a while?"

Clyde said: "He said the big interests were out to get him."

"What big interests?"

"Why, the major and that bunch," said Clyde. "The big interests."

"Oh, hell!" said Long Tom "That's just talk. They're supposed to hold a meeting, or something, and agree? They'd never agree on anything. If they ambushed Billy tonight, it would be the ruin of Major Morrison, as far as getting to be governor. The major would piss right down his leg if he thought they were out to kill Billy while he was in town, the first one to be accused. If anybody, it might be Avery Carns. He's very bitter. More likely it's Danner, pure and simple. That son-of-a-bitch. He's killed nine or ten men. He drinks a quart of whiskey a day. You can't tell what a son-of-a-bitch like that would get into his head. I think Billy is smart to leave for a while, but there's no sense in blowing it all out of its true shape."

Clyde could hear people talking down the street and started down that way.

"No, you stay right here," Long Tom said.

312

Who are you to be giving me orders? Clyde thought, but he knew better than say it. Not that he was afraid, but Long Tom was generally right.

"There goes the sheriff," said Nehf.

There were other voices.

"What's goin' on down there?" Ace Carter asked.

"A man's been shot," someone said, coming up the street.

"Who?" Long Tom asked.

"I don't know any more about it. I just heard 'em say somebody was shot."

Oh God, thought Clyde, *don't let it be Billy.*

Then another fellow came along, and Long Tom got hold of him.

"Who are you?" he asked.

"Al Stevenson."

It was actually too dark to see, even at arm's length.

"What's going on?" Long Tom asked.

"Why, I was sleeping in a wagon when I heard this commotion in the sheriff's office. Somebody came on the run and said a man had been killed. Pete Wall was asleep in the office. He got up and went for the sheriff. That's all I know."

Clyde headed down the street. There were men with lanterns in the alley behind Baker's store. Quite a number of people seemed to be moving that way. Then with a throb of light, a glow that almost died and then hung to life, the street lights came on. Suddenly it was bright. Everything could be seen. There were at least a dozen fellows who had come out in groups along the street. Harry Woodling, a cowboy from the Paint Creek Ranch, old Simon Arbogast's outfit, was telling people: "It was Ted Danner. Billy Buttons killed Ted Danner."

Long Tom got hold of Woodling, and, when Tom got hold of anybody, it was no mistake because his hand was like a vise.

"How do you know?"

"He's down there dead as a rail."

"You see Billy do it?"

"I saw him right after the shot. He came walkin' out from behind the blacksmith shop, and he had the gun in his hand! You could smell the burnt powder ten or twenty steps away. It was strong, as if you'd burned a handful of matches."

"Like hell you saw him!" Long Tom exclaimed. "It was too dark to see anybody."

"No, it was Billy. He looked me right in the face. He came right up and didn't say a word."

"Are you testifying Billy Buttons killed a man?" Long Tom demanded.

All of a sudden the excitement drained out of Woodling and was replaced by a cold fear. With his mouth open, he looked at Long Tom, and around at Clyde, Ace, and Kid Nehf.

"I ain't accusing him. It was kind of dark, as you say. I'm just telling you fellows. I wouldn't repeat it to a soul."

"Why, of course you won't, Harry, and long life to you," said Long Tom.

Ike Thrift, the Association detective, wearing his special deputy's badge, strode over. A sawed-off shotgun hung in the crook of his arm. He said to Woodling: "I hear you were a witness."

"No, I didn't witness anything. I was on my way over to the Square Deal when I heard somebody shoot."

"I understand you saw who fired the shot?"

"No, I didn't see anything."

"Didn't you just state that you observed a man walk by with a gun in his hand?"

"No, I saw somebody, but there was no telling who it was. It was too dark to see anything or anybody."

"Go over to the sheriff's office and don't discuss this!"

Thrift, swaggering and loud, motioning with his shotgun, looked like a man on the kill and no mistake. Next to Danner, he was the most dangerous man the company had. Which made him *the* most dangerous, because Danner was shot dead. He wanted to show he could handle things, that he was able to take over as king of the roost, and, if they paid *him* a hundred and fifty a month plus fees, he wouldn't lie around town and drink a quart a day! He looked around and saw Clyde, and Clyde wanted to get back out of sight, but all of a sudden he was alone. Long Tom and all the others had drifted away, not wanting it known they'd been in conversation with Harry Woodling.

"Buttons!"

There was no way out, so Clyde stood his ground.

314

"Where's your brother?"

When he didn't answer, Thrift, a powerful man, seized him one-handed and spun him around, but Clyde was strong, too, and got away.

"Leave me alone," he demanded.

"Answer my question!"

Clyde was stubborn and didn't answer. He saw the shotgun, but he wasn't cowed by it. He backed around to where there were a number of people, knowing Thrift wouldn't fire into a crowd. Instead, Thrift used the barrel as a club and tried to strike Clyde alongside the neck, but Clyde grabbed it with both hands. He pushed the muzzle straight into the sidewalk, then he rammed his knee on it, and nearly wrenched it from Thrift's grasp. Thrift managed to keep hold, however, and Clyde, standing up, swung his left hand in an arc, for balance and protection, and it struck Hap Stearns, who had come up, squarely alongside the neck. It was as much a shove as a blow, a big, sweeping haymaker. Thrift had to backpeddle for balance. He stepped off the edge of the sidewalk and sat down with a shock that knocked his hat loose and his eyes out of focus. He stared, and his mouth hung open.

"Why, Clyde knocked him flat on his ass!" someone said.

Later it was repeated so often Clyde came to believe that he really had.

Recovering, Thrift lunged to his feet. "Why, you son-of-a-bitch! You whelp!" But he was baffled as to direction. He seemed to see Clyde, but he couldn't get going at the correct angle. He scraped his skin and went to one knee on the edge of the walk. He still had the sawed-off shotgun and was swinging it around, as if he intended to use it. Men looked for cover, but big Jack Fowler, a boss teamster for the Diamond D, reached over from behind with both hands, grabbed it, and jerked it away from him.

"Use your head, you damned fool!" said Fowler.

"Give me that gun!" Thrift cried.

"There's your gun!" and Fowler pitched it, *splash!* — twenty feet into a watering trough.

"I'm doing my job as deputy, and that's kid's a suspect."

"Suspect of what?"

Turning on Clyde, Thrift shouted: "Where's your brother?"

Clyde shouted back: "You're no deputy. You're nothing but a Company regulator. You're in the hire of the dudes."

Long Tom got hold of Clyde. "Wait a second."

"Huh?"

"Go ahead and answer his question. You got nothing to hide."

"I don't know where he is."

"There's your answer, deputy," said Long Tom. "He don't know where he is."

Thrift sensed that the crowd was against him, but he didn't want to back down. He still had a gun in his holster. It gave him something to hitch up and show that, by God, he might just shoot somebody dead, but he didn't demean himself by fishing around for his shotgun, or even glance at the trough where Fowler had thrown it. "You better come with me," Thrift told Clyde.

"No, I ain't comin' with you!" said Clyde.

By then Sheriff Hankey came striding up the street.

"Here's his brother," said Thrift.

"Do you know where Billy is?" the sheriff asked.

"No! He left the hotel, and I ain't seen him."

"If you do know where he is, you better tell me. If this town organizes and runs him down, he won't have a chance."

"He never tells me anything."

Someone laughed and added: "And nobody tells Billy anything, ain't that so, Sheriff?" But Hankey chose to ignore the remark.

Nothing happened for a while. The sheriff delayed. He kept glancing at Clyde but asked no more questions. A wagon was on its way up the short street from the Baker Mercantile, and Hankey decided to wait for it, direct its progress. He walked to the middle of the street. With lanterns still lit, men on foot alongside, it came up the street.

George Deever was driving. He was night man at the stable. Pete Wall and Mace Kuykendall were in charge, keeping the crowd away. It was a flatbed wagon, Boland's dray, and there was a body on it covered by a blanket. The wagon banged one wheel at a time over deep ruts, and the covered body kept jouncing and working its way back, until finally George had to stop while the body was pushed forward. The lights came on in the Ferris Furniture store. **Harvey Ferris, Cabinetry, Furniture, Lumber & Undertaking**. Ferris himself opened the double doors, as if expecting them to drive right up the ramp.

"No, bring the table outside," Hankey directed. "We'll put the body on it and carry it in. We don't want to disturb anything prior to the inquest."

"You'll have to lift the body, anyhow."

The sheriff ignored Ferris. He saw Doc Adams, inside, smoking a cigar. Adams seemed tired and preoccupied.

"Is that all right, Doctor?"

"Yes, that's all right. Here, let me see. We can carry him in."

Clyde didn't move. He didn't want to see. Just the shape of it under the blanket made him sick. Standing all by himself, he could hear them saying: "He was shot from the back."

"He was *not* shot from the back. The bullet went all through. That's why the blood. . . ."

A catcall of laughter was followed by: "Well, there they go again!"

Boe came outside and stood leaning on his cane. He saw Clyde and came over. He seemed perfectly sober.

"I'll represent at the inquest. Do they have witnesses?"

Ace Carter, who had also been staying back, said: "No, they have no witnesses at all."

Clyde sat in the lobby and waited for bad news. He woke up when somebody said: "Sleep of the innocent."

Boe stood over him.

"What happened?" Clyde asked.

"The undersheriff was killed in the line of duty by party or parties unknown."

"Didn't they accuse Billy at all?"

"Oh, his name came up."

"What did the judge say?"

Alf Bunting was there. He and Boe seemed to be the best of friends. "Uncle Curtis is far down the river gunning for an elusive mallard," Bunting replied.

"Vainly the fowler's eye," said Boe.

Clyde followed them into the dining room, full of steamy breakfast smells, and joined them at their table. While waiting for the

Chinaman to come over for their orders, Clyde said to Bunting: "What do *you* think? Do you think Billy was guilty?"

"The coroner's jury merely said. . . ."

Boe interrupted: "Guilt is never a presumption."

"Huh?" said Clyde.

Boe went on, addressing Bunting, apparently picking up some former line of conversation: "One is reminded of a question frequently asked . . . is a lawyer justified in defending a client he knows to be guilty? This very question was propounded to the great Samuel Johnson by Boswell, his biographer, who was then in London arguing a case before Lords. Johnson answered that the lawyer could not know whether his client was guilty, because it was this very question that the trial was set up to determine. By refusing a client because he is guilty, the lawyer presumes to know more than the court, and hence to place himself above the law. The attorneys, of all people, should not commit such a fallacy in logic."

Bunting responded: "On the other hand, the defendant might know he committed a murder."

"Not at all," countered Boe. "The world is full of people who believe themselves guilty of one thing or another, and only flatter themselves thereby." He turned to explain to Clyde: "A man may believe himself guilty of murder in the first degree, but the facts may show him devoid of the use of reason, in whole or in part. It is axiomatic that the mad believe themselves sane. Why, even under the canon law," he added, returning his gaze to Bunting, "my friend, Bishop Laswell, points out that mortal sin . . . which corresponds to a capital crime of the statutes . . . requires full knowledge and compliance of the will, a feat of philosophy and mind most men are incapable of, hence hell must be a select region, like the Royal Society of Great Britain."

"Same," said Clyde, when the others ordered waffles and ham, although he had never tasted, or even seen, a waffle before. Boe went on talking.

"Now, if you do essay the practice of criminal law, you will walk into many a hopeless situation . . . eye-witnesses, plain motives. Hence, time and again your only hope of winning an acquittal is through the bringing forth of a surprise . . . something that puts it in a new light . . . preferably something that will shock and appall, render the issue to the second class. Rape is the best thing of all."

The Chinese waiter brought the waffles and ham, and Clyde watched while Boe covered both with maple syrup, so he did, too. Bunting, however, put syrup only on the waffles. Clyde realized that putting syrup on the ham was a mistake. It showed his ignorance.

"Two connoisseurs," said Boe.

"I'd just thought I'd see how it was," said Clyde. They watched him, and he ate some of the ham. "Too sweet."

Boe went on: "You must remember that sitting as a juror even in the most sanguine of cases soon becomes a very deadening experience," and he went on talking and talking about how to win acquittals in murder cases, and it mainly came down to never telling the jury anything, but letting them discover it themselves, and apparently whether a man had really done it was of no importance at all. It was very baffling to Clyde.

"Now, one further thing. If you essay into the practice of criminal law, fear not to be grandiloquent! It is expected. Memorize some Shakespeare and paraphrase . . . quote Robert G. Ingersoll. Don't come down to them. Hold yourself to an eminence. It's what they want. All their lives they want to say . . . 'I heard such and such plead the X Y Z case.' Use satire, be funny. Tear somebody to pieces. If he's the local sheriff or prosecutor, well and good. A laughing jury is not a hanging jury. But beware. Homicide humor has to be sharp as daggers; caustic as acid. And, above all, be generous. Let the presentation get away with bloody butchery in the rules of evidence . . . and then in their every objection it will be apparent that they, not you, would prevent the whole truth being known."

"This one," said Bunting, "was a masterpiece!"

"Thank you," said Boe. "Thank you very much, indeed."

319

CHAPTER TWENTY-TWO

In the hot mid-morning everybody seemed to be leaving town. The stores were very busy. Ranchers from as far as seventy miles away had wagons backed against the loading platforms for winter supplies. A few men came and went at Ferris's where Danner was laid out in the back room, but the excitement had died away.

"I'm not sure I'm ready to go," said Ma when Clyde drove around. "Why don't we stay for the evening services? Reverend Griffin's not a Baptist, but. . . ."

Clyde was disgusted and showed it. "He's nothing. He's an old fake. He talks against liquor and drinks on the sly."

"You don't know that. It's only gossip." But she decided to get her things in the buggy, to leave. "What'd you do to your hand?" asked Ma.

It was from his tussle with Ike Thrift. His left hand was all puffy down to the fingertips.

Ma let out a wail and said: "You haven't been fighting, haven't you? Yes, you have, you been fighting! Oh, dear God, is there no end to it? It's this awful country. I'll be so glad to be shut of it. Yes, I'll sing hallelujah to bid it a final good bye! What were you fighting about?"

"Oh, hell, there wasn't any fight!"

"Don't you swear at me. I won't stand to have profane language used at me."

Then she started in on Billy, about how Pa had thought it was cute when Billy used strong language as a little boy, and she went on to Billy's bad companions, and now just see what it had come to. She'd never be able to hold up her head in public again, but, thank God, they were leaving the country and going where nobody had ever heard the name of Billy Buttons.

"Billy ain't so bad," protested Clyde. "He just wasn't going to let the big outfits run him out of the country."

"They say he killed another man last night, do you realize that?"

"What do you mean . . . another? The jury found him not guilty! And as for last night, there was no testimony, or evidence."

"Well, I hope not, but if he didn't do it, then his friends did, and he has to share the guilt. And guilt is one thing that's divisible by ten thousand parts without getting less." She got to going on about Billy's friends, and how they were the curse of him, and his being popular, having people follow him around and admire him. "Even when he was small, he could spit better, and ride better, and shoot better, and play cards better. Now look where it's taken him! That poor girl. His wife. I feel sorry for her. The life he'll lead her. If she ever finds him after last night. A fugitive. Yes, he is, whether they got a warrant out or not, he's a fugitive. The people in this country are at the end of the trail as far as he's concerned. Where is she? At the hotel? I suppose we better go around and talk to her. We have to offer her home and succor. . . ."

"No," said Clyde, "she took the stage to Billings. She took it with Boe, Blankenship, and Missus Neeley, they all got on."

Ma started saying, oh, dear, dear, dear, that her own daughter-in-law had gone away without even calling to pay her respects, her husband's own mother, and what kind of a person was that?

"You didn't go around and see *her*, either," Clyde said.

"It's not my place. It's her place. But, oh, dear, I suppose it's just as well. What would we agree about? I can't even get agreement out of you, my own flesh and blood. It'll be better if she just goes away, and stays away . . . if she can go back to Indiana and close the curtain on this part of her life entirely." Then she started in on Clyde, saying now that he'd been shown the example of Billy, maybe it all wouldn't go to waste if he took it to heart. "You can't be smarter than the whole world. You can't just kick people aside."

"Oh, stop talking about Billy." Clyde felt as if he'd go and get drunk if he had to hear one more word about Billy.

"Anyhow," Ma went on, "our time here is just about over. We'll be sold out in another month or two, and, God willing, we'll have a new life. We'll be gone from this country, and it will be your opportunity and God-given privilege of expatiating" — it was one of her favorite words — "all the evil Billy has done."

She went on and on about it being her one last and final hope that Clyde would become a doctor, so he could bring healing to the afflicted and the suffering. And when he did become a doctor, she only prayed that he would not be prideful, but would always bear in his mind that he was not smarter than other folks, but only one of God's instruments whose privilege it was to do His deeds through the intercession of divine grace.

"No, I'm not goin' to be any god-damned doctor!"

Clyde said it. It just came out of him. But there it was, and he knew he meant it.

"What?" Ma cried.

"I'm not going to be a doctor, and I'm not leaving the country. They think they're going to run the Buttons out. Well, they're not going to. Because I'm going to stay. I'm going to stay put."

She recovered and almost blew him out of the buggy in her vehemence. "You are *not* going to stay put! I'm selling! And we're getting out! You'll go to school as I say!"

"No, you can sell, if you want to. But I'm not moving! They can come out with their paper, but getting me out will be another thing. Because I'm holding fast. Possession is nine points of the law, and more than that in this country."

Clyde decided he wouldn't go to Billings for a lawyer, as Billy suggested. No, he'd go to Boston. He'd go and hire Alf Bunting. It just all of a sudden flashed in his mind that Bunting was his man. He'd save his money and pay over the fee spot cash. He vowed not to run in debt for anything.

"That's fool talk," Ma was saying. "I'm selling the ranch, and that's the end of it!"

"You can't. It's not clear. Pa never left a will. It never went through court."

"It's mine, and everybody knows it is. I'll sell. . . ."

"It's the Buttons' ranch. They'll get it over my dead body."

"And that's just what they will do!"

"See, you admitted it! You admitted those big outfits and their sheriff . . . dear, old, dirty Uncle Earl . . . and all the rest are set on chasing us out, dead or alive."

After a solid half hour of silence, driving the team and buggy across the fine-dust flats of the river bottoms, very bright in the autumn sun, Clyde said: "Everything will work out. The longer I hold fast, the easier it will be. Why don't you go back East on a visit? Pa always wanted you to, and you got it coming. You can spend your winter there, visiting around. I'll sort of hole up until spring."

"You can't spend the whole winter alone."

"I won't be alone."

"It will be just the same as alone with poor old Tom."

"No. I'll find somebody."

He could get Long Tom Cooper to stay with him. He could get Ace Carter, Grover Nelson, and some of those fellows, too, but he didn't want them. It would be playing into the Omaha's hands. They'd just love to make out he had a rustler spread. But Long Tom would be all right. He didn't mention it to Ma, though. She'd say he would go the way of Billy all over again. And that wasn't true. He could never do what Billy could, not in a hundred years. He didn't even want to. As he drove and drove, it got to seeming that Billy was already a thousand miles away, and getting farther. Clyde was his own man. He was the last of the Buttons, and he'd do what he had to do.

Dan Cushman was born in Osceola, Michigan, and grew up on the Cree Indian reservation in Montana. He graduated from the University of Montana with a Bachelor of Science degree in 1934 and pursued a career in mining as a prospector, assayer, and geologist before turning to journalism. In the early 1940s his novelette-length stories began appearing regularly in such Fiction House magazines as *North-West Romances* and *Frontier Stories*. Later in the decade his North-Western and Western stories as well as fiction set in the Far East and Africa began appearing in *Action Stories*, *Adventure*, and *Short Stories*. A collection of some of his best North-Western and Western fiction has recently been published, *Voyageurs of the Midnight Sun* (1995), with a Foreword by John Jakes who cites Cushman as a major influence in his own work. The character Comanche John, a Montana road agent featured in numerous rollicking magazine adventures, also appears in Cushman's first novel, *Montana, Here I Be* (1950) and in two later novels. *Stay Away, Joe,* which first appeared in 1953, is an amusing novel about the mixture, and occasional collision, of Indian culture and Anglo-American culture among the Métis (French Indians) living on a reservation in Montana. The novel became a bestseller and remains a classic to this day, greatly loved especially by Indian peoples for its truthfulness and humor. Yet, while humor became Cushman's hallmark in such later novels as *The Old Copper Collar* (1957) and *Goodbye, Old Dry* (1959), he also produced significant historical fiction in *The Silver Mountain* (1957), concerned with the mining and politics of silver in Montana in the 1890s. This novel won a Gold Spur Award from the Western Writers of America. His fiction remains notable for its breadth, ranging all the way from a story of the cattle frontier in *Tall Wyoming* (1957) to a poignant and memorable portrait of small town life in Michigan just before the Great War in *The Grand and the Glorious* (1963). More recent fiction such as *Rusty Irons* (1984) combines both the humor for which he is best known and the darker hues to be found in *The Silver Mountain*. His most recent novels are *In Alaska With Shipwreck Kelly* (1995) and *Valley of the Thousand Smokes* (1996).